I0772715

Cover Design by Dar Albert https://www.wickedsmartdesigns.com/

Map Design by Dar Albert https://www.wickedsmartdesigns.com/

ISBN-13: 978-1726412315

ISBN-10: 1726412318

10 9 8 7 6 5 4 3 2 1

✻ Created with Vellum

ALSO BY LYNN CRANDALL

Touch of Breeze (novella)

Nutcracker Sweet (novella)

Two Days Until Midnight (novella)

Love Between Universes, An Out Of This World Christmas (novella)

At Midnight (anthology)

Captured by Christmas (anthology)

Fierce Hearts series

Secrets

Cravings

Heartfelt

Probabilities

Unstoppable

Snowbound (novella)

Finding Finn (short)

Aegar Investigations series

Dancing with Detective Danger

Always and Forever Love

Love in Dunes Bay series

Then There Was You

Meant To Be You

Could It Be You

Dark Sides

Touch Me, Book One

Hear Me, Book Two (releasing in May 2025)

See Me (releasing later in 2025)

To Mike, my Happily-Ever-After. Thank you for reading for me as my unpaid editor and proofreader and always encouraging me in all ways.

RESIDENTIAL
PAYSON'S HOUSE
WHERRYITE RIVER
DOWNTOWN
HILLS
FANCY THIS
COFFEE IS
AURALIA POLICE
SHEPPARD MEDIA TOWER
CITY BLD.
COMMUNITY CENTER
BEST BOND CO.
N
W
E
S
CITY OF
AURALIA
BRADEN'S HOUSE
CASINO CONSTRUCTION
RESIDENTIAL
PRINCIPLE IDUSTRIES

PROLOGUE

$\mathcal{P}$AYSON SILVER SHIVERED in her nightgown. The ground around her quaked and cracked open. She stumbled as the earth slanted beneath her bare feet, and she leaped to another spot of ground.

Clouds of dust enveloped her and filled her lungs. She struggled, coughing, trying to catch her breath. She opened her mouth to scream for her mommy, but no sound came out. Chaos of people running and buildings toppling over made her want to run but she didn't dare take a step.

People carrying children, holding onto one another, and calling names ran past her, without even looking at her.

Another large piece of ground jutted up past her, and another crater opened. She slapped her hands over her ears, but that didn't block the screams of those tumbling into the gaping hole.

Sirens blared, but she heard voices. A group of Elders gathered in a tight circle beside her, but even they, the leaders of the people, didn't notice her.

"We have to ensure the preservation of our kind or the future of humanity will be destroyed," said one in the group.

"It's too late," said another. "The devastation is the work of Dark Aspects, what we've warned might happen if they continued to seek power and wealth above all else. They have released powerful dark energies and it is tearing apart the fabric of our lives. We knew this was coming but we've done very little to prevent it."

Another spoke up. "It's time for us to leave the island of Atlantis and relocate somewhere isolated and safe, so that we can pass on the essence of our society that is full of love and light and peace."

Payson shrunk to a squat, ducking rocks hurtling from the surrounding mountains and chunks of falling buildings.

"Yes, we'll resettle and prepare the Aeon DNA, as we've planned. The Aeon children born in the future will have the special abilities needed to counteract Dark Sides influence if it persists and grows, despite this cataclysm. We failed to suppress darkness, but the children will give the world another chance."

"We would be foolish if we failed to acknowledge that those who created this destruction of our civilization will have made plans for their survival," an Elder said.

"Are we certain if we embed the correct DNA sequence it will be triggered if darkness proliferates in the future?" a tall, willowy female Elder asked.

"Yes. The process has been perfected."

The female elder peered into Payson's face. "It's okay," she said, then turned back to the group.

Huh? She saw me? Payson ran after the group as they wove through the ruins of the city toward the harbor. She tried to yell for their attention, but she couldn't get her voice to work. Dust funneled up and blocked her sight of them.

Her lungs ached, and she searched for someone to help her. Then a loud cracking sound filled the air and a huge rock broke loose from a nearby building and crashed toward her.

Payson screamed, loud and long.

"Payson, what are you hollering about?" Her mother shook her shoulders and an image flashed in her mind of her mom as a teenager, slouched alone behind a shelf of books in her high school library. Payson's heart nearly split with sadness. Not her sorrow, her mother's. Stunned, Payson stared at her mother's angry face. "You woke me up."

In the glow of her nightlight, Payson saw her bed, her blankets, her room. "I had a nightmare."

"Just a dream, girl. How old are you?"

"Ten." She rubbed her eyes and sniffed.

"You're too old to be afraid of dreams. Go back to sleep." Her mother left her in the dark, and with a knowing she'd never had before.

She grabbed her teddy bear up close. Waves of understanding about the world, her purpose in life, and awareness of how much promise existed for a better world, crashed through her, over and over.

What she'd seen in her sleep was more than a dream, it was the past, and it was real, she simply knew that. She was an Aeon, a descendant of the highly evolved human society of Atlantis, and she was here now, equipped with a special touch, to save the planet from destruction by Dark Sides.

* * *

Seventeen-year-old Payson

PAYSON LISTENED OUTSIDE her parent's bedroom door, holding her breath. Snoring from the other side was her cue. Her parents were asleep.

She had to get out. It was ten-thirty on a school night but she didn't care. She texted Braden. *Can you meet me now?*

His response flashed immediately. *Hi Payson. Course.*

She escaped out the back door into the Michigan summer night, longing for relief from anxiety tightening her chest. As long as she could remember, Braden Powers had lived next door. He understood her and she him. She had to talk with him, and she knew he'd be waiting at their spot.

Streetlights lit the way and the slap, slap of her shoes against the pavement grounded her. She needed that too to keep her sanity.

She shoved her pesky long hair out of her eyes and surveyed the shadows of wind-tossed branches. An eerie fog muted the night. Shivers slipped up and down her spine. Her Aeon senses told her something more was there. Sometimes it amazed her that her genetics dated all the way back to Atlantis. It was just part of who she was, like the way she had a knowing of human potential and keen awareness of the fragile balance of darkness and light.

The *something more* buzzed in her like a vibration of a tuning fork. It was a giveaway that a Dark Aspect was near. It was her natural enemy. She offered light and love to the world, while a Dark Aspect, or DA as she and Braden referred to them, presented the opposite.

Payson shivered. Dark Aspects were a part of life. Thoughts of them circled her brain all the time, and sometimes she felt like a walking talking field guide to dealing with them.

Some of them were Aeons who had chosen Dark Sides. Others were simply average people who had lost their center. Regardless, a DA was one who had given over to the darkness, and it was who she fought to prevent her city of Auralia from slipping into chaos. Braden did, too. He was also an Aeon, which was why they'd always been so close.

As an Aeon, Payson instinctively radiated enlightenment, offering a choice for an elevated life to others around her. Dark Aspects tended to multiply by association, in a similar way creating an atmosphere of bigotry, intolerance, scarcity, hatred, greed, and fear. She couldn't avoid them, but she had to remain guarded against their influence. Still, sometimes she just wanted to hunt them down and take them out. But that would be counterproductive.

Payson focused her thoughts on her inner knowing, and smiled to herself. The inner knowing guided her. It informed her that all people had light and dark in them, and that what dominated was a result of personal choice.

She glanced over her shoulders at the same time she expanded her inner love and light, hoping to touch the DAs following her. All she had to do was focus her attention on the qualities inside her. Her ability to send light out beyond her body was an effective skill for boosting light, but also a tool that stymied DAs. That idea gave her hope. She sensed a compulsion in DAs to challenge an Aeon and defy the light. The threat was not injury or death, but of being overwhelmed and stumbling into darkness. The light inside her had no limits, but it could deplete and then she would weaken temporarily.

At the end of her street she treaded through the overgrown lawn of the empty house—a part of an unsettled estate she and Braden had years ago made their safe, private space—and walked through the back door. A vibration, similar to the buzz DAs emitted but gentle and soothing, ran through her. Flutters went off in her stomach, knowing Braden was already there. As Aeons, they could detect each other through vibration.

She found him in the living room.

"Payson, what's up? I was playing basketball with Cooper." Braden got up off the floor and grabbed her hand. "Are you okay?"

Her hand slipped into his familiar touch, and sparks ignited in other parts of her body. "I'm sorry I interrupted your time with your good friend."

"Not a problem. He lives right next door and we can play anytime. Are you okay?" he repeated.

"Oh sure, I'm fine. It's just same old, same old." At the touch of his hand, an image had flashed in her mind's eye. The image of him struggling to constrain his thoughts while his parents fought twisted her insides, but she kept it to herself. He had to keep a lid on his maleficence ability and not interfere in their minds.

He pulled her down to sit beside him on a makeshift couch—two old beanbag chairs sitting side-by-side. "Parent trouble again?"

That he knew so well what she went through thrummed through her. "I don't know what I'd do if I didn't have you. Sometimes life sucks."

．　．　．

PAYSON'S WORDS HIT Braden's gut hard. He knew when she'd asked him to meet her that her parents were involved in some way. They did not understand her. Yeah, he was an Aeon tasked with building love, but sometimes he just wanted to punch her parents. Like the time they'd had her tested for autism because she didn't touch them much and they'd wanted a diagnosis to put her in an institution. Restraint had been his friend then. He had to be careful, because with his mind control ability he could make them hurt themselves without meaning to.

"Mom told Dad I'd done some voodoo stuff on her." Payson scrunched up her nose. It was one of her cute moves that made him want to grab her up. It ranked right up on his list of things he liked about her along with her soft, brown skin and long dark hair.

"Voodoo stuff? Like what?"

She smacked his bicep hard.

"Ow! Why did you do that?"

"You know I don't do voodoo. I didn't use any kind of psychic skill on her. She'd been drinking and lost her balance. She hit her head on the counter top on her way to the floor." Payson's striking pale brown eyes misted.

Braden lifted her chin and kissed her. Her soft lips incited a riot in his body, but he put on the brakes. He and Payson were high school seniors but they'd agreed way back when their hormones first spurted to life that they would do nothing more than cuddle and kiss. Their friendship was rock solid and they wanted that to continue, not confuse it with sex.

Payson pulled back from the kiss and gave him that beautiful smile of hers. "That was nice."

"Yes, it was." His stomach clenched. He couldn't protect her from her parents' ignorance. "Did your dad get upset too?"

"He ordered me to apologize. I couldn't. The words wouldn't come out, Braden. It was a lie." She blinked, and blinked again. "They don't love me and it hurts. But it's just the way of things."

"I know." He did know. Their world was a harsh place, even with their Aeon ability to expand joy and peace. They were sensitive. They were different, and people didn't understand sensitive or like different. "It's why I've never told my parents about my abilities. But I never feel loved or accepted by my own parents."

A barely noticeable sensation juddered in his gut at the same time he heard noise at the back of the house. Payson's eyes widened, telling him the vibration had registered with her too.

Before he could jump to his feet, Diane Butler stepped into the room. He didn't know which surprised him the most, that she knew about this place or that her vibration was different.

"Oh, the love birds are at it again." Her lips twisted into a snarl. "Must be nice." She leaned against the wall, staring through daggers.

Braden exchanged a quick glance with Payson. He suspected they were thinking the same thing and it wasn't completely insane. An Aeon also, Diane was turning DA. Her vibration felt like crap in his belly.

"Hard night, Diane?" He softened his voice. He knew her family situation was hard, harder than his or Payson's.

She scoffed. "You don't know anything about me, so don't act all syrupy."

Payson sat erect. "Don't act like we don't know, Diane. Your parents are dead and your grandmother resents that you have to live with her. What did she call you this time? Or did she hit you again? I saw your bruises last week."

Braden nodded his head. "Yeah, I know. I'm sorry your life is extreme." The vibration emitting from Diane ramped up, jangling his nerves. In his peripheral vision he saw Payson close her eyes. Her vibration intensified, reminding him he could expand his light energy, too, to help Diane.

Diane stomped her foot. "Shut up!" She raised her hands and twisted a stream of energy at Payson, knocking her in the face.

Payson fell backward. "Ow! Why did you do that? Don't use your telekinesis on me."

"Don't aim your energy at me. I'm not just a quick-fix. You don't know what my life is like. Besides, you have each other. I'm alone, all alone."

Heaviness sank like bricks on Braden's shoulders. He cringed, wondering why she'd apparently been watching them. How else would she know they came here regularly? "I wish you could see that we're with you, Diane."

"Don't let the darkness in your grandmother take you down." Payson's urging was gentle but to the point.

Diane dipped her head. "I'm trying. I'm not like you, Payson. Nobody likes me and I hurt so much." Her words were an ache in his soul that quivered in the air.

Braden walked to her and put his hand to her shoulder. "I like you, and so does she," he said, gesturing to Payson.

She lifted her gaze and with teary eyes revealed the problem. She jerked away, shrugging off his hand. "Payson. Always Payson. Don't think you can help me. I'm fine."

"Why are you here then?" Braden wasn't ready to give up. Diane's unhappiness wasn't something for him to ignore.

She avoided his gaze and chewed a fingernail. "My grandmother sent me to the store." She held up a bag from the corner liquor store. "I wasn't ready to go home yet. I didn't know you two would be in here, though I should have guessed." Diane's eyes darkened. "Maybe I'll go home and mesmerize my grandma to leave me alone, just blank out her brain. Then I'll drink this stuff myself."

Diane's vibration sharpened.

"Don't talk like that. Your ability to mesmerize people's minds is powerful. It's not something to take lightly."

"Don't lecture me."

"Diane, you can stay," Braden said. "We don't own this building."

"Don't treat me like an idiot. I know you two come here to be alone. Don't worry about me."

Diane stalked out of the house, leaving a trail of sorrow and pain that swept over him like the smell of a rotting orange.

"Come back down here," Payson said, patting the seat beside her. "That was so sad and so troubling."

He plopped down next to her and tried to catch his breath. "I'm worried about her."

"I am too." Payson shook her head. "You were very kind, but she has to accept the truth that she is her worst obstacle to happiness. She sounds jealous, and jealousy is a destructive thing. It's the kind of thing DAs feed on."

Braden needed to touch Payson's soft skin. "She's right, though. We do have each other in a very wonderful way. It helps." She rested her head against his chest and his heart stammered.

"I love you, Braden."

Her words drifted through him like a beautiful fragrance. "I love you, Payson." She lifted her face and love poured into him. The gentle, vibrant flow pulsed between them as a shared heartbeat.

He raised his palm to her and she placed hers against it. "Always." It was his promise to be with her and love her no matter what.

"Always," she said.

CHAPTER 1

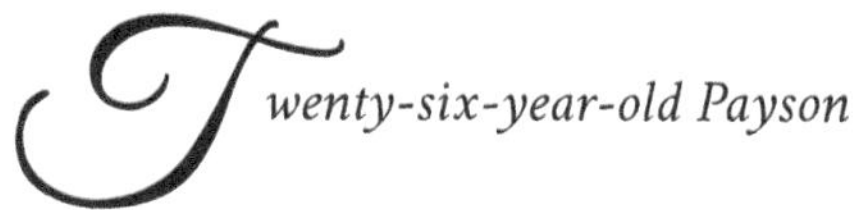

wenty-six-year-old Payson

PAYSON LOOKED DOWN over the city from her favorite vantage point at the top of the Sheppard Media Tower, and worried her bottom lip. In the light of dawn, she perched at the edge of the large deck and scanned the downtown streets.

From fifteen stories up, any city could look like a happy place. What she saw told her it was not so for the city of Auralia.

A summer breeze tossed her long hair across her face. She shivered. Changes in the quality of energy thrumming in the air prickled her skin. She could see dark energies thriving in the fistfight in a parking lot, hear it in a woman's screams for help, sense it in its chaotic pulse that throbbed in her bones. Urgency thudded in her chest.

Her eyes closed, she opened her mind to other Aeons in the city and sensed her energy connection with theirs, like lines of light spreading from her in a web across the city. The gentle pulsing of their high energy hummed in her body, assuring her each one was out there living from light. Awareness bloomed in her chest of how each one brought something different to their mission of balancing dark and light. Hers was working as a bounty hunter.

But Dark Sides energies—the capacity in humans to live for personal power above all else—intensifying these days called her and her fellow Aeons to step up their game right now. Hurry, hurry screamed through her to take stronger actions against the darkness before it was too late.

Payson checked the time on her phone, expecting Braden at any minute.

She ran her gaze across the scene below her—tall buildings that didn't quite reach the tower, cars filling the streets. But in her mind, she saw a seaport bustling with activity, large sailing ships, and buildings reaching upward sitting next to shiny dome buildings. Suddenly, the scene shifted and devastation rushed through her. She rocked on her perch and blinked hard at the reminder of the past.

She had lived her whole life knowing the popular legend of the lost continent of Atlantis, but also knowing most believed it was a cute story, or just a myth, even a parable to warn people away from the evils of challenging laws and traditions.

Her gut clenched and she turned to find Diane Butler strutting toward her. "Great view, huh?" she said.

Payson jumped down to the deck and braced herself for an assault on her senses. Diane carried darkness around as some people wore a smell. "What are you doing here?"

"The same reason you're here. To get a bird's eye view of Auralia." Diane brushed by her and stopped just short of the low brick wall that stood between the deck and thin air. "It's exhilarating to stand above it all."

"Uh huh. I didn't know you had access to this," Payson said, sweeping her arms in circles.

Diane gave Payson a frown over her shoulder. "You have permission?"

"I do. I like to come up here to get perspective. But I need the keycode."

Diane narrowed her eyes. "I go where I want. The keypad is not an obstacle." She spun around to face Payson and slanted her head. "I can always find you, Payson." Her voice held a quality that matched her thorny vibration, but Payson just shrugged and expanded her inner flow of light and love to spread to Diane.

Payson saw Diane gasp and held the flow, hoping Diane would accept it. She had so much hope for her and so much to discuss. "We're not so different, Diane."

"Ha! You're short, I'm tall. I'm white; you're a mixture of your father's Indian genes and your mother's Caucasian ones. I'm a lobbyist and you're ah, ah," she looked down her nose, "a bounty hunter."

Payson blew past Diane's surface argument. "We both carry the same genes and the mission to save the world from the destructive ways of our ancestors."

Diane wrapped her arms around her chest. "What are you blathering about? Ancestors? Mission? Destruction?" She stepped closer.

Payson stiffened. "You know the story. You're a part of it, whether or not you actively work with the Aeons. Your ability to control energy and mesmerize minds could be useful in reducing darkness in Auralia."

Loud and mocking laughter spurted out of Diane. "Shut up."

"No, I won't. We need your help to protect Auralia. You need to join us, not just hover around dropping sarcasm now and again." Diane's anger put burrs on the vibration whining in Payson's body. "Our ancestors sought power and wealth. You can be different."

"Ha! Sounds like some pretty smart ancestors. I don't see your point."

She wanted to shake Diane into acknowledgment. "It's important to remember the reason we're here. Those dark individuals used their knowledge to destroy the beauty and promise of Atlantis."

"Oh, really. Well, that's a myth, and even if it were true, how could we be here today? Tell me that, Payson." Diane slammed a hand on her hip and glared.

Payson dipped her gaze. "Some Atlanteans envisioned what was coming and left before catastrophe hit. They settled in a remote area in Europe and centered their lives on taking care of the planet, doing good, and hoping to save the world from becoming dark again."

Diane punctuated the air with her finger. "Fake, fake, fake."

Pain jabbed in Payson's chest. "I'll tell you why I want to come up here. I want to see the effects of darkness on Auralia. I want to be prepared for what's coming. The destruction is here, now."

Diane pursed her lips and stood silent. Her vibration pounded inside Payson, battering her heart. "You're a fool. I know who I am. I'm a successful businesswoman. I have powerful people wrapped around my finger. I have my own plans and you can't stop me." She lunged toward Payson and slapped her.

The impact of the hit sent shockwaves through Payson. Her reflexes went to work and she drove a punch of her own at Diane's gut. Diane doubled over and slumped to the ground.

"Violence? The goody-two-shoes isn't so good after all."

Payson took in a big breath and let it out. Deliberately, she filled with peace and reached a hand to Diane. "Being full of light doesn't mean I'm a push-over."

Diane slapped her hand away and stood up. For one tiny second her face drooped, and Payson caught a glimpse of her dejection.

Then it was gone.

"I really, really don't like you. You're wrong about us being alike. I'm nothing like you."

Many things came together in serial flashes for Payson, and hung in the air between them: Diane's vulnerability, her defenses, her delusions. They all stood there with Diane, taking away her conscious choice. "You don't know me."

Diane glared. "Kiss my ass." She rammed her shoulder into Payson as she marched toward the elevator door. "Hi, Braden."

Braden glanced at Diane, then grabbed Payson's gaze. "What's going on here?" He sprinted to Payson.

"Oh she's fine," Diane called across the deck. "I just gave her a little reality check."

The elevator door closed and Braden touched her cheek. "What's this? Your cheek is red." The warmth in his eyes shifted to glacial. "Did she hit you?"

Payson nodded. "She did but I hit her too. I'm all right."

"Let's sit down, okay?" He took her hand and sat her on top of the short wall. "Do you want to tell me about it?"

"I think she's been following me. That's the only explanation for why she knew I might be up here this morning." Braden rubbed his thumb over her fingers. "I don't know how she got access."

"Hmmm…maybe one of her DAs deciphered the access code. I'd say she could have blasted the keypad but it was fine a minute ago." He wrapped his arm around her shoulders, and pulled her against his body. "I'm sorry she invaded your space."

Noises from the city waking up lifted from the streets. "I can't explain it, but I feel closer to the city up here."

"I know. Kind of like putting a finger on the city's pulse without any of the distractions down there."

"Yes, exactly." She breathed in his scent and let it calm her vibration. "Darkness is growing, without a doubt. It hit me strong this morning. It drove me to urge Diane to see it too. I rehashed the history of our ancestors and let her know how I feel about the Aeons' role in lighting up the city. It only made her more defensive."

"There's nothing wrong with trying. It's too bad she's resistant to the truth." Braden stroked her hair and the chaos of Diane slipped away.

"Our ancestors are very real to me, Braden. I feel them in my bones. When I was young and finding it hard to be around my parents, I longed for them."

"I feel the connection too. It's a part of us we can't deny any more than we can ignore what is happening to the city." He kissed her forehead, then lit up her heart with his smile. Braden's smile gleamed in his eyes and radiated in his face like sunshine. "But for now, I vote for getting breakfast. Then I have to get to work."

"Me, too. You go ahead. I have one more thing to do and then I'll be ready. You go ahead."

"Okay, you better hurry. I'm ready for eggs and bacon."

He left her with a glow. She couldn't drop the images she'd seen earlier in her head. Of course, she'd been born thousands of years after her ancestors. But maybe if she'd had them around, she would have felt like she belonged. Those long-dead strangers could have told her there was nothing wrong with her.

Instead, her parents had looked for ways to deal with their strange daughter who talked about things she couldn't have known. Payson clenched her teeth, remembering an early time when she'd asked her mother why the neighbor's wife didn't like her.

"Payson, what do you mean, Mrs. Trautman doesn't like me? Did she say something to you?"

"No, Mommy. I heard her brain talking about you when she touched me."

"Oh, Payson. I've told you not to lie, so many times."

"I'm not lying, Mommy. Her brain told me she doesn't like it when you leave Pixie outside and she barks too much."

"There is no way Mrs. Trautman's brain told you that. Now go to your room and write two paragraphs about what happens when you lie."

Payson found her center and drew strength from the light that was always there, and stood, sighing. Neither her mother nor her father accepted that she was different but still lovable.

Payson stubbed her foot against the low brick wall around the deck, breathing through remembered chaos in her home. Still, Auralia was her hometown, and in the relative safety of it, she'd been able to use her special skills and her work in service of the Aeon mission.

She swallowed anxiety. Now that safety was gone. Something had happened, and she wasn't sure she knew what, but DAs thrived and lived among average people discreetly doing their thing to debilitate hope and good will. Some of them were unaware of how their choices had darkened their soul, but nonetheless they made a mark. The increase in poverty, crime, and violence oozed in her gut like tar.

She closed her eyes and sent out her light energy to the people below. The energy tingled in her body and spread to her limbs, her feet, her fingers. She opened her eyes and saw her energy spread like an invisible blanket of golden light. Hope proliferated like delicate, flowering vines all around her.

"Good morning, Auralia," she whispered.

She took the elevator down to the building's street level and stepped into the lobby, where she almost ran into the building owner, Carl Sheppard.

"Good morning, Payson. Did you enjoy your gaze over the city?" The CEO of Sheppard Media was a wealthy businessman with a lot of heart, who gave her hope.

"I did. Thank you for giving me access to the deck. I love it up there, Carl."

He shook his head. His smile slipped into a sober expression. "Payson, fulfilling your request was the least I could do. I can never do enough for you. You brought back my daughter to me."

It had been six weeks since she'd located his runaway teen, but his eyes instantly misted. "It's what I do, Carl. I find people for a living. I'm very glad to have been able to find her and convince her the best place for her was back with you." She gave him a grin. "Which, by the way, was pretty easy to do at that point."

His gaze dropped. "It makes me sick to think that some drug dealing pimp had gotten hold of her when she ran away."

"I know. Are you two working things out?" If any father could learn from his mistakes with his children, it would be Carl. His inner strength came from his light energy, not ego.

"We're talking with the counselor you suggested, Claire Eve Kelly. Her methods are very effective, so yes, my relationship with my daughter is already improving."

Sheppard's assistant walked up behind him. "Mr. Sheppard, your early appointment is waiting in your office."

Sheppard nodded. "My day starts early, as I see yours does too. Nice seeing you, Payson."

Payson waved as he walked away, then headed out of the building. She had appointments to keep too. First, breakfast with Braden. Then she needed to review her initial information on a missing young woman and talk with the mother. Later she'd pick up Braden, then retrieve a family's nest egg.

CHAPTER 2

HERE'S A REASON why a female bounty hunter should never bring her boyfriend on a case.

He's apt to go all knight-in-shining-armor.

Payson shook her head. He wasn't going to win this one. "No, Braden, you're not going with me. I need you to stay here in the car."

Braden frowned. "I'm a cop, a detective. I detect stuff. I can help you find what you're looking for, and watch your back in case the perps show up."

She ran her hand over his cheek, and savored the butterflies that leaped to life in her stomach. "No. I'm in charge. This is my case. Me, bounty hunter, you, stay-in-car. I can take care of myself. You know that."

He slanted her a smile and his gold-specked hazel eyes sparkled. "I do know. But—"

"There are no buts. As a recovery agent, I can do things you can't. I want you for backup and to drive my car, but do more than that and you'd be putting your job and mine at risk." He couldn't argue, really. They had agreed years ago they would keep their work separate from their relationship. It was the professional thing to do.

A warm, late afternoon summer breeze wafted through the open window in her silver Volt, lifting locks of his dark wavy hair. The grove of trees situated just off the country road gave them cover. Shade from the maple and oak tree branches cooled the interior of her car just enough to keep from sweltering. Payson watched Braden consider her argument and waited for the moment he'd see her point.

The clients, Mr. and Mrs. Blaine, who had hired her to find their stolen restored 1941 Willys coupe, had given up hope of ever finding it. The Willys held sentimental value to them because a great-great grandfather had discovered it rusted and littered with dried leaves and brought it back to its shiny glory. Beyond the family heirloom aspect, the car's value of nearly $100,000 was a college education and part of a retirement fund. Its theft disrupted the family's hopes and dreams, and was exactly the kind of activity DAs would do just for kicks.

But she'd found it. She'd used her ability to connect with the vehicle when the owners had given her documents and photos. Her research and that connection had led her here.

"You're right."

There it was. She knew Braden would come around. "Thanks. I know that, but I'm glad you see it my way."

"That's what I love about you. You're so humble." He moved closer into a quick kiss. His lips firm against hers pushed her already racing pulse.

Adrenaline pulsed through her. She climbed out of the car, double-checking the Ruger LC9 in her holster at her back and the knife strapped to her leg. Leaning in the car, she grabbed the set of keys that belonged to the owners from the console and shoved them in her pocket. "If I need you I'll whistle. If you see me driving the car off the property, follow me."

He saluted, and she turned away, all business.

Exhilaration filled her like fresh air. She stepped carefully through the overgrown grass up to a small house, her gun raised. At five-foot-four inches, she had to stand on tip-toes to see inside through a side window. A kitchen stood on the other side of a small living room area.

She slid along the outside wall around a corner and looked through another window into a bedroom.

So far, so good. The house looked empty. She sensed the case coming together inside her, and she glanced around for an outbuilding. It was only about two-thirty in the afternoon, but clouds were building in the sky. Cicadas filled the air with their signature buzzing. Shadows stretched across the property, lending a sense of foreboding to the landscape.

Her heart did flip-flops when she found what she wanted. Her sights focused on a garage sitting at the back of the property. Its roof was covered with moss and the garage door sagged. Hmm. No lock? She paused, scanning the yard for signs of people and took note of the tire tracks in the grass. They came from the road and ended at the garage door. Bingo!

She walked the circumference of the building, poised for the perp's appearance and searching for a way in other than the obvious. The windows were boarded up and there was no side door.

At the front again, Payson crouched, scanning around the garage door for signs of a security system. Surely the robbers hadn't left the valuable car unsecured. They'd stolen the Willys by disarming a sophisticated alarm system and driving it out of the owners' pristine storage facility. They'd left no prints, so she suspected they were experienced car thieves. This silly garage raised her suspicions.

Payson straightened and took deep breaths, in and out, intentionally grounding herself, imagining her feet connecting with the earth. She engaged her psychometric ability and pressed her hands against the garage door. An image of it sliding up flashed in her mind. In her mind's eye, the open door revealed the interior, where a glossy, green Willys sat.

It was here, just on the other side of the garage door. Her ability confirmed the vehicle in the visual was the missing one she was after.

She held the video-like image, watching for signs of security measures.

C'mon, we need to finish up here. Don't lock the car.
What? You're crazy.

No, I'm smart. We may need to drive it out of here in a hurry. Leave it.

The image dropped, but the sense of urgency and darkness emanating from it rattled Payson's insides. The voices of the two men in her vision chilled her bones. A quality of heartless determination warned her to be on her best game.

A chaotic hum went off in her body and set her nerves on edge. At least one DA was nearby, but she wasn't afraid. Maybe the source was far enough away not to cause problems.

She yanked on the garage door and it rolled up, complaining on its tracks all the way. True to her vision, the car stood in the middle of the floor.

She didn't waste time assessing its condition. It didn't matter. All she had to do was deliver it to the owners. She took a step.

"Hold it right there."

Drat. In her excitement she'd let down her guard. She twisted her head around to see a man standing behind her, aiming an AK14 at her back.

"Drop the gun. What are you doing here?" His voice was smooth and deep. It sent shivers through her body. She let her gun slip from her fingers as she turned around.

"I asked you a question." Cool, expressionless, 'Mr. Smith' shoved his gun into her shoulder.

She sighed, detecting strong darkness in him. His sharp vibration hurt her heart. She chose her next move, and expanded her light, setting her intention for it to engulf him. It was one way of disarming a DA. "You probably guessed what I'm doing. I'm here to retrieve a stolen car."

"You're a cop!" Mr. Smith's eyes widened. He grabbed her long ponytail and jerked her against the wall.

"Ow!" Note to self. Rethink wearing a ponytail when working in the field. "No. I'm a recovery agent."

Smith shoved his rifle harder into her skin, and got twitchy. "That's worse. Get down on your knees," he ordered, his voice steady.

Suddenly, a second man dropped through the roof, hollering and just missing the Willys.

The noise must have alerted Braden. His light energy floated to her, filled her, and helped her sustain her flow of light. She grabbed the end of Smith's rifle and ripped it out of his grip. "Freeze!"

She shoved him to the ground. "Put your hands behind your head." She shuffled around to keep him in her sight. "You, the clumsy guy hiding over there. Come out right now, your hands in the air."

A young man in camo stood up at the back of the garage holding his hands above his head. "Don't shoot." Blood trickling from scrapes and cuts on his forehead flowed into one eye. Payson suppressed amusement and aimed her light at him.

"I won't as long you cooperate."

He walked toward her, but tripped over a wire she hadn't noticed, and released a shrieking alarm.

She cringed at the sound and hoped it wouldn't bring Braden running to her. It wasn't time for a cop.

"Grab her," commanded Smith, the older man of the two, who appeared to be in charge.

The younger man lunged for her, and pulled her feet out from under her. She landed flat on her back and hit her head, but not hard enough to daze her. She balled her hands. She had to get control of the situation.

The other man took the gun and trained it on her. "Find something to tie her up with."

"Listen, Mr. Smith, we can work this out."

"My name's not Smith."

"Hmm. You look like him. I'll take the car and let you go, free and clear." Payson didn't mean it, but persuasion was useful in her line of work, even if it meant bending the truth.

The young man scrambled to wrap rope around her feet and hands. Sweat beaded on his face. "You never said anything about shooting someone."

"Shut up," Smith barked. "It doesn't matter. The boss has reasons for stealing the car. That's all that matters. We'll deliver it and stay alive. Now stand back."

Payson chortled. "You're not going to get any money for this heist. Do you know how much this car is worth?"

Smith stared at her. "That mouth is going to get you killed."

He scuffed toward the Willys and ran his fingers over the finish where the young man had fallen.

"I didn't scratch it. Can we get out of here?" The young man's eyes twitched.

Payson flooded him with light and peace. His eyes convulsed. She kept up the stream, hoping it would override the fear inside him, while she discreetly inched her hands toward her knife.

Buzzing sharpened to a jagged edge in Payson. Smith slanted his head and smirked. "Put her in the car. Maybe the boss would like to meet her."

"Oh, man," the young guy whined. "Of course he's gonna like her. Look at her. But we shouldn't do this."

The man twisted and smacked him with the gun, then took hold of Payson's hands and pulled her to her feet. She head butted him, knocking him backward long enough for her to reach her knife. She aimed at the man's thigh and flung it.

"Aahh," he screamed and stutter-stepped, while pulling the trigger.

A sharp pain sliced through Payson's shoulder and she struggled to stay upright. The bullet had just nicked her shoulder, but the men were down. She kicked the gun away from Smith and pulled the knife out to cut herself free.

"Okay, Smith, to hell with this." She kicked the man over and punched him in the face, then stomped on the other one's back. "Stay down." A quick shove to Smith to face him into the ground, and she pulled the keys from her pocket. Quickly, she tore off the bottom of her shirt and wrapped it around her bleeding arm.

With one backward glance at the men out cold, she picked up her gun and got behind the wheel. The engine roared to attention. She pressed on the clutch, thrust the gearshift into reverse, and backed out of the garage. Quickly shifting into drive, she peeled out on the grassy driveway and floored it. In her rearview mirror, she watched the two men stumble to their feet, but it didn't matter. She had not only taken back their prize, she'd stolen their gun.

Out on the road, she didn't waste any time on anticipating Braden joining her. He'd first call in the crime and alert Auralia police of the thieves. She alerted the Blaines that she was on her way and drove straight to the people waiting for news of their car.

Twenty minutes later, she pulled in to their driveway and honked the horn twice. Original to the coupe, the horn sounded a quaint beep-beep.

This was the part of her work that made her heart sing. The moment when her client got a happy surprise.

The front door swung open and twelve Blaines—one son, two daughters, three cousins, one aunt and an uncle, one grandfather and one grandmother—poured out. Mr. and Mrs. Blaine brought up the rear.

"You found her? Payson, Payson. Oh, my, Payson. You're bleeding."

Payson shrugged. "It's nothing. Here's your baby."

Mr. Blaine wrapped her in a bear hug. "I never thought..." He choked on his words and tears meandered down his rugged face.

"I told you I would bring her home." Her heart expanded in the satisfaction of righting the wrong done to the family, and in the glow of their appreciation.

Mrs. Blaine stood staring at the car. "Look at the sun sparkling off the finish. She's happy to be home." She put her hands to her heart. "This is a miracle, Payson." She patted Payson's arm. An image flashed. Payson saw Mr. and Mrs. Blaine staring into the empty garage.

Mr. Blaine shook his head. "I can't believe the Willys was stolen. This is terrible."

"What are we going to do? What about our money?" Mrs. Blaine's tears wet her cheeks.

The thieves had come close to stealing more than a vehicle, they almost ruined lives. Payson's heart expanded. She'd changed that.

One of their daughters and a niece grabbed her shoulders, shaking her. "You have no idea how important the Willys is to our family."

Laughter came from deep inside her, bubbling out. "I do understand. I'm very happy you have your car back." When another daughter came to her holding a pen and a checkbook, her smile dropped.

"I'm sure my father discussed your fee with you. Whatever we owe you it should be more."

"You owe me nothing. I don't charge for missing persons or displaced possessions. Please put away your checkbook." She waved her off. "If you want to do something for me, please continue to love one another and pass it on to others." The family's gratitude lit up their faces. It boosted the peace and hope inside her. Their focus on helping each other and commitment to family may have seemed small to them, but in a world where balance of light and dark was everything, the importance of their values was significant.

She waved when she saw Braden drive up and park in the street.

"This is my ride." She waved him up and savored the bounce to his long stride.

"Hey, folks."

"This is Braden. He was my back-up."

Braden grinned and offered his hand to the family members gathered in the yard. "Not that she needed any back-up." He eyed her shoulder. "Are you all right?"

She nodded and he draped his arm around her waist. It was warm and comfortable.

"As much as I'd like to stay awhile and enjoy your company, Braden and I need to get going. I need to follow up with the police. They will be in touch with you soon."

She slid into the passenger seat in her car and let Braden drive. The excitement of the hunt and the retrieval was turning into fatigue. As adrenaline boost dissipated into a sense of tranquility, she leaned back against the seat and enjoyed Braden's closeness. "Thanks for your support today. Things went a bit crazy, but nothing I couldn't handle. The men implied they weren't getting paid for the job, but rather were under some threat."

"Interesting. One was a DA, I felt that. He was a pretty intense dude."

"Yeah, I called him Mr. Smith, you know, like in the movie."

Braden laughed. "Oh yeah, I can see that. It's not funny that you got shot, though." He kissed the tips of his fingers and pressed them softly to her wound.

"Don't worry. I felt your energy, and that was nice."

He took her hand in his and rubbed his thumb over her skin. It tingled at his touch. "No problem. I'm going to drive back to the station so you can go on with your day."

"Do you have work you need to do before five o'clock quitting time?" Relaxation drifted through her body. Her eyelids fluttered, then closed.

"I have someone I want to check on. But you could go home. I have my car in the parking garage. It's going to take me about an hour to talk to the guy."

"Shouldn't you interrogate Mr. Smith and his partner? I'm interested to know if they would give away the name of the person who hired them, but it's not within my purview now that they're in custody."

"Yeah, good idea."

"Can you find me a room to work in at the police station? I have to be there anyway." Now that the Willys was home, urgings rose for finding the missing daughter. Prioritizing her cases was difficult and driven moment by moment by the cases themselves. But until checked off, they all churned in the back of her mind. "We could each drive to my house after you're done."

"Affirmative." He pulled her toward him.

She nuzzled under his chin, her pulse picking up from a whiff of his spicy scent. "Maybe we could pick up a pizza and turn in early."

He met her gaze. "I'm not tired."

She grinned. "Neither am I."

CHAPTER 3

$\mathcal{B}$RADEN SAT ACROSS the table from Mr. Smith at the Auralia Police Department and held his gaze. The heavy penetrating vibration emitting from the man challenged the intensity of his inner light, but Braden thought of Payson. Thoughts of her strengthened him.

"You know, I could compel you to tell me who you're working for, or you could make it easy on yourself." Braden wouldn't use his mind control, though it was tempting. He wanted to give the thug a chance to make a positive choice.

"Go to hell." Mr. Smith rattled his handcuffs. "I'm not giving you squat."

Braden jumped to his feet, his muscles rigid, and circled the man. "Listen, stupid. Do you really think your boss is going to save your day? You're just a bug on the windshield."

"So you say." The man smirked, as though he were relaxing on a patio in the sunshine.

Braden gritted his teeth. "Oh, smart guy, huh? Well, let's think a minute. You aren't getting paid for the job, that's for sure. On top of that, you failed. You're going to pay for that mistake. This loyalty you've got going isn't going to come back in your direction. Give me a name and I can help you."

Mr. Smith's mind-scrambling vibration lost its edge. "Man, I can't." His face scrunched into what looked like pain.

Braden slammed his palms onto the table. "You have to. Why can't you see that?"

"Let me out of here. Please, before it's too late. They're going to kill me."

"I know. That's why you have to give me a name."

Watching Smith deteriorate right in front of him tortured Braden. His pulse raced while intense energy rose inside the interrogation room.

Terror widened Smith's eyes. "I can't tell you. It's too late. I can feel it."

Pressure engulfed the room, making it hard for Braden to breathe. It was Dark Sides energy, flooding the room. It had to come from a DA, but from where?

Braden grabbed Smith's shoulders and poured light energy to his soul. "I feel it too. Tell me while you can. I can help you."

A light bulb burst and the man shrieked. His face slumped and his body fell limp.

Braden stuck his head out the door. "I need help, now." He ran back to Mr. Smith and checked his pulse.

Another officer ran into the room. "What happened?"

"He fainted. His pulse is weak."

"I'll get medical."

"I didn't do anything that would have made him pass out."

The medic surveyed him. "You didn't hit him?"

Braden rolled his fingers open, palms up, then turned them over. "See for yourself. I didn't touch him."

"Okay, I get it. Medical will take care of things."

Alone in the room in the aftermath of something crazy, Braden expanded his light to Mr. Smith and his cohort. Clearly, they were deep in Dark Sides. He shuddered. Payson was right. Dark Sides was growing, and he couldn't even protect Smith inside the jail.

He headed toward his office, looking for something to absorb his mind. Payson's run-in with the men who had stolen the Willys reminded Braden of a young man, Nick Ward, he'd taken on as a project and then quickly neglected to stay in touch.

His gut twisted. He had let his workload take priority over his community work, and regret soured his stomach. Now, right now, that was going to change.

He perused his computer, making sure Nick's contact info was the same. Nick was in the database because he had been charged with theft and other petty crimes. The guy had a rough life but was trying to make positive changes, so Braden had struck up a quasi-Big Brother relationship to support him, even though Nick was in his twenties. It was a very informal attempt on his part. No play dates or anything, just an occasional drop into Nick's life to make sure he wasn't too deep into his former life of gangs and crime.

He moved around a lot, so Braden wanted to confirm he could find him at the same house. Sure enough, his last known address was different. He noted the change, and walked out to his car. He pulled at his collar, guilt tripping in his gut. It was going to be quite lame to show up in Nick's life after so many weeks had passed since his last visit. With the recent rising crime rate in Auralia, work had kept him very busy, making it hard to fit in time for Nick.

Regret pinned his thoughts with should-ofs, could-ofs, and didn'ts all the way to Nick's neighborhood.

He parked his burgundy Highlander in the street in front of a convenient mart slash fast-food place. This was Nick's hangout, or at least had been weeks ago.

People of different ages clustered in groups talking. He spotted Nick in one group of young men and climbed out, heading in his direction. Nick's back was facing Braden, but others standing around eyed him up and down. He wasn't trying to hide his *copliness*. He wouldn't be a bit surprised if someone offered him a doughnut.

"Hey Nick," he said from about three yards away.

All heads turned toward him. One guy pointed at him and gave Nick a push.

Nick glared at Braden. "Hey. What do you want?" He took a pull on his cigarette and blew the smoke in Braden's face.

"I thought you quit those things." Braden's chest tightened. An unmistakable ragged buzz emanated from Nick.

"Yeah." Nick sniffed twice. "I did. But I'm back with them."

The dual meaning of Nick's words didn't get by Braden and either did the sniffing. Odds were good that Nick was back with his gang and snorting meth again. Braden nodded away from the crowd. "I see. You got a minute? Nothing important, just want to talk."

Nick rolled his eyes and sniffed again. Braden didn't blame him for attitude. But he breathed an inner sigh of relief as Nick followed him.

Words stuck in Braden's throat. How could he make inroads with Nick when he'd probably blown it? "I'm sorry I've been MIA. But I hope you'll give me another chance to be friends. I care about you."

Nick laughed and rubbed his nose, a disgusted chuckle twisting his lips. "Friends? Man, you don't even know me. I got friends, and they don't let me down." He scrubbed his foot against the dirt. The hard edge didn't disguise the pain knitted in his brow or his sharp brown eyes.

Braden's instinct reached out to Nick, wrapping him in light, but he sat on his urge to wrap an arm around him and promise to be better. "I know I've messed up. I'm not going to give you excuses, I know I failed you. Could we start over?"

Nick turned his gaze away, looking at nothing. "Why?"

Braden swallowed hard over the question. "Because I do care. I want to be involved in your life and help you when you need it." Nick had history. People had let him down, left him. His life experiences guided him, sometimes in wrong directions. He expected to be disappointed and rejected. That's what Braden's meager efforts had been about, replacing the negativity with healthy experiences that would give him a chance at a good life. "I hope it's not too late."

Nick looked into Braden's eyes, aiming questions at him. "No. It's not. I know you're good for me…when you show up."

Relief filtered through Braden, unwinding the knots in his gut. He offered Nick his hand. "Thank you. I'm going to do better by you."

Nick gave him a hearty handshake and smiled. "All right, then. When?"

Braden laughed. "Saturday. Burgers at my house. I'll pick you up at your apartment."

"Pick me up here."

"Sure, man. See you then."

The guilt still lay on his shoulders, but Braden felt lighter going to his Highlander. He had faced the facts soon after he'd called Nick from his group. The kid wasn't going to say anything that would assure him he wasn't back into criminal activity. Nick had in fact implied he was. That didn't sit easy in his heart, but at least he had made chinks in his walls.

The Highlander made little noises inside the dash and he smacked it. "Stop it." It wasn't a new vehicle but it got him around and that was all that mattered. A little quiet would be nice, though.

He cruised through traffic on his way back to the station, his thoughts pulling toward Payson. Just thinking of her bright scent, soft hair, and spunk made him squirm to get comfortable in his seat. A break alone with her from the chaos that was becoming normal in Auralia teased his senses. That pizza and night with her was sounding pretty damn perfect.

THE FARTHER FROM the city Payson drove, the more her breathing eased. She checked her rearview mirror and smiled. Braden was following close behind.

The drive to her home from downtown Auralia took only about forty minutes. Her house sat surrounded by nature, away from people and the noises people created. She had her counselor and fellow Aeon Claire Eve Kelly to thank for the awareness of her need for the healing benefits of nature.

Claire Eve's guidance had saved her life. Now she relied on specific strategies Claire Eve had taught her to counteract the physical effects —depression, short temper, anger, hopelessness—of mixing through her work with those who fueled darkness. With awareness of what was at stake for her and the world, Payson thanked her lucky stars for Karate, meditation, nature, and music to clean her energy field and refill it with vitality. But without time talking with Claire Eve, she'd fail and failure was out of the question.

Payson turned into her private lane and savored the way the forest trees and foliage closed in around her as she took the dirt road deeper into her property. At about three-quarters of a mile, the dense forest opened to a spacious front yard. Her nerves settled at the sight of her home. The two-story modern cottage built in the early 1900s was exactly what felt like home. Just looking at the large front porch and how the house sat quaintly among the trees made her heart smile.

She hit the garage door opener, pulled into her garage, and waited for Braden. As soon as he stepped in the garage, she closed the door behind them, effectively securing their safety.

She punched in the passcode at the door and entered one of her favorite places on earth. Her secluded and protected home.

"ZuZu, I'm home," she called to her cat just as the orange tabby came running out of a hall closet. The door to the closet was always open and it was one of her sleeping spots. Payson picked up ZuZu and started rubbing her neck and around her ears. "Sleepy head," she said, kissing her cat and setting her back down.

"Hi, ZuZu." Braden walked into the room, and the cat strolled by his legs and meowed. "She's hungry. There's nothing else she'd want from me," he teased, and put the pizza on the counter.

Payson took her time relaxing. Her home was one of the few places she could let down her guard and simply relax without fear of being attacked by a DA or a disgruntled skip. Even though windows and sliding glass doors made up the entire back wall, she didn't feel vulnerable.

She took a whiff of pizza. "It smells great. Hungry?"

"Yeah." He smirked, and twisted a lock of her hair. Her pulse fluttered. "I'm thinking of something else first. How does warmed up pizza sound?"

"Interesting." She looked into his eyes and forgot about her appetite. "What are you proposing?"

He pulled off his shirt and unbuckled his belt. "Skinny dip."

She shot him a coy smile and shrugged off her clothes. His gaze drifted up and down her body. He gave her a lopsided grin.

"You really get to me, sweetheart. I never get used to seeing you naked." He pulled the elastic band from her ponytail, releasing her hair to cascade over her shoulders. He plunged his face into the long locks and moaned. "I could stay here forever."

She trembled and grasped his face for a silent moment. She didn't want to rush their time together. She strolled through her living room, taking in the spectacular natural beauty outside the glass wall. Love swept through her veins. She leaned her hand against the glass and watched the stream outside spill over the rock wall into a small pond, and tuned into the gurgling as the stream rushed around rocks.

The soothing sounds brought her peace, while at the same time her senses enlivened as she opened the sliding door and stepped onto her deck. She beckoned Braden with her fingers, and he followed her down the winding stairs to the dock at the side of the pond. She dove into the brisk water, then popped to the surface quickly, just as Braden's splash went up. Submerged, he swam past her and came up for air, sputtering.

"It's brisk! Feels good." His muscled body grabbed her gaze. His body was as familiar as her own, but it never failed to stir her thoughts.

Braden did a breaststroke to the other side of the pond while she swam farther into the middle, luxuriating in the freedom with each stroke.

She closed her eyes and sunk. Deep in the delicious feel of the water, she swam until a rush of water told her she was in the waterfall.

Coming up for air, she swam through the curtain of water into the small cave hidden behind it. Crashing water drowned out birdsong and crackling from the forest she knew so well. Payson dipped her head to the crystal surface and blew tiny bubbles. A delighted giggle escaped her throat. Immersion in nature never got old.

Visible in the sparkling clean water, Braden wrapped his hands around her legs and slid up her body, tiny rivulets of water running from his hair down his chest.

They stood feet to feet, planted to the wet, rocky cave floor, naked skin to naked skin. Heavy lidded, his gaze locked on hers, and her inner light responded to his, swelling with peace and love. Her pulse sprinted, aching in her body taking over. He took her head in his hands and touched his lips to hers, stealing her breath. His hands traced the curves of her body and grabbed her behind, pulling her closer still.

Payson took his lower lip in her mouth, then opened her lips to his darting tongue. Passion expanded her breaths as his chest heaved against her body.

Instinctively, she arched backward and Braden held her in one arm while drawing his fingers through her cleavage, inciting her nerves to riot. He drew her back up, his eyes blazing.

"I'm going to go insane, Payson." His voice hoarse and his muscles taut made her giggle.

"Oh, I see." She stroked his hardness. "How nice. Me too." She stepped to the edge of the tumbling water and pointed to the shore of the pond. "Race you?"

Without a word, Braden sliced into the water and took off toward the other side. She watched his elegant movements through the pond, then swam toward the shore, her heart thudding in her ears.

By the time she reached the stretch of grass along the pond, Braden was gathering beach towels from the storage cabinet near the dock. He handed her one and laid out two of the towels on the grass. He stretched out on the place he'd made for them and Payson paused. The early evening light bathed him in a golden ambiance, highlighting his muscled torso. The sight of him spurred impulses she couldn't, didn't want to, resist.

He reached for her. "C'mere."

"Well, when you say something so romantic," she teased, "how could I resist?" She took his hand and he pulled her to his side.

He draped his arm around her shoulders and she took in his presence. His light and love flowing around them intoxicated her. With

Braden, oneness meant something more than physical closeness. It meant they opened to each other's souls with no censor or agenda, and disappeared in the moment.

She squirmed under his caresses to her breasts. Her breath caught, as he lingered there to lick water droplets from her skin. Urgency drove her. She had to taste him. She drew him up to her mouth and parted her lips. He pressed his lips to hers, open mouthed and heated. She poured out her love in a deep kiss that took away all her breath.

Braden moaned and drew back. His gaze trailed over her and he reached his hand to massage firmly and rhythmically between her legs. She drew in a sharp breath, then relaxed against his touch.

"I love you, Payson," he murmured. He stretched his body on top of her, and his heart pounding against her drew her nearer. His words floated on the stillness of the evening, sending shivers rolling through her.

She closed her eyes and relished his thrust inside her. His body was warm. "Braden," she whispered.

She wrapped her legs around him, wanting him close, so close. She pressed her body to him and the sounds of his labored breathing matched the pace of her pulse as tension built. Awareness bloomed in her, knowing each of them as individuals offered full-bodied love, each holding nothing back and coming together in such a way that there was nothing else. Braden wasn't taking anything from her, he was giving her a gift. Payson's heart filled with love from Braden and overflowed with love for him, giving all that she was.

In one tiny second, thoughts stepped forward in her mind as though someone had pressed the pause button. All the years she and Braden had been together flashed in a recollection of times they'd made love, and yet there remained a quality of newness each time. Her heart warmed. The pause broke and explicit joy quivered through her. He shuddered as they climaxed together, throb after throb, so raw, so keen, and waves of pleasure took her in.

She lay limp beneath him, listening to his breathing slow, mirroring her own. A rarified moment embraced them, and she couldn't want anything more.

Braden slipped to her side and rested his head on his arm. "Are you warm enough?"

She chuckled. "Plenty. Look up. It's beautiful." Above the trees, streaks of tangerine and honey painted the sky.

"Mm…nice sunset." He stretched his arm across her body and sighed. "I love making love with you. Want to do it again?"

She shoved him over. "You nut."

CHAPTER 4

$\mathcal{P}$AYSON PULLED BACK the covers on her bed. "Get up, sleepy head. It's time for work."

Braden startled awake, lying naked in her bed and peering up at her through squinted eyes. "Do I smell coffee?"

"You do. I made breakfast too. Blueberry pancakes with real maple syrup." She tugged at his arm, laughter spilling out of her heart. "Out of bed."

He quickly roused and pulled her down beside him. "Not so fast. Lie with me, just for a minute."

Her heart swelled. She leaned her face against his bare chest and breathed in the warm and masculine scent of his skin. It teased her to forget everything but him. She cuddled deep into his neck and delighted in his embrace.

Braden groaned. "Mmm, you smell good." He tugged at the buttons on her shirt. "It's unfortunate that you're dressed." He shifted to lean on his elbow and looked down at her. "I love waking up like this. Too bad we both have to get to work." He smiled and woke up all parts of her body.

"Yeah, too bad." She kissed the tip of his nose.

"You know, we could make moments like this permanent." He lowered his gaze. "We could get married."

Her pulse skipped a beat. They had discussed it before. "No, we can't. Not when the darkness is still growing. We don't know what our future will look like." She lifted his chin. "Besides, taking a step like that could send Diane over the edge. I'm afraid what she might do if she realized there was no hope of you two getting together."

He rolled his eyes. "There is no way I'm ever going to leave you, and I would never couple with Diane. To be honest, sometimes I wonder if I really care about saving the city from darkness. It's becoming just all blah, blah, blah. No matter how hard we work for light, darkness keeps growing. Maybe we should get married and have a bunch of kids, live a life worth living."

She ran her fingers over his brow. "Sometimes I feel the same way. Sometimes I feel like chucking it all. I want to know why I am one who has to deal with the Dark Sides. I never get an answer."

"Exactly." He sighed.

"But, being an Aeon isn't something we can quit. It's who we are. Could you honestly let the city fall? Could you let people lose all hope, virtue, and love? I know it's hard, but we've got each other. Your love means everything to me."

His expression softened. "When you put it that way, well, no, I don't want that. I do want to get married, but I see your point. I can wait, for now."

"I love you." She'd been in love with Braden since high school and college, but every time she told him, he responded as though it was a new revelation.

He brushed her hair back from her face and placed a soft, slow kiss to her lips. Her heart tripped as he pulled back. "I love you."

Suddenly, her cat landed smack dab on his back. "Ackk! Geez, ZuZu. Good morning." He rolled over and wiggled his toes as the cat played with them.

Payson sighed and climbed out of bed. "See you in the kitchen. Pancakes await."

She poured herself a mug of coffee and sat at the island to sip it, listening to the sounds of Braden climbing out of bed and readying to come to breakfast. The light of her love effused her spirit.

The marriage talk ended as they usually did, at a dead end. She couldn't promise to love, honor, and cherish as long as Dark Sides continued to threaten life itself. It didn't feel right. So for now, they each would keep their place. His was a condo near downtown. She surveyed her home and looked out the large expanse of glass into the deep green of the forest. A mother duck and her four babies waddled out of the trees and slipped into the pond. Wildlife frequenting the spot always delighted her. She didn't want to leave this place to live with Braden and he wanted to live close to his work.

His footsteps landing crisply on the stairs lifted her lips. He stepped into the kitchen, whistling.

"You look happy," he said. He poured himself a mug of coffee, but stopped to kiss beneath her ear before sitting across from her, a lock of his dark hair falling over one eye.

"I know sexy when I see it." Her eyes pinned his. "I like sexy."

Braden almost spit out his coffee. "Thanks."

Payson set a plate of pancakes in front him and he stuffed a bite in his mouth. "These are yummy. Thanks for making breakfast."

"Sure. Do you want to come over tonight?" He didn't spend every night in her home, but even though it was a frequent thing, she never wanted to take anything about Braden for granted.

"I'm going to be late tonight. I've got a ton of work today and a stake-out later." He slanted her a grin. "You're welcome to come to my place. It's closer."

"I'll text you."

He wiped his mouth and leaned back in his chair, his gaze solidly on her. "What's your case? Another scumbag bail-jumper?" He touched her hand, sending warmth through her. "He doesn't know yet that he's about to get nailed by the best registered bail recovery agent in the country."

"Scumbag, huh? Spoken like a cop," she mused. "The skip is wanted for a domestic abuse charge. He's almost the lowest of the low. He beat up his pregnant wife and sent her to the hospital. I'm eager to put him behind bars." Pins stabbed at her heart. She and Braden tended to get harsh when it came to criminals, but they had to walk a fine line. Investing too much in negativity would affect them as much as it would any average human. "We can't afford to sink to the level of the criminals we encounter."

He pursed his lips and his expression went sober. "I know. I feel the darkness of my work inside me sometimes." He brightened and pulled out a box from his pocket. "Which is why I want to give you this."

He slid the box to her. Inside she found a pendant——a circle that held the yin and yang symbol. She smiled. "Balance."

"Just a reminder for you. And for me when I look at you wearing it." His deep blue eyes gleamed and held her gaze.

"Thank you." The weight of their role in life loomed heavy between them, but the assurance in his eyes promised her they were up to the challenge and just needed to remain aware, vigilant, as always.

"I love you," he said again, and shoved away from the table.

She met him half way and slipped into his embrace. Her body molded to his like it was coming home. "I love you." His lips touched hers tenderly, then dove into a long, simmering kiss.

She stepped away and nodded. "Have a good day at work and be careful."

A smile stretched across his face. "You, too."

BRADEN TOOK THE stairs two at a time to his third floor office. The pleasant beginning to his morning lingered, but with each step, he assumed more of a working attitude. His mind sorted through his present investigation of an uptick in criminal activities in the city. His assignment was to find the people behind a string of robberies. No one had been hurt yet, but for the victims, having property stolen was an assault to their boundaries and sense of safety as well as a loss.

"Good morning, Zane." He nodded to a fellow detective, his closest friend in the department, and walked directly to the coffee area. He poured a cup and sniffed it, then frowned.

"What's the matter, Braden? You don't like the coffee?" Zane sat with his feet up on his desk. "I made it myself."

"That explains the smell," Braden joked.

"No one is forcing you to drink it."

Braden chuckled and set his mug on his desk, ready to dig in to his files.

"Hey, I heard about what happened during your interview with a thief Payson brought in yesterday," Zane said. "Weird, huh?"

Braden was careful with his response. "It was. Did you hear how the guy is this morning?"

"Oh, you didn't, I take it." Zane swiveled in his seat. "He and the other guy with him died last night."

His muscles froze. "What? They're dead? Both of them?"

"Yeah. Medical checked on the one guy during the night and when they found him dead, they checked the other one. Both of them dead, huddled on the floor in their cells."

"Cause of death?" His thoughts scrambled. How could this be?

"Brain hemorrhage, both of them."

"So they both sustained blunt force trauma sometime?"

"No evidence of head wounds, just internal bleeding. It seems too coincidental that both would have had embolisms, but that's what the coroner suggested."

Braden couldn't quiet the panic in his gut, remembering Mr. Smith hollering in pain. "Thanks for telling me. I don't know what to think. They were fine at the scene when they were put in squad cars for transport."

Zane scratched his head. "There's no finger pointing at you or Payson. It's just a freaky accident."

Braden stared without seeing at his computer screen. He had decided against telling Payson about the incident with Mr. Smith because it was police business at that point, and they didn't share their cases. But now, it seemed suspiciously Dark Sides tactics had been used to keep the thieves silent. Need to know what was going on troubled inside him.

He turned his focus to the files regarding the recent robberies, just to stop questions from firing off in his mind.

The first one he clicked open sagged his shoulders. The victim, a young woman in her early twenties, told police three men had stopped her on the street outside her apartment as she was leaving and asked her for a cigarette. When she told them she didn't have one, they pulled out a gun and demanded her purse, watch, wedding rings, and cellphone. He'd interviewed her and gotten descriptions of the robbers, but she'd been pretty rattled and had not given him much to go on.

He stared at the file, anger building. A thin line had stood between the victim's life and her death in that hold-up. Thugs had preyed upon the vulnerable. The idea of it balled his fists. "I'm going to get these guys."

"Sounds serious." Zane swiveled his chair to face him. "Are you talking about the robberies?"

Braden gritted his teeth. "I hate this crap. I know seeing the worst of the worst is a part of the job, but sometimes I want to cut through all the bull-shit."

"I know how you feel. If we didn't have an obligation to the law, what we could accomplish, right?"

Braden's chest burned, as his mind followed the narrow line between right and wrong. They existed so close to each other, mere choices apart. He shrugged. "I probably shouldn't think like that. It's not like I'm going to turn vigilante." It was true. He would never cross the line. If he put his mind to it, he could force people to follow the law. But it wouldn't build light. Individuals had to make their own conscious choice for good.

He stopped breathing at a memory of his parents' deaths. He'd learned the hard way about the misuse of his ability. Trembling, he had to get out of the room.

In the bathroom down the hall, he leaned against a sink and cried inside. He had tried to save his parents from two escaped prisoners who had broken into their house and demanded money. Inside he was the nineteen-year-old son, paralyzed with fear as the men hit his mother, then shoved his father to the floor and kicked him. His maleficence presence rose in fury and he used it to stop the violent men. It had backfired.

Braden's shoulders shook, hearing his parents' screams. His anger had let loose the negative side of his mind control and incited a level of violence in the men he could never have imagined. When the men turned on him, his father yelled at him to run, run away and not look back.

And he had done just that. The blast of the shotguns killing his parents followed him all the way to the abandoned house down the street to Payson. She had sensed the outrageous violence and his mind-numbing rage at his part in it. She nursed him back to life after his devastating taste of failure with his mind control.

The memory always ran in the back of his mind. He had to hang on to it as a reminder of what his ability could do when he lost control. His parents had been just people, not loving parents, but they hadn't deserved to die in such a vicious way. That was his doing.

He threw cold water on his face and checked in the mirror for signs of his heartache. Remorse mixed with anger raced through his blood vessels. It helped him stand and return to his desk.

"Hey, guy, are you all right? Where did you disappear to?" Zane asked.

"Yeah, I'm fine. I guess Payson's pancakes didn't set well in my gut. You know what we were talking about, taking the law into our own hands. I wouldn't do that. I just get irritated."

The burning in his chest simmered, not completely dissipating.

Zane turned back to his desk. "Yeah, I know."

Maybe I can use this anger. The frustration roiling in Braden's gut ramped up adrenaline in his blood vessels. His senses heightened. He could breathe better.

He opened another file and ran his gaze over the case details. The second in the string of robberies, it was a home invasion. Three suspects, young men again, had smashed through a window after failing to kick in a door. The victim was a father of two young children. He'd tried to get his own gun but before he could, one of the suspects had grabbed his son and pointed a gun to his head, demanding the father freeze while they grabbed electronics and ran.

Braden slammed his fist on his desk and printed the incident report. "I'm going to talk to a victim and see if I can get a better description of the perps."

"Good luck," Zane said, as Braden grabbed the report from the printer and headed out.

A few steps down the hall and he stopped short.

Diane stood in his path. "Braden. I was just running by to talk to you."

"Hey, what's up?"

"Do you have a few minutes to talk, alone?" Diane pursed her lips, eyeing him with troubled brown eyes.

"I don't really. I was just leaving. Maybe later?"

"Yeah, sure. How about lunch, my treat?" She shifted her weight from one high-heel to the other. Restless, just like always.

"I can do that. Noon? How about we meet at Coffee Is?"

Diane's eyelids fluttered. "Okay. I'll see you later." She pivoted and marched out of the hall into the elevator.

Wondering what just happened, Braden waited until he was certain Diane would be out of the building before taking the stairs. She was a tough one to understand sometimes. Her terrible childhood was behind her, but it had left its mark. Her smiles were empty, her attitude was flippant, her drinking was excessive.

Those problems didn't mean he would leave Diane in the lurch. He ran down the stairs, still fueled by the fire in his belly. He straightened his shoulders and flexed his muscles.

He was on a mission to ferret out the identity of the robbers, dismissing traffic, swerving in and out of it as an obstacle to his objective: getting to the scene of the home invasion.

He pulled into the driveway in front of the house and surveyed the property. Summer roses bloomed in reds, pinks, and yellows along the edge of the driveway. The exterior of the small, attractive home looked serene, untouched by trauma.

He knocked on the front door. Steps approached, then someone unlocked the deadbolt, and cracked open the door.

He flashed his badge. "I'm Detective Powers from Auralia PD. I'd like to talk."

The door opened. "Come in. I'm Ted Hicks."

Braden followed the man into the living room. A boarded up window at the side of the room grabbed his attention. His muscles tensed. In contrast to the exterior, evidence of trauma and violence lingered in the room.

"Have a seat." Ted gestured to a chair and took a seat on the couch, his body stiff, his movements jerky.

Poor guy. The robbers really messed him up. *I want to strangle the robbers for threatening this family.* "I'm going to take just a bit of your time. I know it's hard to go back through what happened to you and your family."

Ted's gaze dropped and he nodded slowly, as though movement of any kind required painful exertion.

"Just tell me anything that comes to mind. Don't censor or think something is unimportant. Tell me what happened, blow by blow."

Ted pulled in a deep breath and let it out. "I don't know where to... to...to start."

Braden's gut clenched as Ted stammered. He could help him by connecting to his mind. With his mind-control, he could convince the man's brain to let go of his fears and the fog of trauma. He could influence Ted to trust him.

He waited. Yes, he could relieve Ted's mind, or with a single destructive thought of his own, send Ted out into the world with a vendetta.

"Take your time. Where were you and the kids that night? What were you doing before the intruders broke in?"

"My wife was gone for the evening. The kids and I were sitting on the couch watching an old movie on TV. We were laughing because the movie was a comedy." His voice broke. He closed his eyes, and wrung his hands.

Braden shifted on the couch. He couldn't just sit there and let this man suffer when he could ease it. He slowed his breathing and opened his mind to his ability, and set his intention to hold a positive, welcoming space for Ted.

He held the space without pushing in any way, and subtle things happened immediately. Ted straightened his back and opened his eyes. Heaviness registered in Braden's body but he held his positive intention and added a slight suggestion. *You can trust me.*

"We jumped, my son and daughter and I, when we heard a loud noise at the front door." He pointed to the door just around the corner in the hall, then put his hands to his head. "I didn't have time to think or call for help or get my children to safety. Oh, God!"

Braden intensified his grasp on the open channel stretching from him to Ted. *You're safe now.* "Very scary. I'm sorry this happened to you." Braden waited for Ted to relax more in the supportive energy.

"I'm sorry. I guess I'm still rattled."

"It's okay. What happened next?"

"I ran to the hall closet and got my gun, then everything happened at once. The window broke. Glass splintered all over and," his eyes widened and his voice rose, "one of the robbers saw my gun and grabbed my son. He pointed a gun at his head and told me to drop mine or they'd shoot him. I let the gun fall."

Braden nodded. "You did the right thing." The energy of his ability pulsed strongly. *You did the right thing. You did the right thing.*

Ted took in the words without knowing it was happening. He sighed heavily and his shoulders relaxed. "I still see my son's eyes and feel my daughter trembling."

"You saved them, though. You took care of them. Did you look into the robbers eyes?" *Don't back away. See.*

Ted sat quietly, frowning. "First I saw just their clothing and dark masks. One of the men was black with brown eyes. The other two men were white. I don't know what color eyes they had, but each one glared as though they hated me. The one holding my son was thin. I looked up at him, so he was taller than me, and I'm five-foot-nine. He kept sniffing. He smelled like cigarettes. The other two guys had longer hair that poked out from their masks. One had brown and one had kind of reddish hair. They were about the same height as the black guy."

"Anything else you remember about them?" The more details Ted remembered the fuller the picture emerged in Braden's mind.

Ted's eyes lit up. "The guy who held my son had a flinty voice. His movements were swift but smooth. One of the white guys had a gravelly voice and the other one didn't speak. He just stood there until the black guy passed my son to him and ordered him to watch us. Then the black guy started loading up our electronics with the other guy. He cut himself on a shard of glass from the window."

Ted crossed the room to the boarded up window and crouched on the floor. "I wonder if there is any blood here."

Braden joined him. "Could we be so lucky? I'd expect if there was any physical evidence like that, the crime scene investigators would have found it."

Ted grimaced. "The robbers shoved my entertainment center away from the wall when they were unplugging things. I'm afraid I messed with the crime scene without meaning to. I started putting things back where they belonged without thinking. I didn't tell the investigators."

"It's okay. You were in shock. The important thing is you remember now." Braden pulled on gloves from his pocket, moved the furniture away from the wall, and inspected the carpeting up close. "They're small but here are some drops of blood." He pointed to a bloodstain. He ran his eyes along the back of the TV center, close to the floor. His heart leapt. "And here is a fingerprint partially in blood. Concrete evidence, Ted."

"Concrete evidence."

Braden closed his connection to Ted and slapped him on the back. "Great job. Hang back while I call this in and get investigators to collect it. I'll stick around until they arrive. They should be here soon." He nodded at Ted. "Thank you for going back to those horrible moments. It paid off."

Braden beamed inside. He'd used his ability and it had gone well for Ted.

CHAPTER 5

*P*AYSON DIDN'T WANT to wake from the dream of her morning with Braden. She pulled her car into street parking and headed to where she'd be able to think. She walked into Coffee Is in downtown Auralia, humming a tune. Voicing her happiness strengthened her connection with her surroundings. She felt a part of things.

She spotted her friend and owner of the coffee shop, Skye Stone. Skye also was an Aeon who had a healing touch and could read auras. She lifted her hand. "Hi, Skye."

Skye waved from the counter. "Take a seat. I'll be right over." Her brown eyes sparkled and she tossed locks of her long black hair over her shoulder.

Skye was beautiful, and the soothing hum of her vibration gently touched Payson's heart with peace. She settled in at a table near the window where sunshine slanted across the wooden floor, and connected to the positive energy all around.

"Here you go. My treat." Skye set coffee on the table in front of her. "I guessed you'd like to try this variety. It's from the Sierra Madre de Chiapas mountain range in Central America."

Payson sipped the hot coffee. "Mmm ... wonderful. Very robust.

You know what I like." She patted the table. "Can you sit? I can't stay long."

Skye scanned the room, then pulled out a chair. "Sure. It looks like customers are fine. What are you up to today? Hunting the usual suspects? Drug dealers, perverts, and identity thieves?"

Payson smirked. "Domestic violence." She sobered. "You forgot white collar criminals. It all sounds so bleak. I do work among some bad dudes and dudettes that challenge my attitude."

"I do too. Serving the public is not always jolly." Skye grinned. "But I get to see good people too, like you and the rest of our little band of light warriors."

"I like that description." She held up her pendant. "Braden gave me this to remind me to stay balanced."

"That's beautiful. What a great reminder. That Braden has style. I need one of those too." Her eyes suddenly lit up. "We should all get matching tattoos of the yin and yang symbol."

Payson sucked in a breath at a sharp dissonance vibrating in her body. "Don't count me in on that."

Payson's body tensed on alert. Diane walked up from behind her, set her to-go coffee cup on the table, and took a seat.

"Hi, Diane." Worry sprouted immediately, filling her with fear. A look from Skye told her she felt it too.

"Why are we talking tattoos?" Diane frowned. "I'm not into inking my body or putting myself through that pain."

Skye shifted in her chair. "It was just a thought."

Diane's smugness was a defense. Payson tried not to judge. Strictly speaking, Diane belonged to the small group of Aeons, but she acted as though she couldn't care less about them or what they did. "Yeah, I was showing Skye my new pendant."

Diane glanced at her necklace. "Yin and yang? I certainly wouldn't ink *that* on my body, for sure. Where did you get that?" Her eyes turned almost black and her lip curled.

Payson's chest tightened at Diane's warning frown. "Braden gave it to me. He wanted to remind me to stay balanced." *Why do I feel under the lights? And why am I not surprised by Diane's disdain?* She knew the answers to her questions. Diane had been jealous of her for years and was obsessed with Braden.

"Oh." Diane sipped her coffee, then started tapping her long, deep red fingernails on the tabletop.

"Balance is important," Skye added, a somber smile stretching across her earthy face.

"Well, of course you would think so, Skye. With your Northern Cheyenne heritage—"

Skye cut off Diane before she finished. "Excuse me. Balance is not simply a Native American philosophy, it is something everyone should strive for in our lives." Skye's eyes flamed and she stared at Diane.

"Don't get so snooty. I didn't mean anything offensive. I'm just saying it's natural for you." Diane stared back at Skye, taunting, and Payson wriggled, hoping she wouldn't take the bait.

Their antagonism hurt like metal burrs in Payson's stomach. But this was how it always went with Diane. And with the strength of the dark vibration Diane was giving off, Payson feared for her. "Diane, we're not getting tattoos. So, what's going on with you?"

Diane ignored her. "Braden gave that to you," she restated low and ponderous. "Always you and Braden."

Skye sniggered. "What's eating you? Payson and Braden have been a couple for a long time. They will marry sometime. Do you feel they're slighting you?"

Diane snapped her head to face Skye, her brunette bob swishing in her face. "Shut up. You know I'm an outsider among your little group of Aeons. The truth is, the only one of you who cares about me is Braden." She turned to Payson and her voice hardened. "So you're getting married, to Braden. You stole him from me. You fed him lies about me."

Payson's heart sank. "It's not true. We all care about you. I don't understand why you think I've tried to poison Braden's mind. But I am concerned about you. You rarely come around." She wanted to pound the truth into her but instead she simply spoke gently. "I'm worried you're slipping away from our mission."

Diane scoffed. "There is no *our mission.*" She shoved away from the table. "I'm living my life my way and everything is great. I'm a very successful lobbyist. You can ask anyone important. My work with prestigious developers and corporations goes way beyond anything you've ever dreamed of in your little Aeon mind." Disgust dripped off her tongue. "Stay away from Braden," she warned and marched out the door.

"Wow, that was some dark stuff. I know you felt it too. I could see her negativity making little pinpricks in your aura. And her aura, well, it was painful to see it filled with red blotches. She's in trouble emotionally." Skye rolled her eyes. "I'm speechless. Especially with her demand you stay away from Braden."

"I'm sad and worried. She gave off a much stronger negative energy this time than I've felt with her before. I suspected she was going dark, but I didn't know she'd already gone so far into it."

"Well, she made it clear she's no longer one of us." Skye rubbed her temples. "That's not good for her or the city. We know Auralia is already showing signs of the effects of more DAs. Crime is up. The city council is squabbling about the proposed redevelopment of Old Town. I can feel the friction growing. Diane is powerful, so the strengthening of darkness in her can only make things more chaotic."

"Yes, you're right. All the more reason to send her love, though I don't know if she can accept it anymore."

Skye shivered. "We can't let the city be a breeding ground for darkness."

Payson stared at the dark liquid in her cup, knowing it had gone cold. "No, we can't. We should probably talk with the others and give them a head's up."

"Yeah. I've got to get back to work now, but I'll send texts to everyone that we need to talk."

"Thanks."

Payson left Coffee Is with the weight of Diane's remarks bearing down on her shoulders. She paused on the sidewalk and breathed in deeply. Heat shimmered from the pavement and she looked up to take in the blue sky and sunshine. While Diane's words lingered like a rabid animal, all around her was light and she had to remember that. She leaned against her car and quickly called Braden.

His phone rang once and he answered. "Hi, babe. What's up?"

"Sorry to bother you. I know you're working." His voice was cheery, but unlike normal, the connection between them felt a step removed. Her breath froze.

"I always have time for you."

"I ran into Diane at Coffee Is. Something is terribly wrong with her. It scared me."

"Oh. What happened?"

"She thinks I'm coming between you and her, for one thing." She couldn't breathe. It wasn't just because of Diane, it was something about Braden too.

"What? There's nothing between Diane and I. That's crazy talk."

"I know. Could I come over to your place tonight?"

"Of course."

"Are you okay?"

"Yeah. I'm great. Why do you ask?"

"Just wondered. Something feels different, Braden."

"I am psyched. Maybe that's what you're feeling. I just got a boost in the robbery investigations."

She'd have to sit with this feeling to know for certain if he was right. "Great! We can talk tonight. I love you."

"I love you right back."

Nerves fired in her body. Braden was her rock. She couldn't imagine her life without him in it as he'd always been. But she couldn't ignore the rattling in her body that suggested a shift in his energy.

Payson closed her eyes and intentionally let love fill her and spill into the world. She envisioned the invisible field of light spreading out from her and blanketing the city. She deliberately connected to other Aeons and sensed the light glowing brighter. No one would see it, but it offered everyone a touch of its brilliance. It was all she could do right now to protect Braden.

Inside her mind, she flipped a switch to refocus on a case, and climbed behind the wheel.

Excitement fluttered in her gut. The work was already in progress for an assignment Keegan Barnes, an Aeon and owner of Best Bond Company, had emailed her a few days ago. She had been able to pinpoint her skip's last known address and make calls. The skip, Jimmie Jones, lived with his mother. According to his info sheet, he was twenty-eight years old, about five-foot-eleven, and had brown, longish hair. The mother had insisted that Jimmie wasn't around, but during one of the calls, Payson had heard a man's voice in the background. Maybe it was Jimmie. Instead of asking for him, she had sweet-talked the mother into believing she would be kind to her son and it would be better for him to let her bring him in to police custody. Now it was a matter of checking in with the mom to make sure their plan was still in place.

She picked up her phone and called.

"Hello, Payson."

"Hello, Mrs. Jones. Are you ready for me?"

"Yes." Mrs. Jones sniffled. "I don't want my son hurt."

"I'm not going to hurt him. I know you love him. Is he there now?"

"He is. I talked to him, and he agreed to go with you."

"I'll be right there." The woman hung up and Payson crossed her fingers that Jimmie wouldn't burn her.

The home was minutes away, so she accelerated and drove as fast as she dared. Her heart raced as she pulled into the driveway and sped to the door, poised to run around back if Jimmie panicked.

She knocked hard and the door opened. She recognized the man standing in the doorway from his mug shot. It was Jimmie, looking scrubby in sweatpants, a gray T-shirt, and a days-old beard.

"Mr. Jones. I'm recovery agent Payson Silver."

Jimmie nodded and motioned for her to step inside. "I'm only doing this to make my mom happy. I don't belong in jail."

"That's not what the court says, sir. I'm going to walk you out of here without restraints for your mother's sake. But one wrong move and I'll put you on the ground."

"Do what you're told," said the older woman standing in the room.

"Mrs. Jones?" Payson didn't hold out her hand. She was getting control over her psychometry, but she knew better than to touch this distraught woman and open herself to all matter of images that could leave her wasted.

"Yes. I'm Jimmie's mom."

"Thank you for caring about your son." Payson turned to the son. "You're doing the right thing." This time she had to touch, but she set her intention as solidly as she could on building an invisible wall between Jimmie and herself. It didn't always work but it was her only protection. She took his arm. "Let's go."

Jimmie jerked and pulled his arm back. His eyes went wide. "Mom, I can't go. My old lady lied, I never hurt her. I just can't do it."

Payson grabbed him again and yanked him close. Jagged fear shot through her. "Jimmie, this is only going to go bad for you. Stop resisting." She wanted to cuff him right then, but she channeled Obi-Wan Kenobi-type energy instead. "I know this is hard but you can do it."

He breathed in short gasps and shook his head. "No, no I can't." He pulled out of Payson's grip and punched her face.

His fist ploughing into her cheek thrust her against a wall and her feet went out from under her. Dazed, Payson sat with her back against the wall and tried to gather her senses. An image pounded in her head. *A young woman crashed into a stairway, holding her belly. Tears streamed down her cheeks and Jimmie kicked at her feet. "Get up!"*

Payson shuddered and clenched her teeth. As a reflex, she grounded herself and shook off the disruptive energy.

Jimmie ran out the back door into the garage, his eyes on the late-model Ford.

Two steps behind him, Payson pulled out her gun from its belt holster and shoved it into the back of Jimmie's head. "Don't move.

"Okay, okay. Don't hurt me, please." His voice wavered.

"Lift your hands and spread your legs." She kicked at his legs, and kneed him in his lower back. "How does it feel to be a punching bag?

Go ahead, run. It will give me an opportunity to smack the daylights out of you. Then I'll drag your ass to the police station anyway."

"No, I'm not going to give you an excuse to mess me up, bitch."

"That's it." Payson expanded her light, love, and peace and directed it to envelope Jimmie. He wasn't DA, just an angry uncivilized man. He would feel the loving vibration. If it worked how she wanted, the love moving through him could prompt remorse and all the guilt that would go with it.

She grabbed his wrists and secured them with zip ties from her pocket.

"Mom, I feel like shit. Please help me." Jimmie hung his head.

"It's okay, Jimmie." His mother stepped close. "You have to go. It's no use running anymore."

Jimmie's shoulders slumped. "Okay, Mom. I love you."

Payson tucked him into the back seat. With Jimmie behind her, she sat poised for trouble, but he rode quietly during the drive. She called ahead to let the APD know she was bringing him in. At the station, she intentionally sent out light and walked him in to booking, where Pete Bacotti, an officer she knew well, took Jimmie.

Not everyone being held in the building was a DA, but still a high level of dark energy permeated the interior. She quickly filled out the necessary paperwork and turned it in. "Thanks, Pete."

"No problem. Thanks for bringing him in. You have a good afternoon."

Outside, Payson checked her phone. She had a text from Skye about meeting and another from her good friend and fellow Aeon, Ainsley Durham. *Please stop by Fancy This when you can. I have an object to show you.*

Ainsley owned a pawnshop in Old Town. The quaint gathering of unique and specialty stores, bakeries, restaurants, and gift shops was one of Payson's favorite spots in the city. On the occasions Ainsley called on Payson's ability to learn more about the history of objects she got in her shop, she looked forward to immersing in the upbeat energies of the area. Using her psychometry for Ainsley's work gave her a fun way to help, even though sometimes the objects told sad stories.

She texted her back. *I'll be there soon.*

Ainsley's reply popped in. *Great. I'll be here.*

Before leaving the station, she took time to text Keegan that she'd delivered Jimmie Jones and would be expecting her pay in her account. He quickly let her know he'd tend to it.

Getting paid was a good thing, but her sense of job-well-done came from serving justice. The covenant of justice was alive in her. It meant something. She valued that it at least made an attempt to balance right and wrong by holding people accountable for breaking the agreement to protect the greater good by abiding by the laws of society.

If only people understood that their words and actions build a safe and beautiful world or tear it to shreds.

Her heart heavied with thoughts of another case, as she drove to Fancy This. Adele Freeport, the mother of a missing daughter, had asked for help in learning the truth about what happened. Bounty hunting paid the bills, but what really lit Payson up was her work with locating missing persons. Reuniting a lost loved one with his or her family was why she got out of bed in the morning. That, and having her first cup of coffee.

As she breezed into Fancy This a few minutes later, she perused the merchandise while Ainsley waited on a customer. Strolling along the display cases and merchandise shelves, Payson enjoyed the interesting array of objects. She imagined histories of an art deco pair of lamps. The lampshades were decorated with oval shapes and scalloping along the bottom. She guessed them to be from the nineteen-twenty's era.

"Looking to buy, Payson?" Ainsley walked up beside her, smiling. A warmth shimmered between them, unspoken but so good it lifted her spirits. Gratitude glowed inside her for Ainsley's light, and for every time the action was repeated between Aeons.

"No, but these are adorable." She couldn't help but gush.

"Yes. I hope they find a home soon. I'm sure some customer will like their vintage rose moiré fabric and Irish crocheted flowers."

Payson put a hand on her heart. "You know your stuff. I know I like the small pink and silver finials and the beaded fringe."

"It's hand-beaded fringe." Ainsley spoke as though the lamps were her family. "But you're here to read the picture frame, right?"

"I am." She scanned the items on display.

"Oh, it's not on the floor." Ainsley threaded her way to a back room and Payson followed. "Here it is."

"It's lovely." Payson took four cleansing breaths, in and out, then focused on the frame. "I really enjoy helping people connect with the objects they love."

Ainsley grinned. "I know you do. Reconnecting with objects brings them closer to more of their memories and that helps them ground more to their lives."

"Tell me about the frame, but nothing other than its description, please." She had been through this with Ainsley on more than one occasion, so this process was not new. A telling of the object was like an introduction minus a handshake or hug. The distance gave her an initial sense of the piece without getting overwhelmed with impressions.

"It's constructed of wood. Two pillars come up from the base to suspend the frame. The actual frame is crowned with an arching piece of wood." Ainsley traced the crown with her fingers. "The carvings on the base, pedestals, and crown are art nouveau. The photograph is old."

"Okay." Payson took hold of the frame. She closed her eyes and sunk into her senses. She fingered the floral design carved into the crown and opened her eyes. She noted the places where the soft gray paint was worn. She ran her fingertips over the pedestals. "I'll tell you what I'm seeing and what I'm hearing."

Payson opened to receive impressions and didn't have to wait long. "A young woman is placing a photo of two children on a shelf. The same photo still in it." The scene in Payson's mind came alive. "The children reach for their mother just as she sets the frame on a buffet. She bends to grab them up in a group hug. The mother is walking to the kitchen, where she gives the children slices of apples on small plates."

Payson's heart melted with the next image flash. "The mother is sitting in a large upholstered chair holding both children on her lap and singing with them. Their eyes are bright and there is joy in the music. The little boy wriggles in her arms and stretches his feet to the floor."

"'Yes, you can go outside and play,' the mother says, patting his arm, smiling."

"The little girl asks if she can go play too. Her bob is tidy and adorable."

"'Yes. Stay in the backyard, both of you.'"

Another flash. "This time I see a young man sitting with the woman as the children, now a few years older, sit on a cherry-wood-trimmed gold upholstered settee, crying.

"'I'm very sorry for your loss, Ma'am. Your husband was a good man,' a man says and gestures to a boxy carriage sitting in the street. 'The movers are ready to get you and your children settled into your sister's house.'"

Payson blinked, watching the scene progress in her vision. "The movers are packing china, clothes, and much more, sweeping up the woman's life into wooden boxes, trunks, and gunnysacks." She opened her mind specifically to seeing the picture frame. "The picture frame is being packed amongst trinket boxes and perfume bottles. I'm trying to focus on the frame as it moves in time." Payson cleared her throat. A burst of images made her shiver. "The frame is still packed in the box. The box is stacked with other boxes." The images stopped abruptly, and she glanced at Ainsley.

"What's happening?" Ainsley chewed on her fingernails.

"I think the box's history with the woman has ended."

"Oh, I want to know more." Ainsley's chewing shifted to her bottom lip.

"I do, too." Payson closed her eyes tightly. Her mind cast around in time to learn what she could about the family. Names were called out.

"'Helen, Edward is calling for you.' Someone is talking to the mom about her son."

Payson waited, allowing for more input from the past. "Here is a burst of more images about the mother, Helen. She's upstairs in a dimmed room and the boy now looks about sixteen. He's lying in bed, wheezing. Helen is talking to him. 'The doctor will be here soon, my son.'" Payson touched her chest. "Helen wiped his forehead with a cloth."

Flash, flash.

"Is there more?" Ainsley whispered.

"The bedroom door is cracked open and I think the daughter is going inside. She looks about eighteen. 'Mother, you must come down and eat. It's been days.' She's kneeling beside her mother, who is sitting in a chair beside an empty bed, staring."

Ainsley gasped. "Oh, no."

Heartache broke open Payson's heart. Sorrow overwhelmed her as though she were in the room.

"'Elizabeth,' the mother whispered. 'I can't eat.'"

"'Mother, Edward is gone. But we are still together.'"

"I see a gravestone." Ainsley sobbed but Payson pressed further. "I'm trying to see the name on the stone. Edward Fitzhugh Adams. He died in 1900." Payson opened her eyes.

Ainsley's eyes glistened, wet with tears. "Wow, Payson. That is so sad."

"I know. But it's far in the past, remember. I hope the information is helpful."

"It was fascinating listening. But there's still no way I can reunite the photo and frame with the owner."

"Not yet, anyway. But the frame wants to be here."

"Really?" Ainsley ran her fingers through her long red hair, pulling the strands up straight. "I know. A guy brought it here to pawn. He bought an old warehouse and found it among the things in the warehouse."

Payson smirked. "I don't mean that kind of reason. I'm not the psychic, you are. Everything has energy. The frame's energy gave off its pleasure with being here."

"Interesting. I'll think on that sometime." The light in her eyes shifted. "I read Skye's text about a meeting. I got goosebumps."

The air in the room emptied. "What do you mean?"

"I got a precognition of Diane surrounded by DAs. She was giving them orders to help her do something with Braden."

Shivers trembled through Payson. "Do what with Braden?" She couldn't keep the quiver out of her voice.

Ainsley squinted. "I couldn't make that out. I tried, but everything got fuzzy. Did Skye set up the meeting because of something to do with Diane?"

All her nerves started firing at once and everything in her wanted to run to Braden. Thoughts spun. "Yes. We saw Diane this morning at Coffee Is. Her vibration was chaotic and she warned me to stay away from Braden."

"Oh. So not good." Ainsley shook her head. "She's been MIA for a while, but I had no idea she's been turning darker, though I'm not surprised. The scars have been there for a long time."

"Yes, her childhood was brutal, but she's an Aeon. She has the ability to turn hate into love. We have to help her."

Ainsley frowned. "If it's not too late."

CHAPTER 6

$\mathcal{B}$RADEN CHECKED THE time. It was way too soon to expect to hear from Will at Crime Scene Investigations. Will had assured him he would be notified as soon as they had a DNA match to the blood from the Hick's home and a name to the finger-print—if they found them. He'd tried to get them to push the testing process to seventy-two hours, but they couldn't promise any sooner than seven days. He knew that was standard but that didn't mean he could suppress the impatience clenching tiny muscles in his cheek. He rubbed his temples and resigned to the wait.

Standing in line at Coffee Is, he shifted from one foot to the other. Expecting Diane to walk through the door any minute, he smiled at Skye. "Hey, busy crowd, huh?"

"Hi." Her eyes narrowed. "Good to see you. What would you like?"

"Chicken salad on pumpernickel and a small side salad with house vinaigrette." He checked the time again.

"Are you expecting someone?" Skye sent the order to the kitchen and eyed him.

"I'm supposed to meet Diane for lunch, her request." His senses picked up Skye's Aeon vibration, but it felt muted. *Curious.* The intense buzz from the morning still pumped through him, though.

Skye knitted her brow. "Did you read my text about meeting with the others?"

"Yeah. Payson told me about what happened with Diane this morning. Go figure."

"I don't think what happened with her is something we can dismiss. Do you agree?"

"Yes. Maybe I'll learn something at lunch."

She nodded. "I hope so. Apparently Diane has a thing for you."

That made his stomach twist. "It's not mutual." He checked the line again. "Sorry. I better get out of the way."

"I'll bring your food when it's ready." She smiled, and with it, his mind eased.

He turned away just in time to hear the man behind him in the line mutter.

"It's about time you realized others are in line. Move out of the way." The man glared at him.

The words hit his gut. "What did you say?" He stepped closer to the man.

"I said get out of the way." The man's nostrils flared.

Braden grabbed him by the shirt. "I am. Calm down."

"Let go of me." The man raised his fist and bared his teeth.

Braden caught Skye's expression. It hit him just as hard as the man's initial sarcasm. Fear shone in her brown eyes, and her lips formed a straight line.

He released the man's shirt and took a step back. "I'm sorry, sir. Skye, I'm sorry." He couldn't get to the back of the room fast enough. How did he come so unglued? He rubbed his eyes, trying to understand what had just happened.

"Hey, Braden." Diane sat down across from him. "Have you already ordered?"

Her heavy black licorice and dark chocolate scent clouded his thoughts further. "Hi, Diane. How are you?" That stupid question was the only thing he could come up with.

She heaved a sigh. "I'm here. I really need to talk to you."

"Sure. But go order your lunch. I already ordered mine."

He watched as she sashayed toward the counter. He noted her shapely legs, the sway of her hips, and the way her patterned black and red dress hugged her curves. He couldn't deny her attractiveness, or the way everything about her shouted for attention. It didn't mean anything to him. He was only an observer and a friend. But something was different. He chuckled to himself. Maybe it was her aura. If so, Skye would notice.

"Here you go." Skye slid his food in front him with a glass of water, and stood beside him with her hand on one hip. "This is Benjamin Clover. Benjamin, Braden."

The lanky guy standing beside her didn't look the part of a perky coffee house worker. A black T-shirt peeked from beneath his dark green uniform shirt, and he wore tight, black jeans. Piercings, multiple piercings in both ears, his chin, and his lip, joined his sharp eyes to give him a no-nonsense appearance.

Benjamin extended his hand. "Happy to meet you," he said, without cracking a smile.

"Benjamin is our newest employee. He is in training." Skye gave him an approving nod. "I think he's going to work out well."

"Thank you, Skye. I like coffee and I like it here, so I hope things work out." Benjamin made to go. "I better get back to work," he said, and pivoted on his black suedes.

"Must be business is good." Braden nodded toward Benjamin.

"I can't complain. But I hired him for more than his service. He needs guidance." Skye arched an eyebrow. "Diane's here. Maybe it would be better if I stayed away."

"Maybe." He stared up at Skye. "Does she seem different to you?"

Her lips puckered. "Does she to you?"

"Yeah, I think so." He scrubbed his face again, trying to sort his thoughts. "I don't know. I may be having a weird day."

Skye gave him a look. "Is something wrong? Your aura looks peaked. What have you been doing?"

Little hairs rose on the back of his neck. Nerves bristled. "I've been working. You don't need to scan my aura. I'm fine."

Skye raised her hands toward him. "Okay. It's not like I 'scanned' you. You know that. But you're not fine, Braden. I can see it. I'm getting a different vibe from you. That little scene you made at the counter isn't like you."

"What do you mean?"

"You don't lose your temper much. You certainly don't threaten other people. That was very un-Braden-like behavior."

"Yeah." The incident ate at him. But so did the idea that he behaved a certain, predictable way. "Perhaps I'm just expressing more of myself. That guy made me mad."

"I got that." She put her hand to his shoulder and warm, soothing streams of energy emanated from her to him. "You didn't just respond. You reacted. Typically, you give a measured response." She pointed to the scene of his crime. "Is that the Braden you want to be now? Is that what you're saying?"

"No. Maybe." The soothing energy stopped. Turmoil rattled inside his brain.

She pulled her hand away. "I'm sorry. I didn't mean to badger you like that. Maybe being off is in the air today."

"What are you two talking about?" Diane plopped her purse on the table and sat down. "Skye, I like the looks of your new hire. He is new, right?"

Skye's brow creased. "Yes, Benjamin is new."

"Mmm, he's cute. Brooding." She faked a shiver.

"He's too young for you, Diane. Stop ogling him."

"Oh shut up. I'll ogle whomever I feel like. I told you I'm done with you. Now scamper off to your coffee making and muffin baking and leave us alone."

"Diane, stop it. Skye and I were just chatting. I—"

"Don't defend her. She's interfering as usual." Diane spit the words.

"She doesn't need defending, unless it would be from your temper." He waved his hands in front of her. "She's not a threat to you."

"It's okay, Braden. I'm leaving." Skye gave him soft eyes and walked to the kitchen.

He heard Diane's voice going on in the background but not her words. A man standing in line at the counter captured his attention. He wore a black cap pulled low. He kept fidgeting with his clothes, then tweaked his cap. All of Braden's cop instincts narrowed down on the man.

Braden sat still, his muscles tight springs. If the man made a quick move, Braden would be on him. He tuned his ears to the conversation at the checkout.

"I'm not going to hurt you as long as you give me what I want and don't make any wrong moves." The man opened his coat and at the checkout, Benjamin flinched.

The man had a gun, Braden had no doubt. He was robbing Skye's shop.

"Braden, are you listening to me?" Diane's voice was shrill in his ears.

"Yeah, yeah." He glanced at her and held up one finger. "Just a minute."

As a police officer, Braden took seriously his obligation to protect the innocents in the coffee shop, so he weighed his next move carefully. Adrenaline pumped through him, and he reached for his gun, pulling it out of his holster slowly and keeping it low. One slow step at a time, he crept around tables filled with customers oblivious to what was going down. The shop was busy and the last thing he wanted was for anyone to become a hostage. His breaths were measured. He had the advantage.

Suddenly a young woman in line pointed her finger and screamed. "He's got a gun!"

The robber raised his gun and hollered. "Everybody down on the floor."

Braden sighed. *Damn it.* Customers dropped to the floor, shoving tables and chairs aside in a din of floor-scraping and whimpers.

The robber turned back to the register. "Hurry up! Get me my money. Now!"

Quietly, Braden stepped over people hugging the floor and around empty tables. He reached the man and shoved his gun into his back, without breaking a sweat. "Drop the gun and put your hands up."

"What? Who are you?" the man hollered but raised his hands, still clutching the gun.

Out of the corner of his eyes, he saw another man slip inside the shop and aim a gun at him. Before that man could bark any demands, Braden grabbed the gun from the man at the counter with one hand and twisted the robber's arm behind his back. "Freeze," he yelled at the man at the door.

Bravado streamed out of the man's mouth. "My gun is on you, cop! Let him go or I'll put out your lights." The man's eyes drew down into dark fiery slits.

At least he hadn't grabbed a hostage. Urgency hammered in Braden's chest. He had to make his move, fast, but controlled. He saw Skye huddled beneath a table. It twisted his heart to see her so close to danger.

"I said, let him go!" hollered the other man. "You have one minute. Then I'll shoot you and one of these fine people." He nodded to a couple lying on the floor.

Braden wouldn't fire in a crowded room, but the gunman didn't know that. He opened his mind-control and took hold of the man's thoughts. "C'mon, guy, you don't want to do this."

"I don't want to do this."

It was working. Braden pressed harder without words but thoughts. *You don't want to hurt anyone. Just give me your gun.*

"I don't want to hurt anybody. But I have to rob this place. It's my job." The man looked beyond Braden and swallowed hard.

The man resisted his suggestion to surrender. Braden shook his head. It wasn't going to work. With a sharp jab, he sent the man in his grip to the floor, out cold. He jumped across the people on the floor and sailed to the other man's side. He yanked the gun from the man and threw it to Skye. Without missing a beat, he wrapped his arm around the man's neck and squeezed. The man kicked at Braden's legs and struggled to get out of his hold. Braden squeezed harder. "You should reconsider your career choices." He raised his head. "Skye, call 911."

She trained the other gun on the man on the floor, her hands trembling. Anger pushed up into Braden's throat. "Bring me the gun, Skye."

"What about him?"

"I got him. It's okay."

He forced the man he was holding face down to the ground. "Put your hands behind your back."

The man twisted his head. "This is police brutality. I'm going to—"

"Shut up." Braden shoved the man's face into the floor and cuffed him.

Minutes later, beat cops charged in, surveying the scene.

"Oh, Braden," said the first, a familiar face. "You've got two suspects already cuffed and secured."

"Yes. Could you get witness statements? I'll file a report."

"Yeah, we can take it from here."

"Thanks. Talk to the owner for her statement." He walked up to Skye and patted her hand, while the officers cleared the coffee shop. "I'm sorry this happened."

Still trembling, Skye gave him a weak smile. "I've never been robbed before. I'm glad you were here."

He scanned the room, making sure the room was calm. His gaze ran into Diane's. "Oh, I forgot about Diane."

Skye nodded. "Of course, go. She's got stars in her eyes for you, but chronic trauma in her aura. Be careful."

"Thanks for the head's up." Braden hugged Skye. "I'm glad you're okay."

Nerves tensed his stomach as he strode through the room and met up with Diane. "Shall we take our lunch outside?"

She put her hand on her chest. "Braden, you were so commanding." She squeezed his bicep. "But why didn't you tell me the place was being robbed?"

He shrugged and directed her outdoors to a bench just a few steps away. "I went into cop mode, that's all. Did you know those guys?" He motioned for her to sit and bit into his sandwich and chewed.

"Know them? No. Why would you ask?"

"I don't know, just a feeling. One of them seemed to look at you, as though he wondered if you were watching."

"You're imagining things." She frowned. "I saw you talking to Skye. You took care of her, but me you didn't even think of me." She pouted her lips.

Her pout didn't faze him. "Her shop was being robbed. She was in the center of the danger zone. Of course I checked on her."

"Honestly, I don't know why you put up with those people in your little click." Diane pulled tomatoes out of her turkey sandwich and rolled her eyes.

"I like them and we're a team, remember? You're a part of that group. Why haven't you been hanging out with us? We need you."

She reached across the table and placed her hand over his. He flinched inwardly. Her hand sent tiny, sharp spikes into his skin. Her eyes pinned his gaze. "Can we stop talking about them now? I want to talk to you about something personal."

"Of course. What is it?" He pulled his hand away and fumbled with his fork, trying to pick up kale and pineapple chunks from his salad. Heat spread throughout his body. *What the heck?* He swallowed over a lump in his throat and tried to tune out the whirring in his head.

"I want us to be good friends, Braden. I don't know if we can be as long as you're associating with those people."

He felt her eyes boring in to his head. But that was crazy thinking. Her voice was smooth and flowing, like water in a slow stream. "We are friends. We go way back. But I'm not going to ditch the other Aeons because you have hard feelings about them."

The whirring rose in volume that grew like pressure in his skull. He looked away and guzzled water from his glass.

Diane wrapped her leg around his. "I need you to prove that you're my friend and that you won't abandon me as everyone else has."

She moved her leg up and down his calf, slowly. His skin prickled. "Stop that. I'm with Payson and you know it."

"I knew it." She snapped her leg away. "Payson is always sabotaging our relationship. I need proof you won't let her come between us."

He took in Diane's pain. Her perspective differed from his, but he understood where it was coming from. Her childhood. Once again, it was getting the best of her. "I'm sorry it seems like that, but you are my friend. I care about you." He didn't bother to defend Payson. That would only make things worse. Maybe he could help her by accepting her as she was. The tension whirling his thoughts stopped. "How would I prove it?"

She squared him. "Come work for me." Lights came on in her eyes. "I've got a project I could use your investigative skills to ensure its success. There would be good money."

"Work for you? I have a job." He shook his head. She must be on something to think he would work for her. "Thank you for the offer but I'm in the middle of my own investigation at APD. I like my work."

"Come to work for me if you mean what you say about being my friend." Her sentence flowed slowly, like molasses. Her eyes glazed and he couldn't pull away. "Say you'll do it."

His thoughts got hazy. "I'll do it. But my police work comes first."

Diane's deep red shiny lips stretched wide. Her smile reminded him of the Cheshire cat. "You do love me." She gathered her things. "I'll be in touch with what I need from you within the next couple days." She bent to kiss his cheek and left without a goodbye.

Speechless. That's what she'd done to him. Made him speechless. Braden slammed his hand against his head. How could he have forgotten her ability to mesmerize? In the grip of her demand, he'd been unable to turn down her offer. *No, she wasn't mesmerizing me, Diane is simply demanding. She doesn't know any other way.*

AFTER A SHAKEN SKYE CALLED, Payson picked up a late lunch of sandwiches and waters, and took a seat at a table at a plaza down the street from Coffee Is. She lifted her face to the sun, trying to warm away her fears. Cold iced her blood. Braden was tied up with work. She couldn't see him now, but longing to check in with him ached in her chest.

"Thanks for the lunch, Payson." Skye eyed a seat across from her.

Payson hugged her. "How are you doing?"

"I'm okay. I sent Benjamin home. The whole thing was scary for him, and the police closed the shop anyway."

"He's so young and doesn't yet know he is an Aeon. I'm glad he's working for you so we can kind of keep an eye on him."

"I'm glad you found him. He needs our support," Skye said. "And our protection. You should have seen the way Diane looked at him. I'm betting she knows he's an Aeon."

Payson's heart thudded heavy in her chest. Skye was right about Benjamin. But talking with Skye steadied her. Their energies joined as she streamed peace to Skye. They didn't have to talk about it, they simply did it.

"I was just drinking coffee with you that day. There he was a couple of tables away, vibrating at an unmistakable level." She couldn't have ignored his vibration if she had wanted to.

"It's so good you sensed him a few weeks ago, and I could steer him to apply for the job. He has issues already with feeling like an outsider and managing an ability he knows nothing about." Skye took a sip of water. "That's evident in his dark clothing choices and somber attitude."

"I'm tracking him. He's had his dream so he has the knowing or I wouldn't be able to connect with his energy. But probably he doesn't understand anything yet. One of the guys may have to talk to him soon, but we don't know him well enough yet."

"Right. Boy, I'm so glad Braden was in the shop when the robbers showed up. He took care of them so smoothly and no one got hurt."

"Yes, that is lucky." Unease squirmed inside her. "Was he just picking up coffee?" She took a bite of her veggie sandwich, but the green peppers and black olives went down her throat like burned toast.

"No, Diane showed up and they were eating lunch. But before that, he made quite the scene at the counter. It bothered me. We talked about his outburst and he seemed truly confused." Skye exchanged a look with her. "Is something going on?"

"I don't know yet. But I have wondered."

A police officer called for Skye. "I'll be right there," she called.

"Don't worry about Braden. Be sure to let me know if you need me."

"Thanks, I will. Go take care of business." She gave Skye a smile she didn't feel.

The first to admit her center was unbalanced, Payson knew she should go directly for help and call Claire Eve. Instead, she leaned toward taking another case. She needed it, and fast. The deep mental and physical activity of a search and recovery would make a nice distraction. Besides, she'd be doing Keegan a favor if she took on one of her typical cases, one that had a tight deadline and a particularly slippery skip.

It would only take a minute to get a case. She gave up on the sandwich and tossed it in a trash barrel.

Keegan's business wasn't far by car. She pulled her Volt into street parking outside his business. The bell hanging at the top of the door jangled as she opened it, and its familiarity gave her comfort.

"Hey, Payson." Keegan yelled from a back room. A clairaudient, Keegan heard things no one else heard. His ability gave him access to high frequency vibrations, sounds, words spoken at an ethereal level. He could distinguish different motors and likely recognized the sound of her car before she opened the door.

"C'mon and join me." She heard him dribbling a basketball as she walked closer. Alone in the large empty storage room, Keegan lifted up in the air and dunked the ball. He pivoted toward her, his hair flying into his face and his biceps popping as he reached toward her.

"Nothing but net, huh Keegan?"

"You bet. How about a hug?" he asked, and hugged her casually. Looming over her, Keegan was the picture of a professional player. "Just getting some exercise."

They headed toward his desk out front. His business lived in a former printing company warehouse. She dropped into a chair opposite of his desk and savored the familiar scent of musty books and boxes of paper. "I'm here for a case."

"Good. I hoped you'd be by." He swiveled his chair to a filing cabinet and flipped through folders. "I've got one you'll like." He twisted back and laid out the file. "It's a $500,000 bond for Class D drug trafficking. Name, Eddie Crow. Thirty-nine-years-old. Here's his mug shot. Another agent failed to track him down, so the skip is yours if you want it. I already have last known address and family connections. His family runs a restaurant and he has a large network of couriers who shuttle drugs and money to other cities."

The face staring from the mug shot sent chills up and down Payson's spine. She put a finger to the shot and closed her eyes. An image popped up of Eddie punching out a twenty-something man, and yelling at him. *I'll give you one more chance to pay up. Take these bags with you to this address and I'll forget what you owe me.* She couldn't make out the address but the fear thrumming through the young man sickened her stomach. She breathed in and out slowly, letting go of the pain and the image.

"You saw something not so nice, didn't you?" Keegan looked at her with warm blue eyes.

"Yeah. But that's the stuff our work is made of." She stood and reached for the file. "I'll take it."

Keegan grimaced. "Don't you want to know the catch to this big payday?"

"I already know." She laughed. "It's always the same. He missed his court date. His lawyer hasn't heard from him in weeks."

"I knew I could count on you. You're the best," he called to her as she walked away.

Back in her car and on her way to Braden's, Payson kept her thoughts off Diane and went to work lining up her strategy for finding the skip.

She hadn't picked her career; bounty hunting had picked her. Studying criminal justice for six years in college had been part of her plans for becoming a probation officer. The idea of helping ex-cons make a better life had seemed a perfect way to aid the world. After two years of on-the-job experience, the plans had gone sour. The work had proved toxic for her. She knew she couldn't be one of those cops who turned to alcohol to cope with the daily interaction with crime. For her, the work had nearly snuffed out her sense of love and light. With Braden's help, she'd made her way back to find faith in humanity again. And what had meant to be a job between jobs helping Keegan had given her a chance at fighting darkness in a different way.

Lights were on at Braden's apartment but she suspected he wasn't home. She tapped the code into his lock pad and let herself in. "Braden? Are you home?" She glanced around, waiting for a reply.

When none came, she relaxed on the couch and flipped on the television. Headlines from the nightly news lit up the screen.

"We're at city hall, where Auralia city council members heard at a special meeting today from residents who oppose the redevelopment of Old Town and a proposed casino on the Wherryrite River. The Stillwell Development under consideration is spearheaded by Economic Director Tom Brody and has the support of Mayor Joe Farrod. Mayor Farrod told reporters the projects will be an economic boon for the area, but opponents told the council the cost of losing the Old Town character and tourists it attracts was too high."

Payson rested her chin on her hand and listened closer to the story.

"Micky Gomez, president of a local group called Advocates of Community Empowerment, or ACE, told the council there is more value in retaining Old Town shops and services," the anchor continued, "than anything new construction or a casino would offer. Ms. Gomez, why is ACE against the Stillwell project?"

"Old Town is an important economic asset to the community. The shops there are owned by people who live here in town. They care about the city because it's theirs. What's more, the variety of unique shops comprise as staples for residents and tourists. The proposed multi-use building would be targeted to big-box national chains that would diminish our city's attraction."

A member of ACE, Payson watched the attractive and articulate blonde with pride blooming inside her. "You tell them, Micky."

"While the mayor points to economic benefits, Gomez counters with facts that point to different, grimmer possibilities," the reporter said.

Gomez leaned into the microphone. "The mayor claims the casino will bring dollars to our town, but statistics tell us it also can attract criminal activity. ACE members understand that casinos in general can be good for tourism and bring more jobs. But this project needs more study, and the developers are unwilling to disclose their business plans or investors to assure us everything is above board. We don't need more criminals. We don't need more empty promises. We need respect for Old Town. We need the truth."

Payson's gut clenched. Was it possible that while residents were being asked to get on board with the project, insidious plans were progressing to sway the balance of power in Auralia?

The camera cut back to the reporter. "Gomez attempted to persuade the city council to vote against the Stillwell Development and the casino. Both projects belong to Principal Industries, a conglomerate with interests in drug research, plastics, property development, and media. We'll be following this evolving story and keeping you informed."

The clock on the wall told her Braden should be home soon. She closed her eyes and opened to his presence. Her heart stuttered. He was home.

His footsteps sounded in the garage on just the other side of the door, and she waited. She wanted to sense his familiar vibration, but its usual pleasant hum wasn't there with its natural vibrancy. Her heart sank. *No, not Braden.*

He walked in to the living room and shot her a tight grin. "Hi, babe. Sorry I'm late."

She looked up into his eyes, searching. She knew he would notice but she had to look for the signs. Needed to know if he was still the man she knew and loved. "It's okay. I've just been catching up on the news."

He chewed his lower lip and frowned. "That doesn't sound fun."

She pinned his eyes with her presence. "No, not fun but maybe important. Michelle was being interviewed regarding ACE's stand on the development in Old Town and the casino." She rose and stroked his cheek. A day's stubble scraped her skin, dropping a melancholy note in her heart. Everything about him was so familiar and cherished. "How was your day?"

He shrugged. "It was good. I told you on the phone about my break." He peered back at her. "What's up? You're looking at me funny."

Distance stretched between them, palpable. Loneliness bit at her heart. "You're changing. I feel it, Braden. Something is different about you and I think it's your inner balance." Reflex told her to drop her gaze, look away from the impact of her words on him. But she resisted, needing to see the truth.

He knitted his brow and a telltale shadow flitted in his eyes. He stepped back. "Payson, what are you saying? Nothing has changed. Don't judge me."

The dissonance in his energy sharpened. "I'm sorry. That's not what I'm doing." She steadied her voice. "I'm not against you, I love you." Her love wrapped in white light spilled out to him and she focused on that, trying to overwhelm the darkness she sensed growing in him while her heart split into pieces.

"If you love me, don't accuse me. Are you suggesting what I think you are? Are you saying I'm going DA?" He spit the question at her.

"No, not suggesting, Braden, saying. You're not yourself. Something happened to shift your balance today. Can't we please, please look at that? Could you consider the possibility and not take this as my condemnation?" She had to make him see. Not seeing would prevent him from accepting the light she was offering. This couldn't be happening.

Braden turned away. She reached out and touched his shoulder. Instantly, images flashed of Braden leaning across a table and talking in earnest with Diane.

You're not alone, Diane. I'm your friend.

Prove you care about me.

"Oh my god, Braden. Diane used her power on you."

He turned back to her. "Stop it. What is this? Another accusation? Now you think I'm in cahoots with Diane against you? She's my friend and she didn't use her power against me." Rage flashed in his eyes, sinking her hope. "Don't you think I'd know if she did? I'm not stupid."

"She's mesmerized you, just a little bit. Just enough to mess with your balance between dark and light. She's used your big heart to get inside you. She needs help, but right now I'm concerned about you." She swiped away tears brimming. "Please, you have to see this."

He rubbed his fingers against his temples. "So you feel my imbalance." He sighed heavily. "Maybe you're right."

Payson held her breath. She couldn't breathe, waiting for Braden to make a choice and not knowing if he was already gone.

"Diane wouldn't hurt me. Yes, she's having problems, but she wouldn't drag me down. I know we have concerns about her level of darkness, but she's not DA, is she? It's the work, not Diane."

The vibe from Braden thrummed heavily in her brain. Her legs wobbled. "I see. Something with work troubled you today?"

"Just the same old, same old." He faced her directly. "You don't understand. You don't know what I've seen. Children burned by their parents. Women raped and left to die, broken and brutalized."

Payson nodded. "Horrible stuff and we're here to help, not judge."

"I'm so sick of the damage inflicted by criminals on the citizens of Auralia. It hit me hard today how much I hate it, but that hate felt powerful. It wasn't wrong, Payson, it was fuel." A tiny muscle in his cheek clenched.

"When did that hit you?" She pulled in deep breaths and let them out, concentrating harder on allowing light to flow to Braden.

He ran his thumb over his chin. "Hmm...I don't remember."

Braden's nostrils flared and she wanted to puke. "So you had this moment of disgust and you believe it helped you follow the thread to a break in the case. Is that right?" Maybe she was only stalling, hoping something, anything, she could say would bring him back from the edge of falling into darkness.

"Yes. See? It has nothing to do with Diane." He spread his hands wide. He hadn't moved farther away but he also hadn't kissed her yet.

She nodded. "Okay." He couldn't see past what Diane had done. He'd been vulnerable and she'd mesmerized him. Why, Payson didn't know, but it had to have been on purpose. Frustration and fear braided together, closing her throat. It wouldn't do any good to argue with him. Still, she couldn't leave him alone like this. "The police work is having a negative effect on you."

He scratched his head. "Maybe. I don't know. I feel more powerful, not darker."

The tears she'd been trying to ignore misted her eyes. "You have to see what's happening and take action to stop the encroaching darkness. If you don't see it, I can't be around you. I can't be connected to you." Words stuck in her throat.

Confusion flamed in his eyes. He took another step away. "I…I can't believe what you're saying. It's you, Payson. You're the one changing. See that!"

"Just this morning you reminded me to stay balanced." She pulled out the necklace from beneath her shirt. "Remember this?"

He grabbed her shoulders and the darkness growing in him pounded her like a fierce ocean wave. "Of course I remember. Apparently, you haven't realized your work is coloring your perception. Don't do this."

She had to be strong. She ached for him to take her in his arms and hold her so tightly all the fear would drain away in his light.

But he didn't. He couldn't. "I'm not doing anything. You have to grasp what has happened to you." She cupped his face in her hands. "You have to make a choice to move away from the distortion. It's not me. It's you."

He jerked away. "You want me to give up my work? You know I can't do that. It's what I do. I can handle the threats inherent in the work. I'm an Aeon too. I'm filled with light and love."

"Are you?" she whispered.

"I'm the same as always." His eyes slitted. "Don't leave. We can talk through this."

"I have to go. I don't want to, but our mission is too important." She couldn't look at him. Couldn't believe the unthinkable had happened to him, her Braden. "I'll always be yours. But I have to go."

It took every bit of strength she could muster to open the door and walk out.

"Payson!"

CHAPTER 7

BRADEN SLAMMED HIS fist against the door. Limp, he slumped against it. "Payson," he whispered.

She was gone. Her scent, clean and breezy, filled his head. Why hadn't he told her how much he loved her? He should have held her and kissed her. Why hadn't he?

Why did she leave? The question took over his mind and he let it. He wanted to feel nothing, not this gut-tearing loss. Payson had betrayed him with her accusations. How could she think he was turning DA?

What if she was right? Panic scrambled in his belly. He raced to his bathroom mirror and peered at his face. He leaned close to his reflection, looking deeply into his eyes.

"Looks like me." It ate him up wondering what she'd detected. He leaned against the counter, grasping for a way to convince her not to leave him. "I have to talk to her and she'll see she is wrong. I'm the same."

Adrenaline throbbed through him still. Was it power she'd felt from him? Power was a good thing. He needed it to fight for justice for victims of darkness.

"Payson is wrong." He strode to the living room and surveyed it. Her scent lingered, pulling his thoughts back to her eyes. She'd looked so sad. His heart raced.

He punched her number in his phone. It went to voice mail. "Payson. Please call me back. I have to talk to you. I…I…"

He dropped his phone on the couch. Why couldn't he tell her he loved her? He paced in front of the large window, his mind whirring.

Maybe Payson had been right about Diane using her mesmerizing powers on him. But why would she do that to him? She had told him many times he was her only friend. Could his desire to help her have blinded him to a danger she possessed?

The lights of the city outside his window glowed in the night. Somehow time had passed since he'd gotten home and it was night-time. His stomach had the nerve to remind him he'd missed dinner, but the idea of trying to swallow made his throat clench.

He stared at the glittering night, emptiness gripping him. He plodded to his bedroom, alone. Raw and angry, he peeled off his clothes and left them in a pile. The unthinkable had slammed him in his gut. Payson was gone.

He slid beneath his covers and rolled into a ball. He couldn't help it. She was his everything. Now what?

His phone rang from the living room and he dashed to answer it without looking at the number. "Payson?"

"No, Braden. It's me. Diane. I guess you were expecting Payson to call?"

"What do you want?" He hadn't meant to snap at her, but he wanted only to talk to Payson.

"Am I interrupting something?"

"No, sorry. But it is late. I was sleeping." He'd lied but he had to get her off the phone.

"Okay, I'll be quick. I'd like to see you tomorrow to talk about our new business relationship. I'm very excited."

Yeah, he gathered she was eager to get started. "I can't imagine what you'll need me to do. How can a cop help a lobbyist?"

"You'll see."

Her voice shivered through him, raising his pulse. "I don't know how much time I can give you. My work is demanding."

"You won't be doing any lobbying, so you can relax about that." She let loose a throaty chuckle and he could see her glossy red lipsticked lips smiling wide.

"I'm willing to give it a try." He sighed, bored with this meaningless discussion.

"I'll make it worth your while. You'll see. So can you stop into my office tomorrow morning?"

He vaguely recalled the location of her office, and he didn't know his plans for morning, but at this point, he would say anything to get her to hang up. "Yeah. Sure. Good bye."

"Good night, Braden."

Her voice prompted a visual of her licking her lips. He didn't know what to do with that thought. He rolled onto his back and stared up at the ceiling. The night offered no comfort from the ache pounding in his chest. Thoughts took over, and all he could think of was Payson. Her beautiful terra cotta skin, her champagne eyes, her long, glistening hair. But that was her look. Her body. He loved so much more about her. He loved her warm touch. Her fire. Her loving heart.

Misery pulled him into a ball again. *I could use my ability to change her mind.* The thought startled him. *Where did that come from?* He would never do such a thing to Payson. Would he?

He pulled at his hair. *No. I would not. I'm not a DA. I don't manipulate people. Especially not Payson.* Besides, if he truly believed she was wrong about him he wouldn't need to override her beliefs, he just needed to talk to her. She would see. She would feel it in her body that he was soundly balanced.

Grief and fear wearied him to his bones, but he wanted so much to stay alert in case Payson returned his call. He checked the time. Two in the morning. He had to admit she wasn't going to call him back tonight.

Love was not supposed to be a drain. Uneasiness stirred his

nerves, and he rolled and tossed until he had to get up and do something, regardless of the hour. His phone alerted, sending his pulse flying. He had missed a call? He grabbed it, hopeful. But it was the lab from APD, not Payson.

He trudged to his study and flipped on the light to check his voicemail.

"Braden, this is Will. I've got your results from the blood found at the Hick's residence. Sorry to call so late, or early, however you want to look at it, but I told you I'd let you know when I got them."

It was no use trying to sleep. When all else failed, there was always work to occupy his mind and burn off nervous energy, and this call spurred his curiosity. A quick call to Will could tell him the identity of the perp in the home invasion case. Why wait?

Will answered his phone.

"Sorry I missed your call, Will, but I appreciate you calling. What do you have for me?"

"I've got a match to the partial print, nothing yet for the DNA. The print belongs to Nick Ward. Know him?"

"Yeah. He's in the system for a previous theft." Braden didn't share that Nick was a kid he had been trying to set on a different path. Clearly, he'd failed at that plan. "Thanks again."

"You will owe me," Will teased.

"So you're not just doing your job, you're doing me a favor?" Braden sighed. "Okay, I owe you one."

In the kitchen, he shoved the coffee pot under the faucet and stared blankly. "Dumb, dumb, Braden. You let Nick down. You convinced him to trust you and then you got too busy for him." He couldn't face what he'd done to Nick, and he couldn't find his center. This mess in his mind was Payson's doing.

Or was Payson right about him? He sniggered at the irony of his words to Payson to remain balanced. Was he failing at everything important to him?

"Crap," he sputtered as he noticed water overflow the carafe. He dumped it out and set the carafe on the counter, leaning against it and sinking into the empty place inside him.

He couldn't imagine a life without Payson in it. How long would it take to forget the sound of her voice, the memories of good times together?

No.

That could never happen. He dropped his head into his hands, sobs threatening to take him over. How does one cut out a whole lifetime?

He grabbed for the closest thing, a bottle of vitamins, and threw it to the ceramic floor. Quickly, he sent another bottle to the floor, and the thrust opened the flip-top, spewing caplets over the floor. He kicked at them, and anger hardened his resolve. He straightened to his full height. Whether Payson was right or wrong, he'd fix this mess.

THE MIRROR MADE it clear to Payson that she hadn't slept last night. She peered close and tried to erase the shadows under her eyes with make-up. But why was she bothering? The bags were a dead give-away she had been crying. No one would care how she looked, especially not the person who mattered. And even if someone would, she didn't.

In her bedroom, she stood still, immobile. She shuddered. Somehow, she had to get through her day. She couldn't postpone her case from Keegan. But she had no strength. Nothing to pull from, with only emptiness inside.

It didn't help to know that Diane had messed with Braden, making it impossible for her to ignore the change. She brushed away tears drizzling down her cheeks. It only mattered that she had walked out on him. All night the ramifications of his change and the inconceivable fact that his darkness separated them had risen over and over in waves of nausea.

She couldn't let the emptiness sideline her. For now, she had her job. "One step at a time." That's all she had to do, was live one moment at a time and trust the future to be kind.

She dressed in a pair of grey Bermuda shorts and a sleeveless orange cotton top, then dropped to the bed and pulled on a pair of flat, black, goddess sandals. Tears dotted her top.

She loaded her purse with tissues and her phone and blew out a heavy sigh. "Enough. For now anyway."

Twenty minutes later, Payson walked inside Coffee Is, seeking caffeine only. The thought of food turned her stomach and she wasn't up to anything that took effort, including conversation with Skye other than to check in.

At the counter, she paused to sit with the pleasant vibration coming from the barista. "Hi Benjamin. I'm glad the shop is open today. Are you all right? Yesterday must have been frightening."

"It was." He shuddered. "I don't want anything like that to happen here again."

"That makes two of us."

"What can I fix for you?

"Just black coffee, thanks."

He looked like a typical high school senior, but he was not typical. His expression wasn't actually a frown, but except for the artificial smile he gave customers, Benjamin looked as though he wouldn't tolerate any grief. Payson recognized the signs of a young Aeon troubled by a strange life no one understood.

At the checkout, she took her coffee from Skye and paid. One look at Payson and Skye's eyes widened. Payson waved a dismissive hand.

"Don't ask?" Skye searched Payson's face.

"Please." Her composure slipping, Payson headed to a corner table. She knew silence was a lot to ask from Skye, but the words wouldn't come out alone. There would be sobbing too. She wouldn't talk about Braden, not yet.

The click, click of heels sounded behind her the same minute a harsh vibration juddered in her belly.

"Well, well, little Payson."

She froze. Shards of anger wanted to explode out of her. Her breath came in small, tight pulls. She struggled to claim her peace, when she could just lash out. "Diane."

"Oh, she speaks." Diane invaded her sorrow, placing herself in a chair directly across the table.

"Do you want something?" If there were anyone she would prefer not to see here with telltale signs of crying, it would be the person who had hurt Braden.

"I'm just here for coffee." Diane inclined her head and shot her an innocent expression. "Am I bothering you?"

Payson reset her intention to ground herself. "Be careful, Diane. Just because I can keep my boundaries sound between you and I doesn't mean I'm unable to tell you to fuck off."

Diane's eyes flitted. She leaned close. "You don't scare me." Spit flew in tiny drops from her lips.

"I'm not trying to scare you. I don't understand why you have animosity toward me. The only thing I can surmise is you're going darker and darker, and your perspective is telling you I'm a threat to you getting what you want." Breath moved freely in and out of her lungs as she countered Diane's skewed outlook. "I love you, Diane."

Her eyes flashed dark and menacing. "Stop it! It's a lie. What's more, you are no threat. I have what I want and you can't do anything about it." Diane stood, glowering at Payson.

"You mean you have Braden? I know what you've done. Braden is what you want? Why?"

"I deserve to have him. Besides, anything I can do to hurt you, trouble your little Aeon soul, is what I want."

"You may be underestimating me. I won't let you ruin his life."

Diane chuckled and bent close. "Stay away from him," she whispered in Payson's ear. "If you try to interfere with me, I'll kill him."

Payson held tight to her reaction. She sat there, not moving, not speaking, and Diane marched out the door. Her excruciating vibration left Payson's insides scrambled. Diane's dark energy was powerful and growing stronger. Payson wouldn't feed it by fighting with her. Not physically. Not yet.

She swallowed over a hard knot in her throat. Panic jumbled her senses. It was ten o'clock in the morning. She had to talk to Braden.

Can I meet with you? She pressed send and tapped her fingers on the table. The situation was complicated, but she had to see him. It didn't mean she could be in a relationship, just drop back to where they had been before Diane mesmerized him. But she wouldn't leave him, couldn't leave him to flounder alone in darkness.

Her phone alerted her to an incoming text.

Yes. Please come over to my place. I want to talk to you. How bout 6?

How about now?

Better. See you in a few.

Ten minutes later, she knocked on Braden's door. She crossed her fingers that it wasn't too late for saving him.

The door opened and he stood there looking wretched. Her stomach squeezed. She'd caused him pain.

"Come in." He stepped aside and gestured toward the living room. "Have a seat."

She stood just inside the door, nerves sparking like live wires. "Braden, I can't take back what I said yesterday." She closed her eyes, feeling into his energy, praying he had been able to raise it. She opened them again, gratitude flooding her. The low-level rumble still reverberated through him, but it was lighter. He had a chance. She looked into his eyes, weighing her words. "I'm sorry. I—"

"You don't have to apologize." He shifted on his feet. "I honestly don't know what's going on. I'm struggling." He leveled his gaze at her. "If I've let darkness proliferate in me, I have to do something about it. I'll look at that. Diane may not be the innocent person I see. I'm confused right now. But I'm solid on one thing. I don't want to lose you. I love you."

Sobs took her over. He said the words she had needed to hear yesterday. She didn't bother to wipe away tears trickling down her cheeks. "I never wanted to leave you. I love you so much. I shouldn't have just walked away last night. Can you forgive me?"

He pulled her close and melded against her. "No apologies. I understand how important our mission is and that you had to distance yourself if you even simply suspected I had gone DA."

His chest heaved with hers and she took in his pain, not as her own but as shared agony. What could she say? It was true.

She hung onto him as he shook, nuzzling into his neck. Images flashed in her mind's eye, images of him staring at his ceiling, slumped against his kitchen counter, raging at pills scattered on the floor. Each one a vision of him facing the truth of her words and a testament to the impact of her words. She gave the moment space, presence, so they each could acknowledge how devastating darkness could be and how sorrowful it was to be apart, even for only fifteen hours. She'd left him last night at sixish. The nightmare of every second since reverberated thought her.

Finally, she stepped back, resting her hands on his shoulders. "I have to talk to you about Diane."

"Okay, let's sit down."

He took her hand and led her to the couch, and pulled her beside him. She felt his exhaustion, but she had to warn him. "I still feel a level of darkness in you. I know you're yourself again, but please, be intentional with your choices." He nodded, but she went on. "Diane warned me again about staying away from you. She admitted she'd messed with you and that she's not done."

"Oh my God! What is her problem?" He ran his fingers through his hair.

"In a word, darkness. She's been a powerful Aeon but she's never used her power for good. She wants to break up the group and she wants you. That's probably simplified."

"We've known something dark has been at work in Auralia, we just didn't know Diane was at the core of it." He shook his head. "How could I be so blind? I wanted to help her."

Payson wrapped her arms across her middle. "She told me that if I didn't leave you alone she'd kill you."

His eyes went wide. "Holy shit! That's crazy! We have to talk to the others. There's no telling what she'll do." He pulled her close again. "I won't let her hurt you, and for damn sure I'm not going to die. It's you and me." He slanted his head, giving her a knowing look that made her heart stutter, and raised his hand, palm facing her. "Always."

She reached for his hand—

She screamed as the room exploded. The blast threw her into his kitchen, slamming her against cabinets and dropping her to the floor. She lay stunned with the taste of blood on her lips and ringing in her ears. Aching in every muscle stranded her in the middle of chaos. She groped to get her bearings. Smoke blinded her, but she couldn't let it stop her. She crawled around debris of splintered wood and glass to what was left of Braden's living room.

"Braden!" She eeked out his name, then convulsed into coughing. Her raspy voice sounded distant and unfamiliar. Breathing was impossible. She closed her eyes and focused her intention on slow, careful breaths. She had to clear her head and find Braden. *Braden! Oh my God, Braden.*

She took hold of a broken end table and pulled to her feet. Flames licked up the outside wall and ignited panic in her chest. The living room stood in shambles, but she ploughed through it, tossing aside broken furniture and pieces of the exterior wall, searching for Braden.

"Braden! Are you hurt?" Outdoor air blew in through shattered windows and dispersed the smoke. Out of the corner of her eye, she caught movement down the hall. She gasped and her hands flew to her mouth.

Braden lay on the floor, his eyes closed and his skin pale. Panic spiked and Payson took a step toward him, but hesitated. Diane stood at his feet. And she had reinforcements. This was the precognition Ainsley had told her about.

"I warned you to stay away from him, but you just couldn't."

Payson reached out her energy to feel Braden's life force. It hummed faintly, but he was alive.

"He's mine now. I'm not going to let you marry him." Diane sneered at her and passed her hands over Braden's head, then held them there.

"No!" Payson screamed, knowing Diane was using her ability to mesmerize.

She rushed to Braden and attempted to send him light energy, but nothing happened. She reached for him, but one of the DAs with Diane snatched her, holding her back. "Diane, don't do this." Helpless, she watched four DAs pick up Braden and run out of the smoke and fire into the yard.

"How could you do this? How could you rob him of himself?" Payson's heart caved in. "Why?"

"I love him. All I need to do is to get him away from your poisonous thoughts and he'll see my way is better."

"You don't love him. If you knew what love is you'd be unable to steal his life." Payson made another effort to transmit light and love to Diane. She opened her heart and let loose the healing energy of light. She stilled, holding Diane's gaze. It flickered and she fluttered her eyelids, then shook her head and clenched her teeth.

Tremors staggered through Payson. Hopeless resignation sobered her thoughts. Diane's energy had turned so toxic she had automatically rejected the light.

Diane raised her hands in front of Payson. Debris rose around her, hanging mid-air. The room shimmered and energy rippled all around her as Diane moved her hands. Everything, the broken walls and windows, the furniture, the whole apartment came back into order and the rippling stopped. "This never happened," Diane said. "No one will believe you if you try to report it to the police."

"How can you do this? What just happened?"

"I used my powers to destroy the old and create a new reality for Braden. This event is gone, hidden from this new reality. You can't imagine what I can do to you if you ever try to pollute his mind with your memories of what he was to you. Try to release him. Try to engage with the Braden you knew. If you succeed in taking him from me, I'll kill him." Diane cackled and stepped out the sliding door into the backyard with her DAs.

Payson couldn't move. She stood outside of herself, watching her world crumbling. She had to gather her senses. Her first impulse was to call the police to tell them what had happened. What could she say? A Dark Aspect blew up her boyfriend's apartment and kidnapped him because she was in love with him. Four other DAs helped her destroy the apartment and her boyfriend's future, then put everything back together like magic. Yeah, the police would like that story. They'd also like to admit her in to a mental facility.

She had no choice, really. She limped to her car in the driveway and drove away, lost in so many ways. It was daylight, but to her, it was the darkest of nights.

CHAPTER 8

W AKEY, WAKEY."

Diane's voice blared in Braden's ears. His stomach lurched at her nudge. A hangover the size of Texas throbbed in his head. "Damn, woman. Whisper."

"Open your eyes. I need to check on you."

What was she talking about? He slitted his eyes just enough to see her standing at the foot of his bed. The room was dark. He didn't know what time it was. "What do you mean, check on me?" He made to stretch his arms over his head, but stopped mid-lift, his eyes popping open. "Whoa. That hurt." He rose to one elbow, flinching. "What did we do last night? I'm sore all over, including my brain. Whatever it was, I hope it was fun. I don't remember."

She leaned close and slanted her head. "We didn't do anything fun." She stroked his head, as if he were a puppy dog, and he pulled back. "You were hit by a car. And it happened this morning."

"Hit by a car? When, where? Who hit me? Why?"

"Slow down. I'll tell you about it. The doctor said you wouldn't remember." She sat down beside him on the bed. "I took you to the emergency room and I stayed with you. You suffered a concussion and a few scrapes. The doctor let me bring you home after four hours because I promised to watch over you."

Braden scratched his head and searched his mind for memories. Nerves jittered in his belly. Nothing. "Was I driving? Did anyone else get hurt?"

"You were not driving. You and I were walking across the street when a car turned the corner. I jumped out of the way. You were simply in the wrong place at the wrong time." Diane smiled. That smile he recognized.

"You didn't tell me how I got home." He peered into her dark brown eyes, seeking something he couldn't put his finger on.

"Why are you looking at me funny? Don't tell me you don't remember me."

He couldn't stop the questions. Diane's gaze made his skin prickle, but he saw nothing alarming. His gut relaxed. "Sorry. I feel weird. I don't remember the accident. I don't remember the hospital or how I got here. It's hard to explain what I'm feeling. But I know you."

"I understand. The doctor gave you a sedative to keep you calm. He didn't want you to get upset or try to do too much. That sedative is probably still fogging your brain. I had help getting you home and into bed." She frowned. "I'm sorry you feel weird. But you're in your house. I wanted you to be in familiar surroundings. I'm here with you. You're fine."

He remembered that silky voice. It glided through his body, calming his anxiety. "Thank you, Diane. Thanks for taking care of me."

"Of course. Do you remember anything else? The doctor said you probably would, but it might take time."

He scanned the room, looking for a sense of belonging here. Again, blank. He closed his eyes, waiting for memories. The fog slowly thinned. "Well, I know I'm a cop." That had to be a good sign. "I work for you too. You're a successful lobbyist and businesswoman. Yeah. Yeah. I have memories of my cases, the people I'm investigating. I drive a spider Fiat." He opened his eyes and Diane's gaze grabbed his attention. *Why did it sound as though he were reciting something he had heard?*

"Oh, good. So the accident is the only thing you don't remember."

He squeezed his eyes, focusing. Pain shot in his body. "Oh, God!"

Diane grabbed his arm. "What? What do you see?"

Speechless, Braden saw a black vehicle coming at him, his body flying, then hitting the pavement. And he saw Diane, standing over him, speaking words he couldn't make out. A cloud came over his vision and through it, he saw four men. "Who were the men who helped you?"

"What do you mean? Are you getting memories of the accident?" A sharp edge to her voice vibrated through him.

"Yes. I saw you and some men I don't recognize. Who are they? Were they with you?"

"Us, baby. They were with us. You don't remember them?" Her voice softened. "They work for me."

"I don't remember them." He sat up and took her hand. "Thank you so much for helping bring back memories." He shook his head slowly, the power of having his life back coursed through his blood vessels. He had no sense of how long he had been out, but the emptiness in his brain had scared him.

"Of course. You're important to me. You always have been. Do you remember that?" Her eyes bored into him, begging him to assure her.

He nodded. "You're the most familiar thing to me right now."

Diane laughed. "Thing?"

Her laughter jarred his senses. He shrugged internally. Not everything fit together. He just had to get better. "Sorry. Person. Poor word choice, but I'm trying to thank you."

She slid her gaze up and down his body. "I'm just glad you're okay. I hope you remember that I'm more than just a person, I'm your girlfriend."

"Oh. I don't remember." Her look made him squirm. It just happened and he didn't know why. *Maybe because everything in me hurts.* He rolled over and wrapped in the comfort of knowing this was his bedroom in his house. He checked the clock beside his bed. "It's two o'clock. How long have I been lying in bed?"

"I brought you home around noon and put you to bed. You went right to sleep."

Tense, he closed his eyes again to process the disconnect between her explanation of their relationship and what felt real. If he were honest with himself, the only memory that was solid was that of his police work. Restlessness burned in his muscles. "I have work to do." He paused, and checked under the covers. "You put me in pajamas? I don't remember pajamas."

"Well, they belong to you. I didn't put them on you, darling. You put them on, then crawled in bed." She stood and grinned at him. "You can trust me. I would never invade your privacy, Braden."

Did he believe her? Her words raised his guard. "I'll have to take your word on that. Everything is shaky for me still."

She held out her hand to help him get out of bed. "You can trust your memories of me. Relax."

"Sure." He shoved down an automatic cringe at the touch of her hand. His memories seemed detached, and that was unsettling. Maybe he did need to relax and let them sink in.

He waited to undress until Diane walked out, then he headed to the shower. In his bathroom, he surveyed his naked body, noting cuts on his arms and a knot on his head. They didn't connect with him. But the images of his accident were real, he'd felt it happening.

He stood in the water under the showerhead and planted his hands on the ceramic tiled wall. Could he feel connected if he had no memory of this shower? He stood in the warm spray and accepted that this was home, even if it felt unfamiliar. Acceptance was the only way to go on.

Briskly, he sudsed up and tried to grasp a connection with his body. How weird not to know my body, he thought. *Accept.* The word stepped forward in his mind. It repeated like a mantra. *Braden, accept.* It was so appealing, hypnotic. He relaxed into it and let it comfort him.

He stepped out of the shower invigorated and resolved. He would beat this fog and the disconnected, standing-on-no-ground feeling and focus on work. His work was familiar.

He dressed, tuning out the sense that the suits hanging in his closet didn't belong to him. The one he picked fit and he liked the way he looked in the mirror.

A knock at his door startled him. "Braden, I'm going to leave. Are you okay?" Diane's voice steadied him, with no bitter aftertaste. He released a deep sigh. He would be okay, especially with Diane's help. He must have been a little nuts to question if he could trust her. He opened the door and smiled.

"Yes, I'm fine. I'm going to go into work for a while."

Her eyes fluttered. "Go into work? Are you sure you're up to it?"

Strength powered through him. "I'm good." He strode down the hall, noting the slate-colored walls and the blue-gray carpeting. The colors hummed inside him.

The same steel gray and blues were repeated in the living room, surrounding him like a cool fog. Long windows spread in rows along the expansive room's walls. Light gray blinds muted exterior lighting. Plump furniture in blues sat in a conversation group in front of a sleek fireplace. The room felt like him. He walked through it and passed a den lined in books on his way to the kitchen. *I do like books.*

"Wow, this is a big kitchen. I don't remember this." A large island surrounded with chrome bar stools stood in the center. White cabinets and chrome appliances completed the modern look. "How can I afford all this on a detective's salary?"

"You work for me too, remember? I pay you well." Diane winked at him as though they shared a secret, but he didn't know what she was implying.

"Actually, no, I don't recall that you pay me." He peered through a large, framed doorway into a formal dining room. "Nope, don't recall that either."

Diane smirked. "You will. It's your home. I helped you find it and decorate it."

He ran his hand over the marble counter-top and memories

appeared of Diane helping him cook something. The memory eased into place as a commonplace occurrence.

But enough of the tour. His mind buzzed with thoughts of work. "We can talk more about my house, my car, whatever you want later. Now, I've got things to do."

He headed toward a door out in a mudroom, as though he'd done it many times before, and stepped into a spacious garage. "Is this mine?" He eyed the black Fiat waiting for him.

"Of course." Diane smirked. "Another benefit of working for me. Don't you remember?"

He slid into the seat and put his hands on the steering wheel. A comfortable familiarity eased his questions. Things were falling into place. "Yes, I remember." He pulled the door shut and opened the window, enjoying the feel of things. "I'm a kid who just opened birthday gifts. It's weird."

"That will wear off." Diane punched the garage door opener hanging on the wall and the security pad next to it.

More familiarity sifted through him. The sound of her heels striking against the pavement drew his attention as she marched past him and waved.

He leaned out the window. "Wait. Where will I find you?" Anxiety began hammering in his gut.

She opened the door to her black Cadillac and stood there, a serene expression in her eyes. "You don't remember?"

Braden paused, sinking into his brain, searching. He smiled at a memory. "Yes. I know where you live and where you work."

PAYSON PACED THROUGH her living room, back and forth, struggling to calm frantic nerves jittering in her gut. She drove home four hours ago in a daze. Disbelief battled with reality, keeping her moving. What could she do? Diane. Diane. Oh my God, Diane had blown up her life when she'd blown up Braden's condo and blocked his mind.

Strategies to get him back had gone in circles in the long hours since Diane had made good on her threats. What would happen if she asked for help from the others? What if doing so sent Diane over the edge? "Oh my God, what if she kills him out of spite?"

She could still see the explosion replaying in her mind. Could still see Braden lying on the floor. And could still see Diane's anger distorting her features.

"How could I not have known how dark Diane had gone?" She shrieked at the emptiness inside her house and inside her body.

Tears leaked down her cheeks, and she pounded the walls, sobbing. "Braden, oh my God, Braden."

ZuZu stood on the carpet and meowed up at her. Payson grabbed her and ploughed her face into the soft fur.

She held ZuZu tight and sunk to the floor. ZuZu's heartbeat gave her something steady to grab onto. She breathed in and out deliberately, and tuned her mind to ZuZu's pulse. Despair pulled strength from her body. Crying wracked her body and there was nothing to stop it. ZuZu jutted her head against Payson's face, then she walked away, leaving her to lie flat on the floor. Aloneness ached in her soul. "I can't do this alone."

She pulled herself up and called Claire Eve. As luck would have it, Claire Eve had an opening in her schedule and she offered to make a house call. Claire Eve couldn't erase what had happened, but she'd always been there when needed.

Claire Eve had caught Payson gently in her youth as she was falling deeper and deeper into despair, and used her ability of wisdom of the ages and a healing touch. The memories of those days trembled through her, reminding her of how her high sensitivities to everything left her overwhelmed, invaded, and bombarded as her normal. Claire Eve was not her mother, but in a sense, she was the mother Payson had never had. While her own mother had believed she was a liar and a crazy person, Claire Eve had understood and accepted her. The nightmare in which she learned at ten-years-old of her true nature had given her a promise of Claire Eve. So even in her very difficult younger years, Payson knew she would find a woman who would help her. Even now, that promise steadied her.

Within thirty minutes, Claire Eve knocked on Payson's front door. "Hi, Payson."

"Thank you for coming." Attractively willowy, with muscles exuding strength, her auburn hair was styled simply in a short, tousled cut that always looked good. Dressed in tailored dark grey trousers topped with a cobalt Tee and soft-looking black wrap sweater, Claire Eve looked comfortable all the way down to her black leather Mary Janes. She was the perfect mixture of classic and functional.

The depth in her green eyes assured Payson her therapist cared about others, and the gleam in them spoke of Claire Eve's joy in living.

Claire Eve hugged her and Payson's sorrow took over. A lump formed in her throat and she couldn't speak.

"You're so very sad, aren't you?" Claire Eve's energy held Payson's devastation and loss. The energy accepted it all, limp body, helpless, and fear, and Payson's aloneness began to shift.

"Come have a seat," she said, leading Claire Eve to the couch. "Would you like water?" Maybe if she did something she could stop feeling so much.

"Not right now. Sit with me." Claire Eve patted the spot next to her. "Tell me what happened."

Claire Eve's warm, vibrant energy wafted around her, clear and clean. Payson drew in a full breath and blew it out, aware of the energy rising in the room, like the scent of air after a rain.

She poured out her story, blow by painful blow, and Claire Eve listened, all her attention on Payson. With the last bit of the incident spoken, Payson got a glass of water for them both. "Thank you for listening, Claire Eve. I feel lighter."

Claire sipped her water, then put the glass on the end table and shook her head. "You love Braden so much and you've loved each other for a very long time. It's so hard to think of a life without him, I'm sure."

The words plucked at her heart, so full of truth. "I can't do it. I mean, I know I have it in me to move on without him. I'm strong." Her voice dropped. "I guess I can't imagine life without him. I don't want to."

"I know you're strong and that you can move on, but I'm wondering if you can do both, not one or the other. Be strong, go on with your next move. What would you do?" Claire Eve's eyes were crystal emerald pools. They soothed Payson's sore heart and invited her to think differently. In Claire Eve's eyes and embraced by her high energy, Payson could see possibilities.

"Well, he's not dead. I don't have to feel as though he is, nor do I have to accept Diane's plans for him. It's not right for her to enslave him to her will and deprive him of what he has always loved."

Claire Eve smiled. "No, it's not right." She slanted her head. "But acting against her will is dangerous. She's proven her Dark Sides has taken over and there is nothing she won't do to have Braden under her control. It's very personal for her because of her childhood wounding. She was robbed of her parent's love, and she was rejected by her grandmother. She lost hope for being someone's special person long ago. She needed it from the family who was supposed to cherish her. Now, she's taking what she believes will make her feel loved."

Payson pounded her fists on the couch. "I'm tired of making allowances for her behavior. Everyone has a burden to bear in life, but there are always possibilities available for growth. She is causing harm, she's making darkness proliferate in Auralia. It's my job to stop her."

"You can't face her alone, Payson. When she took over Braden's mind, she didn't kill him but she took his life. That action would have a profound effect on her spirit. In her present imbalanced state, she could be lethal."

"Right. But together we Aeons can stop her and her DAs." Payson's thoughts rolled, strategies forming.

Claire Eve got quiet and took another sip of water. Payson waited for her encouragement. But Claire Eve sat still, gazing out into the nature outside Payson's house. Her silence prompted anxiety in Payson's chest.

Finally, Claire Eve gave her a somber look. "Yes, your group of

Aeons can work together and you can go after Diane. But you won't reach her in her darkness if you don't go there with her. Stand in it beside her and know it as well as you know your light."

"What are telling me? That I have to go dark in order to defeat Diane's negative impact on Braden? I don't want to do that."

"I know. I'm not telling you what to do, that's up to you. Maybe you can sit with what to do and see what happens."

Payson's resolve sank. "What if I can't stay present with the idea? I'm so angry." Just as Braden had been, and she'd feared darkness in him. Her thoughts spun.

"Of course. Your anger is understandable, not wrong. It can inform you if you let it. Observe it and don't let it make your decisions." Her voice remained lighthearted and full of support. "I believe in you. You'll be fine. Remember, getting Braden back is not a given or even your best move potentially. This is a doorway into yourself, Payson. Let it happen."

Payson gritted her teeth. Her mind closed to letting go of Braden. "I'm not ready to give up on Braden. I can't."

Claire Eve rose and walked toward the door. "That's okay. You have a choice. I don't expect you to simply switch your point of view. I want for you to experience an organic energetic movement inside that guides you." She searched through her purse for her keys.

"Thank you for talking with me."

"Of course. I enjoy talking with you. I have hope that what is best for you and Braden will occur. I want you to have a happy-ever-after."

Alone again in her quiet space, Payson's muscles tensed. She didn't know where to find Braden, but she was a bounty hunter, for Christ's sake. She would find Braden.

First, she had to talk to her fellow Aeons, and fortunately, they already planned a meeting for tonight.

CHAPTER 9

THE MEETING WITH the others wasn't going to happen until six o'clock, but Payson couldn't delay notifying the others what Diane had done. She rolled her shoulders, loathe to make the announcement, knowing they would all want to rally around her pain. It took so much strength not to crumple again, and with all of their sympathy wrapping her, it might be too easy to sink.

She shoved the thought out of her mind. If that happened, so be it. She'd accept their support for the goodness that it would be. Her fingers shook as she texted her group.

Heads Up. Diane has gone over the edge. She took Braden with her.

A sob caught in her throat as she hit send. She shook her head, reminding herself it was time to be strong.

Within seconds, her phone rang. "Hi, Skye."

"I'm coming over. If that's okay, I'll be there in thirty minutes. If it's not okay with you, I'm coming anyway."

Payson didn't bother to dissuade Skye. "Ordinarily that would make me laugh. That would be fine, but what about Coffee Is?"

"Shut up. Don't even think about me. I'll see you soon."

Payson occupied her mind with making coffee and checking for snacks she could offer Skye. Her brain chugged along like ancient mechanical gears. She stood at the opened refrigerator door and stared. Pointless. Everything was pointless. The love she had shared with Braden had been a source of meaning. Now what?

ZuZu drifted between her legs. She shook some kibble into her dish and rubbed behind her ears. "Love you, my faithful friend. It means a lot that you're here with me, sweetie."

A sharp knock at the door startled her, but she relaxed when Skye came in and walked directly to her, reaching her arms around her shoulders.

"Payson, what happened?" Skye wiped away tears brimming Payson's eyes. "Let's sit. Your aura is pale green and dotted with black spots. Not good."

Payson breathed in air and the light energy that emanated from Skye. It was a salve that bolstered her own light. "A few hours ago Diane invaded Braden's apartment. She blew it up using her chaos energy, and mesmerized him. He's gone, Skye."

Skye's hand flew to her mouth. "Oh my God. I warned Braden to be careful. But this, oh my God, he's one of us. We need him. But listen to me. I can't imagine what you're going through."

"Thank you for that. I talked to Claire Eve. She helped me process what happened, but I'm still working on that." She stood to her feet. "Diane threatened to hurt me too. But it's Braden I'm worried about. She said if I try to reconnect with him or succeed in eliminating the block, she'll kill him."

Skye scowled. "Not going to happen. We'll figure out something, some way to intervene for Braden and take care of Diane too."

The starch in Payson's spine disintegrated. She slumped to the couch and dropped her head into her hands. "How do I go on? It hurts so much. I keep seeing Braden lying on the floor, blank."

"Let me help you." Skye grabbed her hands and held them. The warmth from Skye's healing touch went through her body. "One moment at a time, Payson. I can't instantly heal the problem, but my touch can support you enough to give you strength and clarity. And one day at a time is how you and all of us will go from here."

Another rap on her door sounded and Skye went to answer it.

Before she got to the door, Keegan walked in with Cooper Munson, another bounty hunter and Aeon. Payson's heart melted.

They both walked to her and hugged her, first Keegan, then Cooper.

"Payson, we got your text and came right over." Keegan took a seat and shook his head. "I want to know every detail, but how about we wait to discuss what happened until the meeting."

She nodded. "Thank you. In short, Diane has mesmerized Braden."

Tall, black, and muscled, Cooper looked the part of a tough guy, but actually, he was a sensitive empath, prone to moments of overwhelming sorrow and sadness from the world around him. He kneeled in front of her. Sun glistened off his bald head. "I feel your loss, Payson. But I have peace to share." His deep voice resonated warmly inside her. His large stature gave him a commanding presence. When she first met him, his empathy tortured him with the pain and anger of others, but these days it just softened his heart and made him an understanding friend.

Cooper kissed the top of her head and took a seat.

"Thank you all for coming." Payson stifled a sob. "I'm eager to take action, but I don't expect anyone else to get involved. It would be dangerous. I can't ask you to put yourself in harm's way."

"Well," Keegan started, "that's the beauty of our little band of Aeons. We're with you in this. You don't have to ask."

"That's right." Skye nodded.

"I second, no third that. And I have no doubt Ainsley will agree. She couldn't leave the store, but her heart is here." Cooper slapped his hands as though dusting them off. "Now, I know you, Payson. You want to go after Diane. You can't wait to put a stop to her devious plans. So I'm not going to ask you to wait until we've formulated a plan before you make a move."

Keegan chuckled. "Right. But please keep us informed." He scanned the group. "It's going to be an especially dangerous endeavor now that we're not only working to raise the world's energetic level, but also saving Braden from Diane."

"Yes, we all need to watch each other's back, I agree." Payson's energy grew. She could feel it lifting as the others amplified their light. It warmed her heart.

"The first thing I want to do is update your security system, Payson." Keegan raised his hands. "No argument. When you actively challenge Diane, she's going to respond with lethal force. You know that now."

"He's right." Cooper pursed his lips and the dark brown of his eyes deepened. "She'll send her DAs to stop you. Your home needs to be your fortress."

"What about the rest of you? Are all of you going to fortify your safety? I'm not special," Payson said.

Skye nodded. "In this case, you are. Diane is making you a target. She hates us all, but she specifically wants you out of the picture. So, accept the guys' offer. Don't be a martyr. Please."

"Okay. It's a good idea. Thank you. But we need to make sure everyone's home is secured. Agreed?"

"Okay, we'll do a security check on each of our homes, but we begin with yours. Agreed?'

Payson decided not to argue the point. "Agreed."

Cooper and Keegan exchanged a glance and stood. "Good. Let's get started, Keegan," Cooper said.

"You are the best, all of you," Payson said.

Skye raised her hand. "I vote we reschedule our meeting for tomorrow. I can stay with you until the guys finish updating your security."

"You don't have to," Payson protested. "I'll be fine."

"I could use some time away from Coffee Is."

Payson had to admit that the others' energy had renewed her faith and hope. The two shined inside her like guides. "Thanks, that would be nice, Skye. If only I could see Braden and find him well."

ACTIVITY AT THE Auralia Police Department settled Braden's nerves. Phone ringing, chatter, and keyboarding were sounds he knew well. Considering his memory challenges, that was a plus to being at work so soon after his accident. He didn't remember his hospital stay, but this place helped him remember who he was—Detective Braden Powers. It was more than a title and a job, it was an identity. He needed that to hold him to the earth.

He turned to Zane and watched him talking on the phone. His memory of him was slim, but he had one at least. Curiously, Zane had simply waved and hadn't acted surprised to see him when he walked in to the room. Braden rocked his head, trying to ease the tension in his neck and dismiss the thought. His brain was too shaky to try to understand why no one cared he had shown up late or what his injury had meant to his coworkers.

He turned his attention to a list of robbery suspects he had made before his accident. He added the name Nick Ward, a rock landing in his gut.

Whoa, that was weird. How did he know that name? He closed his eyes and concentrated. Nick Ward. The name was familiar, but he couldn't grab hold of a face or a reason. Still, he couldn't deny the graveness weighing inside him. It had something to do with Nick.

He punched the name in to the National Crime Information Center's database and a photo and details popped up. He stared at the image of a young man. Black, short hair, twenty-two. His short Record of Arrests and Prosecutions, his RAP sheet, listed petty thefts and one armed robbery charge. In his mind's eye, he saw himself interviewing a man. More clarity sifted in, and he knew the reason he added Nick to the list of suspects. A man in an interview he had conducted recently had described Nick. Nick had pointed a gun at the man and his kids.

"Hello, Braden. It's earth to Braden." Zane knocked on his desk. "Are you feeling okay? Diane told us you were in an accident earlier, but that you were released to work."

Braden jumped, his heart raced. He attempted to cover his reaction. "You caught me. I was in a zone."

"Sorry. I didn't mean to startle you, but I did speak to you first. You just didn't hear me. I didn't want to make a big deal about it. A young woman, said her name was Diane, told me you two were together when it happened." Zane crooked his neck. "Strange thing, she asked me to keep Payson out of conversation because she had something to do with the accident. That is hard to believe."

"Payson?" A pain throbbed in his temple. He searched his mind for memories of a Payson, but came up with nothing. "It's not important."

"Okay, well, I'm glad you're up to working, what with the recent crime spree."

"I'm fine, just a little slow. I'm trying to get a gut instinct about a suspect." Braden turned back to the photo.

Zane looked over Braden's shoulder. "Oh, that's Nick. You've been working with him. You've forgotten him? You saw him just the other day." Zane ran his finger in circles beside his head. "You sure you're all right? Maybe it's too soon to come to work."

Nerves jittered in Braden's chest. "No. I'm fine. Yeah, I know Nick. Of course I know Nick." The more times he said it, the surer he was of his connection to Nick. "I'm just trying to refamiliarize myself with the robberies and the suspects."

"I'm sorry. I shouldn't razz you like that. Sorry you got hit by a car."

Braden squirmed. "It's okay. I didn't know Diane had talked to you. I feel weird about my memory loss, but I'm myself."

Zane flashed him a smile. "Good. If you need help on anything, say so." He turned back to his computer.

"Thanks again." He couldn't sit any longer. Something burned inside him, something that required action. He holstered his Glock 22 behind his back, grabbed his phone, and strode out of the office, a destination calling.

He ran down the stairs and out to his car, a sense of purpose pumping through his veins. He needed this exhilaration to get his brain back.

Nick's home address was his destination. Vague recollections of taking Nick for hamburgers shifted his disconnect to resignation that nothing could have kept the young man from his destiny. Nick had been born a bad seed and theft was in his nature.

Moments later, he turned onto the street in a part of town he recognized. The black Fiat obviously made him conspicuous. What an odd choice of vehicle for a cop.

He remembered walking these streets and conversing with the residents. They were hard-working people. The homes were small just like the lots, and wore signs of a little neglect. It hadn't yet slipped into seedy because the residents cared. They held blue-collar jobs and were the sort who'd been hard hit by the economy. He didn't know how he knew this, but he did.

Everything was slipping. Homes needed new roofs. Fences were sagging, and old cars dotted bare yards. The city needed to put more effort into revitalizing this area or it would become a place with no heart. That's when the creep factor would go up. Scumbags would make it their home, and bad things would happen. Hatred churned in his mind for all that scumbags meant.

He parked across the street and a few houses away from Nick's last known address. It was close enough to keep an eye on but not so close he'd be made before he even knocked.

All his nerves went on alert as he climbed up the stoop and banged on the front door. Sounds came from inside, low voices and steps.

The door opened and a middle-aged woman stood expressionless. "Hello."

"Good afternoon, Ma'am." He held up his badge. "I'm Detective Powers. Could I talk to you for a minute?"

She didn't move. "What about?"

"Do you know a Nick Ward?"

Her eyes narrowed for a split second. "He's not here." She started to shut the door, but Braden stuck his foot out, blocking it.

"Does he live here? When could I find him here or do you have another address where I might find him?" He spoke the words as emotionless as possible. But when he heard feet pounding the ground around the side of the house, he jumped off the stoop. "Damn it!"

CHAPTER 10

$\mathcal{A}$ YOUNG MAN jumped out a window and sprinted toward a fence. Braden couldn't get a fix on whether or not it was Nick, but he took off after him, adrenaline fueling his pace.

"Stop! Police!" Braden reached the suspect just as he finished climbing over the fence and dropped to the ground on the other side. The guy never stopped moving.

Braden slammed his hands against the metal fence. "Freeze, before you break a leg."

The young man turned to look over his shoulder and Braden recognized his face.

"Nick, stop!"

Nick flashed his middle finger, then stumbled over his feet. He quickly recovered from his near-fall, but in the meantime, Braden climbed over and closed the gap enough to grab his jacket and throw him to the ground.

"I told you to stop! Why did you run?" Braden shoved him onto his back and snapped on cuffs. "On your feet." He muscled Nick into a stand.

"I didn't do anything! You got nothing on me. It figures you'd come after me, even after you told me you're my friend."

Braden stared into Nick's face. His words didn't mean anything. He was probably lying. "I know you aren't that dumb. You think I'd knock on your door and chase you down just for kicks? We both know better than that. Let's go."

"Where are you taking me?" The young man's eyes widened nearly imperceptibly.

"Nick, you keep quiet. How did you end up getting caught? Officer, can I be of help?" another man asked.

Braden startled, feeling exposed. The other man had been able to sneak up behind him. "What's your name?"

"Warren."

"Warren what? You live around here?"

The man's face bothered Braden. It was mid-afternoon but this white guy's face was darkened as though it was dusk. His clothes were nondescript—a hoodie and jeans—but his muscular body was evident beneath them. His legs were spread, giving him a solid and imposing stance.

"Warren Brown. This is my neighborhood." His voice was burned toast—all dry and rough.

"Your neighborhood, as in you live here?" To Braden's ears, the implication went beyond residing here to commanding some kind of control. "You're interfering in police business."

Warren slanted his head and stared into Braden's eyes. A cold shiver sliced through him like a bad memory. The sound of Warren's voice resonated in him. His thoughts blurred. Grappling with his foggy head, he worked to summon focus.

Rustling behind his back returned his attention to Nick, but he was running, handcuffs still restraining him, in the direction of the next street over.

"Nick, stop! I just want to talk," Braden hollered. Again, Nick looked over his shoulder past Braden and at Warren, his eyes wide with fear. "Stop!" He didn't like that look on Nick's face, and Braden also didn't like the heavy traffic he was running toward.

Nick never hesitated, and instantly he was in danger, with cars blaring their horns and swerving to avoid him.

Braden reached the road and held up his hand, trying to stop traffic. A sickening *thwack* dropped a hard rock to the pit of his stomach. Nick sailed up, then plunged to the pavement.

A woman climbed out of a car stopped in the street. "I didn't see him. Oh my God, I didn't see him."

Braden raced to Nick. Blood flowed down his face from a wound to his head. He checked his pulse and his breathing, then bent his head. Nick's body lay lifeless.

"Is he dead?" the woman asked, her voice trembling.

Braden stood to talk to her. "Just a minute, please."

He called Zane to tell him about Nick and to ask for medical.

He turned his attention to Brown, who was still standing in the grass between houses. He lifted his hood over his head and stared back at him.

"Hey, come here!" Braden called. "I want to talk to you."

Warren turned and jogged away.

"I said come here! Brown!" He shook his head, knowing something was off with the man, but he couldn't leave the scene. He kept his sights on Brown until he disappeared into a convenient store down a block.

While he waited for EMT, he tried to calm the woman. "You didn't do anything wrong, Ma'am. I saw it happen. I'm a cop. EMTs will arrive soon and they will help you. I'm sure you're really shook up."

"Thank you, officer. I am." Her eyes darted from Nick's body to the people gathered and to her feet, while she wrung her hands over and over. "I didn't see that young man. He just wasn't there, and he slammed into my car." Tears streamed down her face.

Braden's gut tightened at sirens blaring closer. The ambulance coming was for Nick. It couldn't be, his heart kept shouting.

The woman took a step closer to him. "I don't know what to do. This is terrible."

"You're going to be all right. Here, see, the EMTs are on the scene. They will take of you as soon as they check on the boy."

"You mean the body?" She stared at the EMTs surrounding Nick.

Braden knew she needed attention fast. She was going into shock.

He gestured to a second medical team and they took her to their vehicle.

"What happened here?" Zane approached him, questions on his face.

Braden couldn't get words out. He was a cop. He was supposed to remain stoic, so he kept a tight hold on anger and sorrow boiling in his gut. It was a subtle thing, but it helped to have Zane stand with him while the paramedics loaded the body into their vehicle. "Geez, I'm sorry, man. I know you tried to help Nick. Tough break."

Braden relayed the story, ignoring the lump in his throat. This was his doing. He shouldn't have let the other man distract him.

"Why do they always run?" Yates asked. "The usual reason is they're just plain dumb."

"Maybe." Guilt reminded him of how he had put Nick in a box moments ago and labeled it Hopeless. At the time, it had seemed right. Now something told him it was wrong. "I don't think so. He got spooked. He wasn't simply fleeing the law, he was running for his life." *But why? Why did Nick run? He'd been arrested before. What was different this time?*

A warm breeze lifted branches of trees lining the street. The sun was past the high point in the sky and shadows were growing. All around him circled a typical day. But something was definitely not normal. Braden focused his gaze on the place where the other man, Warren Brown, had stood, a dark and menacing thundercloud. Worse, he seemed vaguely familiar, but Braden couldn't pin him to a memory. Diane told him memory loss was due to his concussion and that it would be temporary. Still, he had only a hazy memory of the accident that took his memories, and the possibility that this not-knowing would be his norm now made him shiver.

Yates jabbed his arm. "You all right?"

"Yeah. I'm going to look for some security cameras and see if I can get footage. Thanks for your help. I'll see you back at the department."

Zane shook his head. "No, why don't you go home. Don't push yourself. We can continue with the investigation tomorrow."

Braden had to admit that Zane had a point. The weight of his body made it difficult to stand. But anything could happen, so he wouldn't take a chance on video getting recorded over or stolen. "You're right. But I can manage."

Braden slipped behind the wheel and pushed the accelerator until the power of his Fiat satisfied his need to get to the convenient mart as quickly as possible. His hands on the wheel felt awkward and he couldn't get comfortable in the seat. Had his entire body forgotten what it felt like to drive his car?

Once inside the store, he right off found a camera and approached the clerk.

He showed his badge. "I'm Detective Powers. Do you have security footage of the last two days I could look at?"

"We keep the footage for a week, then we record over it. If you can wait a minute, I'll give it to you on a thumb drive."

"Thanks, I'll wait." He grabbed a bottle of water. "Let me pay for this first, okay?"

Braden took a swig of water and stared out the window. Drivers were filling their cars' gas tanks and paying at the pump. Off to the side, a group of young people stood chatting in groups. He choked on his water. Nick had been one of those kids in the parking lot hanging out. Now he was dead.

"Here you go." The clerk tapped on his shoulder. "Are you all right? You look like you've seen a ghost or something. Did one of those kids out there do something?"

"No. I just zoned out." He took the drive from the clerk. "Thanks. I owe you, man."

He pulled out of the parking lot and took off for his home, emotions wrestling in him. Could he have done better by Nick and prevented his death or was Nick a victim of a lifestyle destined to fail? Two perspectives, but what did he believe? The confusion was driving him insane.

The closer he got to his street, the more his shoulders sagged. Deliberate and slow, he parked in the garage. He walked inside and plopped his things on the counter. Every movement he'd made, every effort he'd used to get through his first day back from his accident had left him drained. Adrenaline he had leaned on now leveled out and all he was was bone-weary fatigue and bewilderment.

I must be having real problems from the accident. Home, he glanced around the place Diane had told him was his house, seemed unfamiliar. There was no sense of belonging in this house. He could find his way from room to room, drawer to drawer, cupboard to cupboard, but he was a robot going through the motions.

He stretched out on the couch and tried to bring up useful thoughts about his incident with Nick earlier and connect it to information. Warren Brown had done something to scare Nick. That would be the direction he would take, unearthing everything he could about Brown. He closed his eyes and saw Nick's terrified expression in his mind. His heart pounded loudly in his head. All he could do was lie flat on his back, thoughts and emotions whirling, trying to find a stronger sense of identity.

"Get up, Braden. You're not the only guy who has had a concussion, so get over it," he lectured himself about persevering. "Turn on your computer and do a search in NCIC. It'll be easy."

Even to his ears, his words sounded sluggish.

A robot on overload, Braden stared at the pile of papers on his desk, papers from which Diane was waiting for him to cull information. The thumb drive of the security feed from the convenience store in Nick's neighborhood sat on top of the pile. He checked the time from his phone. Four o'clock in the morning. Too early to get ready for work. But sleep was nowhere around. Not now.

CHAPTER 11

$\mathcal{P}$AYSON'S NEXT MOVE had become clear to her during the restless night, and it had only clarified more with her morning coffee.

She closed her eyes in the elevator up to Diane's office in the Kurl building, and focused on the white light inside her body. In her mind she watched a small ball of light grow and grow, filling her with light, peace, and love.

A tone signaled her arrival on the tenth floor where Diane's office was located. Her heart skipped, warning her she was heading into the lions' den.

But she was on a mission and nothing could stop her, not even the seriously dark energies inside Diane and her minions. Their darkness was a black hole that could eat up light. It was aggressive, but she worried about people already walking the line between dark and light. They were more vulnerable to its appeal.

Pressure built inside her. One full day and night had passed since Diane had taken Braden's mind. A deadline loomed. She had ten days to get him back before he'd go completely DA. After that, she knew she could continue to offer him light, but his ability to see the choice would diminish. He would be hardened.

She had never visited Diane's office and Payson didn't know what to expect. She marched down the hall; marching had to account for something considering what she was up against. The closer she got, the more prominent the whirring, like a buzz saw, screeched in her body. She fortified her light. It was the best defense and offense she had going for her.

She put her hand to the door with Braden in her thoughts. He'd lost his free will and she meant to get it back for him.

Inside the office suite, she scanned the large outer office, and breezed by the receptionist's desk.

"Can I help you?" A tall blonde stood and tried to intercept her. "Do you have an appointment with Ms. Butler?"

"No," she said without turning. The DA vibration in the room shuddered like a small-scale earthquake. It did nothing to dim her light, though. Her sandals made quiet swishing sounds on the umber-colored carpeting spreading to the tawny painted walls.

She easily found Diane's office and walked in. "Diane, I want to talk to you."

Diane smirked. "Hello, Payson. Have a seat." She gestured to a suede chair sitting on the opposite side of her large, caramel-colored wooden desk. "What would you like to discuss?"

Payson ignored the offer of a seat, power drumming through her. "Braden. What have you done with him? Where is he?"

Diane sighed heavily. "I have nothing to add to what I told you already."

"Stop stonewalling. Where is he?" It was much easier to face Diane when the walls weren't on fire and Braden wasn't hurt, lying on the floor. "Give me proof he's all right or I'll talk to the police." She didn't yell. She planted her hands on the desk and leaned in, pinning Diane with her gaze.

Thrumming in her head grew strong as Diane narrowed her eyes. "You're threatening me? It would be fatal to underestimate me, Miss Payson." She relaxed back in her chair and twirled a pen. "Braden is well. But he is mine now. Forget about him. You'll have to get used to living without him. Alone, like I've been all my life. Let him go." Her lips exaggerated the words she spoke. "Let him go. Braden doesn't belong with you."

Payson drew down to a deep awareness of the energy fueling her strength. It tingled inside her fingers and spread from her head to her toes. It flowed like soothing liquid sunshine, helping her remain grounded and sane in the presence of a sort of insanity. Diane's efforts to mesmerize her failed.

"I can live without Braden, Diane. But I will not stand by and allow you to take away his free will, his right to choose how he wants to make his life." Her words sounded solid to her. She hoped she was convincing Diane that she stood unwavering with the stuff to back them up.

Diane rolled her eyes and Payson sighed internally. She saw the effects of using her power of light. It had helped her resist Diane's will and undermine her determination.

"Humph," Diane frowned. "Braden's old life is gone along with his memories. I've given him a new home, a new car, and a job, along with fitting memories. He won't question any of it. He accepts it all as his status quo."

Payson refused to give in to the despair that slithered around her throat. "You supplanted his life with made up memories and sparkly toys, is that what you're saying? Are you one of the new toys?" Payson gritted her teeth to keep her mind from imagining Diane's arms around Braden's broad shoulders in an intimate embrace. "Why did you need to blow up his apartment? Wasn't that a bit over-the-top drama even for you? Did you need the explosion to get a hold on Braden's mind?"

Diane's gaze dipped, briefly, and she pursed her lips.

"That's it, isn't it? You used trauma as a seed to a successful mind block, didn't you?"

Diane lifted her chin. "You understand that he no longer knows you. You aren't even a memory." She twisted her lips, completely ignoring Payson's theory, and paused. The air went out of the room. "If you try to reach him, you'll hurt him and I will know. I'll end his life."

Icy cold chilled Payson's bones. "You like to make threats. This whole thing between you and me and Braden is a problem only in your mind. It's not a competition. Let him go and give him the chance to choose. He deserves that. It's the right thing to do, Diane, for him and you."

"Ha!" Diane slapped her desk and walked around it until her face was only inches from Payson's. "Right thing? Who says, you? You have no authority over him." She raised her hand and made to slap Payson, but Payson caught her arm. "Let me go!" Diane tried to rip away her arm from Payson's grip.

Images burst into Payson's mind, instantly flooding her with misery. She saw Diane cowering in a corner of her bedroom while her grandmother kicked her and shouted obscenities. *"You're a freak, Diane, and I wish you'd never been born, you bitch, you shit-faced brat! You killed your parents with all your neediness. If they hadn't needed to get away from you, they wouldn't have been driving that night. They wouldn't have been killed."*

Payson stifled a flinch and released Diane's hand. The temptation to find satisfaction in hurting Diane's arm glimmered in her gut on the embers of the chaotic images. Even knowing it originated with Diane's dark energy didn't make it easy for Payson to let it pass. "Thank you for sharing what you've done to Braden." Her composure intact, she went to the door with Diane's rage stabbing her over and over.

"Get out!" Diane yelled.

Payson tensed with the sound of Diane grabbing her stapler. She ducked just before Diane flung it at her, and the stapler put a hole in the wall. "I'm going."

"I hate you, you bitch!"

Payson held her center as she walked out, leaving the door open behind her. Her stomach twisted as she mulled over the premeditated disaster she'd let loose simply by loving Braden. She stood alone in the elevator, doubled-over and leaning one hand on the wall. If she let go, her knees would give out, then she would just have to get back up.

· · ·

UNDER THE SHADE of a sprawling oak tree, Payson pulled her cap down low and scrunched down in the driver's seat. From her vantage point across from the APD, she could see every car that drove into the parking lot and every person who took the employee entrance into the building or out.

Even with the shade, without the car running she had no AC and sweat dampened her neck. Any amount of discomfort was nothing compared to the aching need to see Braden. She'd sit on a briar bush for a glimpse of him. She had to see him.

Across the street people strolled, probably shopping and heading toward food and drinks at the downtown restaurants and bars. She could imagine them chatting with friends at lunch and playing with their children in the nearby Central City Park. The afternoon after the explosion, life continued and no one even noticed that her heart ached, or that her life-long love was gone.

The door at the employee entrance opened and her stomach knotted. She held her breath. Two seconds hung in the heat, then Braden stepped out. *Oh my God. It's him.* Her heart froze and tears misted her eyes. "Braden," she whispered. Everything around her suspended and she had to bite her fingers to keep from calling out to him.

She couldn't stop herself. She opened the car door and climbed out, torn between running to him and standing still behind the door for fear of triggering something awful.

She took in his form, muscled and strong from his shoulders and chest to his slim waist. His stride, so Braden, stretched long and confident, but without his usual saunter. Instead he had a swagger she'd never seen before.

From her spot, she couldn't really know if he was okay, but nothing raised alarms. He was alive. He had no apparent wounds. She shrugged. Diane hadn't lied about his health, at least.

She watched Braden get into a car—a Fiat? Her stomach squeezed tighter. The Braden she knew not only couldn't spend that kind of money on a vehicle, he wouldn't. He preferred less showy and practical to flamboyant.

Payson slipped back inside her car, recognition of what this change meant spreading through her body like hypothermia.

Saving Braden's life was one thing, but saving the essence of who he was as an Aeon would take all her skills and then some.

She pounded her fist on the steering wheel. There was no time to make a plan or to twiddle the time away. She grabbed her phone and wrote a group text. *Can we meet for lunch at Coffee Is? It's urgent. Noon?*

Instantly, her insides groaned. Waiting, waiting, waiting. She grabbed clumps of her hair and pulled, willing the others to reply.

She stared at her phone, hoping for responses.

First Ainsley's text popped in. *I'll be there.*

She pulled in shallow breaths, grateful but still waiting for the others. Each new text raised her hopes for enacting a plan swiftly. Texts popped up from the others, one after the other.

I've got the back room reserved. It was Skye.

Payson rested her phone against her chest and closed her eyes after reading the last text, a response from Skye. Her mind whirred with possibilities for ways of restoring Braden's life. She checked the time. She wouldn't have to wait long now.

Parking was sparse during the mid-day, so Payson had to search for a spot. She left her car along a street down a few blocks from Coffee Is and strolled in that direction. She took note of cars driving by—a green van, a red sports car, an SUV full of kids staring at their cellphone screens. Reflections in store windows let her know who made up crowds of pedestrians. Her awareness was natural for an Aeon, but vigilance also was a natural extension of her job. Like a cop, she was always working, and carried pepper spray and zip ties in her pocket.

A block farther, she heard screams erupt behind her.

"He stole my purse! Help me! Oh, my."

Almost on a reflex, Payson turned. She raced to the woman calling for help. Her mind flew, assessing the situation in a split second. The woman looked about late seventies. A few feet away from her ran a large young man. His energy surged raggedly with darkness, striking in her chest.

Payson shot after him. "Stop!" she shouted. "I have a gun!"

The man kept running. He wheeled and ran into traffic.

She didn't hesitate to follow him. Her breaths came in heavy, deep pulls as she dodged traffic, horns blaring at her. Her thoughts streamed along with her pace.

Her height worked in her favor. A small, female bounty hunter wasn't exactly threatening to the criminals she hunted. She gritted her teeth as she chased the thief. She'd be damned if she'd let this butthead steal from the woman. There might not be much money in the purse but it might have money from the woman's latest Social Security account or something precious like a granddaughter's lock of hair.

"I told you to stop," she growled a step behind him, then grabbed the man's collar and jerked hard. Icy fear attached to a blurry image of a prison cell sped through her fingertips and into her midriff, and she instantly released him. He fell backward, stumbling over the curb. She landed a solid kick to his shoulder and kept her foot on top of his chest. More shocks ran up her leg and she let them pass like clouds. "Stay down. What are you thinking stealing a senior citizen's purse?" she hollered, looking down into his dusty face. Her energy field was coherent, thankfully. If it weren't, she'd have a hard time holding her own boundaries so that she wouldn't take on the negative shit wafting off the man. She stood above him, picked up the purse, and pulled money out of her pocket, then tossed a ten-dollar bill on his chest. "You need money? Get a job."

The small crowd that stood around the scene applauded her, and Payson nodded, relieved to hear sirens approaching. She zip tied his hands and kept an on eye on him until the police arrived.

"Hi, officers. I'm Payson Silver."

"You're the recovery agent I've heard about. Someone called APD to report a robbery." He glanced around. "I see you have witnesses."

"Yes." She motioned to Gladys. "The woman over there can tell you her story. This purse belongs to her. I just happened to be nearby."

Another officer cuffed the robber, and nodded toward her. He ran his gaze over her. "I can't get over it. You fool people every time into underestimating you, don't you? The bad guys don't think a petite woman poses a threat."

She chuckled. "Yeah, I know. It's my advantage. Excuse me." Payson saw the older woman standing alone off to the side and strode toward her, impressions from the purse flashing in her mind. A picture of a young couple lay inside. Made of soft, black leather, it was old, the image of the woman as a young adult told her. Her mother had given it to her and her mother's mother had given it to her. The purse *belonged* to the family. The term rightful owner registered firmly in her chest. "Here you go. Are you all right? Did he hurt you?"

The woman took the purse. Her hands trembled. "Thank you. You don't know how much this purse means to me." She laid a hand on Payson's arm and more impressions streamed through her. She shuddered, seeing the woman's life in short glimpses, like slides. Her mother lying in a casket as tears streamed. The woman's name entered Payson's mind. It was Gladys, and she was sitting alone in a dark room, loneliness sagging her face.

Payson sent the thought deliberately to the ground beneath her feet, trying to catch her breath. Gladys lifted her hand and the impressions stopped. She smiled and allowed love to radiate for her. "You don't have to thank me, but you're welcome. It didn't belong to him, right?"

A light glistened in the woman's eyes. "My name is Gladys Noble. What's yours?

"I'm Payson. It's nice to meet you, Gladys."

"You're quite the warrior, Payson."

Her words meant something to Payson. "Thank you," she said, seeing beauty in the woman's face. "The officers will take you home."

The moment expanded in Payson's head to take in traffic noise, construction sounds, and the thick cloud of negative energy that covered the city these days. It called to her seductively, coaxing her thoughts to vibrate with it. *The robber.*

She turned and watched one of the officers direct the robber into the cruiser, just in time to see the young man's face. It was impassive and he lifted his eyes for a minute to glare at her. The subtle pulsing in her head confirmed he wasn't simply out of balance and carrying darkness. He was a Dark Aspect.

A man in a suit climbed out of a black Fiat Spider. Before she saw his face, she knew. It was him. Braden.

A heavy rock dropped to the pit of her stomach.

She couldn't stop staring as he strode toward her alongside the first office she spoke to. His dark slightly wavy hair glistened in the sunlight. Broad shoulders and trim hips beneath his black suit gave him a striking swagger. Well, the suit made his muscled body look good. His new life had already given him the swagger.

Braden extended his hand, but she ignored it. Her mind frazzled at the thought of peering into Braden's present life.

When she didn't accept his handshake, Braden gave her "the smile." His was the kind that cleared skies. A frown in her heart threatened to sink her. Nothing had changed for her. Everything she was reached for him as she'd always known him, but that Braden wasn't the one offering a hand.

"This is Payson Silver. She's been in the newspapers," an officer said.

"Really?" Braden frowned, and gestured to dismiss the officer. "Miss, I'm Detective Powers. I'm told you apprehended the robber. That was either very brave of you or very stupid. Can you tell me what happened?"

She looked up and opened her mouth to speak. The insult didn't faze her, but the lack of recognition in his face choked her throat closed. *He doesn't remember anything and he doesn't even sense who I am.*

His piercing deep blue eyes held her still while answering his question. They'd meant so much to each other for so many years, and yet here he stood smiling and holding her in his gaze, but as a stranger, listening to her relay the incident.

"Okay, I've got what I need, Ms. Silver." He narrowed his eyes. His smile was gone. "I won't keep you any longer. If you're needed for anything further you'll hear from someone." He gestured to a group of uniformed officers. "I'm a detective and this kind of case is not typically one I would handle."

She slanted her head. "Why were you called?" Suspicion was a natural state for a bounty hunter, but his mention of an out-of-the-ordinary event piqued her interest. She could hope for some sign, something about her that had drawn him.

Braden winked at her. "That's police business. But I can suggest you be on the alert for criminal activity. There seems to be an uptick of such things lately. So between you and me, this grab may be connected to other crimes." He tipped his head. "You seem a little familiar. Have I met you somewhere?"

Payson swallowed, twice. Words jammed in her throat. "Maybe."

He fidgeted with his hair, and her heart dipped. "I don't know. Your face seems familiar. What was your name?"

She hesitated. Diane's threat surfaced. *Dare I?* Reason went out the window as longing for him beat in her heart. "Payson, Payson Silver."

His eyes flitted and she held her breath while he said nothing. He shook his head. "That name doesn't ring any bells. I doubt I would forget your face." He put his fingers to his temples. "Well, have a good day."

She watched him stroll to two other officers and chat briefly. Braden's calm exterior amazed her, considering all that had happened to them. He didn't emit the deep vibration of a DA. The pinch in her chest eased. Just a tiny bit. He wasn't a DA, but he wasn't himself, either.

She fingered the black and white yin and yang pendant dangling from a short silver chain around her neck as the squad car pulled away. The reminder was timely. A reminder that light balanced darkness and there was always hope.

She picked up her things and resumed walking toward Coffee Is. Her shoes clicking off her steps on her way, Payson grounded herself and emptied her body of the energy depleting impressions from the day so far. As she pulled open the door, she paused, awareness of her loss screaming inside for relief, and sent warm, invisible love to Braden, without an agenda of breaking the block or bringing him back, only to express her love. Not her despair, not her anger or fear would help him. Only her love could.

She stepped into the small café and immersed herself in its inviting ambience. Payson ran her hand in circles over her grumbling stomach. She hadn't eaten breakfast, but food was not the answer. Knots in her stomach hurt. She ordered coffee and walked to a room off the side of the main dining area.

She sat at the end of a table near a window, and ran her gaze around the room, letting the ambiance settle her nerves. Skye's décor in the main room continued in the private room. An eclectic selection of local artwork hung on the wall and an antique-styled chandelier lit the room. On each table sat a small, quirky lamp set on low to enhance the atmosphere. She looked out the windows and took in the view of a pleasant yard, populated with bird feeders, birdbaths, and a small vegetable garden.

"Hey, you're sitting in here alone. Do you mind if I join you?" Skye set Payson's coffee on the table and sipped her own coffee.

"No, please sit if you can." Steam lifted from the coffee and filled her nose with its rich aroma. She let it sit untouched, as her stomach lurched.

Skye frowned. "Are you all right?"

"Yes. I'm relieved we're meeting for lunch." Diane's terrible laughter haunted her, but she shoved the image away. "I saw Braden earlier."

"Oh. Where? What did he say?"

"Actually, I've seen him twice. I watched him from my car across the street from the police building. We didn't interact." Payson chewed on her lower lip. "I had to see him."

Skye tipped her head. "I understand that. What did you learn?"

"He's not dead and I didn't see any physical injuries. That was a relief."

The energy in Coffee Is typically whirred pleasantly on any given day, but it suddenly fine-tuned at a higher level and she knew the other Aeons were in the building.

Cooper strode in to the room with Ainsley at his side, and right behind walked Keegan. Payson crossed her legs and sat up straight, anticipation fluttering in her gut. "Hi, guys. Thanks for coming."

Keegan's blue eyes went through her. She couldn't hide from him, or the others, for that matter. "So what's up?" he asked.

Ainsley slipped in to a chair beside her and patted her shoulder. "This situation with Diane is something we all need to pay attention to, Payson. I'm happy I could get away from Fancy This for a while."

"Ditto." Cooper tucked his long legs under the table and nodded. "Ainsley is right. If we let Diane take over Braden's mind, it would certainly embolden her to come after the rest of us with a vengeance."

Ainsley's brows knitted. Her eyes glazed, clueing Payson she was getting a reading. Her psychic ability and precognition often caught her up in impressions of things that had already happened as they played into the future. Everyone stopped talking and took notice, as Ainsley got quiet. One minute passed before she came back to the present moment.

"Oh, Payson."

Payson's heart knotted. "You saw."

Ainsley slowly nodded.

"Okay, you had a psychic moment. You saw something. Payson knows what you saw." Keegan drummed his fingers on the tabletop. "Tell us what happened."

"It's not a secret. I talked to Braden this morning." She tried for nonchalant but her strained voice gave her away.

"Oh, dang!" Keegan rolled his eyes. "How, why, where?"

"I ran down a purse snatcher before I came here."

"A purse snatcher?" Cooper pursed his lips. "Let me guess, the cops came and Detective Braden showed up. That must have been surreal."

She wanted to feel nothing, but then, that wouldn't be right. Numb was the antithesis of being alive, but being alive with a range of emotions was so hard sometimes. "It was okay, sort of. He…he didn't know me. It was pretty awful."

Skye came up behind her and wrapped her arms around her shoulders. "Can I do something?"

Payson dropped her gaze to her coffee and steadied her breathing. When she looked up, all eyes around the table were on her. "It was hard to see him as he is now, mesmerized and distant." Her voice caught in her throat.

"I know. You'll be fine. Of course you will be. That's what we do is take care of ourselves." Keegan sighed. "But it doesn't hurt to lean on your friends, Payson. Say the words and I'll close my office for the afternoon and spend it with you."

That got to her. Her breath troubled in her chest. "You're so kind, but yes, I will take care of myself. I need to reach him before it's too late."

"Right." Keegan switched gears. "I heard murmurs from Diane earlier today. It sounded like she was trying to strengthen her hold on Braden. I kept hearing her repeat the word *accept*. Her tone was hypnotic."

"You heard her deepening her control over him. That's, umm, terrible." Thud, thud, thud. All she could hear was her heart pounding in her ears. She pulled at her collar, trying to cool down. Words formed at the tip of her tongue. *I'm going to stop you any way I can.*

Cooper grabbed her attention. "What's going on, Payson? You look flushed. I don't want to invade your privacy, but I'm getting hot too."

Payson looked from Keegan to Ainsley to Cooper to Skye, and saw compassion in each face. "Yes, I'm hot. I'm angry. Diane and her DAs are a menace." The pronouncement she made echoed in her mind. If she had been honest, she would have said she wanted very much to claw out Diane's eyes.

They each listened without speaking as she told them what Diane had said she'd done to Braden and that she had threatened to do more. Her voice went up a note on the scale as she put words to her anger, and she didn't care. She was earnest, not hysterical.

Skye pursed her lips and narrowed her eyes. Payson wriggled under her gaze. She could imagine gears turning in Skye's brain.

"So the bottom line is Diane's power is growing and she's determined to keep Braden close and under her control," Skye said. "But she's also very insecure. She needs Braden, just as much as she needs to break you, Payson."

Ainsley nodded. "She needs to break all of us in order to boost her chances of manifesting more darkness. It's not just an obsession, it's become her mission."

The words took hold in Payson's gut. "So that's how we'll stop her." The fire burning in her to strike Diane hard fizzled. "Our best chance of breaking Diane's hold on Braden is what we need to do to save our city from darkness. We need to try to save Diane."

"Wait, what?" Cooper quirked one eyebrow.

Ainsley touched Cooper's shoulder. "No, it's not crazy. I get it. Instead of fighting fire with fire, fight it with water."

Keegan pointed a finger at Payson and nodded. "Right. So instead of going after her, use our abilities to support her emotionally."

"Yes." Payson nodded. "I can't let my fears fuel rage. As you all just saw, rage clouds my mind and influences my level of light energy."

"Self-defeating." Skye crossed her arms over her chest. "We could lose ourselves to darkness."

Cooper's gaze softened. "This is not actually creating a plan, Payson. This is non-action. Is that what you think is best?"

She leaned forward and hugged her middle. "I don't see it as inactive and limp. I see it as intentional and powerful recourse." Excitement burbled up as she recognized the rightness of the *nonplan*. "As Aeons, we've always been alert to using our abilities to bring more light to the world. But we've haven't been forthright with our mission."

"For good reason." Skye's eyes widened. "DAs are highly aggressive. We have not wanted to engage them or prompt them to hurt people. If they were to kill us, we wouldn't be able to help the world."

"That's true." Seeing with more clarity, Payson couldn't contain her eagerness. It expanded in her and made demands. She had to make them see her point. "Listen, that has been our way, but things have to change. I'm not suggesting we launch missiles at DAs. I am saying change up our methods from defensive to offensive, in a very intentional, light-minded way."

Around the table, heads nodded, and Payson's heart swelled.

"I like the nonplan, Payson." Keegan grinned. "I feel very *Guardians of the Universe.*" He slapped his hand in the middle of the table. "Or maybe it's more like, All for One and One for All-ish."

"Okay, I'll buy that." Payson laid her hand on top of Keegan's.

Skye rolled her eyes. "Okay, just call me Gamora."

Cooper and Ainsley chuckled and added their hands.

Keegan sat back and ran his thumb over his chin. "Seriously, what is our next move? Volunteer at a soup kitchen? Coach a youth baseball team?"

"Or softball team," Ainsley suggested. "Girls play ball too."

"Those are possibilities, but we could simply be more connected to what's happening around us. People need hope, so you, Keegan, could tune into sounds, then follow up."

"So if my ears are ringing, pay attention to what my spirit guides want to tell me."

"Yes."

"Open myself to receiving empathic information when I'm at the grocery store and support the emotions I'm having," Cooper said.

"Exactly." Payson turned to Ainsley. "You could consider opening to your precognition more and let us know if there's a situation we could direct our light to."

"And I could look intentionally at auras of people around me and use my healing touch." Skye beamed. "This concept feels very organic."

"Good, then it won't feel awkward or forced." Payson dipped her gaze, the possibilities for good fueling her creative thoughts. "I believe a start would be we all do our individual meditations faithfully every morning before we begin our days."

A grin stretched across Cooper's face. "I like that idea. Simultaneous meditation joins our energy and would strengthen each of us. We could ask Claire Eve to join in too."

"Yes, her light is very powerful. Okay, we'll start tomorrow." Peace flowed in Payson's body.

"Works for me." Ainsley nodded. "We all agree?"

"We each could send Braden light and love," she almost whispered.

Cooper nodded. "We don't have to wait until tomorrow to do that."

Without speaking, Payson took hold of Skye's hand and around the table the others followed. She closed her eyes and centered her focus on the ball of light pulsing inside her. Energy expanded to fill her completely, and peace flowed around the circle to her hands. They tingled and from the light emerged peace and love. A tear slipped down her cheek. Braden, I love you. We're all here for you.

The energy peaked, and her inner light slowly grew smaller inside her. "Thank you everyone. I'm hopeful for Braden."

"Onward and upward, right?" Ainsley grabbed her purse and left along with Keegan and Cooper.

"I've got to get back to work." Skye smiled at Payson. "We're going to get Braden back. He's too strong to be locked out of his life for long."

Payson savored the moment of a plan coming together and friends' support. But a grave awareness weighed in her chest. It grew like an approaching cloud of locusts. She would at some point have to use all of her skills in a face-to-face with Diane.

CHAPTER 12

"MAYBE IT'S a mid-afternoon slump, but I don't remember any of this, Diane. You're going to have to bring me up to speed." Braden surveyed what Diane had called *his office* seeing nothing that rang familiar, and scanned the papers in a file she laid on *his* desk.

She stepped close to him and rested her hand on his shoulder. Her thick scent overwhelmed his senses and he took a step away.

She blinked. She slid close, pressing her body to his. She nipped at his ear and ran her tongue around the outer opening, sensuous and coaxing. His shoulders relaxed and her eyes met his.

"It's wonderful to work so closely." Her chest rose and fell, seductively. She traced a finger over the outline of his lips and dipped a finger into his mouth.

His body reacted as though it knew hers well. His pulse pounded in his chest and his gaze held on her open mouth.

Diane ran one hand down over his butt, down his leg, and rubbed his crotch, just as she took his face in other hand and kissed him hard.

He groaned and moved with her mouth in a kiss that wouldn't let him go.

Slowly, she took a step back and fluttered her lids at him. She chewed on one red fingernail. "Oh my. That was a dream."

He couldn't catch his breath. "I don't know how to describe that kiss."

"You don't have to." She touched her lips to his again, but he withheld his kiss. He didn't know why, but his insides started chittering like mad. "Um, I don't think we should indulge like this at the office."

"Why not? I am the boss."

"It makes me nervous. I should get to work."

"Okay, darling, sit down in your chair, accept that it is yours. Everything is going to be fine. Trust me."

He did as she suggested. "You're right." He pulled in deep breaths almost without thought. He let them out slowly, and repeated two more times. Familiarity with his desk and computer sifted through him. He nodded. "It's working. Thank you, Diane. I'm so grateful you're with me."

"Of course. I'm glad I can be helpful. That's what girlfriends are for, among other things." The look in her eyes sent shivers through him, like shock waves. If they were a couple, why didn't her kiss feel familiar? Heat danced through him. Her kiss certainly wasn't hard to take.

His brain fogged, and he looked to her for something. Was it reassurance? He didn't have words to put to his need.

Diane laughed. "Don't worry about anything. I'm here and I'll always be here to steer you right. If you need me just holler." She opened the door at the side of his office. "This is my office, so I'm nearby. Now get to work on that list I put on your desk."

His thoughts scrambled. "List?"

"You remember. The list of members of the opposition to the project I'm working on for a client. It's in the file folder there in front of you."

He opened the folder and scanned the list but didn't take in the names. He shook his head. "This means nothing to me." He leaned back in chair and eyed her. "What exactly do I do for you? I mean, I know I work for you. I remember that. But what do I do?"

"You investigate. Just as you do for the APD. I want information about each of the individuals on that list."

"What kind of information?" As he listened to her explain, memories of his everyday grew stronger. He grabbed the structure of his routine and hung on. He needed it to abate the loss grumbling in his gut. That was another thing he couldn't put to words. He didn't have a reason for the emptiness he woke up with and that nagged his insides.

"I'm going to be here a little longer. I've got meetings this afternoon. Would you like to come to dinner at my house?" He could swear her eyes darkened. *Eerie.*

He checked the time. It was two o'clock. He had only just gotten here, but his concentration just wasn't there. "I should probably stick around. I need to catch up." He chuckled internally, guessing he must have to catch up considering he had been sidelined by a concussion.

"I'll send directions to my house to your phone, just in case you get lost." She opened a drawer in her desk and pulled out a phone. "Here, I got you a new cellphone. Yours got ruined when you were hit by the car."

He took it and stared at it. He'd had no thoughts of a phone. *Weird.* He strained to bring back memories of the accident. Inexplicably, adrenaline streamed stronger in his veins. It erased the anxiety that popped up with his effort to remember. He leaned further into its flow, grateful for the strength it imbued.

"It's okay, Braden. Everything is fine. Your contacts and stuff from your old phone are there." Diane ran her gaze over his face. "So, you'll come to dinner?"

"Yeah, sure." He barely had given her invitation a second thought, but what else would he do?

"Okay, good. I want to discuss our meeting with a retailer in Old Town. He needs persuading."

"Persuading?"

"Yes, you remember. You're good with words, clarifying the right choice for people I want to work with."

"I presume you'll give me details over dinner."

"Of course. I'll see you later."

He had a vague awareness of Diane leaving as he stared at his computer screen. Energy flowed briskly through his body. He couldn't sit any longer. Sitting and sorting through his hazed brain was like twirling his thumbs.

Nick's death made him twitchy. He had to know why it bothered him so much. He grabbed the folder of lists Diane had left him and headed to the APD.

BRADEN CHECKED OVER ONE SHOULDER, then the other. The sounds of the Auralia Police Department all blurred into a mass of white noise. He refocused on the open file on his desk, pushing away the small voice in his head reminding him he should be working on connecting the dots in the mounting number of robberies. No one had an eye on his activities and so what if he chose to do some personal work on the department's clock? He shook his head, trying to jolt his brain into focus, but the recovery agent he'd met earlier kept popping in front of his eyes. It was funny he had never crossed paths with her before, considering they worked in loosely related fields. Then again, Auralia was a fairly large city. Yeah, that had to be why he had never met her before.

Words like hot, babe material, fox, typical words he would use to describe an attractive woman, just didn't speak of Payson. In the brief moments he'd been with her, Payson disturbed him. Her unusual pale brown eyes and diminutive but powerful body got under his skin instantly. He couldn't shake the way she'd looked at him, a little aloof but also sad. He itched to know more about her.

He shook his head again. That's enough distraction. He had to address Dian's work, but what about Nick? Shouldn't he be digging in to it?

He picked up a paper from his desk. Diane had said it was a list of people he needed to investigate because they were against her two large projects. He ran his finger slowly down a list of names under the heading, Advocates for Community Empowerment. He flipped through the pages and counted ten, then started at the top of the list.

It felt good to recognize names on the list. He circled several to begin his investigation.

A yawn took him over and he stretched.

"What's up, Powers, bored?" It was his sergeant. He stopped in front of Braden's desk and stared down at him.

"No, Serg, just needed to stretch." Without breaking eye contact, he discreetly closed the file. He had no doubts his boss would not approve.

"Good. Those robberies aren't going to solve themselves." He rapped on Braden's desk and turned back to his office. "Stay sharp."

"Yes, Sergeant Garcia."

"Excuse me? Luca, detective. Luca. I don't need a title among my detectives. You know that."

Braden, nodded. He did know that?

Between blinking thoughts of Payson in the back of his brain and Diane's demands, he wasn't sure what he knew. He turned back to the list. "Betty Cornelius, Jim—" He stared. One name jumped out at him. "Payson Silver," he muttered. He stared at the name, thoughts clamoring to form but unable to surface. Images of the woman he had met earlier in the day rose again in his mind's eye. Long dark hair that fell in loose waves over her slim shoulders. Smooth, nut-brown skin, and those eyes that reminded him of champagne, framed with full, long lashes.

A pounding in his head started behind his eyes.

The bounty hunter with all the right curves in a petite package. Incongruous in a way that lifted his lips.

The pounding intensified. He put his hand to his head, but he could still see her standing tall, all five—foot—three—inches, as though she were the strongest woman on earth.

Bounty hunters weren't his favorite people on the planet, but they served a purpose. From the way she scrutinized him and his reason for being on the scene, he would bet she was one feisty woman, er, bounty hunter.

Both hands shot to his head. His poor, pounding head. If this keeps up, I'm going to have to make a run to the bathroom before I spill my lunch. Breathe, Braden.

The sound of his phone nearly tore his head in two. He answered it to make it stop ringing. "Detective Powers."

"Ooo, you make me shiver, Detective Powers. Such a sound of authority in your voice."

"Hi, Diane." Her voice on the phone reminded him of their kiss earlier. How could he forget? Though she had told him they were a couple and his body reacted as though intimacy was a regular thing, he had no sense of closeness.

"Oh, so uninspired. I've been working hard on making sure the Principal Industries projects have all the right licenses and permissions. Couldn't you at least sound happy to hear from me?"

"I just saw you earlier and I'm at work. In fact," he covered his cellphone with his cupped hand, "I'm going over the documents you gave me."

"Good. I need to know who I'm up against, so I'm going to want dossiers on everyone on those lists. Especially the one listing the members of ACE."

"ACE?"

She sighed heavily. "Activists for Community Empowerment."

"Oh, how about that. Clever." He tilted his head, checking for pain. "Humph."

"Humph what? Something interesting on the list?" Excitement raised her voice a note.

"No. I've got a whopper of a headache. Anyway…I'll be in touch as soon as I have information."

Silence on the other end of the conversation goaded his curiosity. Diane was never lacking in words.

"Is something wrong?"

The sound of her tongue licking her lips sifted through his brain. "I was wondering about your headache. Did you take something for it?"

"No. It just went away. Nothing to worry about. Headaches come and go."

"You get headaches often?"

This was a strange conversation. Her voice was pinched and she acted unduly interested in his headaches all of sudden. "I don't think so, but my memory still has holes in it from the accident, I guess." He ran his thoughts around that question. "No, I don't get headaches." Funny, he didn't.

"I wonder what caused this one." Ice. Her voice was sharp and cold, like ice.

"Maybe eye strain from reading the names on the freakin lists." Annoyance twisted his patience into a tight ball. This interrogation over a silly headache was stupid.

"Oh. Eyestrain. Yeah, that's probably it." Her voice turned sugary. "Any names pop out at you? I'm just curious."

Oh, yeah. One name in particular. Payson Silver. "No, not so far."

She wouldn't let it go.

"Did you read any names you recognize?"

He had. But a strange heaviness began weighing on his chest as he recalled the names, especially when he thought of Payson. A nudge, like a jab in his gut, told him he should tell Diane, but he didn't want to. "Yes, several. I know people in town, Diane. I'm a cop."

"I think you should stop being a cop and work for me. I need your support in dealing with opponents to the Principal Industries retail development in Old Town and the casino on the river. You have a way with words. You're very persuasive. Work for me."

"I don't have any special way with words, and I do work for you." Distractions—his coffee going cold, his sergeant's stare—grabbed his focus.

"I could use your help fulltime." Diane's words slithered off her tongue.

Why was she giving him the hard press? It didn't matter. He was not about to give up his work just to help Diane give legs to rich people's projects.

"I'm in the preliminary stage of my investigation." He'd decided to ignore her request. "When I have something meaningful, I'll let you know." His head began pounding again. He curled his fingers, wishing it away. It blurred his thinking.

"All right. I guess I'll have to be patient. But not for long, Braden."

His gut tightened. "I know. Have I kept you waiting long before?" He closed his eyes and mentally disconnected. The phone went silent. "Diane?"

Still silence. Not even breathing. *That's strange. I've never known her to leave without having the last word.*

Compulsion to call her back and make nice rattled his nerves. When had he become her slave? Okay, maybe slave was too strong a description of his relationship with her. It didn't feel right, though, that she had given him orders and demanded results. Immediately.

Another inexplicable monster headache thudded in his temples. He leaned back in his chair and closed his eyes, trying to relax so his headache would go away. Robberies to solve, doing his police work—those things were important to him. When, how, did his work for Diane become so, so, important? He couldn't think of any particular time when she had been just an acquaintance, not his girlfriend. Memories strained to come into focus. He rubbed his forehead, trying to think through the pain.

Oh, hell. What next, Braden? You're going to decide Diane is a voodoo princess who has you under a zombie spell?

She was right. It was his job to help her ensure her clients' projects succeeded. Surely this confused state would pass soon.

He couldn't pull forward any details about the Principal Group's projects but he had an awareness of their importance. The casino promised to create jobs and bring in a lot of money to the community. The retail development would offer residents more shopping options while also attracting more visitors' dollars. As Diane told him, what was there to object to? He snickered, thinking of ACE. *I guess some people can't be pleased.*

He fidgeted with the papers in the file. Diane had a point. Somehow, he was able to get things done his way. It was easy to do. Too easy. He'd learned, or Diane had told him he'd learned, to be careful about his thoughts. Beyond that was fuzzy.

Running his fingers through his hair, he dismissed the thoughts of Diane controlling him somehow. He considered the names on the list, and lost interest. He closed the file and shoved it aside to concentrate on information in the robberies file. The list was short, but he would add to it as he waded through records of known thieves.

"Drat!" He walked down the hall to the stairs and ran down to booking. Why hadn't he thought of this sooner? A purse-snatcher had just been picked up yesterday.

Braden nodded at the booking officer behind the counter. "Hi Adya, could you give me the name of the guy who pulled a purse yesterday in the downtown? I'd like to interview him."

"Sure, Braden. Just give me a minute to pull up the arrests info from yesterday."

Braden drummed his fingers on the countertop and composed some questions for the perp

"Name is Ryan Crow."

"Sounds Irish." Braden's brain spun. The surname was familiar. Hadn't he been investigating a Crow family member for Irish mob connections? He squinted, searching his fuzzy memories.

"Well, you can't interview him today. He made bail. He's out."

"What? Who paid his bail?"

"Eddie Crow. Sorry I can't help you out, Braden."

"No problem. I'll track him down. Is your shift about done?"

Adya yawned. "I just got here."

Braden chuckled. "You better get some coffee in you. See 'ya."

A quick trip back to his desk to pick up Diane's file and stick it in a small pile of work to take home and he headed to the door.

Outside, he breathed in evening air and took off for home. The weariness that kept hounding him was taking a toll on his productivity. He swerved into a fast-food drive up window and bought a cheeseburger and fries to take home, but his mind wouldn't let go of the mysteries surrounding him. Why did he feel apart from his life? He rubbed his eyes, wishing his mind to clear and his memories to clarify.

When he pulled into his garage he couldn't wait to down his dinner and relax. Getting his game back was top priority.

He dropped his bag of burger and fries on the table in the kitchen and slumped into the couch to remove his shoes. He dropped his head back against the couch and breathed out a long sigh. *I'm going to take just a minute to collect my thoughts.*

THE PHONE RANG, and Braden's eyes flew open. He picked it up and saw it was Diane. Drat. Dinner. "Diane, I'm sorry, I'm going to miss dinner."

"I know that, because you're not here. Where are you?" Her voice was sharp, and stung Braden's chest.

"I'm home. I kind of lost track of what I was doing. Rain check?"

Diane sighed in his ear. "Of course. As long as you're okay. You are, aren't you?"

"Yes. I'm tired. Today's been a long day. I've got to get my mind clear and make progress on my cases. But I'm so tired."

"Don't worry about your job, Braden. It'll take a lot of work to bring you back to life."

His skin tingled. "Back to life? What do you mean?"

She cleared her throat. "I mean bring you up to speed, that's all. You get some sleep. I'll talk to you in the morning."

Braden relaxed into Diane's words. Gratitude for her help soothed him. She was so right about the effort he had expended today, just trying to focus and stay on task. What would he do without her? His thoughts drifted to the kiss she had given him. Was there more than gratitude, really? The kiss had stirred him, but did he feel passion or was it lust?

He let his eyelids drop. He didn't need to crawl into bed, the couch was fine.

"You have to grasp what has happened to you." Payson cupped his face in her hands. "You have to make a choice to move away from the distortion. It's not me. It's you."

He jerked away. "You want me to give up my work? You know I can't do that. It's what I do. I can handle the threats inherent in the work. I'm an Aeon too. I'm filled with light and love."

"Are you?" she whispered.

"I'm the same as always. Don't leave. We can talk through this."

"I have to go. I don't want to, but our mission is too important. I'll always be yours. But I have to go."

"No, don't go!" Braden sat up on the couch, the sound of his holler ringing in his ears. He cast his gaze around his living room. Bewilderment wrestled with reason in his mind. He dropped his feet to the floor, scratching his head. "It was a dream," he said out loud, still trying to clear the cobwebs in his head. He strode to the nearest window and threw it open, sucking in deep breaths of warm, night air. "I'm in my house. I'm alone."

He draped his arm across the open window and rested his head against it, still reeling from the dream. He couldn't shake it. He would have sworn on his mother's Bible that it was…a memory, not a dream, of something that had really happened. Payson had been with him as if it were an ordinary thing. His gut ached as though he had just lost his lover, his friend.

But it was only a dream.

He swiped at beads of sweat on his forehead. "If it was a mere dream why am I dying inside? I've only just met Payson Silver, but she was really here, or somewhere. And I loved her."

A computer on overload, Braden stared at the pile of papers on his desk, papers from which Diane was waiting for him to cull information. The thumb drive of the security feed from the convenience store in Nick's neighborhood sat on top of the pile. He checked the time from his phone. Four o'clock in the morning. Too early to get ready for work. But there was no sleep for him. Not now. Not with the images of his dream so clear in his mind.

He walked to the kitchen and filled the coffeemaker with water and ground coffee. He pulled on his boxers and opened his laptop, placing the dream images in a compartment in his brain. Everything in him wanted, needed, to make sense of the dream. Instead of dwelling on it, though, he put it in a place for his mind to work on it in the background while he turned his attention to the video he loaded to his laptop.

According to the time stamp, Warren Brown appeared outside the convenient store soon after he ran from Braden. He stood around outside watching, as though he was expecting someone. Warren walked inside and picked a package of cigarettes from the shelf. Actually, he palmed the cigarettes and stuffed them inside his pocket. He nodded as he passed the clerk heading outside, and the clerk nodded back. Braden made a note to contact the clerk and question him about Brown.

Outside, Brown lit a cigarette, and paced at the side of the building.

Braden yawned. This stuff was important to watch but it was slow going and he needed coffee. The beeping from the coffee maker got him to his feet. He poured a cup and sat back down at the table, sipping the hot liquid while peering at the video.

Suddenly he saw something that made him set his cup down. He stared, watching Diane swing her long legs out of the car she parked at the side of the convenience store. Her dark tresses were pulled into a ponytail that bounced as she marched to Brown. Her face animated and angry, she poked her finger in Brown's chest.

The man was many times larger than Diane, but he stood stoic, his lips pursed. He never once raised a hand to her, and when she gestured to him to get in her car, he did so. He slumped in the seat while Diane got behind the wheel and drove out of shot of the camera.

There wasn't much on the video to clue him about what Warren or Diane were up to, but it was clear they were acquaintances. Maybe that would explain why Brown looked familiar to him, though he swore he had never seen him before.

His stomach knotted. He thought he knew Diane, but this interaction with a probable criminal was unexpected. He didn't know her, he guessed, or what she was capable of doing.

He leaned back in his chair and tried to retrieve memories of how he had met Diane. He closed his eyes, and fuzzy images of fire and pain throbbed in his head as he tried to bring them into focus. A memory of an explosion startled him, and another of Diane peering at him through smoke caught his breath.

He squeezed his eyelids tight, and got a glimpse of himself lying on a bed with Diane standing over him. Her lips moving silently, Braden's mind struggled. What was she saying? When did this fire occur and where? What did Diane have to do with it?

So many questions.

He fingered his lower lip, pondering what Diane was up to.

He sat upright, a plan forming. Outside cars and trucks buzzed by, and bus brakes squealed at a corner down the street. While he had been reviewing the security footage, morning in the city arrived. People were on their way to work and kids rode to school. A perfect time for him to do some surveillance outside and inside Diane's office.

In the shower, he aimed steamy, hot water to pour over his head and neck, trying to ease another headache.

CHAPTER 13

SULTRY SUMMER AIR hugged Payson at the top of Sheppard Media Tower like a familiar repeating Blues refrain. Her eyes closed, still, she focused on the light at the center of her body that only she was aware of. Time suspended as she breathed in steady rhythm and accepted the peace and strength that filled her. From deep inside her inner silence, her energy moved out to her fellow Aeons. Their lights met and began pulsing in unison. The energy flowed invisibly over the city. She held the energy and watched it take the form of the lacy vines she imagined hope and guidance could be.

Parts of her never wanted to come out of the meditation. It was beautiful and restful. But awareness of missing energy, that of Braden's, sobered her heart. The sun was up on day three, and another day would pass, and Braden would move closer to the edge of the Dark Sides if she didn't break Diane's hold on him.

That reality took her out of the meditation, and resolve brought her to her feet. From her crow's view, she tuned into the city below.

"Oh my God." Panic wrestled with peace in her chest, a mirror of an uneasy balance all around. Her heart melted. Life was a beautiful thing, just like her flowering vines. But it also was hard. She could help. "Good morning, Auralia."

At street level, Payson strode through groups of people with awareness of the need for her light. She nodded and smiled to anyone who looked at her in passing, and sang little songs in her head. Beneath it all buzzed chaos, growing louder as she neared her car.

She didn't need eyes on anyone in particular to know DAs were near. Out in the open, she was safe from a physical attack, but she wasn't afraid, only annoyed. Their droning darkness agitated her nerves. That was their point, to disrupt her light. DAs never let up, and if her light dimmed, she'd fail in ways she didn't want to give any space to in her mind.

She slipped behind the wheel in her car and thought of her next stop. That thought soothed the creep-factor under her skin, and she headed toward the address she'd gotten from her contacts at APD for Gladys Freeport.

Payson pulled into the parking lot at the seniors' apartment building and took in the boxy, brick building and tiny wooden porches, feeling the weight of its age. At the apartment where Gladys lived, purple and white pansies stood in lines on either side of the tiny covered porch. She knocked on the wooden door and noted a hollow loneliness emanating from the apartment.

The door opened, and Gladys lit up. "Payson, oh my, what brings you here?"

"Hi Gladys, I wanted to stop by and see how you are. Can I come in?"

Gladys ushered her in and gestured to a sagging, plump chair, the only soft place to sit in the small living room. "Please, sit," she said.

"Thank you." Payson sat down on the hardwood floor and crossed her legs. "You sit there. I like the floor."

"I'm going to get you something to drink. Do you like tea or coffee?" Gladys picked up a small pile of newspapers and carried them to a tiny kitchen area.

"Water is fine." Payson swept her gaze around the room, noting the colorful hexagon-shaped pattern of a crocheted afghan draped across the back of the chair. It sent homey warm sensations through her body.

"Here you go." Gladys handed her a glass of water and lowered into the soft chair. "It's so nice to see you. I can thank you again for stopping the robber from stealing my purse. I had enough money in there to get groceries for the week, and some mementoes." Her expression wilted. "My husband died two years ago, and I've lost touch with my family, so I like to keep those reminders close."

"Well, you don't need to thank me again. I am glad I was there to help." Payson sipped the water and deliberately sent Gladys love. "Your family doesn't live in Auralia?"

"I have only one daughter. She and her husband moved away a number of years ago. For his work." Gladys shrugged. "You know how it goes. An old woman doesn't have much to offer a young family, and they live very busy lives."

"I don't know about that. I'm enjoying talking with you."

"You're sweet. I don't mean to complain. It's just that I get lonely. Many of my friends are not well or have died."

"That would be hard." Payson's attention drifted to photos sitting on an end table beside Gladys. "Is that your daughter and your grand-children?"

"Oh, no. This is a very old photograph." Gladys picked up the small frame holding the photo and handed it to Payson.

"Oh." An image flashed in Payson's mind. She recognized the people. "I see now that this is an old photo. Is this your grandmother or great-grandmother?" Excitement fluttered in her belly.

"No, it's older than that. I never knew this woman. Her name was Helen Noble, and she died a long time ago."

"Helen," Payson said, letting the name roll off her tongue. "So she was a distant relative."

"Yes. I just like looking at the picture. I feel connected to family in that way, even though I never knew them," Gladys said, her voice wistful.

Payson allowed images to expand to tell a short story of a discon-nected family. A daughter moving away with her mother to start a new life in another state. Flash, flash. The daughter growing and becoming a mother, happy and full of life. A grandmother sitting with grandchildren, love emanating from her.

"Mother, Faith and I are going to the park," the daughter calls. "Do you want to join us?"

Payson's heart pounded. Where is this scene?

"Yes, Amelia. I need to purchase some fabric. Could we also go to downtown Auralia?"

A woman, an older woman, walked into the room with the mother and her daughter. Wrinkles creased her face, but Payson held her breath, realizing she knew the woman in Gladys's photo.

A hard pounding sound at the front door startled her and the image dropped.

"Mrs. Noble, open the door."

Gladys put her hand to her throat. "Oh my, that's the landlord."

She went to the door and opened it. "Yes, what do you want?"

Dark energies nearly knocked Payson over.

"Rent. You're late, Gladys. If you can't make the rent on time I'll have to evict you." The man's voice sent shivers up and down Payson's spine.

Gladys shrunk. "I paid it already. I don't believe I'm late."

"Your memory is bad. You're late."

Payson marched to the open door. The man's vibration hollered through her. "You've made a mistake." She shoved the door in his face, but he blocked it with his foot.

"No mistake. She's late." He glared at Payson and she saw his intention.

She wavered between kicking him in his privates and acknowledging his right to be dark. She couldn't help but think of Braden and how he would use his mind control to suggest this man leave Gladys alone.

Sadness crept up her gut. Braden had gotten worn down by despair and disgust. Maybe this guy had lost his way, and maybe he had made poor choices. She reached for compassion, when satisfaction of a swift kick tantalized her, tested her.

No. She wouldn't give away her choice to the surrounding shadow.

She put her hand on Gladys and nudged her out of the doorway. She folded her arms over her chest and planted her feet in front of the man. "I have had enough of your threats. If Mrs. Noble says she paid her rent, she paid her rent. You're done here."

The man pursed his lips and shifted on his feet. He engaged a staring contest with Payson, but she held her gaze and smiled. Seconds ticked by, and finally, he shrugged.

"I'll check my records."

Payson shut the door and blew out a cleansing breath. "Are you all right?" she asked Gladys.

"I am. I told you the other day that you're quite the warrior and now you've proven it again." Gladys hugged her. "He was wrong. Thank you for helping me out."

"My pleasure. Before I go, I want to tell you something I think is important for you to know. I have seen a photo of Helen and her children. It's at a pawn shop one of my friends owns called Fancy This. My friend's name is Ainsley, and she would be happy to learn that the picture she has in her shop could find a home where it belongs, with you."

Gladys's hands flew to her mouth. "I don't know what to say."

"There's a chance the information Ainsley has about the photo could help you trace your family line, if you are interested in that."

"Oh, how exciting. I will definitely visit Fancy This. It sounds like an adventure."

Warmth spread from Gladys to Payson. Life sustaining light spread through her body, doing much more for her heart than any strategically placed kick to the DA could have.

"Are you up for an adventure, Gladys?" she asked.

"It's been a long time since I've had one," Gladys said. "I believe I'm due."

. . .

MISTY MEMORIES AND disturbing questions cluttered Braden's head. The more he stayed present with all of it the more he became a coma survivor, just waking up and clueless.

He drove through traffic heading into the center of town. He parked in the parking deck and walked the blocks to the town square where the county and federal courthouses stood not far from the Kurl building where Diane's office was located. He stopped under a tree short of the entrance to her building, just standing and perusing the area.

Withdrawing as much as possible into the trees and shrubbery on the square, he stared up at the skyscraper to the tenth floor where Diane worked. Nothing in particular stood out to him as something to investigate. Businessmen came and went in and out of the tall building, looking very distracted and walking past without seeing him. Lawyers strode briskly to the courthouses, juggling briefcases and cups of coffee.

He scrubbed his foot against the pavement, tiring quickly of waiting for something worth his time to show up.

He pulled in a deep breath and let it out slowly. The air around him was thick. A low humming droned in his ears. *Weird.*

Trying to understand the strange vibration, he dipped his head but kept alert. The glass door on the office building opened and out strode Warren Brown, his eyes downcast.

Inexplicable buzzing in his body distracted Braden's focus, but not so much that he missed the two men in suits who strode from across the square directly into Brown's path and stopped. Brown flinched, and the two men exchanged words with him. Braden strained to hear the conversation but it was muffled. He pulled his phone from his pocket and pointed the camera at the building, like a tourist, but slid it into a position where he could take shots of the group of men. They wouldn't be great, he knew, but it was worth a try.

He crouched down and continued to blend while taking pics, hoping the men would turn and reveal more of their faces.

Finally they did. He heard one of them say, "We're just following Diane's orders." The voice was flat, detached.

Braden quickly snapped shots of the men, struggling to override a compelling urge to run. Nothing notable stood out in their appearance, but doom swarmed around them, stealing Braden's breath.

He slipped deeper in to the bushes, almost instinctively, and watched them usher Brown into a dark blue Cadillac with tinted windows. As the vehicle pulled away from the curb, Braden's pulse raced. To get closer, he moved swiftly, trying to get close enough to see the license plate without being noticed.

He couldn't make out the plate's numbers or letters and slowed his pace. He had enough to take back to the precinct to work on, so he headed to his car. He had photos and a name. The men had mentioned Diane and following her orders.

That didn't sound good for Brown. Diane was a very assertive, driven woman who lobbied for one of the biggest conglomerates in the country, Principle Group. She had underlings, and he had no doubt she ordered them around. Hell, she ordered him around. It didn't mean she was doing anything nefarious. Did it?

If he truly had an answer to that question, he would not be here this morning, sneaking around her office, trying to make the connection between her and Brown. And now between her and the men who took him away.

The words spoken by one of the men with Brown came out menacing. They took away any choice Brown had in whether or not he went with them.

And that stuck in his throat. Brown was someone to investigate, probably had something to do with Nick's death. Even so, the suits ordering him made Braden's teeth itch. The droning resonating in his ears and body was oddly familiar. Not just because it reminded him of Brown's voice just before Nick had run away.

Okay, going nuts, Braden. He ran his fingers through his hair, and pulled into a parking space at the APD.

"Good morning, Detective."

"Hey." He lifted a hand to acknowledge dispatch as he walked by. He took the stairs to the third floor and went directly to his desk. Sitting there, he let the ringing of phones, chatter, and burned coffee soothe the consternation in his chest. He couldn't stop his thoughts from going where they wanted to go, to Payson, and he wondered what she was up to today. A bounty hunter's life was fast paced at times, so if she was working on finding a skip, she could be in disguise right now and walking into dangerous neighborhoods.

That idea didn't fit with petite Payson. She didn't belong running down alleys, splashing through puddles of water and urine, and searching through garbage.

"Braden, yoo-hoo, Braden."

Zane clapped his hands once.

"What?" He snapped to attention, and pulled at his collar.

"I asked, do you have anything on the robberies? Or something on the Nick Ward death? I've got time."

Braden let the thoughts of Payson drift away and dropped the flash drive with the security camera footage on Zane's desk. "Yes. This is something you should look at."

Zane plugged the drive into his laptop and waited for it to load.

"I have these photos too, of Warren Brown, the man who ran from the scene in Nick's neighborhood. I don't know if they'll be much help." He synced his phone to his computer and opened the photo files.

"This is Brown?" Zane pointed to the video. "Who's the woman?"

Diane's name sat on the tip of his tongue but Braden paused. His throat clenched. He swallowed hard.

Zane looked up from his seat. "Do you know her name? She looks pissed." He bent closer the computer screen. "I think this is Diane Butler. *The* Diane Butler with her fingers into very controversial projects headed by high-powered people. The woman who told me about your accident. Do you have a thing with her?" Zane narrowed his eyes.

"I know her, but no, I'm not with her." Braden rolled his shoulders. "Focus on the video." He hoped Zane hadn't noticed his discomfort.

"This business here at the convenient mart is interesting."

"Yeah, I thought so too." He twirled his pen between his fingers. "What about Brown? He seems familiar to me. Let's run him through facial recognition." Braden opened the program and dropped one of the photos into the search. Zane pulled up a chair to his desk and waited with Braden while the program quickly ran Brown through the system.

"We got a hit." Zane frowned. "Not much of a hit. He's in the Bureau of Motor Vehicles database. Yup. He's got a driver's license and a car." Zane chuckled. "He's an organ donor."

A stronger knowing knotted Braden's gut. He jotted down the last known address from the BMV and logged into the NCIC to run a criminal history. "Let's see what we find here." It didn't take long for the results. "Nothing. No hits. He doesn't have a criminal record."

"Hmm. This is unexpected. I thought we'd be able to connect Brown with crime activity or gang operations." Zane sat back in his chair.

"I would have bet the farm on it." The knots in Braden's body tightened. "He scared Nick into running and walked away from the scene."

"Yeah, your instincts are probably right that he's involved somehow with multiple robberies. It just doesn't add up, though. He appears to be an average guy."

"Or more likely, has never been caught committing a crime." Instinct prodded Braden to think critically.

Zane clapped his hand on Braden's shoulder and pulled his chair back to his own desk. "Want me to look deeper into Diane?"

The sight of Brown being scolded by Diane taunted him. "No, I'll check out Diane. And Brown. I've got his address. I'll start with that."

"Do you want me to go with you? It's probably the smart thing to do."

Braden chuckled. "Yeah, maybe. But who says I'm smart? Besides, one-on-one could get me answers that two against one might not."

CHAPTER 14

$\mathcal{P}$AYSON DROPPED ONTO the stool at the kitchen island and tried to rub the weariness out of her eyes. She sipped her coffee and eyed the calendar hanging on the wall. Had she lost track of the days?

The calendar told her five days and nights had passed since Braden had been taken, but it wore on her like weeks or months with no end in sight.

She started her research for finding Eddie Crow, the skip Keegan had given her, but she interrupted it to spend a few hours with Skye distributing meals in areas in the city where homeless people gathered. Another morning, she sang old songs with Keegan at a senior center. Each morning, her group meditated. Each day longing ached for Braden's arms, his lips, his skin.

She couldn't deny that her light was growing in intensity while in service to others, but mornings on top of the tower looking over the city let her know the balance of light and dark still battled fiercely.

And Braden still had not come back to her.

A shiver slid over her as her eyes stopped on the bulletin board hanging on the kitchen wall. Her life with Braden in pictures filled the board with memories. White water rafting, off road cycling, picnicking in Central City Park. Braden's happy face next to hers caught in a selfie.

She hugged her midriff, trying to hold in a giant, world-shattering sob.

Only five days remained before it would be too late to eliminate the block in Braden's head. Five days before the Dark Sides of Diane would completely fill him. If it was true that Braden would never again be in her life, this, this anguish would lay inside her for a long while. But it wouldn't stop her from living her life or prompt her to drop the ball.

She dumped her remaining coffee in to the sink and readied for her morning appointment with Adele Freeport.

Thirty minutes flew by quickly as she showered, dressed, and fed ZuZu.

She backed out of her garage and drove down her lane, past the newly secured gate, and onto the road. She slammed on her brakes. A man stood right in front of her, his face obscured by the shadow of his hoodie. He didn't make a move or speak, but a dissonant vibration emanated from him, scrambling her thoughts. *DA.*

She honked her horn at him, but he didn't budge. *Fine, I'll go around.*

She pressed the gas pedal and made to avoid him, but he held up his hand.

"Stop!" he called. His voice was stern, and sent chills through her.

She rolled down her window. "What do you want?"

"You."

Her pulse raced, but she grounded herself and raised her chin. "Who are you?"

He marched to her door and pulled it open. "My name isn't important. Get out."

He grabbed her arm and yanked her to the ground. The touch of his hand sent images to her mind of faces screwed up in pain and dark, lonely places she couldn't make out. Her heartbeat slowed and words wouldn't come out. Darkness labored her breathing.

"Brown, that's my name. It's a name you won't forget." He

crouched beside her and laughed. "I've heard a lot about you. But you don't look like much. How tall are you, about five-foot-nothing?"

Payson scooched away from him. His vibration rattled inside her, fuzzing her brain and ripping at her gut. Brown was not simply a DA, he was supercharged. He brought darkness so thick it threatened to swallow her whole.

I am peace, I am light, I am love. I am power.

"You bet your ass I am."

"What? What are you talking about?" Brown narrowed his eyes.

Payson climbed to her feet, the light in her expanding her strength and courage. "You're in my way." She kicked at his belly, but Brown grabbed her foot and threw her to the ground, hard.

Her head spun. "I am so damn tired of you and your cohorts causing pain and suffering," she said, lying on her back in the dirt and gravel road.

"Too bad. We're not going anywhere. You think you're in a fight you can win, but you're too weak, too *good*. You don't have what it takes to overpower Dark Sides."

He grabbed her by her neck and effortlessly lifted her up off the ground. Helpless. That's what she felt, like a rag doll. She clung to her inner light and imagined it spreading to envelope Brown.

He threw her across the road into bushes. "Don't try that crap on me. I know what you're trying to do and I'm too powerful. I made my choices and I have no regrets."

"Why are you here?" Her heart saddened. "It's never too late to make different choices. What happened to you that you're so full of hatred?" If he would talk with her, maybe, just maybe, she could make a crack in his darkness.

"An Aeon happened to me. And to my friend. You think you're special. Well, you hurt people, too. Now it's time to pay."

His accusation stymied her. Everything ached and she was tired of trying to make a difference. What was the point?

What is the point? Oh God, Dark Sides is overwhelming me.

He grabbed her again, but she wrenched free and took a pose.

"Oh, you're going to use Karate on me? Okay, let's go."

Before he could collect himself to fight, Payson jabbed at his throat, and he hollered and gagged.

She round-house kicked him in his side, then flicked a kick to his chin. He stumbled, roaring.

Bouncing on her feet, she held her fists ready to punch. He stared at her hard, and an energy wave slammed into her, knocking her over. She couldn't see or move or breathe or scream.

He marched to her and pressed his foot to her chest. "Stay down." He pulled a knife from his other leg. "This is going to hurt you more than me, believe me."

Payson's vision was blurry, but she made out the large knife and its glistening edge. Panic spiked in her chest. He meant to kill her. She mustered the remaining light in her and sent a weak stream to him.

Brown scowled and blinked three times. Then he dragged the knife's edge across her throat. It stung. She felt like prey. Trapped and waiting to die.

Brown stood up and smirked at her. "This is for Diane. Know that I can find you anywhere, anytime I want." He shoved his knife back inside his pant leg, then disappeared into the woods.

Payson stayed on the ground, just breathing and gathering herself into one piece. She hadn't been able to stop Brown and he could have killed her. Her death would be a triumph for Diane. It would embolden her and her DAs.

Braden, where are you? I need you.

A breezed blew across her face and she sucked in a deep breath. Clarity began clearing her mind of helplessness and fear. She wasn't dead and she had resources. Right now, she had work to address, work she had neglected but was determined to work on today. With everything that had been going on since the explosion, she'd let the missing person case simmer at the back of her mind. But concentrating on Adele Freeport's case would be a good distraction and a good place to focus her energy. She climbed into her car and dabbed at the blood on her throat. The cut wasn't deep. She sat immersing in her light. Her strength and confidence grew.

Twenty minutes later, she knocked on the Freeport's front door. Mrs. Freeport welcomed her and led her into the living room.

"Would you like some coffee or tea? I have both."

"Coffee would be nice if it's already made. You don't need to make it just for me." Payson's gaze drifted around the room.

"Okay, I'll be just a few minutes." Mrs. Freeport's energy spun high-pitched and frenetic. The promise Payson and her fellow Aeons had made to consciously spread more light and love prompted her to allow it to stream to Adele.

Payson's heart went out to her. Of course the mother was ramped up. For her, this meeting was her last hope for getting her daughter back.

A plaque caught her eye. "The world is made of tears. Sorrowful and joyful tears."

She spoke the words softly, and stared at them painted on a piece of barn wood. The hand-painted decorative piece sat on a small easel atop an end table in the spacious living room.

Mrs. Freeport, middle-aged and comfortable looking with plump curves, bustled in from the kitchen. She handed a steaming coffee mug to Payson, then sat stiffly with her own on the couch. "My daughter created that piece." She dropped her gaze to the mug in her hands. "It was her last piece. I mean, before she disappeared."

"It's lovely. Where did your daughter get this quote? It's so eloquent." Payson refrained from touching her fingers to the wooden plaque because bursts of impressions about its creator would fill her head. She wasn't ready for that yet. If she touched it, her psychometric ability could take her mind to other places, other times, and out of the present. Right now, she needed to be here with Mrs. Freeport.

"Those are Shana's words. She had, or, I mean, has a way with words."

Payson took a seat across the coffee table. "It's hard, I know, Mrs. Freeport, to find the right words."

"Please, call me Adele. Shana has been gone for two years. The police have stopped investigating her disappearance. Her boyfriend,

Sam Cain, moved on." The woman lifted her gaze to meet Payson's. "I don't like to think of her as—"

"I know," Payson interrupted. She consciously grounded her energy, imagining her toes burrowing into the earth. A hug ached in her, but she didn't want to touch Adele just yet. "We don't know what's happened to your daughter. I will refer to Shana as living. You can too. It's that simple for now." Payson sipped the hot coffee and let it remind her to stay in the moment, not let her brain leave the room to begin the investigation of Shana's disappearance.

Adele's shoulders relaxed. "Thank you. My husband, her father, died last year. He had a heart attack, but I think his heart was broken after no word for more than a year. Now I'm alone, yet I have a daughter."

Payson just listened, letting her say the words she needed to say.

A tear slipped down Adele's cheek. "Thank you so much for coming today. I'm never going to give up hope of finding Shana. When I saw the article about you in the newspaper, I was thrilled to read of your success in finding the stolen car for that family. I just had to try to contact you and ask you for help." The woman perched on the edge of the couch.

Payson smiled. The mention of her recent recovery warmed her heart. "You mean the Willys." In every recovery, those moments of happy endings were what kept her going.

"Yes, yes. That's the one." She slanted her head, her eyes tearing up. "If only you could find Shana."

Payson's stomach clenched. "Happy endings are not a guarantee, sadly." She leaned forward, earnest intention pumping through her body. "But, Mrs. Freeport, I'll do everything I can to find your daughter. My success rate is very high. I can't make promises, because that would be unethical. But there's a reason I'm one of the top recovery agents in the United States and that I have clients from around the world. I'm not telling you that to brag. It's to assure you my chances are good for finding out what happened to your daughter."

Adele's eyes pleaded. "But you will take the case?"

"Yes. I'll start right away."

Adele jumped up and wrapped her arms around Payson's shoulders. "I can't thank you enough."

Bursts of impressions played across Payson's mind. Images of Shana and Adele arguing flitted past, followed by those of mother and daughter walking in a park. The bursts were so real, Payson could feel a spring breeze in the park, hear the angst in the mother-daughter argument. Payson centered herself. Her ability was growing, but now was not the time to go into information it could give her. She had her process and it didn't begin with loading her brain with Adele's memories.

"You don't have to thank me. I'm very interested in finding Shana."

Adele sat back down. "We should discuss the cost."

"I don't charge for missing person cases when it concerns a lost family member."

"What? How can that be?" Adele's eyes widened. "This is your work, finding people. You're a bounty hunter. You charge a fee. I've checked your website."

"Yes, I'm a recovery agent, bounty hunter as you say. I get paid well for locating fugitives, and it funds my true passion, bringing a conclusion to families who have no idea what has happened to their loved ones. That is a kind of pain I wouldn't wish on anyone."

"You sound as if you know that pain too." Adele's lips tightened. "But I don't mean to pry."

Payson's heart rolled over. It was true. So very true, that she shoved away the memory of crystal blue eyes and glossy dark hair. Pushed away especially the bright warm smile. Braden's smile that had felt like sunshine on her face. After five days without him, of Braden being "lost" to her, a keen understanding beat inside her of the devastation and heartache of those who live with loss.

"It's okay. My pain is private, but it doesn't go away." She shifted in her seat. "Now, you said over the phone that you have a box of Shana's things for me. Could I have that?"

Adele disappeared down a hall, while Payson took note of photographs of Shana hanging above the couch. Shana's blue eyes stared back at her from the family portrait. Her smile lit up her face. *Where are you, Shana?*

"I have everything you asked for." Adele marched back into the living room as though on a mission, carrying a lidded cardboard box. She placed it on the coffee table. "The list of her personal information: her full name, her birth date, and place of birth, friends, awards, all the stuff you requested." She started to lift the top of the box. "We could go over it right now if you have time."

"No. I'll take the box with me and spend time alone with the information." She tapped the box. "This is great. Thank you for gathering it. This is where I'll start."

Payson hesitated a moment before turning to leave. Just long enough to see Adele wring her hands. Loss rumbled through her bones, Adele's and her own. She gritted her teeth to prevent words from escaping, when what she wanted was to shout to the heavens, it's not fair!

But no. It was her duty to remain true to her Aeon nature of peace, even if she had to sit on her tongue.

She took in a deep breath and let it out, boosting her flow of love to Adele. She placed her hand on Adele's shoulder. Impressions came in the usual bursts, emotions grabbed at her heart, but she kept her breath steady and let them slide by, struggling not to attach. "I'm in this with you. I promise you I'll be in touch soon. I have other cases I'm working on, but Shana goes to the top of my priorities."

The woman's eyes looked distant and Payson knew the energy of Adele's fear and worry had passed to her. The shift had shocked Adele's system enough to quiet her mind.

"I'll let myself out. You need to rest."

"Yes, I am tired. You'll be in touch?"

Payson smiled, tenderness spreading throughout her. "Yes. Very soon, I hope."

She walked out to her car with satisfaction drowning out her sorrow over Braden. Right now, she had a case to focus on that held the possibility of a payoff that outweighed any paycheck.

Her meeting with Adele Freeport behind her, Payson had all she could do to drive toward home. The afternoon stretched in her mind like an endless airport moving walkway. She had things to do, people to see, places to go, but the drudgery of reconstructing her life sapped her energy.

She pulled at her collar. She could force herself to interact with people but the idea of it constricted her throat. She had to pull herself together and for that, she needed to be alone.

The closer she drove to her home the easier it was for her to breathe. She pulled into her lane and drove up to her house, fully relaxed.

Inside, Payson shrugged off her clothes as she strolled through her living room, turning to nature for refueling.

She took the stairs to the dock and sliced into the water. The coolness made her gasp, but she threw back her head and breathed in fresh air. Quiet was all around, except for the sweet sounds of crickets in the woods. Tears welled in her eyes, remembering the last time swimming in her pond was with Braden. It hurt to remember. She had connected with him so richly, and now nothing.

She slapped the surface of the water. "I will not sink. I will not let Braden disappear into darkness."

The situation was not about her feelings or needs, it was about Braden's life. She closed her eyes, clamping down on her ever-nagging question, why must I take care of everyone? The serenity and ability to let loose of all negative energies in this place was why she'd bought it two years ago, but in this moment it couldn't ease her conflicting feelings.

Thanks to Keegan and Cooper, she now had top-of-the-line security measures, including motion sensor alarms, security cameras, and special doors all around the perimeter that would close automatically if an intruder invaded her property. Of course, outside of her property was a different story as Brown had proved.

All the security measures she'd allowed Cooper and Keegan to install didn't mean she was paranoid. She needed them to keep her safe from possible fall-out from Diane's anger. They all did.

But did she care anymore? She was losing the fight to prevent the

Dark Sides from turning the city into a place of horror. And she'd been fighting so long, with only Braden to keep her standing.

A recollection of the blast at Braden's apartment stopped her breath, and shivers ran up and down her spine. Payson closed her eyes again on the fiery image of Braden out cold lying on the floor and Diane standing over him. She shook her head, her hair splattering water drops across her face. Enough.

She swam across the pond, climbed onto the deck, and sat in the light that filtered through the leaves, struggling to regain her balance. She didn't blame Braden for their failed relationship. How could she?

Some Aeon she was. She couldn't save her best friend from darkness, much less save the world.

From inside she heard ZuZu's meows. "I'm coming, sweetie." She ran up the stairs and into her living room, leaning over to pick up her cat. She pressed her face to ZuZu's soft fur and let the cat's purr rumble in her ears. "Sweetie," she whispered. "I love you. Let's get you something to eat."

After a quick shower, she crawled into her pajamas, regardless of the time, and sat down at the kitchen table with a sandwich, some fruit, and her laptop. She opened social media and began her search for information about Shana.

Shana's name popped up on a number of personal pages that belonged to other people who had posted her as missing and solicited help finding her. Payson took down names and email addresses. She searched for contact information for people who appeared to be bona fide friends. Several still resided in the local area. While many posted requests for help when Shana initially went missing, the activity had dropped off.

She dug deeper, looking for random names in her lists of followers and friends. Quickly, she scrolled through, waiting for something to grab her attention.

Sam Cain. There it was. Nothing more than a name. But that was the point. He'd never directly interacted with Shana on her page, but he had reposted some of her entries.

She punched his name into the search and found his profile in several places. He was thirty-two, a self-employed fitness trainer, and artist.

Payson took a bite of her sandwich and peered at the screen. His photo was the same for each site he was on. Sandy-colored hair, toothy smile, nondescript facial features. *Hmm. Let's just check you out, Sam.*

She grabbed a photo of a car from one of his sites and did an image search. It took her to a website that belonged to the same name, Sam Cain, but a different face, one with a handsome smile and dark hair. Different contact info. Maybe this Sam was Shana's former boyfriend. So what was the connection between the two Sam's?

She took one last bite of her sandwich and washed it down with cold water. The fruit would wait. This was too easy, she had to get out in the field. But first she texted Keegan.

I have a name I'd like you to run through NamUps. Sam Cain.

Minutes later, he texted back. **Will do. I'll also run him in the NCIC db. Be in touch soon.**

Grateful for her friends with useful contacts, Payson turned to the box Shana's mother had given her. Before dipping in, she closed her eyes and hummed a favorite song. Making music helped her ground and center herself, readying for input she would receive. The tune was a simple lullaby. Not one her mother had sung to her. No, her mother wasn't that kind of mother. It was an Indian song her Indian father sang to her when she was young. While she hummed the sweet notes, she heard her father's voice singing the lyrics. *Nini baba nini. Soja baba soja. Mera baba soja. Sleep baby sleep.*

Before touching anything, she scanned the contents of the box. A pair of running shoes. A baseball cap. A silver pendant in the shape of a sun. And a couple books.

She rubbed her fingers over the cover of the first book. It was a classic she was familiar with, *Persuasion*, by Jane Austen. A burst of images flashed across her eyes—Shana, covered in an afghan her grandmother had made for her, engrossed in the pages of the book. Bright, blue eyes with creases in the corner. The slide changed. She was smiling at her mother and they were conversing about her college classes. Another slide and she saw a professor telling her she could be a good writer if she would try harder.

Payson disconnected from the book and picked up another one, this one a book of love sonnets by Pablo Neruda. She flipped open the cover and read an inscription. "Shana, read these sonnets and know that I love you more."

It was unsigned, but images appeared. Shana kissing a young man, the same man she imagined was her boyfriend Sam Cain. Her fingers sifted through his dark hair and her eyes gleamed. The couple walked hand in hand to a small compact car and leaned against it to kiss again.

A piercing stab to Payson's heart stopped her breath. Another burst of images gave her a fleeting look of another man, one who looked like one of the other Sam Cains, who watched the couple from inside a brown, late model Impala. She squeezed her lids tight, trying to bring about a view of the vehicle that would give her the license plate number. She squeezed her lids so hard they started to hurt.

"Drat. I can't get it."

ZuZu threaded between her ankles and meowed. Payson stroked her back. "I'm okay. Just a little annoyed, baby."

It wasn't a lot to work with, but it was a start. Payson stretched her arms over her head and yawned. Dusk was settling over the forest and she caught just a glimpse of the pinks and oranges of a summer sunset from a low place in the trees.

Another day passing and still no Braden. Her body must be invisible, with so much life drained from it.

I should get to work, call Keegan to ask for another assignment. Working as a bounty hunter always sent adrenaline racing through her body. When she took on a skip trace, she had structure, a template to conduct research. She called it SITS, a short cut for Shelter, Income, Transportation, and Social Media. Searching for these fundamental elements of a skip's life gave her a doorway through which she could build an approach. Names, numbers, last known employment contacts, stuff she could take on the ground and make her target. Her ability to read objects enhanced gathering information, but she still wanted the basics.

She knew long ago she enjoyed the thrill of bringing a skip to justice. It was how things worked. But every time she rightfully hunted down and found a skip, she wished it weren't so. Every time a person became something out of balance, in darkness, the whole world grew a bit dimmer. Bringing them to justice gave them a chance to change, but it was also a way for her to bring balance to the world.

ZuZu followed her upstairs, and Payson understood her cat felt anxious. ZuZu was sensitive just as she was, and got twitchy when Payson did. She brushed her teeth, staring at her face in the mirror, hoping to see in her eyes the answer to that question that nagged at her. Why me? She had never found a good answer, not one that settled the wondering. She knew her genes were to blame, as they expressed her connection to the people of Atlantis.

Okay, she could live with that. But still, of all the gene pools she could come from—King Arthur, a Roman peasant, a Pilgrim—why was she born with a purpose so grand it would take over her life? Why was she one of the few here now to save the world?

She knew what Claire Eve would tell her, You're asking the wrong question.

CHAPTER 15

E MIGHT AS well have been driving a hotdog car.

Braden cringed inside as he drove into Warren Brown's neighborhood. Two people mowing lawns and others walking the sidewalks in the morning sunshine stopped to gawk at his Fiat. It didn't shout cop, but it certainly announced his presence as someone who didn't belong.

He sped up. If he couldn't slink in unnoticed, he could at least get to Warren's residence quickly.

Had it been only days ago that he'd come here looking for Nick? He shook his head. Time was all fuzzed up in his mind since his accident. But the image of Nick's face just before his death remained crystal clear, and demanded answers. He rolled his shoulders, determination surging through his body.

He sighted the address he had for Brown and drove by, scanning the apartment complex. Three stories of apartments in decent condition and surrounded by grass and shrubs were absent of any activity. A tall, wooden fence sat at the back of the property and separated it from homes and apartments on the street behind the complex.

Braden nodded, knowing the fence was too high to climb over and there weren't any other ways out of the complex other than the main driveway. He parked on the street and walked the two blocks back to Brown's address.

He strode up the stone path leading to Brown's street-level apartment and knocked hard on the front door. With the noise, Braden felt eyes on him, and he saw faces appear in windows. His skin prickled, but he pushed back his shoulders, unintimidated.

He knocked again. "Detective Braden Powers, open up."

The door opened and Warren stood behind a storm door, frowning. "What do you want?"

"Brown." Braden held up his badge. "I want to talk to you. Please step outside."

Brown complied and spit on the ground. "I know who you are. What do you want?"

Warren gave him a blank expression, but his eyes held Braden's gaze, like a dare. "You interfered in an investigation and your actions resulted in the death of Nick Ward. What were you doing there?" Pressure built in his chest and he drew in a deep breath.

"I was just walking by, Detective." Brown slanted his head at Braden.

"Uh…huh. You spoke to Nick. How did you know him?" The pressure in his chest hardened. Braden shifted his feet and stared back at Brown. "Answer my question here or at the APD, your choice."

Brown rubbed his chin. "Nick was a neighborhood kid. I was looking after him. You're the one who scared him. His death is on you, Powers."

Braden almost choked on a bad taste in his throat. The lies and the avoidance strategy triggered rage in his gut. He balled his hands.

Brown stepped back away from Braden's reach. "You need to be careful. I have friends here, and they won't hesitate to defend me."

"Are you threatening me?" Braden clenched his teeth and took hold of Brown's shoulder. He pressed hard, his fingers digging into Brown's muscles. "Answer my question now. What was your relationship with Nick Ward? Did he work for you?"

"Yes, Nick worked for me. He was one of my guys. He and my

other guys are my disrupters. He ran because he was afraid I was going to hurt him for messing up."

Braden's mind focused hard on him. Brown's breathing came in hard, deliberate pulls. Sweat beaded above his lip, and Braden could taste his fear. "What the hell is a disrupter? Is that a gang?"

Brown's gaze shifted at the same time Braden heard soft footsteps behind. His focus dropped as he turned to the sound. Mid-turn, he saw a man pull back his fist, and he ducked. But Brown pinned his arms behind his back.

"Go ahead," Brown yelled at the other man.

Braden struggled to get loose, but Brown's grip was a vice. The other man slammed his fist into his gut, once, twice. Then Brown threw him to the ground.

"You are a part of the plan, Powers. You're not just an innocent bystander. If you ever use your mind control on me again I'll end you, no matter what Diane wants." Brown bent close to Braden's face, so close he could smell the onions he'd had for lunch. "Does my face bring back memories, Powers?" He laughed and stood over Braden.

The laughter made Braden squirm. Brown's words sickened him. But that was all he had—a *Deja vu* he couldn't sort out and nausea that scared him. His mind blurred as he stared up at Brown. He climbed to his feet, wobbly on his knees. "What does Diane have to do with Nick's death? What do you mean, mind control?"

Warren pressed his finger into Braden's chest. "Stay away from me."

Braden could pull out his gun. He could compel Warren to stop walking away. He could cuff him and take him in for interrogation. But he wasn't in any shape to fight him physically and he was outnumbered. He didn't want to shoot him, because that would complicate getting him to talk.

Obviously, Warren knew things Braden needed to know. But he had something to go forward with, and his brain needed to rest. Maybe then Warren's strange comments about mind control and Diane would make some sense.

He kept up his guard as he walked back to his car and climbed in. He slumped low in the seat and drove straight to his house.

Inside, he sprawled on his bed. He made sure his phone was turned off, wanting no phone calls or texts from Diane to disrupt his sleep. He buried his head under his pillow. If he could spin a cocoon around his body, he would. This whole coming back to life thing, as she had called it, needed peace and quiet.

PAYSON PULLED INTO a parking garage near the community center. Six days without Braden. And he would not be at the ACE meeting either. When Braden left, ACE activities had gone to the back recesses of her mind. They'd joined ACE together and it reminded her of the loss. She sighed. She needed to get a grip. The ACE meeting was important.

But first, she did the thing she could to help him. "Braden, this is for you, my love." Intentionally, spaciously, she sent her love and wrapped him in light and peace. "Always."

She grabbed her purse and files regarding the projects, and headed toward the exit. A quick check at the time quickened her steps. Pressure to be on time nagged at her. It was her pressure, but it just wasn't in her to slink in late.

Then her breath seized. A distinctive low hum vibrated in her chest. It meant only one thing. DAs were nearby.

Two men moved out of the shadows in the garage and stood in Payson's path. Commanding and bleak energy wafted off them, attempting to invade her mind.

Instantly, Payson flooded the space around her with love, encompassing the two DAs. She stood facing them, with no fear, only compassion.

"Where are you going, Payson?" The man slanted his head and stood without moving.

"You know my name. What's yours?" The vibration in her gut continued, but it stayed there, in her gut, substantial but not growing or moving into her mind.

The man laughed and nudged the other man beside him. "She wants to know my name. That's a good one."

The other man glowered. "Why do you ask?"

Payson's heart opened. These men were not evil. They were simply inured with beliefs Diane espoused. "I'm interested, that's all. You know me. I'd like to know you."

They exchanged a glance and nodded. "We're not interested in you or in falling for your tactics to undermine our power."

Her heart cringed. They could only see darkness. "In answer to your question, I'm going to a meeting." She pushed between them, letting their icy energy pass through her and sending it into the ground.

"We're here to stop you."

She didn't have to waste time asking why or what from. DAs under Diane's control just did what they were told to do. She whirled around. "Are you the spokesman? 'Cause if that's so, I'm talking to you." She dropped her things, stepped into a Karate block stance and gestured the man to come at her.

Silently both men came toward her. Payson held her pose. This business with these men crept under her skin. She had a meeting to get to.

Number one man stepped toward her and raised his fists, as though preparing to punch her. When he shoved a fist toward her, she blocked it with one arm and quickly pivoted to the other. She lifted her leg and bent her knee, then smoothly kicked horizontally, landing a roundhouse at number two's midsection, each time hollering sharply.

Back in her block stance, she lowered her eyes and stared at them both. Number one raised his fists again, shoving one fist at her, but she blocked it again, then lifted one bent leg and snapped a hard blow to his groin. He moaned and rolled to the ground.

She didn't wait for number two to regain his composure. While number one groaned, Payson lunged at number two and pounded him first with her right jab, then her left.

He almost lost his footing, stumbling backward, but managed to catch his balance. He came at her like a saber-tooth tiger, open mouthed and growling.

"Hey! What's going on here?"

Payson dropped her stance, her arms falling to her sides. Behind number two stood Braden. He knitted his brow and ran up behind the man, surprising him by knocking his feet out from underneath him and slamming his foot down on his neck. "What do you think you're doing, assaulting this young woman?" He glanced at her. "What happened to your neck?"

"It's just a shallow cut. Something I got on the job. It's nothing." That he had noticed touched her.

"Are you all right?" His gaze didn't move from her cut.

"Yes." He was one of them. Just like them, Braden worked for Diane. Why had he intervened? He was supposed to be like them. Maybe there was a glimmer of hope. She grabbed her things from the floor.

"I was going to ask why they were assaulting this helpless woman, but I see you can take care of yourself." He shot her a smile and she lost her voice. He made a quick call to the APD for assistance.

As Braden's foot remained on number one, Payson took out her pepper spray and aimed it at number two. He shrunk back to the ground.

Braden nodded at her. Her heart nearly crumbled. It felt intimate, familiar, like the pre-Diane Braden. Her brain whirred, trying to make sense of this situation.

Meanwhile, the officers Braden called for arrived. She told them the men had come after her, and she didn't know why.

"I know why," Braden spoke up. "They're scum bags who saw a lone woman. They saw easy prey and acted on their animal instincts."

Payson swallowed hard. He was wrong. The men were DAs doing what they do, cause chaos. He was talking like a cop. But it made a believable explanation. So what was his story? Why had he shown up?

One of the officers handed her his card. "Feel free to call me if you have questions or think of anything more. These two will be interrogated."

"Thank you. It's good to know." She dipped her head. Residual effects of touching and being touched by the DAs made her shiver. It was not as if she could tell the officers that DAs were determined to bring her spirit down into muck, for just that reason. To eliminate her positive influence on the world.

CHAPTER 16

$\mathcal{B}$RADEN WATCHED THE officers drive away with the two men who had tried to hurt Payson and could hardly contain the rage clawing to the surface. Inexplicably. Sure, he was an officer tasked with protecting citizens. This, this intense anger confused him. He barely knew the woman. Worse, the only thing restraining his anger was the sickness in his gut at the idea of Payson being hurt. He turned to her, speechless. A small spot, like a black dot in his mind, started pounding.

"Well, thanks for showing up at—"

"Don't. Don't even thank me for helping out." Awkward, so awkward and he was never awkward. "You had those two guys under your thumbs." All he could do was shake his head.

Payson chuckled and the stuffy air in the garage lifted. "In my line of work it pays to have self-defense skills."

What now? Say goodbye, Braden, you fool. He couldn't take his eyes off her. Her dark hair draped innocently seductive over her shoulders. Her brown eyes glistened with...what? Self-confidence? Yes, but something more he couldn't put a finger on. "I guess we keep running into each other." He cringed at his own words. *Oh, wow, impressive.*

"Weird to keep running into you under similar circumstances," Payson said.

The smile she gave him drifted down into his heart. "I was actually on my way to a meeting. I should probably go." He faced her squarely, the black dot in his head becoming a doorknob. "You sure you're all right?" He looked down into her eyes and couldn't miss the sorrow in them.

"I'm sure I'm fine. Thank you for asking." She bent to pick up her purse and some files. "But like you, I have a meeting to get to. And now I'm late."

"Okay, well, enjoy your meeting."

She was already walking away. "You too," she said without turning around. As though on a undertaking, Payson walked briskly out of the parking garage and turned right.

Slowly walking in the same direction, Braden pulled his thoughts away from her and to his purpose for being here. Doing Diane's beckoning. Payson's rapid clip just ahead of him, he slowed his pace. She was headed in the same direction. This could be trouble.

He climbed the large concrete steps into the city's community center and entered the building. He checked the hall to the right, then the left. No sign of Payson, but the sound of her steps echoed through the hall to the left. Braden's pulse picked up. He was here to check out the ACE meeting. Was Payson doing the same? He stood in the hallway, shifting from his left to his right foot. Uncertain. Of course she was going to the meeting. She was a member of the group. He should have expected to run into her.

So what? He headed toward the meeting room. He was doing the work Diane was paying him for, and he could be a potential concerned citizen as much as anybody.

He opened the door to a meeting in progress, but he couldn't help but peruse the room for Payson. His heart fluttered when he spied her sitting in a row at the back, her attention on the speaker.

A panel of four people sat at a table at the front of the room. He recognized the city mayor, Joel Farrod, and Tim Brody, the economic development director. He didn't recognize the woman at the table or the man speaking.

He slid into the empty seat behind Payson and tapped on her shoulder. "Hey," he whispered.

When she turned around, she startled. She scrunched up her nose, and Braden's brain scrambled. Her look made his body tingle.

"What are you doing here?" Her low voice still managed to sound incredulous.

"I'm interested in learning more about the group." It was true. Besides, what did she care?

Her gaze looked him up and down. She nodded and turned her attention back on the speaker.

The scent of her, warm breezes and clear ocean water, enveloped him so delicately it cleared his head. The doorknob-sized headache subsided. Another breath of her tuned out everything else. He couldn't remember feeling so relaxed.

"For those of you who arrived late, I'll introduce myself again because I see some new faces. I'm Cooper Munson. I am a self-employed recovery agent. As a local businessman, I share your concerns regarding the proposed Stillwell Place development in the Old Town section of Auralia. The shops and restaurants and entertainment venues in that section of the city are well-established and reputable businesses. They offer a taste of Auralia that is time-honored and unique. Mr. Mayor, I ask you to think long and hard about replacing these assets to the community with big-box stores, chain restaurants, and a casino on the Wherryite River."

The room erupted in applause, drawing Braden's full attention. Suddenly, he was interested in learning more. Up to this point, Diane had been his only source regarding the proposed projects headed by Principal Industries.

"Thank you," Cooper said. "Now I'll hand the floor to Mayor Farrod."

Braden had a strange feeling about Cooper. He gave off a casual, laid-back attitude, but he came across as very earnest in his belief that the projects Diane was in the middle of getting licenses and certifications for would threaten quality of life in Auralia.

More than that, as Braden half-listened to the mayor make a case for the development, fuzzy memories of Cooper dribbling a basketball, drinking coffee, and laughing with friends taunted his mind.

"And furthermore, the city of Auralia can't afford to turn away big developers interested in investing here." He motioned to the economic director. "Tim is going to pass out booklets we've compiled that provide background information on Principal Industries that you may be unaware of. You'll read that it is one of the largest conglomerates in the country, with interests in pharmaceuticals, plastics, media, and, of course, property development. Take your time and read through the information. I think you'll appreciate the group's philosophy of using local contractors for construction and opening up local job opportunities."

Tim Brody stopped walking among those gathered. "Any city would more than welcome such a profitable and secure corporation engaged in growing fields of business."

Tim continued to walk and handed a booklet to Payson, then Braden. He thumbed through the slick pages, noticing text from local businessmen and women in support of both the casino and the retail development. The names rang familiar. Several worked with Diane in recruitment for the city and Chamber of Commerce activities.

Braden sighed. It had been a long time since he'd had much interest in city doings. His primary passion was police work, but that hadn't eaten up as much of his life as working for Diane. Memories of participating in negotiations with her and CEOs of corporations and offering his persuasion, she called it, reminded him that his work with her was important to him as well as the city. *Diane has given you much. You're loyal to her causes, man. You'd be nothing but a street cop without her.*

The words sounded in his mind but he felt detached from them. The air around him got thin and he struggled to breathe. Braden stood, tripping clumsily over the legs of his chair, and sped to the door and out to the hall.

"Braden, are you all right?" Payson gathered him in her arms, steadying him. "Do you need some water or something?"

He blinked down at her, trying to clear the blur in his vision. All he saw was Payson standing across a room, a room vaguely familiar but in flames.

"Braden, come with me. Now. The fire is spreading." Payson beckoned him, coughing.

He reached toward Payson, but his hand passed right through her. Suddenly Diane was standing over him. He looked around and found himself lying on the floor, smoke and fire all around.

"He's mine now, Payson." Diane stroked his forehead, over and over. Then the room went black.

"Braden, get up. I'll take you out in the fresh air. Listen to me. I'm here, Braden." Payson's voice pierced the darkness and his confusion.

He sat up with her support. The hall was empty. There were no flames, no smoke. No Diane. "My God, I'm going crazy."

"You just need some air. Let's walk. You can lean on me if you need to."

"I'm okay. I don't know what happened back there. Geez! I haven't been drinking, either."

"Let's take the steps slowly. I don't know what happened to you either, but something did. I should take you to the hospital. I can take you in my car and I'll get your car to you later."

"Hold on. I'm not going to the hospital. They'll run a bunch of tests for symptoms I don't have. No, I'm not going." He let go of her, just to prove to her he didn't need a doctor. He didn't mention the concussion because he knew in his gut that the scene in his head was not an illusion. It wasn't caused by a bump to his head. "See, I'm better already."

"Good. I still think you need to be checked out. You lost consciousness. Are you taking any medications that would cause that?"

"No. I'm good. I appreciate your concern, but I'm good. I'll just find my way to my car and drive home." He couldn't help but be touched by the genuine concern in her expression. How could one woman be so strong and at the same time so sensitive and… Oh, it hit him what he had seen in her eyes. Payson's beautiful appearance was undeniable. But what she had was inner beauty that leaked out all over from her. It drew him to her, despite the warning in his head to keep his distance. And why was that?

"You're not driving yourself home. I'll take you. But someone should stay with you. Do you have someone you can call?"

He smiled. Determination also stuck out all over her. It was so cute. "Okay, you win. You can take me home."

"Payson."

Braden frowned. An unwelcome interruption by the name of Cooper Munson came running out the door and down the steps.

"What's going on? Are you okay, Payson?"

She gave him a strange look. "Yes, I'm fine. Is the meeting over?"

"No, Mickey is leading a discussion about the casino now. I thought you wouldn't want to miss it." Cooper glanced back and forth between Payson and him.

"Who is Mickey?" Braden asked.

Munson eyed him. "The president of ACE."

Braden didn't understand the apprehension in Cooper's eyes or appreciate the implication.

"I'm not going to hurt her." He turned to Payson. "Go back into the meeting. I'll be fine."

"No, I'm not leaving you. Cooper, you can go. I'm going to help Braden get home."

Cooper continued to eye him. Braden knew that face. He couldn't suppress the strong sense that he and Cooper had history, but he didn't know what kind of history. Maybe he had arrested Cooper at one time. His thoughts pivoted. "Hey, Cooper. I'm a cop. I'm not a threat to Payson. Maybe I shouldn't leave her alone with you?"

Cooper broke out laughing. "Trust me, she's safe with me. Safer than with you."

Cooper pointed a finger at him, and when he did, Braden's insides began to warm. It disrupted his thoughts. "Are you accusing me of something? Do I need to take you to the precinct and have a long talk with you, check your background?" Automatically, he bristled. His instincts stepped up to protect Payson.

Payson slammed her hand against his chest and she sent a look to Cooper. "What's all this macho shit, taking-care-of-me about? Must I remind you, Cooper, I don't need your protection?" She turned her eyes on Braden. "Nor yours."

She grabbed his arm and started walking. "See you later, Cooper. Don't worry."

CHAPTER 17

*Y*OU'LL HAVE TO direct me to your place." Payson kept it casual as she glanced at Braden sitting in the passenger seat in her car. She sat on her tongue, staying the words threatening to tumble out. *I haven't seen where you moved after our break up. You moved on without me. Does Diane live with you?*

"It's on Woods Drive. Take a left out of the garage." Nothing in his expression clued her to his state of mind. "It's only about twenty minutes from here."

"Got it. I know where Woods Drive is. There are some very nice homes in that area." He didn't respond, just sat with his eyes focused on the road. "Are you feeling better?"

He rubbed his thumb over the slight stubble on his chin. The subtle rasp stuttered her heart. She had stifled sensual thoughts of Braden since the explosion, but they flitted immediately to life at that little sound. She cleared her throat and waited for his answer.

"I could tell you yes, I'm better." Still facing forward, Braden rubbed his temples.

"But … is there a but there?" She wouldn't do it. It wouldn't be right to touch Braden just to satisfy her curiosity. She wanted to know what images a touch would bring, but she wouldn't invade his privacy.

"There is. The truth is I don't know what happened and, not only that, I don't know why what happened happened."

"Okay, I didn't mean to pry." Tension hung in the air and Payson wanted it to go away, but she wouldn't push him.

He laid his hand on her shoulder, like no time had passed and he had the right to touch her. Confusion woven with heat made her swallow hard again. An image flashed of him lying on the floor passed out while scenes passed through his thoughts. The fire, her begging him to come to her. Chills spiraled down her spine, as Diane hypnotizing Braden filled her mind. It was too much to contain, so she shifted away.

"I didn't mean to give you that impression, Payson." He shook his head. "I'm genuinely perplexed, but my mind is a fuzzball. I've got to sort it out, but I can't." He glanced over at her, his expression distraught.

"I'm sorry that's happening to you. Maybe for now you should rest. If you want to talk we can."

He chuckled. "Thank you. I barely know you and you're being so kind. I don't know what to think, but I appreciate it. I don't mean to be a bother."

"You're not." *Come back to me, live your own life, love me;* all emotion-laced words she kept inside by iron will. "But we're almost to your street. Which way do I turn?"

"Left, then my house is on the right straight ahead. Just pull into the drive and keep going until you reach the house. It's a long drive."

"I see that." An ache throbbed in Payson's chest as she followed the curving drive through patches of trees. Braden's imaginary life had come with a new home.

"This lane ends up at my house. You can pull in."

Silence floated between them for the few minutes it took to reach his house. Her breath caught. "This is your house? It's ... spectacular."

His hand on the door, he paused. He scanned the mansion that was his home, as though for the first time. "Uh, yes, it's comfortable." He climbed out. "Do you want to come in?" He punched in the alarm code and stood at the open front door.

"Yes. I want to make sure you're okay and settled comfortably where you can rest."

"You don't have to, but thank you." He wobbled on his feet and grabbed the doorframe, before stepping inside.

"Oh yeah, I can see you're just fine." Payson consciously grounded herself, then took his arm. She focused hard on her breathing to push away any images, and led Braden to an oversized, overstuffed black leather couch. The scent of leather permeated the luxurious room. "How about the couch?"

"You're making too much of this. I'm fine." But he didn't resist when she helped him lie on the couch. He slipped down into the cushions and rested his head against a puffy, white and black faux fur pillow.

"Can I get you anything? Water? Coffee?" she asked, surveying the sprawling living room. The floor of the sunken room was covered in grey carpeting. A tall ceiling, at least nine feet high, and floor to ceiling bookshelves expanded the spacious feeling of the room. A large, slate fireplace stood at the end of the room and opened to both the living room and adjacent dining room. All the opulence fueled her imagination of the rest of the two-story house. She glanced down at him as he laid quietly, his eyes closed. *All this on a detective's salary?*

She startled when he opened his eyes and smiled. "Thank you but I don't need anything. It would be nice if you would sit with me for a while." He swiveled to sit up, and he motioned to the seat beside him on the couch.

She gripped the back of the chair next to her. His invitation tempted her, but what about Diane's threat? Besides, this was not her life-long friend. This was a nearly turned Aeon. So much chaos trembled inside him and transmitted in swirls to her body.

She smiled at him, and streamed light and love at him. He still had a chance to lean into the light. "Sure." She dropped beside him, not knowing what to do with the awkwardness between them that he seemed oblivious to.

"What were you doing at that meeting, the ACE meeting? Are you actually against the new developments?"

"I am a member of the group because I believe the projects need more scrutiny. Why were you there?"

He sighed. "I wanted to find out what the opposition is thinking. I don't understand why anyone in the community would be against progress, more jobs, and more money coming into the community."

"Did you get answers?"

He nodded. "I get that some people find it hard to accept change."

"Is that what you think? It's simply that ACE is stuck in the past?" Her heart clenched. This sounded like a line from big money and a lobbyist.

"Honestly, until today I hadn't given it much thought. It made sense that the benefits of the development and a casino would be welcomed. They'll provide more jobs, provide more retail options for residents and visitors, and draw more visitors."

She shook her head. "Right. But if you keep exploring, you'll find behind the proposed projects is a company run by people who will change the face of Auralia and the mix of residents, all to fill their own pockets. Sometimes change is about shifting wealth and power, which is not at all about the community." Payson couldn't keep the agitation out of her voice.

He nodded. "Principal Industries is powerful and determined. You and your fellow ACErs won't win."

His words were hollow. It only made her angrier, because he was reciting what Diane had told him, she just knew it in her heart.

She squared him. "I don't believe we'll lose. You could join us and help keep the community safe, uncorrupted, and thriving in ways that benefit the average citizen."

His eyes went blank, and she feared she'd pushed him too much. "It won't matter, but I'll continue to investigate."

"It does matter."

"That I continue to investigate?" He slanted a small grin at her.

"Yes. It will help ensure that big money and their destructive agendas won't rule the city. And even small stands for what we believe in matter to the world."

"You're very earnest." His smile dropped and his blue eyes pierced her. "I barely know you, Payson, but I feel things for you." He broke out laughing. "Okay, that wasn't weird at all."

What could she do about his defenses? They involved so much more than normal fears of rejection. They were knitted into a complete façade, made for him by Diane, and imprisoning him. Diane's threat echoed in her mind. *Try to release him. Try to engage with the Braden you knew. But if you succeed in taking him from me, I'll kill him.*

Payson fisted her hands. The threat made her sick. And she was tired of that fear. "Braden, I'm not someone who you need to impress. I'm interested in what prompted you to say you feel things for me. Could you explain?" Her words flowed from her heart. That was the only way she could relate to him, be there for him. If she relied on her brain to make decisions, she would have dropped him off at the door and hoped never to see him again rather than watch him die because of her.

He drew in a deep breath and visibly collected himself. "Well, what I'm going to tell you is crazy."

The words *trust me* came front and center. She clenched her teeth. He couldn't trust her. Not anymore. Her breaths sped. And if he did, would Diane march through the front door on cue and fling lightning bolts at his head or just whip out a gun and shoot him in his heart?

So she said nothing. Listening and holding a space for truthful interaction was the best she had to offer.

Braden pulled in another deep breath and let it out. "Some very weird things have been happening to me."

"Weird how?"

"Brain fogginess. Headaches, and I never get headaches. They come and go all the time now."

"Now?"

He stared into her eyes, and her pulse tripped. He squinted. "I haven't put it all together yet. I can't, because when I think about … you, my mind blurs. It's as though I'm looking through very thick, steamed-up eyeglasses."

Agonizing seconds ticked by as he spoke each word with deliberation.

"It started the day I ran into you after you tagged a purse snatcher."

Sweat beaded on his brow. She opened her heart to envelop him in invisible light. She released any agenda for him other than healing the damage Diane had inflicted. "You were there investigating a possible connection to a series of robberies. I remember." *Remember? How could she forget?*

"Right." He traced a pattern on the couch cushion. "I couldn't put thoughts of you out of my brain."

"What kind of thoughts?" Payson's insides buzzed with the dark energy Braden struggled to break through. She had to believe he could do this, find the truth and choose to make it his own again.

Strong winds tossed the tree limbs outside the row of living room windows. Exhilaration swirled inside Payson with the drama of the summer storm building and the one churning inside Braden.

"Okay, fuck it." He twisted to face her directly, raw determination in his eyes. "Right in the middle of today's meeting, images took over my mind. It was like looking through a window. Then I saw a fire, Diane, and two men carrying me out of the fire." He held his head. "You called to me, begging me to get up, but Diane stood over me, holding me down somehow." He squinted again. "She said something to you but I can't bring back what she said."

"That happened today? I didn't know."

He ignored her words, then closed his eyes again. "At the meeting I got a feeling I knew Cooper, but I don't."

"Was it like *Deja vu?*" Her heart settled into a steady pace and she kept herself grounded. She had to, for Braden. Calm and acceptance was what he needed most right now.

"No, it was more like memories. And there have been more. I dreamed last night that you and I were lovers."

Payson's heart stopped. Could he be remembering her, them? "Lovers?" she whispered, afraid of breaking something working magic.

One tear meandered down his cheek. He peered at her, his face dripping with sorrow. "You were leaving me. I felt such loss in the dream I nearly broke apart."

She couldn't stop herself. Payson put her hand to his face, gently, yearning to help him. "I'm here now." Tremors twisted sorrowfully through her body, feeling what he'd felt in his dream that wasn't a dream. She closed her eyes to the pain and his memories flashed inside her head. She'd done that to him. She'd left him because of his growing darkness. The wrongness of turning away from him squeezed her stomach like a large snake wrapped around her.

He took her hand in his, coaxing her to see him. See him in his dark hours, in his lostness, his pain, and not turn away.

"So it's true?" His voice gravely, Braden remained with her in their broken place. "I know you? You know me? We didn't just meet?"

Everything in her longed to speak freely. All the parts of her wanted for things to be as they had been, but she had no way to go back. There was only forward and facing the truth, either alone or with him. She could have loved him despite the strengthening of shadow. If she hadn't walked out that night, maybe he wouldn't have been as vulnerable to Diane. Yes, she'd gone back to talk with him, but loss had already weakened him.

Him. The word held the essence of Braden as she'd known him. She wanted him.

But what about the threat?

"Answer me, Payson." Braden's eyes demanded a response. "Can you explain what is happening to me?"

A tiny note of tremulous power resonated with her. Threaded in Braden's demand for help were ribbons of his gift of mind control. The sense of it bloomed in the pit of her stomach, boosting her hope for his clarity. In others, his gift, that of the maleficence and good fortune presence, guided them to right or directed them to wrong. Braden's words carried a power that could persuade an individual to obey his suggestions, spoken or thought. His power had dimmed, probably a result of Diane taking him over. But a glimmer of it had remained, and now, it appeared with his growing awareness of the truth and her steady flow of light, his gift was regaining its full potential.

"I have an idea of what happened, but it isn't such a good idea for me to," she wavered in her intention to tell him, "to tell you what I know," she hedged.

Instead, Payson stood and pulled him to his feet, his face inches away. So close she felt his breath on her skin, she looked into his eyes. "Does this feel all right?"

His eyelids slipped lower. "You holding my hands, standing near enough for me to breathe in your lovely scent? Does it feel good? Yes." He tilted his head and cupped her face in his hands, drawing nearer.

Payson held her breath. Her brain urged her to slow down while the sound of her heartbeat grew loud in her ears. Braden's lips touched hers, then paused millimeters away. She exchanged a sizzling glance with him, and he dove to her mouth, placing a hard, driving kiss. His lips slipped over hers, and she nearly disappeared in the bliss of it. His tongue darted into her mouth and she tasted of him deeply.

Breathless, she pulled away, touching her forehead to his chest. He took her chin between his thumb and index finger, lifting it upward. Her gaze followed the lines of his lips, his cheeks, his classic nose, to collide with his sensuous eyes.

"Thank you, Payson."

THE DELICIOUS TASTE of Payson on his lips evoked a memory. He saw her lying at his side in his bed, her dark hair tousled like a mane against a pillow. Her words of that moment echoed forward. *"I love you, Braden."* They'd given him strength and hope.

"Why are you thanking me?"

He couldn't let go of her. The image was more than a crazed notion. It had emerged organically as a real memory. That knowledge resounded solidly in his body and left no room for doubt. "You answered my question, unequivocally. At least my question about whether or not we knew each other before that day on the street. Why didn't you say something?"

She nibbled on her lower lip, tantalizing him in the worst way. "I couldn't."

He put his hands on her slim shoulders and made her face him.

"Why not?" He rolled his head in a circle, trying to ease the tight muscles in his neck and head.

Payson frowned. "Are you getting another headache?"

"I've had a headache since the meeting."

"All this time?" She caressed his face, and he moved into her touch.

"It subsided in the car, but not for long. Why?"

"I'm not sure, but I suspect the headaches are related to your memory returning. I may have triggered their return." Her eyes dipped. "That day we saw each other in the street, I sent you love."

Braden stepped back. "You sent me love. How would you do that?"

"It's just something I can do. I knew we couldn't be together, but I wanted to help you." She stared into his face. "I wasn't trying to make you love me back. It's not that kind of love, Braden."

"I am so confused. I wish you'd tell me everything. How we know each other. Why you are responsible for my headaches."

She shook her head and locks of her hair slipped over her shoulders. "I'm not responsible. Diane Butler is." She flipped her hair back over shoulders and turned away, pacing the floor. "Oh, I shouldn't be telling you these things. It's too dangerous."

He grabbed her up to him, holding her close and nuzzling her face. "You could never be dangerous. I don't know how I know that, but I do." A warm, gentle peace came over him and he felt the pressure in his head lift. Peace was familiar. He gazed at Payson through new knowledge. Memories of being with her, sharing with her his troubles and being a part of something though he didn't recall what. His body started shaking and his head nearly exploded. "My God!" he hollered.

Instantly Payson's arms swept around him, helping him lower onto the couch. She was talking to him, but he could barely make out the words.

"Braden, relax your mind." The words came from far away. Payson held him close, the warmth of her body heating his skin. "Hang on a little longer. Maybe you can break through the block."

"What do you mean?" he asked, gritting his teeth. "I can't stand the pressure!"

Payson's words came to him, soothingly and calmly. "You have to see the truth for yourself."

"The truth about Diane?" Payson's sweet face dimmed and the room blurred. Braden clawed at his collar, trying to breathe.

"It's okay, Braden. I'm going to leave."

His eyes opened wide. "You can't leave me. I need you. I'm going to pass out." His heart thrummed hard in his chest, ready to burst.

Payson walked away. She opened the door. "No, if I leave your pain will stop. I'm sorry." She pulled the door closed behind her, sucking out all the air in the room.

How could she just leave? Braden dropped to the floor, hands on his head. He spread flat on the floor, rolling in pain from side to side. What did it mean, that the pain would stop if she left? What did her presence have to do with anything?

"Stop!" he hollered. "No more questions, no more thinking." He drew in deep pulls of air and slowly released them. His breathing slowed, and with it his heart stopped pounding. His mind cleared, yet the throbbing pain in his head continued.

Payson had predicted his headache would stop with her departure. The raging pain in his head and tornado in his body had diminished. She'd also accused Diane of giving him the headaches, but how could that be? So much blur in his mind kept him from making connections.

The pain had to stop, no matter the cause. Payson had sent him love, despite the holes in his memory that he couldn't explain. She wanted to help him, but why?

He pounded the floor with both fists. Concentrating wasn't helping. For as long as his short memory could recall, pieces had been missing after his accident. He strained to bring them back. Fuzzy as they were, memories started to return in glimpses after the day in the street with Payson. The timing seemed to correlate with being in her presence and the claim she'd sent him love.

He measured his breathing again, slowly in, slowly out. His breathing was all he focused on. Minutes passed. The clock on the living room wall ticked out the passing seconds. Stillness enveloped him.

He reached into the past with no expectations. Suddenly, memories flowed in. Detached, he watched, as if an observer instead of a participant. He saw his friendship as a child with Payson and why they'd easily become best friends early on. They were a special kind of human. An Aeon. They resonated at the same note. The warm glow that emanated from Payson was in him too. But he'd lost it. Darkness sifted into his energy field and he watched it happen as he worked with rapists, killers, kidnappers, and every kind of low-life. That'd been all he'd seen eventually.

He laid flat on the floor, wasted, but knowing everything. He knew what Diane was, a Dark Aspect, and he knew she had used her gift of mesmerizing to cloud his mind and seize control over him. And he saw the connection between Payson and Diane, and why being near Payson ignited excruciating headaches.

Diane had used the trauma of an explosion to empower a hypnotic block in his mind. She'd made it impossible for Payson to be near him without hurting him. And she had stolen his memories. Hell, she'd stolen his life.

CHAPTER 18

SHAKEN, PAYSON LEFT Braden's house. She'd known the threat of seeing him, but only because she had been there when Diane had mesmerized Braden's brain and experienced the extraordinary power of the block.

Sitting in her car, she tried to stop the quaking in her body. Diane's words slammed inside her head. *"Stay away from him. Never tell him anything about his past. If you do, he'll die."*

Payson dropped her head against the headrest in her seat. Yes, she'd heard the words six days ago and she'd witnessed Diane's powerful block, but she'd never seen the curse almost tear open Braden's mind.

Tears blurred her eyes. He'd suffered so much pain, she couldn't leave him fast enough, desperate to remove the threat to his life: her.

Through her tears and with quaking fingers, she texted Claire Eve. **Could I talk with you as soon as possible?**

Desperation gnawed at her heart over the cruelness of Braden's block. Need to talk to Claire Eve clamored in her head.

She startled as her phone chimed. **I can talk now. Meet me in my office.**

Relief sifted through her. *Oh, Claire Eve. Thank you.*

Moments later, she walked into Claire Eve's office. The scent of sandalwood wafted around her. Everything about Claire Eve's demeanor was genuine and grounded. Her counseling approach gave her a sense of coming home to a home she hadn't known. One that welcomed her as she was with no judgment or criticism, only support and guidance.

"Payson." Claire Eve bent to hug her and she couldn't hold back her tears.

"Thank you for seeing me."

Claire Eve slid into an overstuffed chair and gestured to her. "Have a seat, please. Tell me what's happening." She knitted her brow and propped her elbow on her knee, resting her chin on her hand.

Payson's shoulders relaxed. She let out a long breath, one she'd been holding. Her thoughts settled. Her pulse slowed. But sorrow still lay heavy in her chest. "I've been sending Braden love."

"Oh." Claire Eve pursed her lips. "You were not the source of his increasing pain. You offered him love that gave him a choice Diane wanted to prevent. It was a beautiful, kind thing to do. It doesn't surprise me you would have that impulse."

Silence hung heavily as the thought of what she'd done formed into words while Claire Eve sat waiting.

"You mean any average woman would have scratched his eyes out for forgetting we were lovers, but not me because it's not in my nature as an Aeon?" Guilt swelled inside her. "I let him down six days ago. I walked away from Braden when he needed help."

"Seven days ago. I believe you are forgetting that you went back to him for that very reason." Claire Eve's gentle tone remained steady.

"But it was too late. Diane took away any chance he had of fulfilling his role as an Aeon."

"And that is your fault, Payson?"

She could barely whisper. "Yes. I left him vulnerable. I know we've been over this, but I can't let go of the fact that I abandoned him."

"You'll think about it and talk about it for as long as you need. It's the way things work, you know."

Payson nodded. "But there's more. Sending him love the other day jostled his memory of the truth, and triggered the curse."

"Curse? Do you mean the hypnotic block?"

"Yes. We've seen each other again, and each time he remembers a bit more. He's asking questions. But all that is connected to me and the past is bringing on terrible headaches. He even passed out earlier today." Her heartbeat spun erratically. Shame warmed her cheeks, and she couldn't bring herself to tell Claire Eve what she had done. Then it burbled out of her. "I kissed him."

"You're very brave, Payson, to challenge the block and try to break it."

"I thought I had a chance of doing that, but I also was simply drawn to him. I wanted him to remember. But, I have to be careful with my choices. I have to pause and assess whether or not I'm making a choice at all, or simply letting myself try to bring him back to me."

"That is such powerful thinking. Did it work?"

"It did something. Braden started hollering, his head hurt so bad. I had to leave before I killed him."

"Did he see the correlation and ask you to leave?"

"No, he begged me to stay, but I knew I was hurting him."

Clair Eve stared out the window, pursing her lips again. A siren from a passing emergency vehicle sounded out in the street. A car with a bad muffler roared by. Claire Eve turned her gaze back on Payson. "You're questioning your decision to send Braden love because maybe it set things in motion that were selfish and harmful. You feel your kiss caused him unbearable pain. How did it feel when you did those things?"

Payson swiped at the tears drifting down her cheeks. "It felt right. Organic, like I didn't need to sit on it and weigh the pros and cons."

"How would it be if that is all you must do? Follow your gut, then let go of what happens next."

"But I'm an Aeon. I'm supposed to do no harm." Her guilt resisted reason.

"Payson, you still have choices in life. Being an Aeon means you have more insight and compassion and interior space than the average human with which to make choices. You can choose to draw on those skills and abilities or not. You are not responsible for fixing everyone and everything wrong on the planet. But you do a marvelous job of using your abilities for the good of others, even when it seems like you're creating chaos."

"Chaos is part of bringing about positive change. I know this, but I lose track of it sometimes." She sat still in the chair, allowing Claire Eve's words to settle in her.

Claire Eve chuckled. "You're an Aeon, but you're still human. You're not ever going to be all perfect. We're supposed to be balanced. And in the balance between darkness and light, we contain both. That's healthy."

Payson sighed, letting the confusion and self-doubt shift away. "Sometimes I wish I could erect an invisible wall of protection all around me so that darkness couldn't slime me and bring me down."

"Maybe you'll figure out a way to do that." Claire Eve's eyes twinkled. She could always be counted on for wise words, healthy interaction, and deep healing.

As Payson hugged her good-bye, she paused, her self-confidence renewed, her mind clarified. "I love you." She didn't care if she wasn't supposed to. "It's not simply transference, either."

"I know. I love you too."

She checked the time, then headed toward Coffee Is for a quick meal and with any luck, an opportunity to chat with Skye and Benjamin. The skip assignment Keegan had given her ran strategies through her mind. Since Claire Eve had helped her release unhealthy thoughts and beliefs, Payson's excitement rose for tackling the assignment.

BRADEN SAT OUTSIDE HIS HOUSE, his bare feet relishing the touch of soft grass and the scent of the early evening summer breeze. Nature would help him now that he was empty of confusion and of behaving as someone he wasn't. It would refill him, help him breathe and move his muscles and think, things he hadn't been able to do when Payson left him hours ago. The knowledge of how he'd been changed, duped into slavery for Diane, clattered in his body as he sat listless.

On the lawn chair beside him, his cellphone rang. He knew the ringtone, the same one that rang several times during the past few hours. It was Diane. He ignored it, letting it go to voicemail again. He had nothing to say to her right now. He felt nothing but disgust for himself, and he needed to sit with just that until he no longer needed to.

Then he'd find Payson. The need to talk with her, and only her, gripped his heart so hard it hurt.

The phone rang again. "Leave me alone," he hollered, grabbing it and throwing it to the ground. He jumped to his feet, no longer able to contain the pain of what had happened, what he'd done, what he'd lost.

He marched inside and upstairs to his bedroom. He pulled on his running shoes and did some warm-up stretches, then went out front and sprinted down the sidewalk, his insides wailing. He couldn't care less where his feet took him, he just had to move or he would explode.

He ran past landscaped lawns, past a community playground, running, running. Sweat dripped into his eyes, and he concentrated on his heavy breathing and the plodding sound of his feet on pavement. Echoes of the words he had used and the attitude he had adopted under Diane's block drove him on. Past restaurants, banks, and downtown shops. He slowed his pace, realizing how far he'd run and suddenly knowing where he was going. The façade above Coffee Is snagged his attention.

Could I be so lucky? He shook his head. *Probably not.* He pulled the door open and stepped into the shop and waves of familiarity crashed through him. He remembered this place and the people he had been with.

A lively hum vibrated inside him and this time he knew what it meant. A smile stretched muscles stiff from frowning and somberness as he scanned the interior, his gaze drawn to a table in the back. He stared without moving. The woman with the long, black hair at the table slowly turned in her chair, her eyes meeting his. He held his breath, waiting for the right words to form. "Payson?" was all he could say. He took a step in her direction.

Payson stood and came to him. "Braden. You found me."

"I did. I knew where to go." He took her hands, and love streamed. "I know now, everything."

She stepped closer, cupping his face in her hand. "I'm so sorry."

He put a finger to her mouth. "Shh ... you have nothing to apologize for and I have everything to say I'm sorry for."

"Hey, you two. Can you tear apart long enough to join me?" Skye gestured them to the table. "Coffee is on the house. And whatever else you want, Braden. Benjamin, can you bring us coffees?"

"Will do," the young man called back. "Anything special?"

"You know what I like," Skye said.

"Just black coffee for me. You too Braden?" Payson arched an eyebrow.

"Yes. Thank you, Skye. It feels good to be here and remember my place with friends and fellow Aeons."

"So you're back, memories and all?" Skye quirked an eyebrow.

"Yes, as far as I can tell." He exchanged a smile with Skye, but he quickly turned back to Payson. Unsure of a lot of things, he was certain he wanted never to leave her side, but he didn't know what she wanted. Could they get back to what they'd shared before, before he'd lost himself? He pulled out the chair for her and she took her seat at the table. "May I?" he asked, pointing to the chair beside her.

"Of course."

"So, Braden. Are you the elephant in the room tonight?"

He chuckled. He had always liked Skye. "By that you mean you feel uncomfortable with my presence?"

Skye slanted her head. "More like, uncomfortable with your absence over the last week or so, and here you are all of a sudden, back at our table and sitting beside Payson."

"I understand." Shadows of his past week flitted in his mind, sending shivers slithering through him. "I'll have to earn your trust. I hope I've learned valuable lessons from what happened to me so I can be a better man now. I may stumble for a while, but I hope you and the others," he swallowed hard and turned to Payson, "can wait for me to catch up."

"Here you go." Benjamin slid coffees in front of them.

A bright whir emanated from him, and Braden's curiosity piqued to know more about this budding Aeon. "How are you, Benjamin? Things going well?"

Benjamin shrugged one shoulder. "Things are going. Got to mind the customers, making those espressos and such," he said, going toward the counter.

Skye pursed her lips and stared at him. "Braden, do you mind if I read your aura?"

"It's sobering to realize I forgot about Aeon abilities under Diane's block, even my own." He nodded to Skye and she closed her eyes. He couldn't blame her for making sure he was safe to be around.

He stared at Payson, yearning to touch her.

Skye's eyes snapped open. "Whoa, a flash of turquoise just then. You reached out with your energy to connect with Payson. It felt very nice. Overall, your aura is a rippled orange. That fits your ability to control people with your intention. The rippled means your aura is in fair shape. If it were in good shape it would be smooth, but you're on your way to healing."

"I think that ability had something to do with why Diane took me. She referred to my persuasiveness and wanted to use me to control other people to benefit her business."

"Did you know about your ability while Diane was in control?" Payson tilted her head, drawing his attention to her perfect bow-shaped lips.

"No." Inwardly shaking his head to clear it, he refocused. "I noticed a couple times that what I wanted would happen, such as for her to hang up the phone, but I thought it was a coincidence."

Skye knitted her brow. "So your ability still had power, but not as much, probably because you weren't focusing it."

"That makes sense, since you weren't aware of it." Payson fingered a long lock of hair. He couldn't not notice the sheen of the dark strands.

"Thank you for letting me take a look," Skye said. "You are being forthright with us. But, you should know that although your aura looks coherent, there are also splotches of white. You have a lack of harmony in your body and mind."

"I'm still processing what happened and reconciling my role in being vulnerable to Diane's Dark Sides."

Skye waved her fingers in the air. "We're talking all clinical and wordy wordy, but what you're saying sounds healthy to me. You've been put through a lot of disruptive experiences, and taking responsibility where due is not the same as blaming yourself. Remember that."

He shrugged. He wasn't done with self-loathing and there was no reason to discuss it with Skye. He eyed Payson. "I don't want to interrupt you two any further." *Not true. I came here for a reason.* He couldn't do anything until he'd squared things with Payson.

"I have a skip I need to find." Payson's gaze dropped to papers lying on the table. "We need to talk, but I can't right now. How about I call you when I have more time?"

The searing, just under the skin static of his life upending and then falling back into familiar territory, juddered through him. It wouldn't be right to force his need on her. "Yes, later, then." He shoved back his chair.

Payson put her hand on his shoulder. "You don't have to leave. I could use your professional input."

"You bounty hunter, me stay-in-car." The memory from days ago lit in his head.

"Still true, but things change. While you were away, all of us decided to expand our challenge to the Dark Sides. You and I could pool our resources and have a greater impact on justice."

"Sounds good. What do you have?" The gravity of what had happened to his life-long relationship with Payson spun inside him. It pulled his muscles tight, and he suspected her gesture didn't mean the whole ordeal was over. As much as he wanted to jump back into where they'd left off, it couldn't happen with a wish. But she wanted his help. She wasn't dismissing him out of hand. He would take what he could get. It was enough for now.

"The skip's name is Eddie Crow. He's thirty-eight years old and Irish. He's due in court regarding charges for Class D drug trafficking."

"You have last known addresses, I see. That is downtown." He pointed to one of the addresses.

"Yeah, I looked it up." Payson nodded. "His family runs the Aisling's Irish Pearl restaurant and he's purported to live in an apartment above it. I didn't find any criminal records on the members of the family. I'll send you the information I have."

"I know that name. Eddie Crow, and that face," he said, pointing to Eddie's mug shot. "He's connected to money laundering and drug distribution." A suspicion spiked in Braden's mind. He squinted, trying to pull up information. "I'm not sure, but I think this guy is on my list of suspects for the robberies I've been investigating."

"I'll find him," Payson said, shoving the papers into a file and closing it. "He's apparently not lying low if you're right about the robberies."

Skye leaned closer across the table. "Email me a copy of these documents and I'll put out my feelers. A couple new customers come to mind. They are pretty friendly types, but their energy gives me the creeps. One of them speaks with a bit of an accent, could be Irish."

"Thanks, both of you, for your input." Payson's gaze swept the room, then she carried her dinner dishes and trash to a bin.

Panic jittered through him. "Are you going after this Eddie guy now?"

Payson picked up her file and looked into his face. His breath caught. Losing her and then getting a second chance made everything acute and close up. He couldn't help but cherish the snap in her eyes, the strength in her gaze.

"Yeah. My schedule is getting backed up. I'm going to check off Eddie Crow tonight."

"I could come with you."

"This is not police business yet, Braden."

"Funny. You remember that cockeyed remark of mine when I ran into you downtown."

She held his gaze. "I do."

"I'm so sorry. It was a rude thing to say."

"You didn't say it. Another Braden did."

Her light and love pulsed so strongly his own joined in and time paused. "Thank you."

"Honestly, I can handle my assignment."

"Okay, so we'll talk later," he mumbled, losing the starch in his bones. The idea of Payson out at night hunting a drug dealer didn't exactly make him feel all warm and fuzzy.

"Yes. Later. I want to talk with you, Braden. And don't give me that look."

"What look?" He was stupid to try to deny his concern.

"The one that says you think I'm going to be in danger. I can take care of myself."

A smile in his heart beamed. She knew him, and as long as she did, he would not lose himself again. He took her elbow and directed her out the doors, into the summer evening. "You're right. The Payson I know can kick ass. But that doesn't mean I like the prospects of you going after Eddie alone. I talked with a robbery suspect today, Warren Brown. He admitted that he runs a group of individuals he calls disrupters. I tried to press him to give me more details about what that meant, but he didn't budge."

"Did you say Warren Brown?"

"Yeah, he thinks he's a tough guy."

"He's the guy who gave me this." Payson touched the cut on her neck. "He is very powerful."

"What? You didn't tell me about him?" He gave her cut a closer inspection. "I don't like what he did to you."

"Me either. He said he did for Diane, which makes his connection to her very clear. It happened while you were with Diane."

Braden shook his head. "Diane? That's awful. I'm so sorry."

"It wasn't your doing. I'm okay. Brown gave us both grief."

"He has a roll, clearly, in the level of darkness in Auralia."

Braden's thoughts drifted, knocked around by learning Brown had hurt Payson. What he would do to protect her, to turn back the clock to before Diane had mesmerized him.

Payson rubbed her finger across her lips and he couldn't focus.

"Disrupters doesn't sound like a good thing. Disrupters could mean—"

"People who commit diversions otherwise known as robberies that serve the purpose of making people apprehensive and scared. Fear would make people more vulnerable to DA influence. Exactly why I don't want you out alone. Diane is still out there."

She turned to face him, stopping him in his tracks, and laid her hands flat on his chest. Warmth spread from his chest outward to the rest of his body. "Do you feel that? I am strong in my heart and soul. My confidence comes from my beliefs. We connect in this energy for as long as you sustain positive energy within yourself."

Her words massaged him, brought him to a place of faith and power. "Right. The truth of myself comes back stronger to me when I'm around you."

"It's always been that way for both of us. Remember?" A sorrowful note in her voice made him wish, so hard, that he could erase the last seven days of his life and start from here as though nothing terrible had torn them apart.

"I'm remembering. It's painful. I know all of the things that have happened to us are going to remain a part of us. But we're more than that past."

"We are. Much more."

CHAPTER 19

$\mathcal{P}$AYSON PARKED DOWN an alley two blocks from the Aisling's Irish Pearl, dressed in jeans and a plain grey T-shirt. A short brown wig covered her hair, and she walked in to the pub wearing her running shoes.

An Irish tune greeted her from the overhead speakers.

"My name is Jesse. One, tonight, Miss?" A young man in a crew-neck and skinny jeans smiled.

"I'd like a seat at the bar." She scanned the room to get a feel for the place, noting the emergency exit at the back wall.

"Okay, it's right through there. Enjoy your evening."

She lifted up onto a bar stool, her muscles tense. "I'll have a tonic water with lime," she ordered, and minutes later, the bartender slid her drink toward her.

"I've never seen you in here before." The red-haired woman behind the bar paused in front of Payson.

Payson smiled. "It's my first time. I've heard about this place and thought I'd check it out."

"You'll like it. My name is Meara. I grew up in this restaurant."

"Your parents run it?" It was just small talk, but Payson relied on it put a source at ease. This Meara could be a relative of her skip.

"Ownership of the restaurant has been in my family for many years. Great grandparents on down to my dad and mom now. When I come home from college during breaks, I work here."

"Are you going to be the next owner, you and your siblings?"

Meara chuckled. "I'm not. I'm majoring in graphic design. I have two brothers and many cousins. Surely one or some of them would be better suited to the restaurant business. I want a life of my own."

"You have plans, places to go, things to do?" Payson sipped her drink.

"Exactly." Someone called for a bartender and Meara went to take an order.

Payson checked the time. It was eight o'clock and the restaurant was filling up, but no sign of Eddie Crow. As promised, Skye had emailed her information she'd gotten from one of her new patrons. It told her that Eddie was related to the Aisling family through his mother, Anna, a daughter who had married Davis Crow. Davis and Anna worked in the family business.

Payson read Skye's email, tuning out the noises around her.

The two patrons I mentioned are friends of Eddie's. They've left. Obvious tweakers. I wouldn't want to be in a dark alley with either one. Don't worry. I was coy about getting information, like one tweaker to another.

"Can I refill your drink?" Meara asked, back from other customers.

Payson put aside her phone. "No, I'm fine. So Anna Crow is your aunt?"

Meara stiffened. "Yes, how do you know her?"

"I've heard the name. People say she's a very good cook in your kitchen. Makes wonderful rolls."

"She does." Meara glanced at her through narrowed eyes.

Meara's tense stance and suspicious gaze clued Payson it was time to dig deeper. She expanded her light trying to soothe any needless defenses, leaned closer, and spoke low. "I'll be very honest with you. Though it's true I've heard good things about your aunt's rolls, I'm not here for them. I'm looking for your cousin, Eddie Crow."

Meara slapped a towel against the bar top. "Are you Homeland Security? Someone is always looking for Eddie. What's he done now?"

"I'm not with Homeland Security. I'm a recovery agent. Umm ... he's into some criminal activity and has a court date. My job is to make sure he doesn't miss that date." She frowned. "I'm sorry to bring bad news, Meara, you've been so nice."

"Oh, I understand. I got nervous when you mentioned my aunt because when Eddie is on the run his family is pulled in."

"Does Eddie live upstairs?" Payson pointed up.

"Last I knew. I try to keep out of his sphere." Meara pursed her lips and rested one hand on her hip. "Do you want me to take you up to see if he's there?"

Payson jumped off her stool. Adrenalin surged through her veins. "I don't really want to involve you. If you could show me the way, I'll check out the upstairs myself."

"Follow me." Meara pulled a ring of keys out of her pocket and led her through a hall that ended at a door.

Payson noticed an outside door around the corner with a sign that read Employees Only. "Is this an entrance for Eddie's apartment?"

"Yes. He comes in this back door." She unlocked the door to the upstairs. "His apartment is at the top of the stairs on the right. Be careful."

Quietly, Payson called the APD. "This is recovery agent Payson Silver requesting back up at the apartment above Aisling's Irish Pearl," she told dispatch and supplied the address. "I'm here picking up skip Eddie Crow for Best Bond Company. Suspect skip is armed and dangerous."

"Sending officers now."

A reminder played in Payson's head to wait for the cops to arrive. Her confidence ignored it.

She crept up the stairs, checking her belt holster at her back just once. The shrieking of sirens assured her the police were close.

Voices and noises inside put her on alert. She clenched her fists. Eagerness to secure her subject warred with caution and waiting. Anything could happen and she had to be prepared for that. She stood outside the door, breathing deeply. A slight shift on her feet and her breath froze. A loose floorboard creaked. The room got silent.

"Who's there?" called out a man's voice.

"FedEx delivery." Footsteps approached the door. Payson stiffened, taking a solid stance just before the door opened.

"It's eight o'clock. Aren't you out a little late? Where's the package?" It was Eddie, and he directed a stern look at her.

She slipped her foot in the doorway, just in case, and reached for Eddie's arm, clamping down on the unseen ugliness that threatened to attach to her. Swiftly, she twisted his arm behind his back and pulled him toward her. "Eddie Crow, I'm a recovery agent." She heard the police cruisers arriving.

He hollered loud and kicked at her. "Who are you? You can't just barge in here."

She yanked harder at him, wincing when he landed a hard kick to her shin. She kept her eyes hard on the two other men in the room, ignoring Eddie's protests. One of them pulled a knife from his leg and thrust it at her, but she dodged aside and it clattered to the floor.

She threw Eddie face down to the floor, pressing on his back, and pulled out her nine millimeter. She pinned the two other men with her gaze. "I'll shoot if you don't freeze."

Both men stood motionless, caught off guard by her gun.

"Geez, guys. You gonna let this little snit of a woman take me in?" His accent shaped his words only a little.

She pushed Eddie's head back down. "Shut up," she demanded. Power thrummed through her as she managed the scene.

"Lady, you know we're coming after you as soon as you step out the door." The knife-thrower glared at her with steely eyes. She recognized the face. It was the purse-snatcher.

"I'd advise against that. Ryan Crow."

Ryan frowned, but worse, his darkness throbbed, like a sore overwhelmed with infection. Her whole body ached.

Peace, light, and love to you. She recited the words for his sake as well as her own. "I already notified the police. Just sit tight there on the couch. You get bonus points for not interfering further." She had no authority for taking them in, but they'd threatened her and thrown a knife. They'd be arrested too for assault.

Steps pounding up the stairs echoed in the hallway. "Here, I'm here with the skip."

"Let me go and there'll be money in it for you."

When she didn't respond, Eddie tried another tack. "I have connections. People know me. You're going to regret this, I assure you."

"Auralia Police." One of the two uniformed who stepped up behind Payson announced himself. "Hey, Payson. You got your guy. Good job."

She knew most of the police on the force. Grateful for his respect, she shrugged. "It's my job."

"Did these other two give you some trouble?"

"They tried to." She pointed at Ryan. "He threw a knife at me."

"I take it he missed. We'll handle them."

The two officers cuffed and read all three their rights. Payson grabbed Eddie and the officers grabbed the other two and headed down the stairs.

Sweat beaded on Eddie's face and she smiled to herself, realizing he wasn't the cool cucumber he had made himself out to be.

"You're going to regret this, lady. You don't know my boss. He's not going to be happy with you."

"Is that right? Who is your boss?"

"Somebody you don't want to mess with."

Down the stairs and out to the cars, Eddie continued to threaten and tried to talk himself out of his predicament. It was all background noise to Payson. She needed to stay on task, but thoughts of Braden surfaced over and over. She'd stepped right back into his arms so easily. She wanted to call him just to hear his voice, like nothing had ever happened. But something had. He left her. He. Left. Her.

A quiet part of her retreated from the idea of calling. How could he have done that?

No, now I'm being silly. He'd found her at the café. He'd followed his instincts, instincts that had been stymied.

And he had broken through Diane's block. Her heart warmed, confident Braden would call her. So when she shoved Chatty Cathy into the back of one of the cruisers, she amplified her energy of love and directed it toward him instead of punching him in the face.

BRADEN JUGGLED HIS LARGE, Coffee Is coffee while opening the door to the room where he worked. He set his coffee on his desk and took a sip, so glad he decided to forego the predictable stale coffee at the APD and fuel up with truly good stuff this morning.

Energy buzzed through him and his mind whirled with connecting dots. So many things had clarified since he had come out of the block, including associated leads to criminal activity. He could see, but not prove, Diane's fingers in crimes and would-be crimes. He swallowed hard. He couldn't ignore her forever.

He argued with the bed sheets and blankets most of the night. Antsy for news from Payson that she'd captured her bail jumper without incident, he'd been on alert. He had expected a call from her, but when it hadn't come, he reasoned himself out of calling her. Diane had put her through a lot because of him. Maybe he needed to prove things to her before she could get comfortable.

Oh, crap. I should have called her last night.

He punched in her number and listened as her phone rang, then rang again, and he waited, drumming his fingers on his desk.

"Hi, Braden."

"Hi. I miss you. I didn't call you last night."

He counted four seconds before she responded.

"No, you didn't. But then, I didn't call you."

"I'm sorry. I didn't sleep at all."

"Why not?"

"Can you forgive me?"

"For not sleeping?"

She was going to make this hard. "For not calling. I was unsure what to do." He glanced around the room, looking to see if anyone was listening.

Her sigh put a pin in his worries. "I didn't call you for the same reason."

"Okay, I'm glad we talked about it. Did everything go okay last night?"

"You mean did I get my man? Yes. It was a bit touch and go for a few minutes, but he's in jail now."

His muscles clenched. "What do you mean by touch and go?"

"Eddie was with friends, knife carrying friends. His buddy Ryan Crow, the purse-snatcher, was there too."

"Interesting. Someone took care of his bail. Are you all right?"

"I am. You didn't need to worry. I told you I know what I'm doing." Even though they'd covered this ground, her voice remained warm, soothing, not crisp and annoyed. "I get it. We lost each other. It would be natural for you to be vigilant for any chance of that happening again."

Her words went directly to his fears, easing his anxiety. She allowed him to have qualms, and that in itself was helpful. "Thank you for understanding."

"We can talk any time."

Even with her understanding, a layer of detachment frustrated him. Was it her mistrust that shielded her from him, or a remainder of his mental block? He had to see her. "Do you have time today to meet? Or would you like to go out to dinner tonight?" His nerves rippled. Women didn't make him uncomfortable. But with Payson, his need to do things right rattled him.

Silence on her end hung between them. He knew better than to use his ability to influence her decision, but it was right there, begging.

"I would like that. My schedule today is full, so dinner would be nice. Where and when?"

"I'll figure out the where. I'll pick you up about six, if that works for you."

"It does."

"Do you think you can find your way to my place?" Her teasing tone made him chuckle.

"I remember where you lived eight days ago."

"Good. Six it is, then. I'll text you the security code to use at the gate. And Braden, watch yourself, please. We've created an earthquake and I have no doubt Diane has felt the tremors."

"I'm ready for her." He was more interested in discovering Diane's part in serious criminal activity than confronting her, but it would be inevitable.

"Remember, I'm here for you and you have the support of the others, as well. You're not alone in this."

The concept glided through him with a tinge of familiarity. The sense of belonging echoed from before the block and settled in his cells. "It's a good feeling to know our little band of Aeons can count on one another. Something tells me before everything with Diane concludes, we may all face deep darkness."

She chuckled. "I like that term, band of Aeons."

He hung up, savoring the effects of Payson. He could breathe easier. His heart pumped blood through his body with more vigor. Thoughts were clearer.

He tapped into these effects and sorted through the information he had already gathered regarding the robberies. He saw lines spreading from Diane and forming clusters, each one connecting different people involved in different projects and crimes. And he wondered, where or who was the nexus?

He couldn't put Eddie Crow out of his mind, and checked his suspects in his investigation. Sure enough, he had pulled his name in his preliminary process. Disquiet congealed in his chest. Diane's block had thrown a switch on his investigation, diverting him to another trajectory, unmasking, in a way, her adversaries.

He pulled up the Record of Arrests and Prosecutions, RAP sheet, for Eddie Crow on his laptop. The list was long of his interactions with the criminal justice system since coming to the United States, and included laundering, armed robbery, assault of a police officer, and the recent charge of drug trafficking. Braden compared it to the copies Payson had sent him of paperwork from Keegan's bond company and copied her notes of last known address and acquaintances. "Here it is." Warren Brown stood out at him on Payson's list. This fact added to his suspicions that put

Eddie in a cluster with Brown, which led to a direct association with Diane.

"Hey, Braden." Zane walked into the room and sat down at his desk. "You look like you're deep into something."

"Things are coming together on a couple of fronts." He glanced at Zane. He hesitated to disclose much information to Zane. He had no reason to suspect Zane was anything but a good cop, but he had to use caution. He breathed a sigh, realizing Zane's lack of chaotic energy meant he was okay.

"Need any help?" Zane gulped his coffee, making a face. "This coffee is cold. I'm going to make a new pot."

Braden scrubbed the top of his head, trying to find connection points that weren't obvious. "Thanks for the offer, but I'm still trying to piece things together." He stood and stuffed his phone in his pocket and shoved his gun in its holster. "I'm taking off. See you later."

He stepped out of the building, striding straight to his car. He saw it in the parking lot and it struck him how odd his car was such a flashy model. He stopped. It wasn't his car. He drove an SUV. Where did his SUV go? Clearly the Fiat belonged to Diane, another part of the lie she'd made of his life.

He would hunt down his own vehicle later. The Fiat would do for now. He had a hunch, and his friend at city hall in the planning department, Reid Curtis, could help him follow it. Reid could show him the proposal package for construction of the new development.

"Where are you going?" A man blocked Braden's path to his car, his lips pursed, his eyes menacing. Two other men stepped up beside him, equally tall, built, and glowering.

A vibration like that of an old window air conditioner rattled in his gut. *DAs.* He shoved the man aside, ignoring the question.

Another man in the trio grabbed his upper arm and yanked, stopping him in his tracks. "He asked you a question."

Braden shrugged him off and stared deep into the man's eyes. "I heard him. I have an appointment."

"Yeah, we know. We're taking you to see Diane." The three walls stood in a line blocking his path.

Braden aimed his intention at the group, telling them to back off. His head hurt, holding his objective steady and hard. This was the most forceful and deliberate use of his ability since he had recovered from the block, and the effort shrieked inside him.

The men stood there glaring back. Braden could sense their attempt at refusal of his directive, but he stood firm in his intention.

"If you don't come with us, we'll make it more appealing to you." The man smirked and turned to one of the others. "Say, you still have that address in your head?"

The other man nodded, and all three stared at him. He narrowed his eyes. "What address?"

"Payson's." The first man dropped her name like a rock.

Anger ignited in his gut. He raised his fist. "You stay away from her, you hear me?" His breaths got short and rapid. Of course they wanted Payson, wanted to destroy her goodness. He would not let them. He marched close to the first man, every muscle tensed to beat him to a pulp.

"Oh, you see that boys? Mr. Aeon here is ready to fight for his girl."

The sharp rumble in his ears drove him to end their threat. He needed to end them. *Braden, simmer.* Sanity reined in his anger. He shook his head and backed up. The DAs had almost gotten him. *Are you really so easy, so close to darkness?*

"No." He spoke out loud but he was speaking to himself.

"What do you mean no?"

"I'm not going with you." He slowed his breathing and focused his ability. They didn't stand a chance. They had no defenses against him, even with his rusty ability. He remembered his strength and let confidence expand in his chest.

"You have better things to do, right? I have no quarrel with you and you have none with me." He took another step away. "You have the wrong guy."

The DA slanted his head. "We have the wrong guy." He exchanged looks with the other two DAs. "Let's get out of here. We have better things to do." The three moved out of Braden's way, barely noticing him.

He watched over his shoulder as he went to his car. They continued to walk down the street and around a corner without a backward glance. Braden sighed heavily. The exertion of his mind control ached in his brain and his muscles. But it had worked well.

He slipped behind the wheel, his skin prickling. The car with all its luxury and status repulsed him. "Yuck." He patted the console. "No offense, but you're not my style, I just need wheels. You belong to someone else."

His mind shifted as he drove to city hall, parked, and took the elevator to the third floor where Reid worked. Groups of cubicles dotted a large room that Braden strode through toward Reid's office. Heads raised noting him. Some smiles greeted him; others gave him a distant look of distraction. *Benign attention.* Exactly what he had hoped for. He didn't want to be noticed.

Reid's office door stood open, so Braden strode in. "Hi, Reid."

His friend circled his desk and stretched out his hand. "Braden. Have a seat." He motioned to the one chair that wasn't piled with file folders and papers. He leaned against his desk. "What brings you in here?"

Braden cranked his head around Reid, noting the lack of open space on his desk. "Geez, Reid. Organize much?"

Reid chuckled. "It looks disorganized, but I know exactly where to find things."

"Whatever works. I shouldn't yank your chain. I need a favor."

Reid rolled his eyes, but grinned. "You know I'm happy to help, as long as what you're asking isn't illegal."

"No, it's not." Braden smiled back. "I'm doing background on a development Principal Industries is spearheading. Can I see the proposal submitted for the Stillwell Place development and the casino?"

Reid surveyed his stacks. "Are you looking for anything specific? Maybe I can help."

"No, I can't be any more specific. I want to see the proposal. Is that a problem?" Braden scratched his head, trying to ignore suggestions in his mind that Reid was trying to put him off.

Reid moved some files from a chair to his desk, shoving aside a couple piles to make room. "No, it's just these stacks." He spread his arms and shook his head. "It will take me a couple minutes. Ordinarily, the proposal would be in the file cabinet, but I had it out last night for the Plan Commission's meeting."

Trying for nonchalance, Braden surveyed the office for anything that could clue him into a possible connection between Reid and Diane. Just before giving up, he noticed a pen lying on the desk imprinted with Diane's lobby company, Butler and Associates. His teeth clenched.

He picked up the pen, rolling it between his fingers. "Did you steal this pen? It's a nice looking pen." He pinned Reid in his gaze.

But Reid barely noticed the question, lifting his eyes briefly. "Funny. Of course not. Diane Butler stopped in to check on the same proposal you're interested in. She must have left it behind. Here it is. I knew I had the right pile." He laid the oversized file folder on his desk and opened it.

"Man, you need to join the digital age." He tapped the top of Reid's monitor. "Keep your files at your fingertips in folders on your desktop."

"Again with the jokes. Of course, I use computer files. But I made notes on the proposal documents at the meeting last night. So stop bellyaching and have a look before I kick you out." Reid gave him a light-hearted chuckle again and pointed to the file. "I'm going to refill my coffee. Do you want a cup?"

"No." Braden's head was already in the paperwork. "I'll get started here."

Reid left behind him a trail of brief conversations on the way to wherever the coffee waited, so Braden knew he'd have the proposal to himself for a few minutes. The first thing he saw at the top of page one was the economic director's name listed as the contact person. Braden rubbed his thumb over his chin. *Why would Tim Brody be the lead, not someone from the planning department?*

The comprehensive proposal covered everything from the name of the developer, Principal Industries, to summaries of each component of the Stillwell Place construction. It included types of materials, how many office and retail spaces and apartments—and each space's floor plan and dimensions—in the proposed multi-use buildings.

Interesting but not what I'm looking for.

He flipped through each page and each sketch and illustration until he found the request for contractor bids, market analysis, environmental impact study, and the funding source. He traced the summary outlining the investment of Principal Industries and its request for support from the city. According to the document, the city was offering tax waivers and the creation of an enterprise zone, grants, and large loans.

The information troubled him. He would have to ask Reid some questions, though, before he jumped to false conclusions.

He tore into the section of the proposal in which details were given regarding the construction of the casino. Again, the contact person was Tim Brody. He quickly read through wording similar to the sections describing the multi-use buildings and scanned the proposed funding and cash flow charts.

"Finding what you need?" Reid walked in and sat his coffee cup on a small bare spot on his desk.

"I think so. But I have a couple questions."

"Shoot."

Braden bent over the paperwork and pointed to the cash flow chart for the casino. "These numbers don't make sense to me. It looks like the city's investment and incentives amount to a whole lot more than what the casino and the multi-use developments can produce in the permanent loan period. Or am I wrong?"

Reid closed the office door. "No, you're not wrong. But the city," he gestured air quotes, "believes the non-quantitative value of the projects will pay off in the long run." He dropped his gaze and was suddenly very intrigued by his shoes.

"Oh. Like enhanced ratings in magazines? I can see the headline, 'Auralia, the new hotspot of the Midwest.' And 'Premium water-front housing available in quaint town,' though the quaint will be bulldozed into the ground if this proposal passes, right?"

He looked squarely at Braden. "The city really wants this casino and the property redevelopment. Some members of the city staff believe securing this deal will give them a big gold star on their resume." He stared out the window. "There is significant pressure to acquiesce."

"Significant pressure, meaning just what exactly?" He didn't like the sound of that. Politics could be ugly, but not in Auralia.

"I've been visited by some very influential people."

"Threats! You've been threatened? Who threatened you, Reid?" Braden could swear that steam was about to come out of his ears.

Reid's expression slackened. "I don't remember, exactly. Isn't that funny?"

"No, it's not." Now he knew exactly why Diane had visited Reid. He guessed she'd given Reid orders he objected to, and then she blocked his mind of any alternatives, backed by severe consequences for not cooperating. "What was the threat?"

"I don't want to involve you. I need to keep quiet." His voice hushed. "I have a family."

Braden slammed a fist on the desk. "I'm a cop. I can't just sit back and let you be bullied." He breathed in deep pulls. "But, okay, I understand. You didn't tell me anything."

Reid's expression drooped. "What's happening to our town? I know change is inevitable, but I've lived here all my life and I've always believed the community was safe and free of any serious criminal activity. Now I'm not sure."

Braden nodded. "There is a darkness taking hold. But you're not alone. There are others, including me, who are going to turn the lights on and watch the cockroaches scurry when there is no escaping."

His lips a thin line, Reid grabbed Braden's shoulder. "Thank you."

"I have one more question. I noticed the economic director is listed as the contact for the Principal Industries projects. Is that irregular? Shouldn't the contact be a plan department employee?"

Reid nodded. "Maybe you should find the answer to that yourself."

"Sure. Could we exchange cellphone numbers?"

Reid slanted his head. "Why?"

"So that I can readily keep in touch and you can reach out to me if you need help. I'm not going to share it."

"Okay."

Braden added the number to his contacts and shared his. He held Reid's gaze for a bit longer, then moved to the door. He opened it and stopped. "Take care of yourself."

CHAPTER 20

BREEZES FRESHENED THE summer air and Payson breathed it in, letting it invigorate her as she moved fluidly from the firefly pose into a peacock on her deck outside. Her breaths measured, she executed her yoga poses in detached concentration. The movements rested her brain, improved her flexibility, and kept her muscles toned. Keeping balanced physically and emotionally improved her athleticism, which her work called for, and kept her sane. The sane part hadn't come easily, growing up in a world that didn't understand her.

Her chest pinched and stress tightened her shoulders, remembering how hard life had gotten.

"Payson, you have so much potential. If only you would concentrate on your studies, you could be such a good student."

Payson cringed at the tsk tsk attitude from her English teacher.

"I am trying." The shame of that moment and many, many others scratched at her gut, just as it had years ago.

Another recollection pulled her knees to her chest. *"Payson, come with us. We're all going to the home game. Please, please, please. You never do anything after school with us."*

Her friends had not understood that her freak show life often left her too drained to go out and have fun.

SHALLOW BREATHS DEEPENED, thinking of how one teacher had directed her to Claire Eve, and one particular session echoed up from her past and she was that sad, young girl.

She stomped her foot. "Are you listening to me, Claire Eve? I just told you I can't sleep. A swarm of voices and images fills my brain every night. Every day everything I touch gives me pain. I can't touch people without getting flashes of their lives. I can't even have a life of my own."

Claire Eve stopped her slow twisting at the waist. "Yes, I heard you, Payson. It's very hard at fifteen to have too much input coming at you all day and night."

"Twenty-four-seven." Her fury boiled. "Then why are you asking me to do these silly movements? I need real help."

"I agree. And the Qi Gong movement we're doing, Knocking on the Door of Life, is help. It's a way to find a sense of calm and your own center. Focusing on the movements and the breathing will give you peace from all the sensory input available to you but that is now driving you into a frenzy."

"I can't."

Payson trembled, remembering the frustration of being unable to find the patience to help herself.

"It's a skill that takes practice. Now, bend slightly at your knees, take in a deep breath and let it out slowly. Relax your shoulders."

The memories subsided in gratefulness for Claire Eve. Payson sat in lotus position, just breathing, releasing anything in her energy field that didn't belong to her and imagining herself becoming one with the air around her. Completely relaxed, she enjoyed her ability to sit like that for as long as she chose—ten minutes, twenty minutes, an hour.

Sounds in the cove drifted through her consciousness and she continued to sit. Soft pounding drifted into her awareness. It was ZuZu asking for attention. Or at least a meal.

· · ·

Payson stood and opened the sliding glass door to scoop up her cat. "Lunch time, huh? That's okay. I have work to do anyway." She kissed ZuZu, then placed her in front of her dish and loaded a couple tablespoons of cat food onto the plate.

Her notes and the file she had been working on at the island in her kitchen sat as she'd left them earlier, reminding her of the missing young woman. Her gut told her she knew who was responsible for Shana's disappearance, the suspicious Sam Cain hiding in the bushes spying on her. But she needed more information. For that, she would need to stop by Fancy This and talk with Ainsley.

She brushed her fingers over her cellphone's screen, so eager to update Shana's mother but holding back. Reporting the information she had now wouldn't do much for Adele but kindle more fear.

In her bedroom, she changed from her yoga clothes in to her well-worn jeans and a white T-shirt, and stuffed her files on Shana into a big cloth bag.

"Bye, ZuZu! Kisses."

Driving to town, her attention split. Finding Shana stood paramount. If she were still alive, it was high time for a rescue. But the idea of going to dinner with Braden later kept drawing her thoughts. He hadn't told her where they were going, so she had to pick an outfit that could be casual but sophisticated. Visuals of clothing danced in her mind. She smiled to herself, remembering he had once told her his favorite color. It wasn't blue or green. It was a warm terra-cotta, like her skin.

Her heart clenched. Braden was now and always had been so dear to her. But the absolute terror of the potential consequences of getting back with him reverberated through her. This time had to be different. She had to grow her abilities in order to have true freedom and genuine safety, not just for herself and Braden but also for the people of Auralia.

She parked down the street from Fancy This, refocusing on her work. Entering the store, she kept her hands to herself and took cleansing breaths to keep her energy field coherent.

"Hi Payson." Ainsley set a large blue vase on display and smiled at her.

"Hi. Sorry to barge in without calling ahead. My mind is a block of cheese."

Ainsley laughed. "First of all, you are not barging in. I'm happy to see you. Secondly, block of cheese?"

"I'm going out with Braden tonight." Warmth spread up her neck and into her cheeks.

"Oh. Ohh..." Ainsley pulled her into a hug. "I'm happy for you both." She pulled back and bit her lower lip. "And scared for you both."

Payson shrugged. "I'm scared for him." She held up crossed fingers on both hands. "But I'm hoping for the right and perfect situation for us both. Optimism is good."

"Yes, it is. Just stay aware, please."

"Right. Changing subjects." The cheer in her voice wasn't faked. In her heart, she believed, even though her mind told her to be wary. "Now, the reason I'm here is because I'm looking for help." She squinted. "I'm working a missing person case. Shana's been missing for two years."

"Let's go back to my office and talk." Ainsley strode toward the back of the shop.

Payson let her bag drop on the floor and pulled out her files. She laid photographs of Shana on a table. "I think I know who took her. But I'm having trouble narrowing down a location. Can you help?"

Ainsley closed her eyes as she held one of the pictures in which Shana was sleeping on the couch in her parent's house. She didn't use her precognition very often, even though she was highly skilled, and Payson knew why. Pain in a memory of watching her friend suffer reverberated in her body from a rough experience. It was a time after Ainsley allowed a psychic impression to rise, then had to watch as individuals were killed. After she learned of their actual deaths, it had taken months for Payson and the other Aeons to convince her to crawl out of bed.

Ainsley moaned, her eyes still shut. "I can see her. This is..." She doubled over. "I can see her, but I can't get information about where this is." She sat on the chair, her face scrunched up, eyes shut.

"Can you describe what you see?"

"I see her trying to unlock a door. She gives up and sits on a small, single mattress on the floor." Ainsley's voice got small. "She's crying now."

"Do you see any windows?" Payson hated to put her friend through this.

"Oh, the vision has changed. She's outside in a forest. She is handcuffed to a man, and he's leading her to a car. He has light brown hair. The car is a brown, older model Impala."

Excitement lit in Payson's stomach, but she kept quiet.

"Michigan license plate is BN 2731."

Payson scribbled the number on a piece of paper. Elation filled her.

Ainsley opened her eyes. "That's it. The vision is over." She slumped in her chair. "I wish I could get more."

"This is a great lead, Ainsley. I can do a search with this number. I can't wait to get out there. Shana is alive. The guy I like for her kidnapping has brown hair."

"Remember, this is a vision of a possible future. Real-time changes still affect the future."

"I know, I know." She hugged Ainsley. "Thank you so much. Can I get you a drink of water or something? I'm sorry for what you saw."

"Don't worry about me. Just go find her. I wish I could be of more help."

"Well, what you have given me is confirmation that Shana is alive. And with that license plate number, the perp may be my suspect and he may still be in Michigan. That's a lot of useful information."

"Like I said, go find her, Payson." Her eyes welled with tears and Payson knew that Ainsley now had a stake in Shana's recovery.

She grabbed Ainsley's gaze and stayed there for a long few seconds as she expanded love until it flowed like warm caramel to her. "I will."

Guilt nearly sunk her as she drove to see Keegan at Best Bond

Company. She was in a hurry because of her date with Braden but she wanted to find Shana ASAP.

She walked briskly in to Keegan's, feeling bad for using him as a shortcut. Keegan could help expedite the search for Shana if he had the time. And she knew he would be eager to help if his schedule allowed.

He sat with a client at the front desk, and nodded in the direction of his private office.

Urgency jittered through her. She caught herself tapping her fingers in a frantic pace on the arm of the chair for twenty minutes.

"Payson, what can I do for you?" Keegan's good nature was his best feature, which was saying a lot because he had many. Right now she just wanted to use him…for information gathering.

"I know you've been busy, and I'm sorry for asking, but I need info. I'm chasing my tail."

"What do you need?"

She ran through the information she had gathered on Shana and added Ainsley's vision. "My instinct tells me I know the perp, and it's the guy I asked you about. Now, I feel so close to pinpointing Shana's location that I'm vibrating. I'm hoping you can help with that." She checked her phone for the time. "If you could find info and text me the details, it would really help me out."

"Don't be sorry. No problem. Go. Do. I'm glad to help. You're just using your contacts. SOP."

"I know. But if I didn't have a date, I would do the research myself."

"Oh, Payson." Keegan put his hand on his heart, sorrow in his eyes. "I'm not a mind reader but I am picking up strong guilt vibes and I can hear your words in your head, berating yourself for asking for my help. Want me to ignore this or do you feel like sharing?"

There was no deliberate intrusion with the Aeons, but there also were no secrets. She knew she would feel better if she didn't try to keep her problem from him. "I'm torn." She wriggled her arms and legs. "I desperately want to find this young woman before something more terrible than kidnapping happens. But, I want to keep the date. That makes me a selfish person.

"No, it makes you a woman who wants to save her missing person and save the love of her life. I can help."

"If you help me I'll be able to do both."

He slanted his head. "What's wrong with that? I've got time and why shouldn't you want to keep your date?"

Her heart pounded hard. "It's my job. I should do it."

"There's more, isn't there?" He rested his backside against his desk.

She spread her hands wide. "I don't want to lose him again. Pressure inside is warning that what happened before could happen again at any moment. Diane could show up—"

Keegan sprang to his feet and wrapped an arm around her shoulders. "I know." His words hung heavily. "Do me a favor?"

"Of course."

"Let me do this for you. Go be with Braden. You have catching up to do, or maybe you two need to begin again in order to have the close connection you had before the block. It's the right thing to do. Darkness is presenting in many ways. It's sneaky. We don't need to defeat Diane, but we do need to preserve our lights. You and Braden together make a very strong source of light."

The words powered through her, lifting the guilt. "You're right. Thank you, thank you."

He gave her a dismissive wave. "Will you get out of here?" He flashed a grin that stayed with her as she turned toward the door and strode out to her car.

Her tennis shoes shushed against the sidewalk. Beneath that sound whirred a low hum that jangled her nerves. A DA was near. Her breath caught. She saw it. Diane. Leaning with crossed arms against her car.

"Well, well, well. If it isn't Payson Silver, little Miss Goody Two-Shoes." Diane's eyes glared darkly. "Shouldn't you be off somewhere fighting the big, bad, boogey men?"

The sound of Diane's voice made Payson's teeth ache. The darkness in and around her was thick with rage and malevolence. It would be so easy to slip into negativity and shoot a clever quip at her. Completely unconstructive.

Then again, maybe it would send her arrogance wobbling. "Listen to you. Two clichéd phrases at once."

Diane narrowed her eyes. Payson didn't get any pleasure from slamming the witch, but it did the job of undermining her confidence.

Diane moved away from the car as Payson walked closer. "Cut the crap." She shook her finger in Payson's face. "I warned you there would be consequences if you didn't stay away from Braden." Her words sliced the air, but Payson was unmoved. "I know what you've done to him."

"I've done nothing *to* him. You're the person who tried to rob him of his life. But your block would hold for only so long and it wasn't impervious to genuine love."

Diane's eyes widened into saucers. "What have you done?"

"I thought you said you knew." Payson's throat tightened and Diane's eyes sent daggers in her direction.

"Specifically, what did you do?"

Payson coughed. "I told you. Love gave him back his free will." The ground started spinning as air cut off from her lungs. She closed her eyes. Her special ability couldn't stop Diane using her dark energies from strangling her, but she wasn't defenseless. She imagined a tiny ball of light in her chest. Concentrating on that light, the tightness in her throat lessened. As she focused on the ball of light, it expanded, growing in size and brilliance until it filled her body. She opened her eyes, and she pinned Diane in her gaze.

Diane stumbled back from her. "What are you doing?"

Payson stood firmly on the sidewalk and allowed the brilliance to flow out of her and stretch toward Diane.

Diane shrieked. "Get away from me," she said through gritted teeth.

"I'm not going to hurt you, Diane." A soft place in her knew Diane had only to accept the light and her need to attack would melt away.

But she resisted. Diane stood firmly rooted in her negativity. "You can't hurt me," she said, her voice again slick and viscous like a sweet poison. "Stay away from

Braden." Diane grabbed a handful of Payson's hair and yanked hard.

"Ouch! Let go of me." Payson winced. Diane's grip on her hair tore at her scalp.

Diane kicked Payson's shins, dropping her to the concrete. "You bitch! You think you're so beautiful and perfect. You make me sick. Everything is all your fault."

Images from Diane at a very young age made Payson's eyes flutter rapidly. Anger and suffering overwhelmed her heart. A ruining glare from her father as he yelled at her.

"You're not my kid. Your mother cheated on me."

"No, Daddy. I am your daughter."

"You're a little whore, just like your mother. I don't want you in my house. You're weird, doing your mind control on my dog, making him hate me. Don't even try to do anything on me."

"Please, Daddy, don't kick me out."

"You little beggar. Fine. I won't make you leave, but stay out of my way."

The pain in young Diane reverberated through Payson. Thoughts flashed through her brain like lightning. A child would never succumb to an imbalance of light and dark, but the play of rejection and hatred in a child's body would leave him or her susceptible to their dark aspect.

Diane released her hair and kicked at Payson. "I'm not going to tell you again. I'm biding my time, but not for long."

Payson stood and assumed a Karate fighting stance, then delivered a jab punch to Diane's face and followed with a roundhouse kick. Diane stutter-stepped backward, then crumpled bent over coughing.

"You're responsible."

"No, you're responsible. You don't even know, do you?"

PAYSON SHOOK HER HEAD. "How am I responsible for your hatred? You've had opportunities throughout your life to heal. To do good with your Aeon attributes, but you've been power hungry and selfish. Leave Braden alone."

Diane's eyes swirled with fury. It jabbered in Payson's head, but she got in her car and drove away, leaving Diane alone on the street.

WHAT IS IT like to share a moment so full of acceptance and love your heart glows? Braden knew.

Everything—the music, the clatter of dishes in the kitchen, chatter amongst diners—slipped to the background as he looked into Payson's eyes. Silence filled the space between them, but it was rich and intoxicating.

The right words had to be somewhere inside him. He centered on her beauty, her elegance, and those words formed. "I want to tell you how beautiful you look, Payson, but it wouldn't be enough. Of course you are beautiful, but what I mean to say is, thank you."

"Thank me for what?" She rested her chin on her hand and turned all her attention to him.

"How do I thank you for caring so much about me that you risked your life to defy Diane's cruelty?" His gut clenched, pulling from everything he was to give her the words she deserved to hear.

A tear drifted down her cheek, and she simply waited for him.

His eyelids threatened to close under the weight of his need to make things perfect again. "It took mesmerizing, blanking out my real life, to take me away from you. It was hell. Even without conscious awareness of you, I was lost. And you kept on believing in me and that I was entitled to choice. You gave me that opportunity."

"It didn't belong to Diane, your life." She pursed her lips. "Sometimes during those seven days, one-hundred-sixty-eight hours, give or take, I wondered how I would live without you in my life. I didn't think about that. I didn't want to."

"I can't fathom your courage. Diane could have hurt you, hurt you bad."

"It wasn't courage, Braden, that kept me going, it was love."

He reached for her hand and she grasped his. Her touch melted him. "I know you could live a different life, one without me in it. I think even with Diane's block I'd miss your eyes, the way you scrunch up your face when you're thinking, and how animated you are sharing a thought."

"I'd miss your smile, your hair, the sound of your heart beating in your chest." Payson slanted her head.

Her energy connected with his and thrummed in him like the gentle beating of hummingbird wings. "I'm so grateful we're here together in this moment, thanks to you."

"It wasn't just me, it was you too. You weren't completely lost. You met me half way." She pulled her hand back to her lap, and the mood deepened into sultry.

"You do look very pretty, by the way." He had to say it.

"Thank you."

He ran his gaze over her slim, fit body. Her dark blue dress was sleeveless, so he could admire her toned arms. Her slender neck was almost regal above the neckline, which dipped into a modest V that gave just a peek at the curvature of her breasts. Her black hair fell over her shoulders in loose waves. He shifted in his seat.

She glanced around the dining room. "Radiance. Even the name of the restaurant is lovely. Good choice for dinner. So fitting for the Old Town location. By the way, I've always liked the way you look in a dark suit."

"Good evening." The waiter poured water into crystal goblets. "Are you ready to order or do you need more time?"

The private bubble he sat alone in with Payson burst, and he grabbed for control over his body while Payson laughed at his discomfort, a hearty chuckle that was so her.

The waiter's face was a bewildered smile.

"Excuse us. We just shared a private joke." Braden cleared his throat.

"I'll give you a few minutes." The beautiful moment left on the heels of the waiter.

"So, how was your day?" He rolled his eyes. "I'm sorry. That was lame."

Payson's face gleamed. "No. It's nice. I had a very productive day."

Her eyes danced. "I think I'm very close to finding Shana's location. How was your day?"

"Hold it. You know where Shana is? Do you know if she is alive?" Her excitement meant a lot to him. "You got a break?"

"I think so. I'm waiting for more info from Keegan. He's helping me out."

The sultry got palpable and their gazes stilled. He rubbed the back of one hand over his mouth, then rested it on the table again.

Her fingers slid around his. Her eyes never left his face and her small, secret smile never slipped. "Do you want to get out of here? It's a lovely restaurant and I love the eclectic menu. But do you want to just leave?"

He brought her hand to his lips and kissed it with his heart. "Yes." He dropped a tip onto the table and gestured to their waiter. "We need to leave. I apologize, but I've left you a tip."

The waiter picked up the money, his eyes widening. "Thank you, sir. This is very generous."

In his car, he sat behind the wheel with his emotions roiling. "Where do you want to go?"

"I'm not hungry are you?"

He chuckled. "No."

"How about my house or your house? We could talk." She slanted her head at him, sending his heart tripping faster.

"Hmm…which one is closer?"

"I like how you think." Her voice was throaty, velvety. "That would be yours. But I think my place is probably safer."

His stomach knotted. "Oh, yeah. That."

She ran her hand through his hair and caressed the contours of his face. "Let's go."

He sped through the streets in Old Town, then wound his way through the rural countryside, listening to Payson talk about Shana. She was alive with the prospect of bringing the young woman home.

And it was enough just to listen. The sound of her voice made a sweet melody for his soul.

Then she quieted and watched outside the window. He didn't feel any tension or need to fill the silence with small talk. She rested her head against the seat and sighed.

"Thank you for listening."

"Thank you for sharing. You know, there's nothing wrong with small talk. But engaged conversation, as I have with you, is so much more meaningful. It's not been a part of my life for only days, but it feels like years." He swallowed hard.

"I like it too. It has a different feel, even when we just talk about work." Payson turned her head back toward the window.

He drove down her lane, heavy hearted. "I didn't mean to bring up bad times, Payson. I understand they're pretty fresh."

"We are going to have to talk about it for as many times as we need to talk about it. It's okay. We also should discuss how we're going to deal with Diane." She gestured toward the fence at the end of her drive. "Remember the passcode?"

He answered by rolling down his window and punching in the number. The gates opened, then closed as he drove through and deeper into the forest. When he reached the open space outside her front door, he could breathe fuller. A dim glow emanated from his insides. "I like it here."

Payson walked him to the garage and punched a code into a key pad and pressed the garage door opener. As the door rose he saw his SUV.

He rubbed his chin. "You found my Highlander."

She grinned. "I did, right where you left it. I brought it here from your condo with Cooper soon after the explosion. I hoped you would want it back."

"Thank you. Indeed I do."

She unlocked the door to her house and stepped inside. The low lights were safety measures, he knew. But they gave the room a luminous welcome-home feeling.

Payson dropped her keys on a small, wooden, leaf-shaped dish on the counter. A memory popped in his mind. "Oh, my gosh. You kept the dish. I don't remember that you did that."

She turned her face up to his. "I got it out of storage after Diane, well, you know. Of course I kept it. You made it for me. Remember?"

His breath caught. "I do. I made it for you in woodworking class in high school." He took hold of her hand. "I wish I could see what you see when you touch this dish."

"I see a young you, all gawky and so much fun, coming through the school hall to me, your hands behind your back."

"I was very proud of what I'd carved, but I felt stupid when it came to giving it to you."

"Silly boy. If you could see what I see you'd know that I loved it then." She locked her fingers in his and pulled him closer. "I loved it when you were gone from me. Seven days. A lifetime." A tear meandered down her cheek.

"Tears. I've hurt you so much."

She moved closer. Only nano-millimeters between them, her warm breath caressed his face.

"No. There has been pain, for both of us. But you didn't hurt me."

Love flowed palpably from her. Hunger for her in his body and soul cried for satiety.

Her scent, lilacs and rain, whispered around him. It wasn't a cloying, heavy scent. It was bright and delicate like Payson. He cupped her face in his hands and drew down to touch his lips to hers, gently. Desire sparked, and instantly she melted against him. He held her, the beating of her heart matching the rising heat in his body. The kiss, all sensuous and dreamy, lingered.

She pulled back, a slight smile lifting her lips, and sighed. Her eyes drifted open, revealing gleaming pools of champagne.

"Come with me," she purred, and took his hand, leading him to her bedroom.

He stepped in the room just behind her and swooped her into his arms. He nuzzled behind her ears while she moaned sweetly.

Beside the bed, he set her on her feet and ran his hands across her back and over her hips, savoring the sweet curves. She loosened his tie, pulled it over his head, and dropped it to the floor. Her eyes turned up to him, she licked her lips, slowly.

"My God, woman." Holding back was no longer an option. He

unzipped her dress and watched as it slipped to the floor, revealing her bare breasts and blue lacy underwear. "You're stunning."

She kicked off her shoes and the last of her clothing, and waited on tiptoe as he unbuttoned his shirt. At the third button, she started bouncing and took over removing his shirt. She ran her hands gently over his chest, taking a moment to kiss him on the shoulder, in the space above his heart, and then dipping her hands to unzip his pants.

His breath raced in time to hers. He devoured her mouth as they inched back on the bed until his mind was nearly crazed with, not just passion, mind-numbing desire. A need clamored to show her, not just tell her, how much he loved her.

He flipped her on top of him. Diminutive and delicate, she weighed hardly anything. He cupped her breasts and kissed each tip, first one, then the other. She squirmed and pressed the length of her body to his. Every inch of him hardened at the feel of Payson.

His Payson. His love.

He arched his neck as she lingered her kisses to his thighs and took her time kissing him lower.

Frantic, he urged her to his side and he stretched out on top of her glistening form. She grabbed his head and kissed his lips long and luxuriously.

She whimpered. "Braden, what are you waiting for?"

"You," he said, his voice coming out rough. He teased her, entering her slowly, stroking unhurried, deliberately, cherishing every moment of intimacy.

She kneaded his shoulders and grasped at his back. Tiny lights in her eyes sparked and he drove deep into her.

"Braden. You're so beautiful." Her voice husky, spoke to his heart.

"I love you, Payson."

They rocked as one, together in shared, deep connection, saying things that no words could express. Awareness of all of her intensified, eliminating any layers of separation between them. One by one, each of his chakras whirled in sync with hers, elevating his consciousness and connection. His energy swirled with Payson's, distinct and separate but touching, caressing, mingling soulfully.

His body burned for her, and finally, together, they exploded in bliss, his arms holding her close and hers holding him.

He lay there, still, enjoying the chaos of her damp hair and the gratitude flooding through him.

Laughter bubbled from her lips. "That was fun," she murmured.

Braden slipped to her side and pulled the sheet around them both, snuggling close. He brushed her hair off her face, certain she could comprehend the depth of his feelings in the moment.

"I love you, Braden," she whispered so softly he barely heard the words.

He nodded. So many terrible things had happened to them, things that had parted them. Silently, they lay close, and he wondered if she was thinking what he was.

Would Diane make good on her promise to kill him? Would this be their last time together?

CHAPTER 21

PAYSON FOUGHT HER nerves in the dark. It took all her control to lie still. The peace and joy of making love with Braden had been perfect. She imagined how her life could be fulfilled and lovely if she and Braden could be together as average individuals without the danger and complications of their Aeon mission. She kept that dream to herself and lay beside him, trying not to disturb his sleep.

The steady sound of his breath, simple and unaffected, endeared him further. The idea of losing him again pierced her heart. But she was an Aeon, for Christ's sake. She was complete in herself. She had a role to fulfill for the sake of humanity. And yet here she lay, beside her best friend and lover, unable to stop the fear the sent her pulse racing.

She wrapped her arms around her middle, her eyes closed, demanding peace. *Stop thinking.* It wasn't an inner scream. It wasn't even a cry. It was a simple statement, voicing what she needed. Because what was done was done. She and Braden had ignored Diane's command. If she came after them, so be it. Despite what might happen, Payson had chosen to be with Braden again. And again. To be with Braden meant everything to her.

Or at least almost everything. There was that mission of trying to raise humanity's consciousness a notch.

Faintly, she heard her cellphone chirp. She checked the clock on her bed stand. It read five in the morning. Her heart skipped, and she quietly slipped out of bed.

She padded in to the kitchen and checked a text from Keegan. **I found the info you needed. Call me when you get this. You might want to book a flight for Denver.**

Excitement skittered in her gut. Frozen in place, she glanced down the hall to where she had left Braden sleeping and back to the text. ZuZu rubbed against her leg.

"You poor sweetie. It's early. You don't need to get up yet." ZuZu looked up at her, blinking with sleepy eyes and meowed. "Of course I'll feed you."

Payson ran her hand over ZuZu's fur, torn between decisions. Absently, she poured kibble into ZuZu's bowl.

She couldn't leave Braden alone. If Diane came after him, he would need her by his side.

She pulled her fingers through her tangles. "But I have to go," she said as though talking to ZuZu.

A hand on her bare shoulder made her jump.

"Where do you have to go?" Adorably drowsy, Braden squinted at her.

She stood on tiptoes to kiss him, then leaned her head against his bare chest. Her heart responded, lilting.

But she had to ignore her impulse to drag him back to bed. Her phone chirped again but she ignored it. "Keegan found the information I need to track down Shana. If this email gives me last known address, then I need to get there fast. I don't want to lose the perp or my missing person."

"You better read the email." Braden rubbed his eyes. "I'll make coffee."

"Thank you." She glanced at him as he opened cupboards and drawers. But she knew he would manage. He had been here many times before his block happened.

Keegan had attached a document that gave her the name of the person the Impala was registered to. She stared at the name. Sam Cain. Keegan had also sent two photos. One matched the visual she'd gotten from Shana's book. He was her boyfriend. The other was a mug shot. The face was a match with the photos of one of the Sam Cains she'd found on social media.

Reading Keegan's email sent adrenaline pumping through her, strengthening with each word. **I found multiple Sam Cains but narrowed it down to two. One who has no record but was finger-printed for a job at a local school district. Never had a speeding ticket even. Another Sam Cain you found on social media was not a real account. Nothing there. The third Sam Cain, the sandy-haired one, has a record. Sam Cain is an alias. His name is Darius Jasper. He was arrested for spying on female students in the restroom at an artist collective studio. Never charged. Arrested for car theft, but released. It turned out the car belonged to his mother and she didn't press charges. He was arrested and charged with stalking. He was found guilty and spent six months in jail for the misdemeanor. He's used his credit card in Colorado within the last week. Gower, Colorado.**

Payson's heart swelled. She quickly emailed back. **That's a lot of info. Thank you. This gives me direction. I owe you.**

"Anything helpful?" Braden called from the kitchen. "You know, you could have asked me for help." He pointed at his chest. "Cop. Access to info."

"I know. I have my sources. I can't always rely on you."

"Oh. I get that."

The minute she'd said it she'd wanted to take it back, but it was true. "I didn't mean it like that. I count on you for many things, but it's important to use more than one source. Anyway, Keegan found a trail." She opened her laptop and checked online for a map.

Braden placed a mug of coffee beside her and looked over her shoulder at the map she pulled up. "In Colorado?"

"Yes, Gower, Colorado."

He pointed. "There it is. Click on it."

"Population six thousand. It looks a bit remote, close to the mountains." She sipped her coffee. "Mmm … you make good coffee." She smiled up at him. "I could get used to this."

His eyes glinted. "Is that an invitation of some sort?"

His gaze pinned hers and held it. Her stomach clenched. "What if it is?" She was walking on thin ice.

He dropped into a chair next to her at the table. "It's not simple for us, is it? Assuming you understood that when I said invitation, I meant a commitment."

She shook her head. "No. There are many things to consider before we get to the point of a quote, invitation."

Braden rubbed his brow with one finger and she rested her hand on his shoulder. "I don't want to bring you problems again. We have to be careful."

"It would be a good life, me with you. I know that, Braden. But the decision must support our mission and—"

"Not kill either of us." He smoothed strands of hair away from her face, and the touch of his skin ran through her like electricity.

She cleared her throat. "Back to work. I'm going to book a flight for today, if possible."

"Of course." He knitted his brow. "I could go with you."

"You're in the middle of an investigation. Can you get away?"

"It's not the best time to leave, but I'll be worried about you. Diane could show up at anytime, anywhere. I hate the idea of you being alone with her."

"Um." She hesitated, unsure if it was fair to mention yesterday's encounter. He was already stressed, and she didn't want him to worry. "Diane approached me yesterday."

Braden nearly choked on his gulp of coffee. "When, where? What did she say?"

Payson rested her hand on his. "It was the same old stuff. She warned me to stay away from you."

He stood up fast and started pacing. "Why are you just now telling me? That's it. I'm not letting you out of my sight again. I'm going with you to Colorado."

"Honestly, I didn't tell you because I didn't want to spoil our time together. I'm tired of that woman interfering in my life."

"I am too, in my life. But mostly in *our* life." He pulled her to her feet. "I can't lose you again."

"I don't want to lose you either. Her tactic of separating us is strengthening her ability to darken the world."

He wrapped her in his arms and she molded to his muscled contours. She breathed in the scent of his skin and let it fill her and cleanse her of bleak thoughts of Diane.

He sat back down in the chair, a tiny muscle in his cheek twitching. "So did she hurt you?"

"Yes, but I handled her."

His expression relaxed and he sighed heavily. "You are powerful. I forget that." He lifted his eyes, and the emotion in them gripped her heart. "You are so precious to me, I naturally treat you like a porcelain doll."

"I understand that feeling. I feel similarly about you, even though you're very powerful and strong. I don't want you to run into Diane alone while I'm gone, either. What happened to you was devastating. But we're different for it. Better equipped."

"You're right. So, am I going with you to Colorado or not?"

"Not. Your presence here will help keep Diane in check. Besides, if things go as I hope they do, I'll be right back."

He swept his finger down her nose, then gave her a quick kiss. Sensations twirled through her instantly, and she couldn't harness a spontaneous smile.

"I should get out of here. It's early, but I might as well make use of the time. I have a list of things to do for work."

"Thank you for a wonderful evening, Braden." She laced her arm around his and hung on a long minute. She longed for him to stay.

He wrapped her in his arms and together they made silent promises: to be strong, to be back, not to let Diane part them.

· · ·

BRADEN WATCHED EDDIE Crow through the two-way window at APD settling into his seat. Eddie was no DA, but at the rate he was going he would be a full-fledged one soon. He wasn't just a two-bit criminal.

He checked the control panel on the wall to confirm the digital recorder was in the off position. He didn't want this interview with Eddie recorded. The walls were closing in and he didn't know whom he could trust. He unlocked the interrogation room door and sauntered in, slowly parking himself in the chair across the table. He set Eddie's RAP sheet down and stared at it.

Eddie rattled the cuffs on his wrists. "Hello! Person here waiting for you. What are you doing?"

Braden didn't look up. *Good. It worked.* The silent treatment was part of his strategy to make Eddie ill at ease. "You're building quite the career for yourself. Simple battery when you were fifteen, dismissed. Breaking and entering with six months in juvenile detention. Felony theft at eighteen. Aggravated battery. Illegal possession of a firearm and controlled substance." He lifted his gaze to meet Eddie's. "Now you're in here for drug trafficking. Is this the career path you dreamed of when you were ten, Eddie? I doubt it's what your dad and mom wanted for you."

"So what of it?"

"You're almost middle aged, you're looking at five years for the drug trafficking. What happens when you come out? You're one murder away from life in prison. The clock is ticking. It's time to make different choices, don't you think?"

Eddie twisted his lips and tried to lean closer. "I'm no murderer. Besides, I'm not going to jail for trafficking or anything else." He slumped back in his chair.

"I'm not stupid. You think I don't know you've got connections you believe have your back?" He pointed a finger at Eddie. "You are simply a means to achieve their goals. As long as you keep making them money and taking the fall, you serve a purpose. But there are many others just like you lined up. Now you're in here, probably going away, you'll be forgotten before the prison cell locks.

Remember the sound of the cell door closing and knowing you're trapped, caged? It makes me claustrophobic just thinking about it. Are you claustrophobic?" Braden fake-shivered.

Eddie's expression wilted. He twisted his neck in a circle. "Do you have a point?"

Braden lifted his gaze to the ceiling, exhaling slowly. This was the tiny pause in Eddie's awareness he'd hoped for. He could have used his ability to force Eddie to open up, but it wouldn't have affected the level of negativity in him because it wouldn't have been a free-will choice.

"Give me names. Who you're working for and what you know about their operation. I'll take a personal interest in your safety and successful return to society."

"Humph. After I'm in prison for five years, you'll help me get a job? Doesn't sound like much of a deal."

"It's an offer to help you start a new life, Eddie." His insides churned. He wanted so much to see changes in Eddie.

"What life? I'll get killed in prison. You can't protect me inside."

"I said I'd take a personal interest in your safety. I mean that." Braden gave substance to his promise by expanding his innate inner light to reach Eddie's heart. It required focused concentration. Even with all his effort, it wasn't a sure thing. Eddie's lack of awareness and the effects of darkness in him would be hard to overcome. He could imagine the gears in Eddie's head, as his old patterns moved autonomously to keep him stuck. "Give me something."

Eddie let his head drop back and blew out a sigh. "I need reassurances." He lifted his head and gave Braden a tired regard.

"Give me information first."

"I don't know much. It's not as though I'm in the loop. But, I overhead a conversation." He sighed heavily again. "Imagine all the money flowing at the casino after it's up and running. Imagine the clientele."

Braden's mind spun. "Money laundering. High-profile criminals coming to town for entertainment, meetings, and work. Who was having the conversation you overheard. Do you have a part in this?"

"Me? No. I'm low level. There were three voices. I only recognized two—Joel Farrod and Tim Brody."

"Where did you hear this conversation?"

"The restaurant, Ainsley's Bar and Grill. They were having drinks near me."

"The mayor and the economic development director." Braden slammed his palms on the table. "You heard them discussing criminal opportunities?"

Eddie tightened his lips. Braden waited, grappling with his agitation.

"Something like that. I'll just say Principal Industries' projects aren't planned for construction on the river for the view." He rolled his head. "I've given you plenty. What are you going to do for me?"

"First, I have to check out this information. I need to be careful with it. I don't want this getting around in such a way that the higher ups in the organization trace it back to you."

Eddie smirked. "Sounds good."

"So for now, you're going back to your cell where you'll await your hearing. That won't raise any alarms." He scribbled his cellphone number on a corner of the RAP sheet and ripped it off. "Stay in touch."

He motioned to the guard and shoved back from the table, mindful of the flow of light energy sifting through Eddie. "You have no idea what you've done for yourself here, but I do. Thank you."

Braden took the stairs two at a time and sped to his office. Too many tasks to get done warred inside him. His breaths came fast.

"Zane, you're here." He ran his fingers through his hair.

Zane looked up from his desk. "Uh, yeah. How did your interrogation go with Eddie?"

"Oh, it went. You know how these things are." He stood at Zane's desk, thoughts whirling.

"Do you need something?" Zane stretched back in his chair.

"I think so." He paused, uncertain. "I need to keep track of Eddie Crow. His hearing is scheduled for tomorrow. I don't want anything to happen to him."

"Dude." Zane sat upright, throwing a glance over his left shoulder, then his right. "Why are you worried about that?"

"I can't say. But I have good reasons. It's a matter of life and death."

"Well, then, I'll do my part. What do you have in mind?"

"Pay off the guards. Put him in sick bay."

Zane chuckled. "Paying the guards to keep him safe is a bad idea. Especially if you're trying to keep a secret."

"You're not helping." Braden had trouble standing still with fireworks for nerves.

"I could make him sick. Nothing fatal, just stomach issues."

"That's a workable idea. How?"

Zane stood and began rummaging through his drawers. "Don't worry about it. I'll take care of it."

"Thanks. Don't get caught. I'm nervous about getting you involved as it is."

He exchanged a look with Zane. "Don't worry. Watch yourself, Braden." He grabbed a small bottle from his drawer.

"Ipecac? What are you doing with emetic syrup in your drawer?"

"I got it when one of my informants was poisoned, he believed. I didn't want to take any chances of him dying on me. A dose of this will cause vomiting and a certain visit to the infirmary for Eddie."

"Perfect." As Zane walked out, Braden picked up his cell and placed a call to Reid over at city planning. It rang twice, then Reid answered.

"Hi, Braden. How can I help you?" His voice was shaky, unsure.

Braden's fists clenched. He hated what his friend was going through. "I was wondering if you could meet me this afternoon at Coffee Is."

The phone was quiet except for the sound of Reid breathing.

"Just a little social interaction. Whenever you have some time. What do you say?"

Reid released a long breath. "That sounds good. How about in fifteen minutes. Can you make that?"

"I can. See you soon." Braden paused, collecting his focus. His friend needed protection, and that mattered.

CHAPTER 22

$\mathcal{B}$RADEN WALKED INTO Coffee Is and caught Skye's eye. She was talking to customers, smiling and laughing. Tension eased in his muscles. He moved unhurried to order coffee, then leaned with one foot against the wall until his name was called.

An empty table at the back looked good. He settled in, his eyes aimed at Skye. She took the hint and hurried over.

"Hey, Braden."

"Hi, have a seat." He nodded to the counter up front. "Where's Benjamin?"

She slipped into a chair beside him. "He didn't look well today, so I sent him home." She touched his arm briefly. "Nice to see you. You wanted to talk to me?"

"Yeah, but nothing special. I've been busy since I got back, so to speak, and haven't spent much time with you."

"Oh, well, I understand." She scrunched her forehead. "How are things going?"

He gave his answer some thought, and nodded slowly. "Payson has been," he picked his words carefully, "kind. In the memories that are returning, that quality in her stands out."

"I imagine it's quite the contrast between what you were immersed in with Diane."

He bowed his head. "I didn't even know what was happening. My mind was distracted." His muscles slackened. "I can't take it all back." He lifted his head and looked directly into Skye's unshielded brown eyes. "But I'm here now. I'm grateful for you and the others for giving me a second chance."

She leaned closer, placing her hand again on his arm. Her healing touch helped him expand to contain his remorse. "We believe in second chances, Braden. It's an Aeon's choice. The life of a young Aeon is not easy and we've all experienced difficulties. Yours was particularly brutal, the way your parents died, I mean. No one in our group would judge you for being susceptible to Diane's powers. Deep inside, you may have unprocessed rage and guilt, you get triggered just like anyone might. It's hard to live with that. Her ability to mesmerize in a way relieves the suffering Aeon's have lived with, similarly to my healing touch, but in a negative way. There is no freedom in distraction."

"No," he muttered. The energy of acceptance moved through him with such force his hands spread open. "Sometimes I want a magic wand to make all the pain disappear. Thank you for your help. Anything I can do for you?"

"Another time, my friend, I'm sure," she said, and returned to her customers.

Reid came in and glanced around. Braden waved to catch his attention.

"Saved you a seat," he said as Reid strolled up.

Reid surveyed the room, holding his fingers to his mouth. "Hi. I'm going to get coffee. I'll be right back."

His clipped speech and vigilant glance said more than his words. He didn't feel safe.

He came back carrying a very large to-go cup of coffee and dropped into a chair across the table. "Is this just a social meet as you said, or do you have business to discuss?" Reid took a slow sip of coffee. A dish dropped in the kitchen and Reid jerked, startled.

Braden leaned in over the table and touched Reid's forearm. "There's no one here you need to fear. I would know if there were."

Reid closed his eyes and let out a trembling gush of air. "You would know that? How?"

"Let's just say I have a cop's instinct. Detecting certain kinds of people is part of my work. But to answer your question, I would like this to be purely social, but it's urgent we talk business. I have some information for you and I'm hoping you have some for me. I'm sorry I misled you. I guess I didn't want to alarm you."

Reid's eyes widened, his pupils large and dark. "Okay, your instincts were right about me. To be direct, I'm scared to talk to you, but what do you want from me?"

"I've learned that Tim Brody and Mayor Farrod are involved with criminal factions. I know that Principal Industries is linked to organized crime, and I know money laundering will be an ongoing activity at the proposed casino."

Reid licked his lips, then pursed them. He rubbed the back of his hand across them.

"You don't have to say anything. I did what you suggested, did my job, and discovered this information."

Reid's shoulders slumped. "I can't talk about anything. I told you that."

"I understand. But I'm trying to put together a puzzle that contains a lot of pieces. It's important that I figure it out, but I need some help."

"What do you need?" He shook his head, clearly torn and under duress, but Braden believed Reid could be brave. His energy was light and comfortable.

"I need to be able to connect Principal Industries with a name of someone with a criminal background. I know there is someone at the top of organized crime with his or her fingers in the Stillwell Development, someone who is attempting to embed criminal activities in Auralia. Can you give me a name?"

Reid let his head drop to his hands and said nothing. Braden glanced around the room and noticed Skye appraising them. He nodded, hoping he deduced her look correctly. Reid was sick at heart and needed help.

She made her way across the room and came up beside Reid, placing a hand on his shoulder. He flinched, but Skye ignored it. "How are you two doing? Need a refill?"

She's brilliant. Braden had great respect for all the Aeons in his group, but when he saw them in action, it always made his day. "I could use one. You too, Reid?"

While she poured coffee into Braden's cup, she left her hand on Reid's shoulder. It wasn't just a gesture to garner a good tip, her hand was sending healing energy to his sore soul. The high energy was something Reid couldn't know was happening because he was unable to detect it. Braden expanded the light in his heart, sending it to him with Skye's healing energy, and their combined efforts embraced him in invisible light and love. It was Reid's choice to accept it, and Braden hoped subconsciously he'd feel it, thereby accepting it.

"Uh, yeah. Thanks." Reid gave Skye a thin smile.

"There you go. You boys enjoy your coffee. Be sure to say so if you'd like something from the bakery."

Reid watched Skye thread through the tables. "Yeah, I can give you a name."

He knew it. With a little bit of healing, Reid could bring forward more of his true self.

Reid turned his gaze on Braden. "It's Barry Russell. He's in charge of the casino development. He's CEO of Principal Industries and more. The more you'll have to find out for yourself."

Another thing Reid wouldn't know was that he had just strengthened the light in himself through his choice, and was sending it out into the world, including to Braden. The beauty of it didn't escape his attention. "Okay, that's fair. Thank you, Reid." He sipped his coffee, appreciating the immense courage Reid had displayed. "I would like you to gather up some of your things, take whatever work you need, and get your family out of Auralia for a few days, maybe weeks."

"What? I can't leave now." He pressed his palms to the table, his eyes darting here and there.

"No, you have to leave now. Give some explanation why you won't be into work. Don't tell me or anyone else where you're going, but keep in touch with me." Braden handed him a cellphone. "Use only this phone if you need to call me. It's a number that can't be traced to you. I'm going after these people. It's going to get rough around here. You've already been threatened, you said. Get out now."

Pain dulled Reid's eyes. "Why are these things happening? Our young people are out of control and running wild doing crazy, stupid stuff. City leaders and business people are doing bad things. I don't understand how or why this beautiful old town got so dangerous."

"You're saying what adults have said for hundreds of years. Our kids are not the cause of a crumbling society. And some people get corrupted by power. It's the natural way of things, when people allow negativity to grow inside their hearts," Braden said, sadness flitting in his gut at his own words. "It's been the truth for as long as time."

Reid creased his brow. "It is not that simple. It's a combination of factors, including outside forces we have little control over."

"You're right, and I'm not suggesting the concept is simple. But it is true."

Reid sighed, shaking his head. "You may be right. If you are, I need to consider my own beliefs about who should be in power and in what the community should invest."

"Perhaps. Have safe travels." Braden watched Reid leave, his thoughts automatically sorting into actions he needed to take.

He waved at Skye and headed out the door, his fists balling and unballing. He'd had run-ins with organized crime before but the name Barry Russell didn't sound familiar. On his way to Diane's building, he called Zane.

"I have a name I'd like you to run a check on," he said when Zane picked up.

"Shoot."

"Barry Russell. He's the CEO of Principal Industries and is heading the casino project. I expect you'll find him in the system." He could hear Zane tap computer keys.

"Yup. Your Barry Russell is a top dog in the Irish Mob. His record goes back a number of years. It includes racketeering, extortion, distribution of illegal substances, robbery, I mean how long do want me to go on?"

"I get the picture. It's what I thought." Braden gripped the steering wheel tighter. "The mob is trying to get a foot hold in Auralia, probably planning to expand their operation here long-term."

"Great." His voice was dry, sardonic. "If I wanted to fight this kind of crime I would have moved to Chicago or New York City. This explains the increase in petty crimes and felonies."

Braden knew the robberies and such were a symptom of the effects of DAs in the community. The DAs' expanding darkness simply created the environment for proliferation of criminal activity. But Diane's DAs were deliberately disrupting the fabric of the community. "I wouldn't be surprised if seemingly unrelated crimes, like the robbery of the Willys, which could have been an opportunity to groom the younger man for crimes, and a domestic abuse skip that Payson handled are a part of the grand scheme to distract from the big plans. I've had enough of this crap. Thanks for the info."

"No problem. Later."

Braden reached Diane's office building and checked the time. Diane's work schedule over the days he'd been her slave had followed a routine. Morning in the office, lunch schmoozing with someone important, and then, afternoon in meetings at Principal Industries. He was relying on her following her routine this afternoon.

Inside he took an elevator to the tenth floor and casually strolled down the hall into his office. No one would take note of him since he'd been here recently, doing her dirty work.

He peeked through the door, holding his breath. If only he had an app that would alert him specifically to her presence, not simply the presence of a DA. *Hey, that's a good idea. I'll have to find a software developer.* Inside her office he began searching for files on her desktop regarding Principal Industries.

He drummed his fingertips against the desk, waiting for results. Finally, a folder popped up. He clicked on it and found levels of files. His fingers flew across the keyboard searching for all files that appeared to be related to Principal Industries. One file grabbed his attention. It was password protected, so surely it held important stuff. He ran a series of different combinations of words and numbers, wondering why he hadn't gone into computer engineering. Finally, he stopped. A random approach wasn't working.

He spun slowly in Diane's chair, eyeing the contents of her office. He had thought he'd known her well, but he hadn't. He had been mesmerized and didn't know anything useful. He knew her birthdate. She wouldn't be that dumb. Photos on the wall pictured her with dignitaries and wealthy businessmen and women.

Nope. He shook his head. *I'm not going to be able to figure out her password to that file.*

He closed the file and perused the other files, landing on one titled CLIENTS/PROJECTS. It opened to show him a list of names and projects with dates. He scrolled down the list, noting the mayor's name, the names of some local bars, the state senator, the local hospital, and the farm bureau—and Principle Industries and its conglomerate of companies. Each person and organization was hyperlinked, so he clicked on the mayor's name. A project management site opened with a specific tile for Joel Farrod. The tile connected to other tiles, including Principal Industries, the state's senator, the economic director, Tim Brody, and others. He paused, staring at two names: Principal Industries and Warren Brown. He quickly opened the tile for Principal Industries and straightened his shoulders. Diane's list associated the mayor with the Stillwell development, with notes listing his personal investment and supportive actions he'd taken. That list included awarding certain bars with liquor licenses and turning his eye from underage drinking dating back to a corresponding date for his initial introduction to Brown.

He sat back in the chair and processed the information. The cloud in and around Auralia grew thicker in his mind as he discovered all the criminal activity at the mayor's office.

He clicked on the Principal Industries tile and perused a list of companies, some he recognized and others he didn't, including some located abroad. He had expected that, but some of the companies were connected to personal names of known felons with organized crime affiliations. The tile also connected Barry Russell to the same organized crime groups, including the Irish Mob.

He closed the tile. And opened the one for Brown. It contained a list of dates, names, and activities that drained blood from Braden's face. Names were familiar because of the individuals' run-in with the law. Nick's name was there. Eddie Crow's. It confirmed the existence of what Brown had called disrupters, but more than that, it was devastating proof of aggressive efforts to destroy lives and turn them to Dark Sides. With a heavy heart, he closed the file.

What he had found on Diane's computer was a web. It encompassed nearly every aspect of Auralia and linked to big boatloads of crap.

Worse. It appeared Diane had them all under her thumb. All but perhaps Barry Russell.

He peered at the screen, willing it to produce more information. There was so much here, and yet he couldn't open the password protected file. He wanted to know what it held.

He sat up straight, a memory returning. Maybe there was another way to find out the information.

He remembered a tip Payson had given him for hiding files. Maybe he could use that tip to unhide a file. Payson called it finding a file hidden in plain sight.

He clicked on system files and perused the list. It was pretty much a foreign language to him. That was okay. All he had to do was find similarities in two files.

He stared at the screen, his eyes tiring, and the clock in his gut ticking. It was one of those word puzzles where the specific correct words blended in with all the others in the puzzle. He could stare and stare and never see the words he wanted.

Until the words would suddenly pop out.

Right there in the list he saw a file named "win32API.dol" and beneath it a file named "win32API.dil". He clicked on the first file. He clicked on the second file because its name was off by one letter.

Hiding in plain sight, as Payson had said. His heart pumped hard as the file opened.

"Holy Chicago." Braden pushed his chair backward. "Oh my God." His heart pounded hard and loud, and all he could do was stare at the first page in the file. It read like an opening to a manifesto for world dominance, using words such as conquests, economic restructuring, and … He brought his fist to his mouth and bit it. He finished reading the first page. "…rightful place as leaders in the world." His pulse thudded so fast in his ears he thought he might be having a heart attack. He gasped for slow, steady breaths, his mind thrashing for a way to make this plan go away.

The implications of the file rose huge in his mind until he could hardly breathe. It was obvious now that not only highly evolved Atlanteans had escaped the end of their civilization, as had been believed, but dark factions, those responsible for the destruction, had also gotten away and their ancestors were carrying on the plan for supremacy.

The development projects were wrong for the town, but they were the tip of an iceberg that had roots in ancient Atlantis. He had to stop the overthrow of his world. He needed to know exactly what these people were planning. Desperation thundering in his chest scrambled his thoughts. Diane would be arriving at the office any time.

He could confront her, shake her hard until she spilled everything he needed to know to stop this madness. He could compel her with his mind to confess. There would be consequences for attempting to take control of her mind if he failed. The idea of it flushed his skin, and for a brief few seconds he heard his parent's screaming at him to run, run away from men in their house.

He wasn't that young boy any more. He couldn't run away.

He frowned. Diane's frequent phone calls, the ones he'd been ignoring for days, had stopped. That might have been another not such great idea of his. At the time, he wanted nothing but to keep her out of his life. The idea that he had kissed her brought bile up his throat. He swiped at his mouth. Now he realized by ignoring Diane he could have put all the Aeons, but especially Payson, in danger by making her angry.

He closed his eyes and grounded himself as best he could, sending his light to anchor in the earth. His nerves slowly calmed.

"Duh, Braden. Copy the file." He raced to his desk and grabbed a thumb drive. At Diane's computer, he tapped his foot against the floor, feeling every second tick by.

Finally, the file finished downloading and he shoved the drive in to his pocket.

Turmoil and chaos vibrated inside his body. The sound of heels clicking on the tiled floor in the hallway outside the door sent shivers up and down his back. Quickly, he closed all the open windows and left the chair as it had been, then slid into his adjoining office and sat at his desk.

Diane burst into her office and stepped around her desk. She turned her head and met his gaze. "Braden, you're here. Why haven't you answered my calls?" She crossed her arms over her chest and strode into his office, glaring.

The chaos inside him pulled his muscles tight. Fear jittered under his skin. He tuned to his center, where a tiny light shone in his mind's eye. "I didn't want to talk to you." The words came from the tiny light.

She scowled at him fiercely. "What do you mean? Tell me what's going on, Braden. You know I need you. Did Payson get to you?" She dropped her arms to her sides, her eyes turning innocent. "You can't listen to her."

He stood and leaned across the desk and ignored her reference to Payson. "You tell me what's going on, Diane. Tell me about Barry Russell." The force of his ability filled his mind, demanding Diane answer his question.

She flinched. "He's the CEO of Principal Industries. We're working with him, remember? He's my top client and he's helping Auralia prosper."

The lies stabbed his gut. He could see them now. "I know that." His intention escalated the demand to answer truthfully. The effort challenged him, but his authority of his power strengthened. "Don't lie to me. Is Barry your boss, not simply your client?"

She clenched her teeth. Her resistance a wall of rock, it flung his energy back at him. "Don't try to use your ability to bend my will. It won't work." She pointed a finger at him. Her trembling hand told a different story. She was weakening.

Braden closed his eyes and shifted his intention to the light inside him, letting it grow and flow toward Diane. "Is Russell your boss?"

Her eyes glazed for two seconds, then cleared. "No. He's my client."

The power he aimed at her dropped. "If you're going to continue to lie to me I have nothing more to say."

She grabbed at his arm, clenching it tightly. "Don't leave." She raised a hand, and pressure began to build in his body, pressure to comply. He had to get away.

He marched to his office door. "I'm not your pawn anymore." He didn't raise his voice, he just spoke the words with certainty.

She sputtered. "You're not making sense. Come into my office and lie down on the couch. I think you're having a nervous breakdown or you're overdoing things before healing from the concussion. Let me help."

Braden snickered. "Concussion." He stole another glance at her eyes. "I'm fine."

"Fine," she spouted. "You can't fool me. I know what you are, Braden. You can't hide forever from the truth."

He knew better than to take the bait, but this new tack was interesting. "What am I hiding from?"

"You're a killer."

His heart cringed. She had aimed her arrow at his past. "You don't know me at all."

"I know you killed your parents with your mind control. I know how much you hate yourself because of their deaths. I can turn that hatred into something useful, like making sure nothing bad happens to you again."

"No, Diane. I'm not the bad guy here." He left her standing alone.

His phone rang as he headed out of the building. It was Sargent Garcia. "Yes, Luca?"

"You need to get here fast. Something has happened to Eddie Crow."

Braden couldn't get to the APD fast enough. He parked haphazardly and bounded up the stairs, where he found Zane sitting head-in-hands at his desk. He looked up. "Braden. I couldn't stop them. Eddie Crow is dead."

"What happened?" Braden couldn't breathe.

"Someone shot him. Surveillance videos show only static. I'm sorry."

"You didn't do anything wrong." He slumped into his chair, awareness of encroaching Dark Sides sickening him. "No suspects."

"Nope, just a dead guy. This is bad, Braden. I mean, really bad. Whoever killed him got inside and took him out without leaving any trail. I don't know if I've ever felt so helpless."

Braden nodded. "A perfect storm."

PAYSON STRODE TO her rental car at the Gower Regional Airport with full-on focus for locating Shana. But she couldn't ignore the sunshine and warm breezes of Colorado. It wasn't her first visit to the state, but it was her first in a while and she had never been to Gower.

During her three-hour flight, she memorized Darius Jasper's personal data and mug shot. She left Auralia sleepy in the early morning, but she had been too pumped to nap. Striding off the plane and out of the airport toward the rental lot, adrenaline sharpened her senses. She slid behind the wheel of the rental, and placed a call to the local PD. She wanted to give them a head's up that she was in town and let them know what she was up to. It was part of her routine. Cooperation with the locals was not only good etiquette, it was essential. It gave her a better opportunity to complete the investigation safely and without any chance of locals getting territorial. She would locate the suspect and his captive. The police would do the rest.

The call done, Payson programmed the GPS to the address Keegan found and headed out of the parking lot.

Gower sat in a valley at the edge of the Rocky Mountains. According to the chamber of commerce website, plenty of activities were available to enjoy in the city. But many miles of protected public lands with hiking in a variety of terrains made it an outdoor-lover's dream.

The wind flowing through the windows tossed her hair, so she tucked it behind her ears, enjoying the cool mountain fresh air.

Thoughts of Braden entered her mind, and she smiled, imagining getting all outdoorsy with him in the foothills and mountains. A vacation out here together would be a wish come true.

Payson sighed and set aside the pleasant thoughts. Not all of her had faith in their future, but right now she needed to focus on her job.

Her directions led into a rural area outside of Gower. Her rental, a four-wheel drive vehicle, downshifted as the incline steepened. The road wound around rock outcroppings and forests of spruce and fir. Aspens and balsam poplars grew beside meandering streams.

The deeper she drove into the foothills, the fewer houses she saw. A few more miles up and finally, she approached her destination. She drove by, surveying the property and the domicile—a very small log cabin that could rightly be termed a shack, sitting amidst trees up a long drive. The windows were small and darkened. A tarp lay over one corner of the roof.

Most importantly, a late model, muddy-water colored Impala, license plate number BN 2731, stuck out from beneath another large, scraggly tarp.

"Bingo," Payson whispered. And drove on.

She drove until she found another house. It was small but charming on the outside. She pulled in the short driveway and scanned the property. No warning vibrations went off inside her. She got out and was still standing behind the car door when a man opened the front door.

"Hi!" he hollered. "Can I help you?"

His smile welcomed her as much as his offer. "Hi. Yes, I'll be right there."

She moved toward the front step, taking in the surroundings with her peripheral vision. Yellow and white daisies in a small flower garden in the side yard nodded in the slight wind.

The man held out his hand and she accepted his handshake. "I'm Bob, Bob York. We don't get many visitors."

Images played in her head that eased her wariness. Bob and a woman sitting in the backyard, chatting amicably. Sensations of love and peace filled her. "No, I bet not. You're rather secluded." The scent of bananas spilled out of the house. "Something smells good."

"Oh, my wife is baking banana bread. Do you want to come in?"

"Actually, I'm doing footwork for a survey company, and I am trying to contact someone on my list. Maybe you know the name." She arched her eyebrows.

Bob's wife joined him at the doorway. "Honey, this woman is from a survey company."

"Hello. I'm Sophie."

"Nice to meet you both. I was just asking your husband if he could help me out. I'm looking for a Darius Jasper, he may go by the name Sam Cain. He is supposed to be living around here somewhere but I haven't been able to find him. Do you know him?"

Bob rubbed his chin and exchanged a glance with his wife.

"Sam Cain lives down the road about two miles, but we don't really know him." Sophie frowned. "Some people who live around here are neighborly. It's good to know people just in case someone needs help. But Sam keeps to himself."

"Oh, so you've met him?" Excitement churned again in her body.

"We introduced ourselves to him when we noticed someone was living in that old cabin," Sophie said.

Her husband nodded. "Yeah, we invited him over but he's not sociable."

"Just to make sure I'm on the right track, could you tell me what he looks like?" This typical procedure for Payson, checking with neighbors for information, usually yielded good results. During her plane trip, she'd considered her strategy and decided on her pretense.

"Sure. We haven't seen him in a while, but at that time, about a year ago, he had light brown hair. He's probably about six feet tall. Thin."

She scribbled notes, not that she needed them. "Okay, thanks. Does he live with anyone?"

Sophie shook her head. "No, he seems to live alone."

"Yeah, I've never seen anyone else around that property. What kind of surveying company are you working for?" Bob swatted at a bug.

"Oh, I may not have mentioned that. The company has been hired to gather data regarding areas in close proximity to a proposed luxury resort."

Both Bob and Sophie's eyes widened. "What?" Bob wrapped his arm around Sophie. "Not near us, I hope. Think of the traffic. The road would have to be widened. Stores would want to locate here."

Payson held up her hands. She should have picked something less intrusive. *Darn it. I might as well have told them aliens were invading.* "I'm sorry. No, no. Not even close. The company has to learn everything about land use within a seventy-five mile radius. I'm just collecting data, that's the extent of what is going on now."

Note to self. Lie better next time. Years ago, Braden had told her more than once that she was a good liar. That hadn't set well with her, but if she were truthful, her skill at lying was an important part of her job. Maybe she was off her game. Her gut clenched. What with Diane's actions against Braden and the increasing darkness in Auralia, she shouldn't be surprised that stress was messing with her brain.

Back in the car, she chewed at her lip. *Good recovery. Not such a good cover story.* Her goal while working was to be unmemorable. Causing distress was not unmemorable, it was very memorable. She was now attached to their emotions and they were apt to remember her as the woman who came to their door and told them their world was coming to an end. *Drat! Drat! Drat!*

She blew out a big breath and rolled her shoulders. The thought of Braden hung over her, prompting wishes that she'd let him come on this trip. She was accustomed to doing footwork on her own. And he had his ongoing investigation to work on. But even as she had assured him she didn't need him along, a lump had formed in her throat. Hadn't she told him they were safer together?

Slowly driving toward Sam's cabin, she split her attention to bring focus to her heart. Lovely thoughts of Braden's sculpted face and frisky smile sparked a glow that spread, and she wished him a nice day. The distance between them shrank. Their love kept them connected. That awareness thrummed through her, resting fears.

About a half-mile away from Darius's cabin, she pulled off the road into a grove of Cottonwoods. She climbed out, shoved her gun in her back holster, and picked up a file from the passenger seat. She missed her disguises. Of course she hadn't brought her wealth of disguises cross country with her. Back home she carried them in her trunk. In a moment's notice, she could be a young teen in shorts, thanks to her short height. She could be a young woman out on the town in provocative clothing and high heels. She could be a person with disabilities and carry a cane. The disguises were not to protect her identity so much as to help build a story that would facilitate acceptance.

She shrugged into a safety vest with reflectors and added a black cap, and became a worker for a surveying company.

Moments later as she drove into the suspect's driveway, which was more like a weed-filled dirt patch, she brushed her hand over the gun in her holster, adjusted her cap, and tramped through the overgrown lawn to the front door.

The tattered curtains in a window moved aside a tiny bit and a portion of a face peeked out. The curtain quickly fluttered closed. Payson swallowed hard, her mouth turning dry.

She hammered on the front door and listened for sounds from inside, while teetering on the step, trying to keep eyes on possible activity around back.

Staged whispering sounded inside. She pounded again and rested her hand in place. A visual flashed in her mind and she drew in a sharp breath. "Hello! I'm from a local surveyor's office. I just need some information. Please open the door."

CHAPTER 23

THE SOUND OF a deadbolt unlocking set little hairs on Payson's arms to stand erect. Anything could happen. Be alert, be casual, she repeated her mantra.

Until it was time to be aggressive.

The door cracked open, but a chain lock remained.

"Hello. Could you open the door? I promise I'm not a cop or a salesman." She gave him her best innocent face.

A man peeked through the crack. She sucked in a quiet breath. It was Darius.

"What do you want?" he asked.

She had to get inside. She held up her hands, palms out. "I work for a surveyor company." She pulled at the vest. "See? I'm doing the footwork, going door to door. I'll only take a couple minutes. You'll get fifty dollars for doing a survey." She wanted to spin as small a lie as possible, with few details.

The door closed and she held her breath until she heard the chain lock slide.

"Come in."

She slanted her head and smiled as she stepped inside. "This is a cozy place you have." Pine scent filled the room. She sent her gaze flitting around, noting two closed doors. "You have two bedrooms? This is nice."

He ignored her question. "I guess. I like privacy."

Payson had everything she needed to know. Her pulse pounded. It was Darius Jasper. The same scraggly sandy hair and unremarkable face from his mug shot.

She tuned her ears to any sounds from another room, but there were none. "You live here alone, right?" She flashed a smile again. "I just need to know for the company. They're sticklers for details. You know how it is." She smirked.

"I'm not a fan of big companies." His dull eyes peered at her.

"Oh, I feel you. I've got to do my job, though. I can't lose it."

He nodded and circled around her. Her mouth got dry. He wasn't a DA, but he was treading a dark path. She felt it in the room—a heavy invisible cloud of misguided intentions sucked up all the air. She expanded the light in her center.

Darius led her to the kitchen—a wall with two cupboards, a small sink, and tiny refrigerator—where he pulled out a chair from a rickety table and slumped into it. "Have a seat."

She remained standing. "Could I have your name?"

"Why do you need my name?" He leaned on an elbow and narrowed his eyes. "What is your company doing a survey for?"

"Like I said, I just need to give them information. I don't know why. But the company was contracted by a real estate developer exploring possibilities of building a resort in the mountains. So what is your name and are you the sole occupant?"

A muffled sound reached her ears. She tightened her grip on her pain. The sound made her heart cringe, but she couldn't let on.

"Umm, I live here alone. When do I get my fifty dollars?"

"When you finish the survey, I'll give the company your name and contact information and they will send you the money."

He shoved away from the table and strode briskly to the front door. "I'm done." He jerked the door open and pointed out."

"Oh, okay. Sorry to intrude."

She barely got out the door before it slammed behind her.

Sprinting to the car would have been her choice, but she still had to be careful and not arouse any flight impulses in Darius.

She drove back to the grove of trees and pulled in to conceal her SUV. She checked in with the Gower Police Department. Tracking the road for any traffic and the Impala in particular, she reminded them of the location and confirmed that her subject was inside, possibly hiding a victim.

"Okay, Ms. Silver, we'll notify the cruiser closest to that location and send more," the dispatcher assured her.

"Please, no sirens. I don't want to announce we're coming."

"I'll inform the officers. We'll be right there."

She disconnected and sat waiting. It made her blood burn to have to sit in the car doing nothing. She crossed her arms over her chest, her pulse racing.

She allowed the image in her mind to open. The visual of Shana restrained inside the dumpy cabin pushed her pulse faster. She checked her firearm to make sure, what? It worked? She knew it was loaded, but it was good to double-check. *Relax. Breathe.* Calm spread through her gut, then her limbs, and through her chest. Adrenaline was powerful stuff, though. Her heart pounded in her ears.

"That's it!" she declared.

She climbed out and shoved her gun back in her holster. Her limbs stiff from tension, she sprinted back toward the cabin. As she got close, she sunk to the ground on her heels, hiding in brush and trees.

Again, waiting ate up her patience. She pulled off her cap and fidgeted with the brim.

She called Braden. His phone rang once, twice, three times.

"Payson. Are you okay?"

The sound of his voice murmured through her. "Yeah. I just wanted to hear your voice. Are you okay?"

"Yeah, I'm fine. But your voice is trembling. You sure you're okay?" His voice deepened. "I wish I were with you."

"I know. I'd like that too. But everything is fine. I found Darius."

"Oh wow! Good job, Payson. How about Shana?"

"She's inside somewhere. I'm waiting for Gower PD."

"Right. I'm with you in my heart."

"Wait, have you heard from Diane?"

Silence.

"Tell me, Braden." Her thoughts scrambled. "I need to know."

"Everything is fine. I have info to share when you get home."

"Be safe, please."

His voice dropped. "You too. Call me when you can."

"I love you too." She heard his concern in his voice but he was fine. She could tell. And his love filled her.

The sound of oncoming vehicles grabbed her breath. She peeked out from the bushes and saw the Gower PD cars racing toward the cabin. Rising to her feet, she motioned wildly, pointing them to the side of the road. Her breath came easier as they complied and came to an abrupt stop down the road. She still wore the reflective vest so she was comfortable walking down the road knowing if Darius looked out the window, he would not be alarmed.

Once past the cabin, she ran up to the group of cruisers. "I'm the recovery agent who called in, Payson Silver."

A lead officer nodded. "I'm in charge. Officer Dakota."

Around them eight officers checked their weapons and were talking approach.

"The man inside is not my problem, the potential victim inside is why I'm here."

"Affirmative. We've read your report. Let's hope this goes well and you get the woman and we get the perp."

Crouching while running to the cabin, Dakota led the men, their weapons ready. "You four take the back, four of you take positions on either side of the front door."

Payson followed on Dakota's heels, hanging back enough to let the officers get inside and secure Darius.

"Gower Police," Dakota yelled through the door. "Open up."

No response. Dakota circled his fingers above his head and the other officers swarmed behind him. With a quick, forceful kick, Dakota splintered the front door.

Payson followed them inside, crossing her fingers that the officers out back poised on alert.

"Clear," called out an officer from one of the rooms.

"Clear," hollered another.

Her pulse in her throat, Payson ran to the back door behind an officer.

"Nothing here," said another officer.

Her heart dropped to the bottom of her feet. This couldn't be. It had been only minutes since she stood in the cabin talking to Darius. Ainsley's impression of Darius leading Shana into the woods reminded her it was possible they had left. She glanced at the Impala under the tarp and walked to it. With a brisk flick, she yanked off the tarp and let it fall to the ground. Empty. The car sat empty, and through the car windows she didn't see any blood or other signs of trouble. Maybe the impression Ainsley saw hadn't transpired yet. Maybe it was a possibility she could prevent. Urgency filled her throat like bile. She pulled at the door handles but they were locked.

She stomped back inside and peered at the floor, examining every foot. Slowly she walked through one room, noting the small single mattress and chest of drawers. She bent to examine the seams in the wood flooring, but came up with nothing telling.

In the next room, she perused every inch. A full-size bed, a large dresser, a closet with few clothes. She touched a shirt hanging from a wooden rod.

She sucked in a breath. Darius stood in her mind, hanging up the shirt. Sweat beaded on his face and he turned toward the bed. Payson froze. A young woman who matched the photos she had of Shana was lying on the bed, naked.

"Where is the lacey thing I gave you? I want you to wear it." Darius licked his lips and pulled a black lace, short negligée from a drawer and tossed it at her.

Payson wrapped her arms around her middle and crouched. Another image appeared. Darius again, tying Shana's wrists to the bed. Her eyes glistened with tears.

"Stop crying." Darius caressed her cheek while Shana tried to turn away.

Payson flinched, as she saw Darius slap her face.

"What's up, Payson?" Dakota asked.

Jerked from the scene in her head, she looked up into his eyes. "I'm concentrating. I know Shana is here, I just can't prove it."

"You're having a gut instinct? Yeah, that's hard."

Suddenly her thoughts turned to Braden. Nausea burbled in her stomach. It wasn't the same, but like Shana, Braden had been held captive. The block Diane made had kept him isolated from people who loved him, removed from his normal life. *Why oh why do people hurt one another?*

She connected to the light inside her and quieted her thoughts. Shana was near. She strode to the other bedroom and stood still. The room was empty of a closet. It was sparse with only the bed and small dresser. She yanked open a drawer and pulled out a blue camisole. As she wrapped her fingers around the fabric, an image flashed.

"Shana, come in here." Darius's voice was sharp.

Payson saw Shana standing barefoot near the bed, wearing the same camisole and a pair of underwear. Her expression was pinched. Fear darkened her eyes.

Faintly she heard the officers searching the cabin. She squeezed her eyes tight, even though the image closed, hoping to create a kind of connection with Shana grounded in the physical objects she'd touched.

Everything in her narrowed down to her sense of Shana. If she was close, so was Darius. Caution was important. Again, she crossed to the other room and dropped to her knees, listening with every cell in her body. She waited. Her body ached, as though she was being shoved through a keyhole, straining to catch a sound alerting her that Darius was holding Shana somewhere in a secret place in the cabin.

Dakota's voice came near and she motioned for him to leave, pleading for silence with her eyes. He nodded.

"Okay, let's wrap this up, guys. There's no one here."

She could have hugged him hard. But she didn't move, still waiting for a break.

Oh, Braden. I need you now.

She said it as prayer, knowing he wouldn't hear her but wanting so much to connect with him. She understood that love was an energy, and therefore had no physical boundary. She let her love flow to him. Their connection came easily and her heart began pumping with more vigor. Warmth glowed inside her. Though apart, she knew they were together, each a force to help the other. Their Aeon abilities made it possible.

Silence was all around and time crept. Still, she remained quiet, motionless. Expectant.

Then it was there. A small whimper and a harsh remark coming from above.

"Shut up! They're gone now. It won't do you any good to holler."

A creaking sound across the hall was followed by footsteps.

"Go wash your face. You look terrible." Darius sneezed. "That attic room is dusty. You need to clean it up."

Payson slid her body across the room, crawling behind the door before either of them entered the hall. From between the door hinges and the wall, she saw him follow Shana into the larger room where the bathroom stood across from the kitchen. She was wearing only a skimpy nightie.

Without hesitation, she tiptoed across the room to the window and pulled back the curtain. Dakota was just outside. She swept her arms back and forth until she got his attention. She gave him the universal sign for *Yes,* a thumbs up.

While she took in the trap door hanging from the ceiling across the hall, Dakota and his men stormed in.

"Hands in the air," he barked.

Darius twisted back toward the hall and came right at her, his eyes wild, his skin ashen. Her legs splayed, rooted to the floor, she aimed her gun at him. "Stop. I don't want to hurt you, Darius."

She truly didn't. What she saw was a man in so much pain he had to project it out into the world. But even he had choices, he just didn't realize it.

Dakota kicked him to the floor and Payson went to Shana, taking her aside. "It's okay. It's over. He isn't going to hurt you anymore."

While two officers cuffed Darius and took him to a vehicle, others tended to Shana and brought her clothes and sandals. Dakota and the remaining officers followed Payson up the ladder hanging from the ceiling and began their evidence collection.

She shivered, standing under the low ceiling in the cramped room. The temperature of the room was stifling. She shivered with the foul sense of darkness filling the room. It was palpable to her. Her arms to her sides, she didn't want to touch anything.

She heard Shana sobbing as officers tried to comfort her. Down the ladder and into the so-called living room, Payson was careful to give Shana space. But she knelt on one knee in front of her and smiled up at her. "I'm Payson. I'm so very glad to see you. These officers are going to take you to the local hospital and I'm going to follow behind. I'll stay by your side until I can take you home to your parents." There would be another time to give her the truth about her father.

"My mom and dad?" she stuttered.

"Yes, they've never given up hope they'd find you."

Shana raised her hands to her face. "It's been so long. I thought I'd never see them again."

An officer interrupted. "We're ready to take you to the hospital now, miss. Just come with me."

On her way out the door, Payson stopped. "Sergeant Dakota, thank you so much for helping me return Shana to her mother."

He tipped his cap. "Great work, Payson. We make a good team."

CRISP MEDICINAL SMELLS and beeping tones punctuated the background while Payson walked the same few steps back and forth in the emergency waiting room at Gower Hospital, awaiting a report from the ER doc about Shana's condition. She inhaled full breaths and exhaled slowly and steadily. She had memorized Adele Freeport's phone number, specifically for this day. Her fingers traced the edges of her cellphone case. Common sense held her back from placing the call. Shana's mother would want to know everything, including her daughter's physical and mental health. Right now, all she would be able to report was that Shana was alive and safe.

Payson's heart expanded. Shana was safe. Jubilation bubbled inside her. She couldn't contain it, she had to call Braden and share it.

"Payson, I've been waiting for your call."

"I got her, Braden. Shana is in the emergency room getting checked out. But she's alive and safe."

"Oh God, you did it." His voice floated to her, and her heart opened wide. "I'm speechless. You saved her life and restored hope in her mother."

"I felt you with me." Joy spilled down her cheeks. "I can't wait to see you."

"I can't wait to hold you. When are you coming home?"

"I don't know. It depends on Shana. The doctors are probably going to admit her, at least for observation."

"Right. Well, we just wait. When you get home we'll celebrate," his voice teased.

"You mean with cake and ice cream and balloons?"

His laughter filled her heart. His voice turned sultry. "No, not what I was thinking of."

"I'm going to hold you to that celebration."

"I hope you do. I miss you."

"I miss you, too."

"Ms. Silver?" A nurse called her, beckoning.

"I have to go. I love you."

A heavy pause hung in the air. "I love you."

Braden's parting words played through her, begging for his presence. She wanted the intimacy of his breath on her skin, the warmth of his arms around her, the sizzle of his lips touching hers. But for now, his words held her solidly to the earth and that would have to be enough.

$\mathcal{O}$UT OF THE lion's den, into the fire, or something like that, Braden quipped to himself. He neared the river where Barry Russell's office was located in a small building in Old Town.

The rumbling in his body began again as he entered the building. He yawned, trying to pop his ears. Pressure pounded against his eardrums.

He stood at the door to Russell's office and read the attached sign. "Stillwell Place." Silently he repeated to himself what he knew: *I am not alone.* The strength of the Aeons was in him, and that connection put him in touch with Payson, Cooper, Keegan, Ainsley, and Skye.

He touched into his light again and linked it with his mind control. He opened the door and stepped into the outer office.

"Can I help you?" A pretty young woman sat at a desk. Her smile could easily distract an unknowing person from the sad fact that she was DA.

Braden's heart hurt. "I'm Detective Powers from the Auralia Police Department." He flashed his badge. "Is your boss available?"

"I'll check." The smile remained as she rose and swayed down the hall. A minute later, she returned. "He'll see you, Detective." Her voice set his nerves on edge, the way it slithered toward him.

He nodded and strengthened his energy field against the secretary and the boss.

"Come in, come in, Detective. I hope this is a friendly visit." The man stepped around his desk.

The pressure on his body hit Braden like a tsunami. It carried a punch of powerful dark intentions wrapped around seductive whispers. "Mr. Russell. Thank you for seeing me."

Russell's stride was long and stately. Braden estimated he stood about six-foot-four. His hair was short and a mixture of red and blonde. His body was muscular, and his handshake hearty. To the unknowing, he appeared a bright and friendly person. But the veil that hid his brooding eyes and angry heart was visible to Braden, all qualities of a powerful DA.

Russell gestured to a chair. "Have a seat," he said, and retraced his steps to his desk. "How can I help you? Are you in need of donations for the Help a Kid program? I always like to do my part to help out the community."

"This isn't a social visit. No, I'm not asking for money. I am investigating a series of robberies."

Russell's brow furrowed. "You don't think I'm involved with robbery, do you?"

Braden ignored the question. "I have some mug shots to show you." He laid photos on the desk. "Warren Brown and Nick Ward. What can you tell me about these men?" He decided to skip asking if he knew them because they both knew he did.

"Uhh ... " He raised a shadowy look at Braden and engaged him in high-power, World Armwrestling Federation-level determination to throw him off. Braden's vision blurred under the pressure. "Listen, I don't know why you're here asking me questions about these two. You obviously have an agenda. I don't like your innuendo."

Braden narrowed his gaze. "It's my job to ask." He planted his feet solidly on the floor. "You don't like my innuendo? How about I be direct?" He pressed harder against Russell's strength. "I'll tell you what I know. Brown is a thug, involved in some capacity with a crime ring. Nick was a young man who worked for Brown and he stole things."

He leaned closer, pushing against the force aimed at him. "Nick is dead. Brown got him killed because I got too close."

"And what does any of this have to do with me? You're wasting my time."

"You know Nick is dead. You know Brown, because he works for you, or should I be specific? He works for your operation."

Almost imperceptibly, Russell's brows arched, then dropped back into place. "Do you mean my project? You're suggesting he is working on the casino?"

Braden exhaled heavily and rolled his eyes. "Don't play dumb with me. You asked me why I'm here." He slanted his head and held his center. "I want to be up front with you. I know you're not merely the CEO of Principal Industries. You're the CEO of an organized crime organization and you have launched plans to expand your illegal activity here. I know you have already established a network of drug runners and couriers who move your money around to other cities. I've met some of them. Shall I remind you of their names? Ryan Crow, for example.

"Ryan doesn't work for me."

"Okay, stick to your story. But I'm going to pin the robberies on you, because I know you're behind them. They are distractions, busy work for APD, while you and the people in your pocket go about securing the city for your operations." Braden took a breath. "I'm not going to let you."

Russell jumped to his feet and pointed a finger toward the door. "You're not so smart telling me what you know. If you're right about me, you should understand that you're dead meat."

It was no small accomplishment to get away from the dark energy swirling around him, but Braden did it. He turned toward the door. "You can't stop me, you know. People, detectives, know what I know."

"No one can protect you, Detective. You should have learned that the first time."

The words hit Braden in the back as he left. It wasn't true, he knew that. But the dark power in Russell made it difficult for him to believe his light could make a difference.

Outside, he gulped fresh air until the suffocating sense of malice left him. He had discovered what he had suspected was true. The facts had told him Russell ran a mob, but Braden needed to be in his presence to confirm he was a DA. Darkness had overwhelmed Russell.

He checked the time. It was almost quitting time for Zane, but curiosity churned in Braden's head. He punched the number for Zane's cellphone.

"Braden. Everything is fine right now." Zane's voice was low.

"You're not alone, are you?" He heard phones ringing and chatter in the background as white noise to Zane's cover.

"It's busy here. But nothing more to tell you about Eddie's shooting."

"Okay. I just wanted to check with you. I pushed Russell's buttons."

"Understood." Zane spoke to someone, then came back on the line. "I have to go. Keep safe, buddy."

"You too."

Braden yawned and rubbed his eyes. The confrontations with Diane and Russell dragged on his body. The sun was still bright in the late afternoon sky, but he couldn't go on. A mixture of weariness and loneliness sapped all he had. If he ran into any DAs, he'd be nearly helpless against their intentions.

The pull to Payson's home was irresistible. He drove out of the city and toward her house as though going home.

At the fence protecting her property he punched in the passcode and let the serenity that was her home and the nature around it fill him.

Inside, ZuZu ran across the living room floor to brush vigorously against his leg. "I miss her, too, ZuZu." He picked up the cat and went to the refrigerator to get cat food. He stood there with the frig door open, perusing the contents. Then the persistent meowing began.

"Okay, okay." He placed ZuZu on the floor and spooned food into her dish.

He checked the cupboards and found Payson's favorite vanilla and almond granola cereal and poured himself a bowl. The almond milk added, he leaned against the counter and ate mouthfuls of the stuff, his muscles relaxing.

Her scent was all around. It was at the same time refreshing and painful. His arms ached to hold her.

He finished his cereal, meandered to the couch, and slumped into it. She had assured him she would call when she had an update, but waiting twisted hard in his gut. He dropped his head against the back of the couch and closed his eyes.

He reached out to her with his energy. The energy made them in sync with one another, able to touch each other. The link surrounded him in love he could rest in. He amplified his light, and satisfaction that he could bring her close pulsed in his heart.

His phone rang and he saw that it was Payson. "Hey! I was just thinking about you."

"Good. I felt your energy. Thank you for that touch. It was reassuring." He could hear her smile.

"For me too."

"Any problems with Diane?" Her voice pinched, but she'd made it sound cheery.

"Nothing but silence."

"That's almost eerie."

"I know. You need to get back here. Things are happening." He had to bite his tongue to keep from spilling everything he had found on Diane's computer and details of his face-to-face with Russell. Shana was enough for her to manage right now. ZuZu jumped into his lap and he smiled. "I'm in your house. ZuZu is lonely for you and so am I."

She chuckled and the sound of it stirred things in his body. "Good. That's one less thing I need to worry about. You'll be safe there."

He heard someone calling her name. "Do you need to go?" His heart dipped, longing to touch her silky skin.

"Yeah. But first, I want to update you. Shana's mother is here. She flew out as soon as I told her. It's made a difference in her daughter's condition."

"Is she hurt? What condition?" He balled his fingers.

"She's physically okay. Emotionally she's been a mess. Darius made her do things and threatened to hurt her family if she tried to escape. The doctor had the nurses do a rape kit examination on her, but the small bit of semen they found didn't have viable sperm. Apparently, Darius is sterile. She was evaluated by a psychiatrist and was diagnosed with severe persistent trauma. Lots of crying and a sense of loss."

He listened, scratching ZuZu's neck. "Of course. So when do you think you'll come home?"

"When her mother arrived she really relaxed. It's helped her process, but she's still very fearful. She's wanted me around and in fact that's who just called my name."

His heart sank. "So you don't know when you'll come home."

"Shana was reevaluated late this afternoon and cleared to leave the hospital in the morning."

"Oh. Great!"

"I'll be home tomorrow." Her voice dropped. "Braden, I can't wait to be with you. Could you meet me when I get back?"

He couldn't suppress his laughter. "You bet! Just let me know where and when."

"ZuZu, Payson's coming home," he said after he disconnected. "How shall we welcome her back?"

He lifted his legs and reclined on the couch. "Flowers, of course. Probably cake. You know Payson loves cake." His thoughts turned to imagining kissing her lips and never parting again.

But first, they had to save Auralia from going completely dark and make it safe for everyone. Life, his life and Payson's, always took a back seat to their mission.

PAYSON UNFURLED FROM the couch in Shana's room early in the morning and headed for coffee in the cafeteria. The liquid made her smile as she sipped it on her way back to the family room across from Shana's room.

Exuberance burbled inside her heart. The muted sounds of Shana and her mother talking reminded Payson how much she loved reuniting missing persons with their loved ones.

Adele tapped her shoulder. "Payson, Shana is asking for you." Adele's touch elicited an image, an experience of the mother first seeing her lost daughter when they were alone earlier.

"Shana, it's Mom." Adele stood over her daughter's bed and whispered. "I love you so much."

"Mom? Mom?" Tears spilled down Shana's face and she reached for her mother.

Adele hugged her daughter, each one hanging on for time that had passed.

Adele reached an arm out to Payson and pulled her into the embrace. "How can I thank you?"

The image dropped, but the joy at the memory remained and added to the many others of lost people she'd been able to return home.

She followed Adele into Shana's room, where the young woman sat on the edge of her bed, thin and pale from her ordeal, but dressed. Payson savored the peaceful expression on her face. Life had returned to her eyes. "Are you about ready to go home?"

"I'm more than ready."

"Good. Our flight leaves today at twelve-forty-five."

Shana began rocking slightly and wringing her hands. "I hope I can avoid any media attention when I get to the Auralia airport."

"I can understand that. I've taken care of it, or I should say my friend, Detective Powers, is handling that."

Adele rubbed her daughter's arm. "Yes, we've worked with him to make sure we have a very calm arrival." Her eyes darted to Payson.

"You'll be surrounded by your mom and me, and Detective Powers and a small group of officers will usher us to a private room when we get off the plane. While we're in that private setting, I'll issue a statement for you. Only a reporter for the local newspaper and one from the local television news will attend that mini press conference. You don't have to do anything or say anything unless you want to. Your mother will be by your side. You don't have to be in the same room, even."

"Thank you." Raw tears trickled down her cheeks. "I'm sorry I'm so emotional." She swiped at her tears.

Payson knelt in front of her. "No apologies, please. You've been through a terrible thing. It's going to take time to recover. That is your main thing to do right now, rest and recover. Let people love on you."

AS THE PLANE touched down on the runway in Auralia, Payson went on alert.

Though she and Shana had worked on her statement during the flight, Shana had slept through most of it. While she slept, Payson had spread peace to her and her mom, supporting their healing process and filling them with so much light they would get through the airport situation with more assurance.

That was for them. Her job was incomplete until she delivered Shana back home, so she relied on her protection mode to guide her.

But there was more for her to address. The character of the air and energy shifted as they entered Auralia space. It tugged at her spirit. Prevailing *dark noise* set her teeth on edge as though touched with a tuning fork.

Inside the terminal, Payson took the lead, glancing around for threats or intrusions.

"Payson." Braden walked up behind her and touched her shoulder. She smiled, her pulse stuttering.

As officers led Shana and her mother to another room, Payson reached her arms up and around his shoulders, pulling him close and drawing from his beautiful spirit. She didn't care that they stood in a public place, she grabbed the moment for herself. "You're here."

"I wish we could get alone, but—"

She put her fingers to his lips. "I know. We can't yet. Thank you for being here and getting things covered to shield Shana and her mom."

"Of course." He pointed across the large open space. "They've been set up in a there by themselves."

His hand against the small of her back sent warmth through her body as he guided her to the room. "Okay. That's good."

"You can deliver your statement when you're ready."

"Braden?" She paused to capture his gaze. "Darkness has escalated in Auralia."

He pursed his lips. "I know. I feel it too. We just have to be ready, as always."

She nodded and entered a private room where she would deliver her statement. Braden introduced her to the reporters and then she watched him recede into the background, alert and watchful.

She addressed the reporters. "Well, shall we do this?"

The young woman newspaper reporter nodded. The newscaster, another young woman, agreed and motioned to her crew. "We're rolling."

The cameraman aimed the camera at the reporter while the newspaper woman began to write on a small tablet.

"I'm here at Auralia Regional Airport welcoming Shana Freeport back home after two years in captivity."

The TV reporter turned to Payson and the cameraman focused on them both.

"I'm with renowned bounty hunter Payson Silver. Ms. Silver located Ms. Freeport and reunited her with her family. Ms. Silver, you must be very gratified."

"As a recovery agent, it is my great pleasure to serve justice. In this case, I am blessed to have been able to work with my contacts and the police department to free Ms. Freeport. Her return home is long overdue."

"Could you give us some details?" the reporter asked.

"The authorities will release details when they're ready. But I will say that Ms. Freeport's ordeal has ended and she and her family would appreciate respect for their privacy as they focus on Shana's return to her life."

She stepped away from the reporters and knocked on the door to the family's room.

Inside, she narrowed her attention to Shana, embracing her in the energy of love. "You're safe. I'm so amazed at your resiliency and courage, Shana." The young woman's blue eyes soaked up Payson's sentiment. "People care about you. Love is all around you and inside you. You're going to be all right."

"Thank you. You saved me. I will never forget you, Payson."

"Of course you won't. I'm not going to disappear."

Shana's brows lifted and life sparkled in her expression. "You'll keep in touch?"

"Certainly. I've also arranged for you to talk to a counselor. Her name is Claire Eve Kelly. She's very good. She'll be contacting you about when she can visit with you." Shana looked at her mother, and Adele nodded. "Now, the officers are going to take you and your mother home and see that you're settled in. Please, trust your future to be kind, sweetie. I'll see you soon."

"Right this way." Two officers ushered the family to a cruiser while Payson and Braden watched until they drove away.

She let out a cleansing breath. "Can we go now?"

He slanted a grin at her and folded a lock of her hair behind her ear. His touch was a gently rolling laugh that drew her in, filling her heart.

"I left my car parked in long-term parking here." She reached for his hand.

He picked up her bag and grasped her hand. "I had help from Keegan getting your car back to your place. I'm going to take you home. "I can't wait to talk with you about my investigation."

"Talk? That's what you can't wait for?" She gave him a teasing grin.

He tilted back his head and let loose a rowdy laugh. "I love the way you think." His arms swept her up and he bent close. His familiar scent washed over her and he kissed her long and hard. Nothing could move her from this spot in time. "Does that answer your question?"

She nodded.

Suddenly Braden howled and grabbed his head. "Payson," he gasped.

A fierce vibration drummed around her. "Braden, we've got to get out of here."

From either side of them, two figures marched toward them. The whirring became audible inside her head. One of the men grabbed her around the throat and squeezed just enough to cut off her voice, while the other one stole Braden's gun out of his holster and aimed at her.

An image of Diane, her face contorted and full of rage, standing in front of the men, ordering them to deliver the threat filled her mind. Helplessness sifted through her, dragging down her strength and her force.

"You've been warned about interacting with each other," spoke one of the men. His voice harsh, it hammered against her brain.

As though from a deep well, Payson heard people gathering around, speaking in staged whispers.

"What's going on here?"

"I don't know, but it's a fight for sure."

"The guy with the gun is bad ass."

The voices sickened her. No one standing up to help. No one calling the police. People just gawked and jeered. The power of the dark ways in Auralia promoted such thoughts. Giving into it empowered darkness.

Payson reached deep inside and found her center. She expanded the electrical fire sparking in her core and let it fill the space around her and out into the parking lot. With her will, she spread the energy to connect with Ainsley, Skye, Cooper, and Keegan. She knew they would feel the energy and respond. She clenched her teeth, drawing more and more energy. The longer she held it, the more her strength grew.

Her eyes on Braden, she watched his face slowly relax and he straightened to his full six-two.

"Thanks for the warning," she gritted out. "Here's yours."

Before he had time to say 'Huh?' she seized the DA's hand from her neck and twisted his arm hard behind his back.

Near simultaneously, Braden kicked the gun out of the other man's grasp, sending it spiraling across the pavement. The man lunged for the gun, but Braden slammed a foot in his face.

The man grunted, but barely slowed. He drew back his right fist, then landed a hard hit to Braden's jaw.

Fury flamed in Payson's gut. The two men had no mercy in them. But they also had no mind of their own. They simply followed orders. She wouldn't take their lives, not ever, if she could free them.

She jumped on the back of the man who had grabbed her and kicked at him, her feet dangling along his sides. He grunted, but stayed on his feet. She slipped down and stabbed a side-kick into his middle. He doubled over and before he could gather himself, she kicked him in the groin.

"You bitch," he grunted, and tipped over, holding his crotch and rolling on the ground.

She pivoted to see Braden had retrieved his gun. He stood over the other man, smirking. "Did Diane send you?" When the man didn't answer, Braden kicked at him.

"Yes, she did."

Payson's breath heaved. "Diane is not happy."

With both men on the ground, she consciously touched them softly with the light inside her, gently offering a way out of the darkness in which they existed. A charge electrified the air as she waited, negative versus positive. But nothing changed. The heaviness and the sandpaper scratching under her skin remained. All she could do was offer the DAs a different choice. They had to accept or not.

Frustration growled in her gut. She exchanged a look with Braden, and he nodded.

"Okay, you two. Get out of here before I arrest you for assault. I'm going to let you make a choice for good or return to your boss and see what happens."

She could see in their eyes their indecision. Fear, too, maybe at failing to fulfill Diane's orders. "C'mon. You've delivered your message. We've been warned. Now get out of here."

One of the men lunged at Payson and stepped into a move with his left hook, but Braden blocked him and hit him hard in the face. Bones crunched, but the man hardly blinked.

The other DA turned and grabbed his companion's arm. "Let's go." He leered at Payson one more time before the two lumbered off.

Braden addressed the few remaining bystanders. "Time to go, folks. There's nothing here to watch."

CHAPTER 25

$\mathcal{B}$RADEN DROVE TO a meeting of the Aeons, his hand on Payson's all the way to the coffee shop. He opened the door for Payson at Coffee Is and together they went to the dining area.

Braden surveyed the room, memories filtering up from deeper in his mind of Ainsley giving Skye the antique chandelier that lit the room, and how it became a game for the Aeons to find quirky lamps to set on the tables. They'd made it their home away from home to gather as a group.

He pulled out a chair for Payson at a grouping of tables at the back, then sat in a chair next to her. "I want to be close to you," he whispered in her ear.

"I want you close too. We've been apart too much." Her smile lit him up.

"Hey, would you mind some company, you two love birds?" Cooper strode across the room with Keegan and they each took a seat across the table. "Good to see you back home, Payson. Way to go with that missing person case."

"Well, she is the *quote* renowned bounty hunter we all know and love." Keegan flashed a broad smile and used air quotes to emphasize the line from the reporter at the airport. "You make me proud, Payson."

"Thanks you guys. Thanks for your help. Whether it's Keegan helping me with background or Ainsley with using precognition to pinpoint my perp, or all the Aeons supporting each other with light and love, it means a lot to me that we can rely on each other."

"All for one and one for all, right?" Keegan beamed.

"Right," Payson said.

Braden sat back, warmed inside with the shared support. They needed it, especially now. "Where are Ainsley and Skye?"

"Skye will be here. She went home to change when the next shift came in. I don't know where Ainsley is. I thought Benjamin would be here today." Cooper ran his hand over his head and frowned. "Why did you call this meeting, Braden?"

"I'll tell you after Skye and Ainsley show up."

"I also invited Claire Eve," Payson said.

"Sure." Cooper gave her thumbs-up. "We've all sought her help at times."

Keegan's smile dropped. He shifted in his seat and rested his head in his hand. Braden shot him a sidelong glance, recognizing the signs that Keegan was picking up something troubling.

"Keegan, are you all right?" He never knew whether to pretend he didn't notice sudden shifts or ask. "I don't mean to intrude, but you look upset."

Cooper's hand went to his chest. "I feel it too."

Keegan lifted his head. "Do you want me to say?"

It was as Braden suspected. "Go ahead."

Keegan pointed toward Braden and frowned. "I hear disturbance in your head. Your thoughts are scattered. Your mind is raw. I don't know what happened to you today, but you went through something very traumatic. It left a mark."

Payson sighed. She looked into his face with troubled eyes, and his heart clenched. "Yeah, Payson and I were attacked at the airport by two DAs. They started with exerting pressure to my mind. But I'm okay. Maybe rattled some."

"Did I hear someone got hurt today? What can I do?" Skye asked, walking in to the room with Ainsley and Claire Eve. They each slid quickly into remaining seats.

Skye passed coffees around the table. "House black for Payson. Mexican half-decaf for Cooper. Two classic teas. Those are yours, Ainsley and Claire Eve." She set cups in front of Keegan and Braden. "Two more House blacks. And mine. A hazelnut Arabica."

"Thanks, Skye. Where's Benjamin? Did he not come in today again?" Ainsley asked.

"Yeah. Sick again." Skye frowned. "He didn't sound good on the phone."

"Maybe one of us should check on him. What's wrong with you, Braden?" Ainsley took a sip of her coffee.

"I'm fine. But the reason I asked you all to meet Payson and me here this afternoon is to discuss things I just discovered."

"You all know the dark energy is intensifying." Payson said. "When I flew in today from Colorado it was very evident. Auralia is sinking deeper and deeper."

"I'm sorry you were attacked." Cooper shook his head. "But I bet you kicked their butts." He grinned.

Braden's gut lurched. "We did. Physical violence isn't always the answer, but the bad news is that Payson's offer of light and love didn't take. The DAs are getting stronger, tougher, and their energy is manifesting devastating situations despite our efforts."

Skye sipped her coffee and rolled her eyes. "When you were out of touch, Braden, the rest of us got busy helping in a variety of ways. Our efforts helped a lot of people. I know that counted for something, but it hasn't been enough, I guess. We don't attack DAs. We don't try to eliminate them proactively. And embracing them in light isn't doing much to stem the darkness they're flooding the town with. The more the DAs succeed in perpetuating negativity, the more prevalent Dark Sides energies become."

Braden clenched his teeth. If Payson had taught him anything, it was never to give up. "Helping the human race evolve is why we are the way we are. I have information that we can work with."

He shared with his friends what he had learned about the mob infiltrating the area. He pulled a folded piece of paper from his pocket and smoothed it open on the table. "If we can identify how these people connect and why they're here in Auralia, maybe we can save the town and the innocent people being affected."

"That sounds like a good approach. Show us how it lays out." Claire Eve leaned closer.

In the center, he wrote 'Diane' and circled it. From that center point, he drew random lines and wrote names from the list of people he'd gathered: Brown, Russell, Crow, Brody, Farrod, Nick Ward. He circled each name and drew more lines wherever he had found a connection.

A somber weight dropped over him, and he wrote his name at the end of a line originating with Diane.

Keegan drummed his fingertips on the tabletop. "A thug, a mob boss, a drug dealer, a mayor and economic director, a dead drug runner. And a lobbyist. That's quite an interesting group of associates."

"Do we know if they're all DAs?" Skye asked.

"I haven't spoken face to face yet with Mayor Farrod or Tim Brody, the economic director, so I haven't confirmed it." Braden rubbed the back of his neck and continued to stare at the paper along with the others.

"I wondered when you went away, Braden, why Diane picked you to mesmerize." Ainsley twirled a lock of her hair.

"That question has been hounding me since the day I broke her block. But, I know I've struggled with anger for a long time. I have to accept responsibility for my anger making me susceptible to her power."

Skye wrinkled her forehead. "I suppose we all have weaknesses. But I wonder why she is determined to keep you two apart? Is it to isolate you from just Payson, whom you love, or is it to keep you from all of us?"

"Yeah, we're good people." Cooper grinned. "But to keep you from your loved one would have potential of not just hurting you and

Payson. When one or two of us are suffering, are we all hindered from our purpose?"

"There's something specific about you, and definitely with Payson. It's something Diane has deep feelings about." Skye narrowed her eyes."

Payson shook her head. "I have no idea what it's about. She's always been jealous of my relationship with Braden."

"Yeah, but maybe for me it's simply my work." A thought sparked in Braden's mind and he drew a line from his name out and wrote APD.

Keegan leaned closer to the paper. "She could use your investigation skills without drawing any attention."

"That's an idea," Skye added.

"That is exactly what my job was. To get intel for her."

Without speaking, Payson took the pencil from him. Slowly, intentionally, she drew another line from his name and added and circled each of their names. "The goal is to weaken the Aeons to expand the reach of Dark Aspects. And Diane is orchestrating it all, beginning with Auralia. She's not simply a DA, she's an Atlantean with a genetic connection to those who destroyed the civilization."

Braden draped his arm around Payson's shoulders. He couldn't breathe. He wanted to bury his head in her soft wavy hair and just be with her.

Claire Eve had been sitting quietly sipping her tea. She knitted her brow, but emanated calm. "You're leading to a conclusion that Diane has bigger plans than darkening Auralia."

Braden hung his head, loathing sinking like a boulder in his heart. "There's more. I waited to tell you until after all the other stuff because this piece is what is fueling everything else."

Ainsley strummed her fingers on the table. "Tell us already."

"I found a disguised file in Diane's computer that reads like a manifesto for a world order change."

"What? Whose manifesto?" Cooper frowned. "It must be Diane's since you found it on her computer."

Ainsley's expression went blank and Braden waited to continue until she came out of her trance. He could guess she was getting a precognitive hit about Diane's plans. He froze when he saw a tear meander down her cheek. He watched the effects of the vision on first her, then on Cooper and Keegan.

Cooper cried softly. "I have so much sorrow and just as much rage. Everything is dying."

Keegan closed his eyes, concentrating. "I hear whispers. This means there is a something secret at play. Words. Take over. Destroy." He opened his eyes and covered his mouth. "I'm stunned."

"I am too. Our mission is so huge and we cannot fail." Braden stared at Payson. "We're living proof that good people of Atlantis survived the cataclysmic event that destroyed all of Atlantis. But I'd never heard a part of the legend about any others surviving. The legend told us that dark factions destroyed the civilization and perished in the event. It's not so, according to the documents in Diane's computer."

"They're here in Auralia," Ainsley said. "They're organized, and if we don't stop the effects of dark energy, they'll kill every Aeon. I saw it happening."

"Why?" Skye's eyes begged for reason.

"It's as it was in the past, I think," Cooper said. "Back then, some Atlanteans were more dark than light and they wanted to rule the world. But their dark energies were chaotic. Like Diane's telekinesis is chaotic and can physically split objects apart."

"It looks like it." Braden shrugged. "I guess we shouldn't be surprised."

"No. It's been in play for a while, I'm sure. Diane is apparently connected with other powerful Atlanteans, perhaps Barry Russell is one, too." Claire Eve shook her head. "But each of you have what you need to counteract Diane's influence and thwart the plan. Try to let that knowledge direct your thoughts and plans."

Braden stared at her. Her expression serene, as though nothing was wrong, much less nearly everything. "I accept that it is our task to go the extra mile, infuse the world with hope, and unhinge the DAs with our light. But it feels like I'm lighting a match inside a large cave."

Her eyes bored into him. "Yours is not a task, Braden." Claire Eve slanted her head. "There is no extra mile."

His insides slid into an invisible lump. "Okay, Yoda. I get it. Be the light, not *try* to be the light."

She aimed kind eyes at him. "No, just be you, Braden." She placed her hand on his, and acceptance expanded him. "You are inseparable from the light."

"I'm tired, Claire Eve. I need a break." It was true. The need ached inside him.

"Then take one." She ran her gaze around the table. "Expressing your own brand of joy is as important to each of you as eating healthy food, serving the community, and standing up to darkness."

Her words released him from *shoulds* and *trying* that he didn't need. "You're right." He inhaled deeply and exhaled.

PAYSON SAT IN the mutual shock vibrating among the Aeons around the table. Her friends' expressions shifted as each one processed what they had learned and sat erect in their seats. She pictured the vines sprouting, twisting around, spreading around them and filling the room with life and hope.

"There are too many DAs to turn," Cooper said. "We don't even know where the core group plotting to take over the city is meeting. They have to be somewhere hatching their secret plan, but where?"

Keegan ran his hand over the back of his neck. "We don't know who they are either. If we did, maybe we could find them. But we'd have to fight. It's too late to influence them to lean into the light."

"We know where the leaders are." Payson nodded. "Mayor Joel Farrod is at the city building in the downtown. Economic Director Tim Brody is also in the city building."

Cooper's eyes glistened. "The bounty hunter finds people. You're probably right, Payson. No offense, Keegan."

"None taken." Keegan waved off Cooper's apology. "Do you think Barry Russell would be in his office at Principal Industries' headquarters or his office on the river?"

"You could listen, Keegan, for clues about where he is." Claire Eve rested her chin on her hand. "You guys have been causing disturbances in Auralia's energy field. The descendants of dark Atlanteans would have the ability to sense it." She slowly twisted a short lock of her auburn hair. "We each, in our own way, have been rocking their boat. They may feel the time is now to let loose their plans, before you Aeons succeed in creating an inhospitable environment for their dark energy to flourish.

"Okay, then, let's each take a spot where we'll probably find a DA prominent in the city. I'll take the mayor and Brody since they're both in about the same place." Cooper rubbed the top of his head. "I could use help."

"Count on me." Skye rested her hand on Cooper's arm.

"Thank you. Between my fighting skills and your healing ability, we should be able to take them off line."

"Don't forget," Claire Eve spoke up. "You also have the power of light and love in you. Don't discount that as a way to diminish their darkness."

"Right. I'll visit Russell. Ainsley, would you want to work with me?" Keegan perched on the edge of his chair.

"Of course. We'll make a good power couple. I'll see what's potentially going to happen and you'll hear things. We'll be totally prepared." Her eyes popped like saucers, full of confidence that plucked at Payson's gut. They all had a chance at turning the tide on the DAs.

Payson jumped at the sound of her ringtone. "It's Adele, Shana's mom."

Payson could hear low voices as the others sat discussing their next step, but she tried to tune them out. Fear in Adele's voice pierced her gut.

"Men came to our house. They were led by a woman in charge." Her voice rose, then cracked. "She and those men abducted Shana. I didn't know what to do. I just called you."

"That was a good choice. I'm so sorry this happened, Adele, but I'll get Shana back. I'll find her and bring her back to you. You have to stay hopeful. That is your one job now."

"I'll try. This is terrible. I just got her back." She sobbed over and over, and Payson wished she could hug her, but instead she extended her light and love to embrace her. And she would go after Diane.

She hung up and turned to Braden. "I want you all to leave Auralia, now."

"What? Why?" Ainsley asked.

Keegan sat back in his seat. "Yeah, why? We just made a plan."

"I know, but I know now that I have to talk to Diane. It's between her and me. I have to find Diane. She has Shana. I need you all to leave town so that I can be sure she can't get to you and neither can any of the others directly involved in her plan."

"I'll go with you." Braden patted her shoulder. "We'll find her. The rest of you, keep us in your light."

"No," Keegan shook his head. "I'm not leaving you guys alone."

"Please. You have to trust me." Certain she was right, Payson had to make them accept her request. "Claire Eve, you know I'm right. I have to be with Diane, alone."

Claire Eve held her gaze. Wisdom emanated from her and Payson soaked it in. It gave her clarity.

"I'm going to go to my lake house and hold light energy. Let me know if you need help." Claire Eve gathered her things to leave. "I think the rest of you should do as Payson asked."

Payson hugged her. She paused, her arms around Claire Eve's shoulder, breathing in her intense and elevated vibration. Tears threatened to spill over her face. "I know I'm strong," she whispered in Claire Eve's ear. "But I'm overwhelmed. So much is at stake. I feel it is my fault because Diane wants me dead. If it weren't for me, the others might not be in danger."

"I don't know if that's true or not, considering she does want to conquer the world. But it's not your fault. Diane is a DA. She isn't thinking from her heart or light, she's acting from her pain and darkness. Remember, your light and love and peace are powerful. You are a light being. Believe it. See it. Now go kick some DA ass."

Payson squeezed Claire Eve once more, then pulled away and turned to the others.

Cooper pulled Skye to her feet. "Well, if you're sure you want to go it alone, you two, then I'll oblige. Skye, Keegan, and Ainsley, let's take a road trip."

"Thank you." Payson turned to Braden. "I need to look for Shana. I need something of hers to connect with. I have some things at my house."

Braden took hold of her hand and energy surged between them. It was the boost she needed. "Then let's go get them."

PAYSON SAT IN the passenger seat in Braden's Highlander, holding a scarf belonging to Shana, her head aching. When she picked up the scarf, she opened to images, and they'd quickly flashed in front of her eyes.

"Diane is holding her at your house. The cussed mansion she replaced your condo with after she mesmerized you."

"Cussed?" He eyed her.

"Yes, cussed. She planted you there and made it your home, a fake home, along with fake stuff that wasn't your style."

"Yeah, I get that." He pulled her hand to his lips and kissed it gently.

Her heart stuttered as Braden sped through traffic. "Could you hurry?" Stress turned her voice into a squeak.

Braden punched the accelerator and the vehicle lurched forward. "Is that better?"

She concentrated on the scarf. Images flashed. Shana tied to a kitchen chair and DAs staring at her. Shana crying, asking for release. It all broke Payson's heart in pieces.

"I hate this. The only reason Diane abducted Shana was to spite me."

"I know. We're going to help them both. If we can turn Diane, she'll let Shana go and leave us alone."

His voice, calm and measured, soothed the anxiety twisting her gut. She knew he was right. "We're almost there. The vibration in the neighborhood is pounding like drummers on a set of quads." The hammering in her head got worse and Payson deepened her breathing. Braden drove up the driveway and climbed out.

Payson kept intentionally allowing her light to build.

Then she heard Shana scream.

"Oh no!" she hollered.

Braden stood at the front door, waiting for her signal to charge in. She gestured toward the backyard and nodded. He returned her nod, but waited.

She raced around the house to the back door and twisted the knob. It was unlocked. A few quiet steps inside and dark energy flooded her. She struggled to breath and proceeded toward the living room, creeping along the wall. Braden's elevated vibration whirred serenely around the room. He was somewhere inside now.

Then she heard his voice on the other side of the wall she was hugging. It was firm, persuasive. He was using his mind-control ability to coax DAs in the house.

"I'm here for Shana. You can release her to me. You don't need to be here."

"That so?" one DA countered. "I think you're mistaken."

Shana sniffed but kept quiet.

Payson held back to let Braden control the scene. If he succeeded in controlling the DAs minds, they would be able to get her out of the house without a big showdown. If it didn't work, she was perched for a fight.

She poured her light and love into the room. With all her angst and desperation pitting against calm, she focused on her strength and power. *I am safe, and there is no fear.*

"You don't want to fight me. We only want the woman. It's okay to let us have her. You can leave," Braden continued.

"No man, I don't want to fight you. You're here for this bitch? You can have her. We don't want her. Let's get out of here." The DA doing all the talking led the other outside.

Payson sucked in air. Braden's mind-control had worked on them.

If these guys were alone and Diane wasn't in the house, then where was she? She ran after the men. It was worth a try. "Hey, you two. Wait."

"What?" One of them gave her dark look. "We're leaving."

"Before you go could you tell me where to find Diane? I think she's looking for me." She brushed her hair out of her face and held her boundaries.

Both DAs chuckled. "Oh, she'll find you when she wants you. Don't worry." They climbed in an SUV and drove off. Payson stood watching them leave. Exhaustion, physical and emotional, weighed heavy on her body. She didn't like the sound of what they had said. It left her with a sense of someone just out of view watching her. She shivered hard and ran back inside.

Her heart dipped. Poor Shana. Diane was using her as a distraction, no doubt. All Payson wanted was to get Shana back home with her mother.

"Shana, I'm going to take you home," Braden said. "I'm just going to get a knife from the kitchen."

She heard him cutting ropes off of Shana's arms and legs. Payson stayed scrunched close to the floor. She would stay there until Braden had Shana out. Shana's energy was thick and bleak. There was no way to know what might set Shana off if Diane had messed with her mind.

"Wait, where are you taking me? I don't want to go with you."

Oh my God. Payson's pulse pounded. Had Diane made a trap? She stood up and walked carefully into the living room. "Hi, Shana. Your mom is worried about you, so let's get you back home." Payson held eye contact with Shana and ice formed in her veins.

"I am home." Shana's eyes were dark. She spoke low and unwavering. "Diane told me all about you two and that she'd rescued me from your plans to keep me with my mother."

"It's true we're going to take you to your mom. She loves you."

Shana spit. "Nobody loves me. Only Diane, and she promised to protect me from my terrible mother. She left me with that pervert Darius Jasper. He hurt me, but my parents never came for me. I hate them."

Payson sensed Braden's light energy flowing while Shana, without knowing, explained what Diane had done to her. She had mesmerized her. They exchanged a glance. He could use his mind control to get her to cooperate.

Braden shook his head and she knew he was right. Shana had to make a choice in order to break Diane's mind block on her.

"I know your story. I took you away from that man, remember? You can trust me."

Shana started to wilt. "Where will I go? Diane told me to wait here, but I'm cold." She surveyed the room. "Where am I?"

"This is my house," Braden said. "I don't know why Diane left you here, but I can take you home. It will be warm there."

"No," she whispered. "I can't go there. My mom doesn't want to see me. Diane told me."

Payson could easily have raked her nails over Diane's face. Diane had done so much harm to people. Every effort Payson had made, every strategy she had tried hadn't stopped her. Failure at making a dent in Diane's darkness or deterring her from her goal clogged her throat. Unreleased sobs of falling short and facing the collateral damage that was this young woman.

"Shana, we can take you to my friend's house. She's a very kind person and she won't make you do anything you don't want to."

"What's her name?" Light glimmered in Shana's eyes.

"Claire Eve. Can I take you to her house now? Your mom won't know where you are and you'll be safe."

Shana nodded, and Payson relaxed. She took Shana's hand and followed Braden out to his vehicle. If they could make it safely to Claire Eve, Shana would be safe. It would be the best place for her because Claire Eve could hold space to contain Shana's extreme trauma from her abduction and support healing from Diane's invasion of her mind.

CHAPTER 26

$\mathcal{B}$RADEN'S SHOULDERS RELAXED watching Claire Eve settle Shana onto the couch and cover her with a blue and green afghan.

"My mom has an afghan like this. She crocheted it." Shana's voice was weak. Braden ran his fingers through his hair. She'd been through so much.

Claire Eve accompanied Braden and Payson to the door. "She'll be fine. I'll take care of her. You finish things with Diane." She nodded. "It's time."

Payson pursed her lips.

He didn't like to see her so tired and worried, but she was strong and he would be at her side. "What if Diane comes here?"

Claire Eve winked. "I'll deal with her. I know her well, you know. She can bluster and blame and threaten, but she's afraid of me." Payson glanced at Shana drifting to sleep on the couch. "We'll be fine. Shana made her choice. Diane's block is broken. Mesmerizing Shana was a strategic move. She wanted to distract you from the DAs plan and weaken you so she could get Braden back. But she also wants to hurt you, Payson, because you represent everything she doesn't have. Remember that."

Braden took Payson's hand and silently they walked to his car. He turned the ignition, awareness of the distorted energy flooding Auralia fueling his need for action. He gripped the wheel harder than he meant to. "I'm not going to let Diane or any other DA hurt you." His eyes fixed on the road ahead. He didn't want to scare her. He just had to remind her she wasn't alone.

"You either, Braden." She rubbed the muscles in his neck. The tightness that had given him a crick in his neck subsided.

He floated his fingers through her long locks. Neither of them knew what was ahead but right now, this is what he needed. Just Payson and the hope pumping through her veins. "If you could stop time right now and stay here with me forever in this moment, would you?"

She leaned her head against his shoulder. "Tempting. But no. What's ahead is why we're here. I have a better understanding now of the parts of me that want to be done with the pressures of our mission and the way we've lived. I've asked the question, why me, so many times and never gotten a satisfying answer. But the question I needed to grasp was what was the best way to use my gifts? As an Aeon, my awareness is unavoidable. Awareness, though, is not a curse, it's a gift that makes everything real."

He accepted her words because he perceived their truth. They soothed him. "I understand your point. Our lives are hard, but they're also beautiful."

"We can save the city, maybe the world, from darkness." She ran her hand down his thigh and left it there. Her warmth thrummed through the fabric of his jeans and warmed his skin. "We're going to win this battle. And we'll still be together."

"You sound so sure." Her hope flowed through him and he knew she was right. "Peace wins, right?"

"Peace wins."

"I love you." He raised his hand, his palm aimed at her. "Always."

Payson smiled and laid her palm against his. "Always, Braden." She turned away. "Take me to Sheppard Media Tower, please. I need to clear my head."

His heart thudded in his throat. No one would ever understand the kind of bond he shared with Payson. He could stop her from climbing to her perch above the city. It wasn't safe. But he wouldn't get in her way. She knew what she was doing, that much he understood. If their world came to an end this night, it would be because they had completed their mission, not because they had hidden from it.

He pulled into street parking at the building. Silently, they got out of the car and went to the front door. Payson used her keycode to unlock the lobby door, then she unlocked the door to the restricted access deck door and strode the few steps to the elevator.

He pressed the button on the elevator pad for the upper deck and counted off the floors they passed. The counting gave his mind something to focus on other than the grave situation they were heading into.

"My connection with the others is strong." Payson leaned against a wall, waiting for the last stop. "That's got to be a good sign."

He could hardly manage his awareness that life was fragile and this was the only moment he had with Payson. The present moment. Up at the top, he didn't know what was going to happen.

"Are you okay?" she asked. Her eyes sought clues.

"I'm fine." He was, except for the buzzsaw vibrating through his body. It would be easy to let fear fire in his chest. The fears would come out in words—were the others all right, was the world already dark outside of the elevator, could he protect Payson and save Diane, was Diane a hopeless case?

As they reached the top level of the building, he heard rain pounding and winds swirling around.

"The sky was clear, but it sounds like it's started to pour. Just what we needed, a storm," he complained. Payson looked into his eyes and he held his breath. "It's not a storm, is it?"

"No." She opened the door and he followed her onto the deck, fighting the circling column of wind. It filled his ears with its roaring power.

"Oh no." Payson groaned.

"Oh my God!" Braden tried to pull her toward him.

She shook her head. "Please, stay here." Payson's beautiful face pleaded with him.

"You don't have to do this alone."

"Please."

"I'll be right here."

PAYSON LEANED INTO the wind and walked steadily toward a point on the deck not quite in the center. Heartache throbbed in her chest at the sight of Diane in the middle of the tower top and Benjamin standing at her side.

"Diane, what is he doing here?" She had to yell into the wind. She reached with her energy stream to connect with Benjamin. His vibration rolled weakly, like a car running on fumes.

Diane smirked. "Benjamin, tell Payson why you're here."

"To be with Diane. She's my friend." His eyes dull, Benjamin's voice was empty of his personality.

"I'm asking you, Diane. Why did you bring him here? It's just you and me, working things out between us. Did you need reinforcements? Obviously, you've mesmerized him."

Diane lifted her chin. "You brought back-up, I see," she said, nodding toward Braden.

"I don't need him for back up." She drew her fingers into tight fists. Her fingernails cut into her palms. "Let Benjamin go." Despite the slow droning energy in Benjamin making it difficult to send him hope, light, and love, she strengthened her intention.

Diane laughed, sending shivers through Payson. "Okay." She draped her arm over Benjamin's shoulder and nuzzled his neck. "Take a walk, sweet boy."

Benjamin marched toward the edge of the tower top, his hair tossing wildly in the wind.

"No! Stop!" Payson screamed. She tried to run to him, but the wind grew stronger, slowing her steps. "Diane, what are you doing? Stop him."

"Go ahead. Use your light and love, Payson."

Her words twisted and turned in Payson's gut. She ignored Diane and ploughed through the turbulence surrounding her. "Benjamin, stop!" She grabbed for his arm, but he shirked her off.

"He won't hear you. He's mine, and he will do whatever I tell him to do. Good job, Ben. You're almost there. Just a few more steps, then climb to the top of the short guard wall."

Payson tried to hold onto Benjamin's arm, and turned to Braden. "Help me," she hollered.

Braden couldn't move. She could see that.

"I'm trying to," he yelled back.

It was up to her to break Diane's mind block on Benjamin. Everything she had strained toward him. Diane's telekinesis was feeding itself with Dark Sides of the city. It weighted Payson down. She gritted her teeth, fighting chaos and death and destruction, and watching, as though through a thick fog, Benjamin step to the edge of her perch. She saw his innocence, his Aeon potential, his right to choose teeter on the edge in his sneakers.

"No!" she tried again to scream but her voice got swallowed up in Diane's power.

Braden touched her arm as he passed her, his footsteps finally taking him closer to Benjamin. He stretched toward Benjamin, inches from him.

"Keep going, Benjamin." Diane's voice was ice.

Braden reached out his arm, striving. Benjamin looked at him, his eyes still blank. With his next step, he disappeared.

"No!" Braden leaned over the edge, gasping.

If Benjamin had screamed, Payson hadn't heard it. It was like the wind had sucked up all sounds, and she stood in a vacuum, staring at Diane, then at Braden.

"You let him fall." Her words were cruel, she knew that. "Why couldn't you be strong? You could have saved Benjamin."

Braden's expression crumpled. "I tried. Diane's powers are too strong."

"You let your anger rule. It wasn't just your work, Braden. It wasn't just Diane and the DAs that made you Diane's prey. You didn't face your self-contempt about your parents' deaths, so you let anger make you vulnerable. You left me, Braden."

"I did. You're right. I'm so sorry, Payson." His voice cracked. "But I'm here now."

"Are you?" Payson wrapped her arms around her body, coldness seeping through her. Sorrow and regret painted Braden's face. "I'm tired of having to take care of the world. Where is my choice? We didn't have a choice, not you and not me. Not any of the Aeons. We were born to fight the Dark Sides."

"I'm tired, Braden. Help me Braden." Diane's voice mocked her. "You disgust me."

Despair fuzzed her brain. Her pulse dropped, and words recited in her head. *You lose.* "Stop. Stop trying to mesmerize me."

"I can do anything with you I want."

Payson's vines surrounded her as she peered back at Diane. Diane's words were cold water in her face. The vines turned a putrid green and the leaves wilted in front of Payson's eyes.

Her heart sobbed. "I want to do what I want. A genuine choice for what is right for me, just me." The wind thrashed around, and inside her, pieces of nightmares, vigilance, and loss compacted into one large boulder in the pit of her soul. The burden of it loomed immense. There was no escaping that fact, and she stayed with it, knowing it well. Knowing it deeply and thoroughly. With that knowing, the boulder broke apart and light shone brilliantly. "Braden?"

"I'm here," he said. "We always have choices, baby."

Braden's voice registered in the center of her chest. "Thank you," she said. In that moment between them, Payson understood more than ever that she and Braden were a promise.

BRADEN CHOKED ON his own saliva as he watched Payson stride toward Diane. He wanted to protect her. He wanted her to stop before Diane hurt her. But this moment was years in the making, and he wouldn't interfere. Not yet.

The wind pitted against her, but Payson walked to the center across from Diane and planted her feet on the concrete deck. "Stop this. I don't want to hurt you."

Diane hollered into the wind and raised her arms, tearing off metal pieces from an air conditioning unit and lifting them to sail around her and Payson. "I'm going to hurt you, Payson. Pity it won't take me very long." Diane thrust her hands toward Payson and with the debris, rocks and papers blew toward her.

Payson ducked. "Missed me." She took another step toward Diane. "I'm sorry, Diane. I never meant to leave you alone in the world."

Diane growled. "Don't try to get inside my head. Don't lie to me. You're not sorry!"

Braden watched Diane's rage made visible in the wind and chaotic energy she tried to wrap around Payson and tear her apart. The sharp wind sliced open Payson's pant legs and blood trickled down her skin.

"I am sorry. I should have taken you out of your Grandma's house. I should have walked with you to school and gone to movies with you."

"You never went shopping with me. You never sat with me in the cafeteria, or picked me for the volleyball team."

Braden shook his head. He couldn't bear to watch Payson get torn apart. She didn't need to take the blame for Diane's unhappy life. "Payson," he whispered.

"Let me make amends. It's not too late to do those things. Just let me make it up to you." Payson's voice was small.

"No! It is too late!" Diane threw another blast of wind and debris straight at Payson.

Braden dove in front of the blast, and it hit him hard, sending him careening toward the edge of the tower. Pain throbbed in his temples. *You belong to me. You belong to Dark Sides.* The words repeated, making him dizzy. "Stop Diane. You can't take my mind. I chose light, not dark. Payson, not you."

"Braden, stay back," Payson screamed.

"Yeah, Braden." Diane's voice was distorted and scornful. "Protect Payson, by all means. Too bad you can't."

"Diane, please, why are you doing this?"

Diane shook her head and pointed at Payson. "You don't even know. If it weren't for you, my parents wouldn't have died."

"What are you talking about? They had an accident. How was that my fault?"

"They told me I couldn't have company. I mesmerized them so that I could invite you to sleep over. It worked and they left. But you didn't come over and they died in the car accident."

Braden groaned. "You're blaming Payson and there is no blame, Diane. You just wanted a normal life. Shit happens."

"No! Payson has to pay." Diane arched her back and gathered up the swirling air in one huge plume. "Say your goodbyes. Payson, you're going to die." She sent the tornado at Payson. It picked her up, dropping pieces of her clothing as she swirled closer to the edge of the tower.

Braden's heart froze when Payson went limp. He had only stayed back in the hope that Diane's rage would calm. He tore at the rocks still lying on the deck and pummeled Diane.

"Bring her back, Diane. She apologized. She's taken responsibility. Let her go." His voice was hoarse from screaming into the wind and Diane's energy froze him in place.

Payson's body hovered close to the edge. He died a thousand times inside, watching and not being able to move.

"Ahhh!" He leaned into the gusting winds and picked up one foot, then another. Diane's expression defied him to come meet her in the middle. He took another look at Payson and expanded his light and love. He could control Diane's mind.

"Diane, you heard what Payson said. She's sorry for hurting you. For leaving you alone in your miserable life. She wants to be your friend and do things with you that friends do. Accept her offer. I know you want to."

The wind drew down to a slow bluster. Payson's body rotated in the slow-motion column of air and debris.

"She doesn't know me. She doesn't know what I've done or what I'm doing right now. If she did, she would take back everything she said."

At the city skyline, the sun was sinking behind tall buildings and evening began to envelope everything. Life and death, light and dark, love and hate were so close. Braden breathed heavily.

"You're wrong. She does know. And she, both of us, Diane, offer you light and love. We'll be genuine friends with no holding back or hurting. You simply have to accept."

Diane's shoulders slumped and Payson began falling toward the concrete deck. He raced toward her and caught her in his arms just in time. He held her close. Her pulse was weak but he felt it beating against his chest.

All he wanted was to lie her down and direct his light and love to her.

But he had to make good on his promise to help save Diane. He put Payson down and strode across the deck to Diane. "Accept, Diane. It's a choice that will change your life for the better."

She sunk to the concrete. "I can't. Stay away from me. You don't understand what's happening." She straightened her shoulders and climbed to her feet. "You had your chance to work with me and you rejected me. Now, you and Payson and all the other Aeons will deal with the consequences. You'll see." She spun on her heels and walked toward the elevator.

Braden's muscles twitched. He had to stop her. He reached with his mind to hold her in place. "You want to stay here with me, Diane. You know you do. You murdered Benjamin. You have to face those consequences, but I'll help you."

She hesitated, stood in place for seconds. "No, I don't." She moved her hands in circles and Benjamin floated up unconscious to stand beside her. She snapped her fingers and his eyes opened. She ran her fingers through his hair. "Sweet boy. You can't stop me, Braden." She tossed her hair over her shoulder and stepped into the elevator with Benjamin. "And this is not over." Her words were clipped, emotionless, and the elevator door closed.

"Payson!" He ran back to Payson and held her. "Payson, you're all right." He rocked her back and forth, sending his light to connect with her. Panic spun in his gut, but he kept up the steady flow.

She moaned and shifted in his arms. "Braden?" She opened her eyes. "You're okay?"

"Yes, and so are you."

She sat up and scanned the deck. His heart drooped.

"Where's Diane? What happened?"

"She left with Benjamin. He's not dead. I'll tell you about it later. Right now I want to get you off this tower and into someplace I can take care of you."

"I need to go to Claire Eve's lake house and get Shana to take her to her parents. We need to check in with the others to make sure they're all right."

He stroked her cheek. "Claire Eve will take her home. As for the others, check your connection. What does it tell you?"

He watched Payson's focus turn inward.

He waited.

A smile lifted her lips. "The others' energy fields are coherent. They're still holding us in their light. Everyone is okay." She tried to get her feet under her but stopped mid-wince.

"Let me help you." She grabbed his outstretched hand, and he pulled her to her feet.

She leaned against him and he wrapped his arms around her. "We're all okay." He breathed in deeply of Payson's scent. "You amaze me.

"I don't feel amazing. We didn't bring Diane out of darkness and for all our efforts to weaken Dark Sides, DAs are stronger." She shook her head. "She has Benjamin. I couldn't stop her."

"All of us Aeons will regroup and find a way to save the city." He kissed a bruise on her cheek, wishing he could kiss away her anguish. "I'm sorry I couldn't stop her either. All she had to do was choose light, but she didn't." He pursed his lips and sat beside her. "You give me hope. You withstood the forces of dark energy that Diane used to try to kill you. I call that downright kick ass."

Her voice was quiet. "I tried to use love and light to help Diane, but she couldn't accept it. Maybe I could never be the one to help her. I've missed my chance."

Braden lifted her chin. "I understand what you're going through, but it's up to Diane. She's been tortured by her own decisions all these years, not your lack of support."

Payson sighed. "I guess that's all anyone could do. We can't actually save anyone, we can only offer our light and love."

"It's a hard truth." He ran his hand over her hair, smoothing the tangles. "But what we offer is still very powerful. Life-changing powerful."

HER BODY RELAXED in his arms. "Yes it is."

"We have loose ends, still. But right now, Payson, I have one thing in mind. Marry me."

Her heart flipped. "What?" She sat erect.

"I'm asking, will you marry me? There is danger still. We don't know what another day or week or month will hold for us. I don't want to leave any question about our relationship going forward." He dropped to one knee. "Please, Payson, be my wife?"

All the danger and chaos and angst of the last week, the last few hours, evaporated from Payson's mind and body. "What about all the problems we need to consider? Is this the right moment for us to decide this?"

"It's the perfect moment to hold tight of our love. It's unreachable by darkness. It's important and life-giving to me. All the other things we're concerned with, our mission, the danger, our work, none of it is important compared to our love."

His eyes held her in place. Surrounded by the light of her little band of light warriors and in the face of uncertainty, she knew.

She looked up into Braden's eyes. "Yes."

He grabbed her up and spun. "She said yes!"

She slipped slowly down his body, warmth everywhere at once, and he bent his head to her lips. He anchored her to the spot with a long, hopeful kiss.

When he pulled back, she whispered. "Always."

He took her hand and kissed it softly. "Always."

ACKNOWLEDGMENTS

From concept, editing, proofreading, and formatting to setting and technical information, and support, I drew from great sources in writing this book. I am so grateful to everyone who worked with me to create this book: editors Tamara Eaton and Danielle Stockdale, HiDee Ekstrom, and Jan Clayton, Jamie Kurtz, Daniel Kurtz, Cara Kurtz, Andrew Kurtz, Lynn McLewin, designer Dar Albert, and Jay Walker. I am especially grateful to Michelle Gomez, the world's best bounty hunter, for sharing her experiences and expertise. You all mean a lot to me.

ABOUT THE AUTHOR

Lynn Crandall started spinning stories as a child when she tried to entertain her younger sister at night when they were supposed to be going to sleep. In the dark, her stories typically took on a scary or paranormal element—didn't do much to put her and her sister to sleep.

Lynn has been a reader and a writer all her life. Her background is in journalism, but whether she writes a magazine or newspaper story, or creates a romance, she loves the power of stories to transport, inspire, and uplift.

Today, she hopes her stories still fail to put readers to sleep, and instead take them on a journey.

For more from Lynn Crandall, visit http://www.lynn-crandall.com Stay up to date with releases, including Dark Sides books two and three, *Hear Me, See Me,* by subscribing to her newsletter.